Texas Bride

by

Brenda Huber

This is a work of fiction. Names, characters, places, and incidents are either the product of the author's imagination or are used fictitiously, and any resemblance to actual persons living or dead, business establishments, events, or locales, is entirely coincidental.

Texas Bride

Cover Art by *Rae Monet, Inc. Design*

The Wild Rose Press
PO Box 708
Adams Basin, NY 14410-0708
Visit us at www.thewildrosepress.com

Publishing History
First Cactus Rose Edition, 2011
PRINT ISBN 1-60154-950-4

Published in the United States of America

Dedication

This one is for my dad, Larry Osborn.

"Every individual has a place to fill in the world and is important in some respect whether he chooses to be so or not."

~*Nathaniel Hawthorne*

Prologue

Carlisle, Oklahoma
Summer 1879

"Damn it, Garrett, you're gonna get yourself shot."

Garrett ignored the gruff rebuke and spurred his horse on. Pushing the animal hard. Too hard. On some level, he knew it...knew it and just didn't give a damn. The dusty, hard-packed dirt road was empty; the thunder of gunfire reverberated through the bustling, sun-baked streets, warning pedestrians to seek cover as nothing else could. The dull thud of pounding hooves trailed him down the now barren streets, but he dared not pull rein long enough to look over his shoulder.

This was all wrong. This wasn't supposed to happen. Nick said he'd be only a few moments. He'd assured Garrett he would do his job, then the three of them—he, Nick, and Eddie—would head home.

Damnation, what had gone wrong?

By the time Garrett drew rein out front of Carlisle First National and Trust, an odd stillness had descended. Blood raged in his ears. His heart, ready to explode, battered his ribcage. He flicked a glance at the cloud of dust disappearing over the horizon and the posse following close behind. His gaze swerved back to the bank door. It was so quiet in there.

Too quiet.

His stomach churned as he swung a leg over his mount's rump, dropping both feet to the hard-packed dirt. Someone shouted a warning, but he paid no heed. He couldn't feel his legs as he raced up the steps and across the boardwalk. Hell, but for the violent pounding of his heart, he could feel little else, be it physical or emotional. Hands shaking, he reached for the doorknob, and for the space of one painful heartbeat, he hesitated. Dread of the unknown crawled up the back of his throat, leaving a sour taste in his mouth. The chill of apprehension raked at his guts with vicious, icy claws.

That momentary hesitation provided Sheriff Taggard enough time to catch up. A bony hand dropped on his shoulder. "You'd best let me head in first, son."

Shrugging Taggard's tight grip off with a raw growl, Garrett forced the door open, bursting inside the room, gun drawn and ready. The coppery tang of fresh blood—a lot of fresh blood—hung heavy in the air. He staggered back a step at the carnage before him. His breathing arrested. His vision swam.

In the lobby, just to Garrett's left, three men sprawled in an unnatural heap. None of them so much as twitched. The teller dangled across the counter, unmoving and covered with blood. Garrett spared them little more than a fleeting glance. Unable to delay the inevitable any longer, his stunned gaze shot across the room.

His world lurched to a standstill. His heart plummeted. He could scarce wrap his mind around the vision before him.

No...no, this was wrong...all wrong. This couldn't be happening.

He raced across the rough-hewn plank flooring. The thud of his boots echoed like hollow heartbeats. Unshed tears burned his eyes and clogged the back of his throat as he dropped to his knees.

Side by side, Nick and Eddie lay on the floor, still gripping their guns. Garrett crumbled inside. It

"Miranda," he stalled. "You shouldn't—"

"I shouldn't what, Garrett?" She lifted a hand, settling it on his chest, just over his pounding heart. "Shouldn't I wonder what it would be like to be held in your arms?" Her bold stare lifted to his. "I do." She forced a swallow, fighting to hide the sudden crack in her self-confidence. Was she doing this right? She'd never before played the wanton.

She eased closer, and this time he didn't step away—he couldn't as his back was to the wall—and she let a small, sanguine smile curve her lips. She knew she was goading him, knew her next words might not get quite the exact reaction she wanted from him—might gall him into turning away from her—but she needed this...needed his kiss like she'd never needed anything else in her life.

"I'm curious, Garrett," she murmured. "I want to know...I *need* to know. Does every man kiss like Draco does? Do all men taste the same?"

His stormy eyes flashed, like lightning just before it reaches down to scorch the earth. He cursed beneath his breath, vehemently, and heat soared in her cheeks. A tiny tendril of uneasiness coiled deep in the pit of her stomach. She'd pushed him too far.

Damn it, she hadn't wanted it like this. She'd wanted him willing, not coerced, but he'd left her no choice.

Garrett's heated stare locked on her mouth, and an animal growl rumbled through him as he snaked an arm around her waist, hauling her hard against him. Her eyes flew wide, and she gasped. His hand tangled, fisting in her hair, dislodging pins, rough and demanding. Their gazes connected for a heartbeat, and, with a tiny flare of fear, she realized she hadn't just pushed his limits. She'd broken his control. Comprehension—apprehension—registered a split second before his lips swooped down to seize hers.

About *Brenda Huber's works...*

"Ms. Huber has the ability to draw you into the story and keep your thoroughly entertained."
~The Romance Reviews
~*~

"Ms. Huber has a gift with weaving emotions and building characters that made me feel like I was part of [the story]."
~Seriously Reviewed says of TEXAS BLAZE
~*~

"One word for Brenda Huber is "WOW"...This reviewer loved and highly recommends *TEXAS BLAZE*. Awesome!"
~Happily Ever After Reviews
~*~

"I loved this historical romance...I was on the edge of my seat during much of the reading. The spectacular and riveting ending, with its surprising revelation, brought the book to the only ending possible. This is an author I will read again."
~The Romance Studio says of TEXAS BLAZE
~*~

"Huber's serial killer is truly twisted and readers will be guessing the person's identity until the last pages of the story...Huber's engaging characters and winsome town will have readers yearning for a sequel."
~Romantic Times says of SHADOWS
~*~

"*MINE* is a sexy, sultry, unforgettable vampire novel that tingles in all the right places. Author Brenda Huber has crafted a tale that will ensnare the mind and enrapture the heart..."
~Long and Short Romance Reviews

didn't matter that the gunfight had been over almost before it had begun. He should have gotten here faster. Eddie's sightless stare riddled him with guilt, damning his soul as nothing else could. He clenched his teeth against the urge to howl his grief aloud. Garrett sucked in a ragged breath, suffocating on air stale with the stench of death.

Dashing the back of his hand across his eye, he blinked and struggled to focus his watery gaze on Nick's face. His oldest brother was clammy, pale as death. But still alive.

Nick struggled to draw a rattling breath. The gaping hole beside the conspicuous U.S. Marshal's star pinned to Nick's shirt left little doubt as to his chance for survival.

The Smith and Wesson Model Three in Nick's hand rattled against the floor as he struggled to speak. He stretched his empty hand toward Garrett, but his arm flopped to the floor at his side, useless. Snatching Nick's hand in a death grip, Garrett gulped for air like a fish pulled from the water. His stomach rolled and pitched. Nick's lips moved, but a death rattle was the only sound that escaped. That sound would haunt Garrett's nightmares for the rest of his life. He doubled over, pressing his ear close to Nick's mouth.

"Colby...Chambers' Gang...Nora..."

Then there was no more. No more breath in Nick's lungs. No more words on Nick's lips. No more life in Nick's glassy, gray eyes.

His brother was gone.

Both of his brothers were gone.

He rocked back on his knees, there between Nick and Eddie, one hand on each of their chests. Their blood soaked his hands, staining his soul. His chin dropped to his chest. He squeezed his burning eyes closed. His own breathing was harsh and ragged, an obscene reminder that his beloved brothers were dead, yet he still lived. Nick's words rang in his stunned mind, and he understood what Nick expected. He needed to find U.S. Marshal Merle Colby, Nick's superior, and tell him the Chambers' Gang was responsible for the robbery...and the murders.

And he needed to tell Nick's wife that Nick was...that he'd...oh, God! His throat closed up tight. Tears scalded the backs of his eyelids. He blinked, dashing the moisture away with the back of his hand.

Offering stark silence to the men staring in morbid fascination at the bodies strewn about the room, Garrett pulled himself to his feet, feeling as if he'd aged a hundred years in the last few minutes. With methodical, ruthless precision, he removed the Colts from his gun belt before bending to place them on the floor. Retrieving the sticky gun from Nick's hand with reverent care, Garrett placed the Model Three in his empty gun belt. Turning, he did the same with Eddie's gun.

Then he faced Nick, the brother he'd idolized all his life.

He unclipped the blood-covered, U.S. Marshal's star from Nick's shirtfront, numb but for the ache where the splintered pieces of his heart pierced his soul. As he straightened once more, Garrett lifted his face to the setting sun, impervious to the warm rays pouring through the shattered window.

The sharp points of the lawman's badge of honor—coated with Nick's blood—cut into Garrett's palm. He was empty inside, beyond physical pain now. Bowing his head, he offered a silent prayer for the dead. Then he let the rage and grief boil inside him. As he lifted his head, his burning gaze promised vengeance. Without a word to the others, he stalked from the bank, the very fabric of his life altered, devastated beyond repair.

No longer the carefree charmer was he.

No longer the youngest of the mischievous McCabe boys.

His innocence died on that blood-soaked bank floor alongside his beloved brothers. The man who stalked from the carnage—a phoenix risen from the ashes—was an avenging angel of death, hell-bent on atonement.

Chapter One

Johnston, Texas
Spring 1885

Garrett split the deck and shuffled the cards, savoring the warmth of the whiskey swimming in his belly. Lifting his gaze from the cards, he watched Antonio tip back in his seat and prop his booted feet up on the corner of the table. Antonio's deep brown eyes surveyed the other patrons inside the Busted Wheel from beneath a thick fringe of dark lashes as he folded his long, lean hands across his middle.

One of the dancing girls wandered close and Garrett chuckled, shaking his head. With a seductive purr, she slipped her fingers through the black hair flowing over his friend's shoulders and down his back. Antonio shot her a wicked wink and then sent her on her way with a few whispered words in her ear and a gentle pat on her generous behind.

Antonio was a real heartbreaker all right. But the women he'd wooed and left in his wake didn't seem to hold any hard feelings...ever. Garrett still couldn't figure out how Antonio managed it.

He shuffled the deck again, more from boredom than necessity. Now that Ethan and Matt had gone home, there wasn't much point in another game. Besides, Ethan had cleaned them all out before heading home to his very beautiful, very pregnant wife.

Garrett settled back in his seat and scanned the room. From this particular table, he enjoyed a wide, unobstructed view of the entire saloon, which suited him just fine. Johnston was a small town and for the most part, quiet, but they'd all learned a valuable lesson over the course of the last few months. Trouble had a way of catching you when you least expected it...not that they were expecting any trouble, of course. But it still paid to be cautious all the same.

The way Garrett figured it, you couldn't stop the devil from visitin'. But that sure as certain didn't mean you had to offer him a seat and a place to hang his hat.

Just as Garret reached for the whiskey bottle again, a flash of movement in the saloon's doorway caught his attention. The double doors burst open, and a young man dressed in a black suit and bow tie rushed inside. The newcomer stood out like a preacher in a brothel, drawing the attention of every man in the establishment. He paid them no heed as he glanced around the shabby interior of the saloon. His unswerving gaze came to rest on the table in the corner, searching for—and locking on—Garrett.

Well, shit...

The suit scurried forward, determination glinting in his gaze. With an inward grimace, Garrett recognized him as Judge Thomas's clerk. Whatever this dandy wanted, it couldn't be good...at least not for Garrett. Dread settled deep into his very bones.

"Marshal McCabe," the clerk addressed him, tugging on his collar. "I have an urgent message for you from Judge Thomas."

Garrett gritted his teeth at the title the clerk had bestowed upon him but didn't bother correcting him. He'd learned some people just couldn't seem to get around to understanding he'd quit being a lawman the day he'd rounded up the last of the Chambers' Gang, put his brother's star to rest in the box under his bed, and turned in his resignation.

The man laid a folded piece of paper on the table at Garrett's elbow, then spun on his heels and scurried out without another word. Garrett's gaze flicked to Antonio. Picking the missive up, he flipped it open and read in silence, then huffed out a resigned sigh, and tossed the paper back on the table between them.

Antonio settled his feet on the floor and sat up straighter. A deep groove dug in between his dark brows. "What's wrong?"

"Thomas wants me over at his place as soon as I can get there." Garrett pushed his chair back, readjusted his gun belt. "He's callin' in a debt I owe him."

Anyone who'd been in Johnston long enough to dust off his hat was well aware Johnston's own Judge Thomas didn't merely enjoy his reputation for being a hard-nosed son of a bitch. He reveled in it. He wasn't above stacking the deck in his favor, and he didn't care how anyone else fared as long as he got what he wanted.

Antonio narrowed his dark brown eyes at Garrett, ready for action. "A debt, huh? Well, why not. My luck at cards tonight wasn't worth a shit anyway. I suppose we better head on over, see what the old bastard wants."

"No, I got this one." The last thing he wanted to do was toss his friend in the judge's path. "I made the deal. I guess the time's come to pay the devil his due."

"You sure?"

"Yeah, don't worry about it," he assured Antonio. Dropping the stack of cards onto the center of the table, he downed one last, bracing shot of rotgut. "You gonna head back to the Bar M tonight?"

Antonio picked up the bottle and poured himself another shot. He shook his head, sending his long hair rippling behind him. Reaching over, he patted the scarred tabletop, drawling, "Nope, I have every intention of sittin' right here and drinkin' myself under this here table." He eyed the buxom, dancing girls, adding, "Then again, I might decide to keep company tonight."

Garrett shot him an envious grin as he picked his hat up and ran a hand through his disheveled hair before settling the hat on his head. He made a beeline to the door, pushing out into the cool evening air. Pausing on the boardwalk, he drew a deep breath, scenting rain on the breeze. Shaking the liquor-induced cobwebs from his head, Garrett gathered Hades' reins and vaulted onto the spirited animal's back.

The gelding had been a present from Ethan, a combination thank you and welcome to the area gift after Garrett had helped to round up Ethan's string when the raider Vega set his stables on fire. Garrett still shook his head at the horse's moniker. He wasn't sure where Ethan came up with the names for his horses, but Garrett found it amusing.

Nevertheless, in this particular instance, the title seemed appropriate. Garrett had spent nigh on to two frustrating weeks before he'd been able to ride the demon gelding without the constant fear of being dusted. They'd come to an understanding, he and the enormous horse. Hades thought himself lord and master. Garrett knew otherwise.

They simply agreed to disagree.

Wheeling the huge horse around, he centered his thoughts on the issues at hand. Hades took less than two minutes to cover the distance between the judge's house and the Busted Wheel. Nowhere near long enough. Garrett took a moment to settle his unease before knocking on the door. Following the aging butler down the hallway, he wondered what price he was about to pay for bartering away his soul.

The Honorable Milton Thomas stood in the middle of his dining room, holding a stack of papers in each hand. More documents were scattered across the gleaming mahogany tabletop. He glanced up over the rim of his wire glasses as Garrett stepped inside the room.

"Marshal McCabe," Judge Thomas snapped, pushing one sheaf of papers into a satchel on the chair beside him, thrusting the other sheaf of papers back onto one of the stacks on the table. The judge's demeanor bespoke a man on the prod. "Time's short, so I'll cut to the chase. I'm calling in that little favor you owe me...the one from Colchester."

Careful not to bat an eyelash, Garrett couldn't help the muscle ticking along his jaw at the mention of *that* particular little favor. He'd been afraid of this. Having the knowledge confirmed had an immediate, sobering effect, counteracting the bottle of whiskey he'd been working his way through all evening. Bells and whistles sounded in his head— accompanied by a full marching band—warning him whatever it was Judge Thomas wanted doin', it was gonna be big.

Or one *hell* of a headache.

"I need you to be in Coopersville in five days to meet a stagecoach. You'll be escorting a passenger to Johnston. I've been called to Washington and have to leave on the morning train, or I'd do it myself." The judge stopped his paper shuffling long enough to scowl once more at Garrett. "This passenger's safety is of the utmost importance to me. I am entrusting you to see that she arrives here without any undue complications."

Garrett's brow wrinkled while he listened to the judge's orders. Something wasn't sitting right. The judge was calling in Colchester for a simple escort? He wasn't buying it, not for one minute. The fine hairs on the back of his neck stood on end.

Then the judge's final comment registered.

"*She*, sir?"

The judge pinned him with a hard stare and nodded, clarifying, "My niece, Marshal McCabe. Miss Miranda Thomas."

Garrett didn't bother to correct the judge about his retired status, knowing it would be useless. As long as Judge Thomas deemed Garrett a U.S. Marshal, a U.S. Marshal he was. Still he couldn't help but frown. What the judge was asking for—what he was willing to trade for it—just didn't make a lick of sense.

He must have let his confusion show. With a hearty sigh, Judge Thomas set aside his paper shuffling and focused his attention on the conversation. "You're wondering why I would call in Colchester for an escort for my niece. Let me assure you, if I know Miranda, there will be nothing simple about it."

Feet planted, hands folded behind his back, hat dangling from two fingers, Garrett watched the judge. He made an effort to smooth out his features as he waited for some kind of explanation to that last odd remark.

The judge seemed to mull the matter over for a long moment, then he grunted and motioned for Garrett to have a seat. He, too, pulled out a chair and sat. "Before I say more, you must understand...I love my niece. I do. She has a kind heart and the best of intentions, of that I have no doubts. She takes after her mother that way. But she is young and head-strong." A small smile curved his lips as he added, "Again, just like her mother."

The judge paused, the smile slipping from his lips. "My brother is sending her to live with me for...an extended holiday. He claims he's at his wits end, says she runs roughshod over him and his household, meddling in things that are of no concern to her. You ask me, Isaiah should have put his foot down and married her off long before now. He should have tied her down with a husband and children of her own, and then she'd be too busy to stir up trouble right and left.

"But he didn't. Far too busy with his own interests and dealings. Now she's gone and gotten herself into hot water once again. Her latest stunt pushed Isaiah over the edge. He's hopeful I'll have a tempering impact on her."

Garrett's stomach knotted. His assignment was to escort the judge's niece—by the judge's own estimations a headstrong hoyden—across the better part of Texas. Something told him it would have been far easier had the judge demanded he walk barefoot across a sun baked creek bed full of stirred up rattlers instead.

Heading into this with no other alternative, he wanted to do it with his eyes open. "May I ask what 'stunt' it was she pulled, your honor?"

The judge eyed him, shrewd and calculating, and Garrett steeled himself for the worst. "My brother finally deemed it time the chit settled down, got married. He arranged a suitable match with a very wealthy, very powerful shipping tycoon. Miranda, however, had other ideas. She discovered her betrothed was being less than honest in his business ventures...the good Lord only knows how...and rather than just keeping her mouth shut and her opinions to herself, she chose to worm her way out of the marriage by shouting of her betrothed's misdeeds from the rooftops, so to speak.

"Needless to say, Boston's elite didn't appreciate having its flaws and shortcomings thrown into the bright light of day. By the time the nabobs finished with both Miranda and her betrothed, the man would have nothing to do with her...an attitude the rest of her father's circle saw fit to adopt. The whole fiasco may have been forgotten, given enough time. Unfortunately, there were several other occurrences that were...troublesome."

"Troublesome?" Garrett echoed the judge's words, beginning to feel like one of those exotic, talking birds he'd read about, but he couldn't seem to help it.

The judge shifted in his seat, a frown darkened his already formidable countenance. "It would seem there were a series of unusual events. Someone tampered with a wheel on her phaeton and later cut the cinch on her saddle. A band of miscreants set upon her carriage in an otherwise upscale neighborhood. Fortunately, a family friend happened to have been close by. In any case, for her own personal safety, it seemed best she leave town with all due haste."

"Did no one confront this man she was to have wed?" Garrett frowned at the judge. Leaning forward, he braced his elbows on his knees and twirled his hat in his hands. "Why weren't charges filed? Those were obvious attempts on her life."

A perturbed scowl lined the judge's face. "It wasn't as simple as that. You see, Miranda has a way of, er, offending certain people. Her former betrothed wasn't the only man she'd embarrassed before the public eye, therefore he wasn't the sole suspect."

Realization dawned.

Realization...and a definite spark of worry.

"Hence we come to the crux of the matter. Due to this unforeseen summons to Washington, I can no longer meet her coach as planned. I'm sure you've heard there are several gangs of bandits attacking the trains, as well as the stagecoaches, between here and Coopersville. As you can well imagine, I've no wish for my young niece to fall victim to the thieving scoundrels."

"I heard Pinkertons were being posted on the trains along that route now, as well as additional U.S. Marshals being relocated to the area. I'm sure security on the trains would be sufficient now. If you don't mind my asking, why doesn't she just take the train and meet you in Washington?"

"She refuses. It seems she gets motion sick every time she gets on a train. Aside from that, I'm going to Washington to deal with a volatile situation. If Miranda were to accompany me, well, let's just say that volatile situation could turn explosive." The judge cleared his throat. "Regardless, Miranda is an accomplished equestrian, and so I can assure you the ride back will be painless. I've wired ahead to Coopersville and instructed her to stay put until you get there."

Then the judge's lips twisted in a mockery of a smile, a smile that sent an eerie chill through Garrett. "Look on the bright side, McCabe. By the time it's all said and done, in all likelihood, I'll end up owing you."

He shoved a foreboding chill aside. He'd been a U.S. Marshal for damned near six years. He'd dealt with renegades, bank robbers, and cold-blooded murderers. How difficult could one woman be? Hell, he should be grateful. It sounded as though he was about to get off easy.

Reaching out to shake his hand, Judge Thomas caught Garrett off guard by patting him on the shoulder in what appeared to be a gesture of sympathy. "Good luck, son."

Dismissed, dumbfounded by the almost affectionate gesture, Garrett strode from the judge's home, crunched his way down the gravel pathway, and vaulted onto Hades' saddle. He rubbed a wary hand over the back of his neck, mystified over that last, odd exchange. He'd known Judge Thomas for as many years as he'd been a marshal. This was the first time the man had ever seemed…well, *human.*

Garrett shook his head, deciding to head home. He'd have to leave at the crack of dawn and had five days' hard riding ahead of him if he intended to make it to Coopersville in time to meet the judge's niece.

He considered what the judge said about his niece, and once again, he scoffed. No woman could be *that* difficult. He was a U. S. Marshal, or he had been once upon a time. Miss Thomas was just a woman, and she would soon fall in line. She didn't stand a chance. He gathered up Hades' reins and settled back in the saddle.

Nope, he grinned, shaking his head.

Not a snowball's chance in hell…

Chapter Two

Miranda was fuming by the time she stepped from the telegraph office onto the rough-planked boardwalk. The blazing sun rode high in a cloudless sky. She blinked, squinting against the glare. A bead of perspiration left a damp trail along her hairline, but she ignored it. Just like she ignored the dampness at the small of her back. Jerking her lace-trimmed, kid gloves back on, she ran her hands down the front of her heavy velvet traveling skirts, trying—unsuccessfully—to smooth some of the wrinkles from the expensive material. She'd never experienced a heat so dry.

Dear Lord, it's miserable here.

Heaving a disgusted sigh, she tromped the short distance back to the coaching station, ignoring the fascinated stares she garnered from passersby. Miranda was accustomed to drawing unwanted attention. Her flaming locks, flawless alabaster skin, and shrewd Kerry-blue eyes pretty much assured her attention.

Moreover, if those fine attributes didn't catch the eye, her lissome figure—curved to perfection in all the right places...or so an overeager suitor had once informed her—never failed to. She'd learned to live with the stares, indeed even the rude gawking, but today she just wished she could blend into the scenery. She kept her eyes riveted on her destination, chin elevated, step determined.

How dare he? How much more did her father—and Uncle Milton—expect her to tolerate before she rebelled altogether?

They should know better by now.

They would not break her no matter what inconvenience they tossed in her path.

When she and her companion, Miss Burns, arrived in Coopersville, a man at the depot notified her that a wire from Uncle Milton waited for her. Said wire, which now rested—crumpled—in her reticule, informed her that her uncle had taken it upon himself to send an escort...some pandering U.S. Marshal firmly lodged beneath her uncle's ruthless thumb, no doubt.

Great! Just bloody fabulous! Now she had to put up with some crotchety old, stick-in-the-mud as well. It was the final blow to her patience. As if being shipped off to live in some rustic, sweltering, sun-baked town with her controlling uncle hadn't been trial enough, her father had already deemed it necessary she have a suitable traveling companion. For propriety's sake, of course.

Thus, she'd gained the company of the severe, disapproving Miss Burns. Miranda was of a mind to believe her father had gone out to find the most unpleasant, unreasonable woman he could, just to add insult to injury. The only time the dour woman deigned to open her mouth was either to lecture Miranda on social conscience, or to quote scripture.

Shaking thoughts of her abrasive traveling companion from her mind, Miranda passed the mercantile and pulled the small watch fob from the silk reticule dangling at her wrist by a thin ribbon. It was nearing one o'clock, and the stage was to depart inside of ten minutes. The next wouldn't be along until sometime tomorrow, or so she'd been informed.

Shoving the timepiece back inside the reticule with a dainty harrumph, she ground her teeth. If her uncle was going to saddle her with another escort, the least he could have done was find one that was punctual. She knew she was being uncharitable, but the long hours cooped up in that tight, stifling stagecoach, forced to make polite conversation with disagreeable strangers, had worn her nerves to frazzled shreds.

So help her, if Mr. Marks made one more stupid joke, or tried to use some feeble excuse to lay his hand on her knee one more time, she'd hit him with her reticule...unladylike behavior or not. As the idea held great appeal, she paused for a moment on the boardwalk and eyed a scattering of small rocks. Two or three wouldn't be too heavy to carry around for a little while...

No, that wouldn't do at all.

Regardless what her father thought, she was not a child given to juvenile pranks and tantrums.

Shaking her head at her own vindictiveness, she squared her shoulders. She'd behave in a lady-like fashion, no matter what adversity she faced. Miranda stopped to check her reflection in the large, smudged display window of a mercantile, poking a few stray wisps back into her chignon. Her skirts were beyond hopeless, but there was no help for that. She couldn't see much of her complexion in the dirty windowpane, but she wouldn't be at all surprised if there were dark smudges beneath her eyes. She couldn't remember the last time she'd been this tired.

Frustrated, Miranda stepped back into the meager flow of traffic. Once back at the depot, she paced beside the stage, glancing at her timepiece in annoyance. Torn by the decision of whether to wait here in this tiny, dust-covered town, or whether to travel on, God willing to a town that at least had a decent hotel—any hotel at all, she didn't ask the driver to unload her baggage.

Miranda glared at her watch again. The marshal Uncle Milton had sent still hadn't arrived.

What was she to do if he didn't show up today? Where would she stay tonight? She chewed on the tip of a gloved finger as she eyed the stagecoach depot. The ramshackle building didn't look like it would stand up to a stiff gust of wind. And the poor excuse for a roof had more holes than a hunk of Swiss cheese.

Miranda cast a weary glance at the pristine sky, then let her gaze wander over the dusty buildings and the sun-baked road. Maybe the holes in the depot roof wouldn't be an issue. It didn't look as if precipitation—in any form—visited this place often.

"Missy?" The stoop-shouldered driver leaned over the side of his perch on the top of the stagecoach. "D'ya'll want me ta unload yer belongin's, or be ye goin' on ta Comp'n with us?"

Miranda glanced both ways down the vacant street. Still no sign of her escort. Making up her mind, she turned back and forced a smile for the decrepit old man. "Leave them on the stage, please. We'll be traveling on."

With that, she stepped forward, allowing the driver's assistant to hand her up into the conveyance. Aside from her companion, the coach was empty. Miranda bit back a groan as she settled into the corner beside a snoring Miss Burns. Her aching muscles protested every movement. For a fleeting moment, Miranda thought perhaps she'd gained an ounce of luck and no other passengers would join her...until the door opened and a tall, lean man climbed up into the conveyance with the natural grace of a predator.

His hair, the color of pale gold, was unbound, cascading well past his shoulders. His chiseled face was tan, his strong jaw covered with golden stubble. His nose was a smidge crooked, with a defined lump just on the bridge. Ice-blue eyes raked over her, and nervous butterflies took flight in her stomach. She clamped down on the urge to squirm in her seat. He blinked and turned away, adjusting his gun belt.

The newcomer sat down across from her, hanging his dusty cowboy hat on his bent knee. Silver studs twinkled at her from the hatband. His black shirt and trousers were dusty beneath his matching black greatcoat. Silver spurs gleamed bright. He folded his arms across his broad chest, and those ice-blue eyes settled on her once more, speculative and imperious.

This next lap of the journey certainly looked to be more promising. Ever inquisitive, her mind filled with questions, intrigued by the man before her. Miranda considered striking up a conversation, yet the aura of danger surrounding him gave her a moment's pause. He embodied all she'd read of the unsavory bandits of the Wild West. Gunfights and bank robberies. Saloons and fisticuffs.

Shaking off those images, she scoffed at her flight of fancy. How much of an unsavory bandit could he be? He was riding a stagecoach, for pity sake. Wouldn't a ruffian of the Wild West have his own trusty mount? Still, questions crowded her brain. Just then, Mr. Marks saw fit to join them, and so she was unable to lend voice to her questions. As Mr. Marks climbed aboard and settled himself against the seat, Miranda tilted her head back and closed her eyes, feigning sleep. Praying he'd take the hint. Her ploy seemed to be working as silence, broken only by Miss Burns' intermittent snoring, filled the coach. A few moments passed as the driver and his assistant shuffled and settled overhead, then the stage began its jolting, bouncing journey once more.

Now and then, Miranda couldn't help but sneak fascinated, furtive glances beneath her lowered lashes at the blond man. The mysterious stranger stared out the window, ignoring his fellow passengers. His strong profile seemed etched in granite. Mr. Marks looked to be growing bored, she noted. Unable to engage Miranda in his monotonous discussions, he made a few half-hearted attempts to draw the stranger into conversation. He met with stony silence and a cool, dismissive stare.

The handsome stranger seemed comfortable keeping his own counsel. She wished Mr. Marks were of such a mind. Interminable minutes ticked by, and she developed a crick in her neck. Miranda had almost given up her ploy, when Mr. Marks heaved a deep sigh and leaned his head against the seat.

Ignoring the pain, she remained motionless, silent as a whisper, until Mr. Marks's breathing drifted into the faint, nasally inhalation of slumber. She lifted a cautious eyelid to consider him. He looked to be sleeping. Both of her eyes popped open. Straightening her head, she rubbed at the ache in her neck, wincing as her muscles screamed in outrage. Nevertheless, she was careful to keep silent, fearful of rousing Mr. Marks and Miss Burns.

With the two of them still awake, it felt a bit awkward—not to mention flat out rude—to ignore the stranger. Therefore, she offered him a tentative smile. He arched a golden eyebrow and returned her smile with a wry twist of his sculpted lips.

Feeling ridiculous—a bit like Little Red Riding Hood striking up a conversation with the Big Bad Wolf, she leaned forward a bit, and furtively whispered, "Hello."

His gaze was warm—perhaps a bit too warm—when he angled his head, tilting it the tiniest bit in acknowledgement. The edge of his appealing mouth curved upward.

"Ma'am," he drawled, smooth and easy.

"I was beginning to think he'd never be quiet."

His grin widened, and humor twinkled in his

captivating eyes.

"I'm Miss Miranda Thomas, by the way."

His bold gaze roved over her face, skimmed her hair, then dipped—albeit briefly—below her chin. His voice was whisper soft, yet deep and oh-so-husky. Wicked. "It's a pleasure to meet you, Miranda." His head angled a bit as he considered her for another long moment. His stare was mesmerizing, making her think once again of him in terms of a big, bad, golden wolf. "You can call me...Draco."

****

Garrett swore a wide, vicious, blue streak as he stormed from the telegraph office. The cowering man behind the counter had confirmed a young woman by the name of Miss Thomas had indeed received a wire not two hours ago. He also stated that he, along with several others, had witnessed her boarding the stagecoach and leaving town all the same.

Garrett's mood—already sour—took a decided turn south. Hades had thrown a shoe, forcing Garrett to walk the last several miles into town, therefore the delay. He was dusty, sweaty, thirsty as a cowpuncher fresh off the trail, and so damned tired a cactus would make for a good pillow just then. Now he had to hunt the damn fool woman down because she couldn't follow a simple order...*stay put.*

Garrett beat his hat against his thigh. A small cloud of dust billowed from his clothes. Shaking his head, he clenched his teeth and headed for the livery to reclaim his horse, the scowl on his face discouraged any in his path from trying to engage him in conversation. Many, in fact, scurried in the opposite direction. Entering the stables, he paused long enough for his eyes to adjust to the dim interior. Garrett aimed his long-legged stride toward the balding, pot-bellied man standing near one of the back stalls.

After the last five grueling days, there was no room in him for pleasantries. "My horse done yet?"

"Just finished." The man offered a tobacco-stained grin when Garrett tossed a few coins in his direction. "He's a might temper'mental, ain't he?"

Garrett said nothing, feeling a might *temper'mental* himself. He took the gelding's reins and led the animal forward, watching each time Hades stepped on its right foreleg. Satisfied, he turned back to the proprietor. "I'm gonna need an extra horse."

The man all but drooled in his excitement at the prospect of more coin to weight his pockets. He hurried to the opposite end of the livery. In a few minutes, he was back, leading a raw-boned, sway-backed mare who'd seen better days. Pushed beyond annoyance, Garrett leveled a cold, hard stare at the man. The owner cleared his throat, shifting foot to foot.

Tugging at his collar, the squat man spun on his heel and dragged the decrepit horse away, calling over his shoulder, "Might be I got one more."

This time, when he returned, a smart-stepping, dappled gray mare nipped at his heels. Garrett gave the horse a thorough, if speedy, examination. He lifted each hoof, running his hand down each fetlock before sliding his palm up over the horse's rump and along its solid back. He sized up the spacing between the animal's eyes, checked its teeth.

Satisfied with the piece of horseflesh, he snapped, "How much?"

"Hundred and twenty," the man crowed, all but dancing in his excitement.

Garrett lifted a brow as he lowered the animal's rear hoof and waited with narrowed eyes. The owner quaked in his muck-covered boots.

Garrett blinked, allowing the man to steal a breath.

"Ninety...including tack," Garrett challenged, pokerfaced.

The owner blanched. "Now, just a blame-fool minute..."

Garrett blinked once, then turned away, leaving the man and his horse behind. As Garrett led Hades through the livery doorway, potbelly came lumbering after him, tugging the dappled mare in his wake. Garrett stifled a grim smile before turning to face the greedy livery owner.

"I could maybe go an even hundred...including tack." The man scowled.

"Ninety-five including tack...and not that worn out shit you got shoved somewhere in the back," Garrett demanded, deadpan, letting a full minute pass as the proprietor stuttered before he dug in his pocket. He counted out the bills, shoved them in the man's considerable paunch. "I need her saddled. *Now.*"

****

Miranda leaned against the painful seat, lifting a rueful brow at the man across from her. She'd employed every trick she could think of, used every feminine wile in her arsenal. Yet she'd been unsuccessful in getting Draco—he'd insisted there was no Mr. before it—to reveal his full name, or anything else about himself other than he was just passing through.

He, however, had wheedled quite a lot from her. He now knew she was from Boston, and she was the eldest of three. She'd revealed her destination of Johnston...and the reason for her travels. He'd even managed to charm the truth of her failed engagement from her. She'd never before faced such a cunning, charismatic interrogator. Her father could, without a doubt, learn a lot from this man.

Time and again, Draco had deflected her questions with clever queries of his own.

Nevertheless, despite his cunning, she'd managed to detect certain significant things about him. From his speech, she'd perceived a faint southern drawl, similar—yet somehow different—from that of those native to this area. She could tell, by the words and phrases he used, by the topics of which he was versed, that he was well educated despite the ruffian's appearance he seemed to be fostering.

"You're toying with me, Draco." She leaned back and crossed her arms over her chest, affecting a petulant pout that had reduced many a strong man to groveling for forgiveness. Her efforts had no visible effect on Draco. He smiled, and she ground her teeth.

"You wound me, my angel. I desire only to please you," he drawled, smooth as churned cream.

Growing uncomfortable with the intense look burning in his eyes, she shifted in her seat. His endearment was far too intimate—as was his tone— but when she protested, he quirked his lips, ignoring her objections.

She'd been talking with him for over an hour, but she hadn't felt the least threatened...not until now. What had changed? She opened her mouth, but before she could speak, the sound of nearby gunshot echoed near the coach. Her startled gaze flew to the window. Her mind raced as the coach jolted to an abrupt halt. All but thrown from their seat, Mr. Marks and Miss Burns woke up, sputtering and babbling in disgruntled unison. Miranda glanced to Draco, reassured when he withdrew his gun from the holster on his hip.

His teasing grins and burning stares were gone.

Her comfort gave way to swift confusion and then to mortified understanding when Draco cocked the weapon and pointed the lethal barrel at Mr. Marks with unerring accuracy. She'd been flirting with a criminal. A bandit. A thief. Oh, but how low she had fallen, indeed.

Marks gulped. Bug-eyed and pale-faced, his hands shot into the air.

Miss Burns clutched her knitting against her chest and huffed, "I demand to know what's going on."

Draco smiled at her, waving the gun in his hand as though its presence should be sufficient answer to her idiotic question.

The pinch-faced Miss Burns scowled. "What's the meaning of this, young man?"

"Why, Miss Burns," Miranda quipped, lifting a caustic brow, her fulminating stare riveted on Draco. "I should think that painfully obvious—we're being robbed."

Draco slid Miranda a charming smile, his eyes gleaming approval at her apparent lack of fear. She could feel a wave of heat burst to life in her cheeks and did her best to ignore it. The mutter of angry voices outside the coach grew louder. Then the scrabble of luggage shifting overhead drew her gaze.

"Ladies, Mr. Marks—if you'd be so kind as to exit the vehicle," Draco directed with a casual wave of his gun.

Marks harrumphed but didn't put up the slightest fight. Miss Burns glowered at Miranda, as though the entire situation was all somehow her fault. If it were the last thing she did, somehow, she'd find a way to pay her father back for forcing her to put up with this loathsome woman. Just as she shifted in her seat, Draco leaned forward, preventing her from moving.

"A moment, my dove," he murmured.

"*Miss Thomas*," she hissed between clenched teeth. Staring at him with cold eyes, Miranda pressed against the seat, eager to put space between them.

He leaned closer, amusement lurking in his eyes

at her prim response. "I would spare you any undue indignities, *angel of my heart.*"

Her eyes narrowed. She tensed. How dare he call her such names...and at gunpoint, no less. Oh, how she longed to slap the arrogant, wicked smile from his face. How satisfying it would be to sting his pride. Still, she was unprepared when he moved, swift as lightning, to kneel at her side. His hip pressed the side of her knee with startling intimacy. Capturing her wrists, he drew her resistant form closer, until she perched on the edge of the seat. Miranda sucked in a sharp breath, torn between wanting to scream and the urge to snarl chastisement for his boldness. That breath, however, shortened the scant space between her breasts and his broad chest. Her teeth snapped closed, and her temper flared.

"My men will insist on a thorough search, darlin'. I want to be able to reassure them I haven't missed *anything* of value."

He grinned, leaning closer, crowding her. His ice-blue eyes burned with sinful intent, and her earlier analogy of the big bad wolf came back to haunt her.

All the better to see you, my dear...

Miranda glared at him, struggling to pull away. But his strength was not to be denied. He pushed her hands behind her, trapping her wrists in one large hand—his grip like steel, caging her in his arms with frightening ease. Her struggles, and consequently his efforts, pushed his chest hard against hers. The tip of his nose brushed hers. His free hand settled on the curve of her waist. His bold gaze lowered to caress her lips. Her breath caught in the back of her throat. His rakish grin widened. His teeth flashed, perfect and white, in the dim coach.

All the better to taste you, my dear...

That was all the warning she got before Draco's

mouth swooped down to seize hers. For a moment, she froze in stunned immobility. His supple lips, warm and smooth, moved over hers, demanding a response. His tongue swept out to stroke her lower lip in bold seduction. Curious. Pleasant. The hand lingering on her waist shifted, gliding up until his hot palm cradled the side of her breast.

She gasped against his lips, shocked to her core.

No one had *ever* dared to touch her so.

The minute her lips parted, his tongue swept inside, plundering where no man had dared trespass before. She was floored. She didn't know how to react. She should slap him. Yes, she should. And yet, the sensations were not all together unpleasant. So caught by surprise was she that, for a moment, she accepted the contact out of sheer curiosity.

Tentative, inquisitive, she swept her tongue against his. Draco's body jolted against her. Releasing her hands, he wrapped both his arms around her waist, fitting her snug against him. He devoured her, slanting his mouth and opening it wider, thrusting his tongue deeper, he overwhelmed her with his ardor. Suddenly afraid, she twisted her head to the side, tearing her lips from his as she pushed against his shoulders. Undeterred and hungry, his lips slid to her jaw, then the curve of her neck.

"Stop it!" She pounded a fist against his shoulder, breathless. For the first time, fear tinged her voice. She heard it and cringed, hating herself for her show of vulnerability. "Let me go this instant."

He hissed a ragged breath against her neck, and released her, slow and reluctant. His face was an impenetrable mask of control, but his voice was hoarse. "I suggest you join the others...*now*."

Her eyes widened, but she scrambled out of the coach, didn't dare so much as a backward glance.

Hurrying over the uneven ground to stand with Miss Burns and Mr. Marks, she watched as four men, their faces obscured by dusty bandanas, rummaged through their luggage. The bandits stole intermittent, curious glances at her, but none approached. Moments later, Draco climbed down from the coach while two of his men clambered back to the top for more trunks.

Sauntering over to stand in front of the sputtering Mr. Marks, Draco ordered, "Please empty your pockets."

"You won't get away with this, you scoundrel," Marks snapped. Ruddy color rushed from his collar to the roots of his hair. "I'll see every last one of you hanged for this."

"Yes, yes...your pockets, if you please," Draco reminded him. He waited while Marks produced a silver pocket watch and small roll of bills, then he added, "Don't be a fool, man, the derringer, too."

Marks shot him a mutinous glare before drawing the tiny pistol from a pocket inside his coat. He slapped it onto Draco's outstretched palm.

"I'm a God-fearing woman," Miss Burns blustered in righteous indignation when the bandit turned to her. "I don't put stock in worldly possessions."

"I would hate to have to search you, madam," Draco warned.

Miss Burns blanched and hurried to empty her pockets and her reticule, dumping out a handful of coins, a jeweled brooch, a man's pocket watch, a man's wallet, and a few crumpled bills. Miranda's mouth fell open, and she gasped when the string of pearls she'd thought she'd misplaced tumbled into Draco's palm. The pearls had belonged to her grandmother. Miranda had been heartbroken over their loss. Draco raised a brow and smirked at the red-faced woman before he moved on.

"You're reticule, my pet." He smiled, holding his hand out, empty palm up.

"You can't very well leave us with nothing." She forced herself to remain calm and searched his eyes, trying to reach some part of his humanity.

He leaned closer until his lips brushed her ear, and he whispered so that even Miss Burns, who stood right next to them, could not hear his comment. "I trust you'll find I haven't taken...*everything*...of value." Then he leaned back and let his audacious gaze slide down over her curves. As his gaze met hers once more, something lingered there, just beneath the surface of those bold eyes. Something that made her swallow and back up a step. "Not just yet, at least."

Then he grinned, staring pointedly at her midriff. Her eyes widened, and she recalled the money belt tied around her waist. Right where he'd run his hands over her. Her lips parted in surprise, and he winked before moving on to take a money clip from the stagecoach driver. Confused, she clamped her lips together. Why would he leave her money belt, when his men seemed intent on scouring the rest of their belongings for the tiniest bauble of value?

Willing herself to remain silent and therefore unnoticed, Miranda bristled as strangers raided her trunks. Careless hands riffled through the contents, tossing her belongings onto the ground. She winced when one of the bandits pulled a weighty tome of poetry free and studied it for a moment before pitching it over his shoulder.

At last, Draco returned to Miranda's side. The smile on his face was well beyond salacious. "You know, darlin', I could take you with me."

She gasped, horrified by the very idea. "You wouldn't dare!"

"I thought you'd understand by now," he crooned

as his impudent gaze dipped to her bodice, reminding her that a short time ago his hand had rested there, rather than just the weight of his stare. "I dare anything."

Miranda's face blazed with heat, but still she hissed, a she-cat baring her claws, "My uncle is Judge Milton Thomas of Johnston, Texas. He would hunt you down and hang you," she warned him.

"I'm thinking for a taste of you, it might be worth it, my love," he murmured. To her utter surprise, he leaned closer and whispered in her ear once more, "Between you and me, my sweet, I wouldn't go about advertising your relationship to the good judge. There are many in these parts that would put a bullet in you *because* you're related."

Then—without giving any clue to his intentions—he shifted, slipping one hand around her waist, cupping the back of her neck with the other. He sealed his lips over hers in a brief, jolting kiss. Grinning shamelessly, he released her before she had time to struggle. Miss Burns' scandalized mutterings pricked her ears, but she was too shocked by Draco's actions to pay the indignant woman any mind.

She couldn't believe he'd gone and kissed her...*again.*

"Definitely worth it," he drawled as he stepped back, all but licking his lips.

The scoundrel.

Without conscious thought, Miranda's hand shot out. She slapped him with all the indignation she could muster, leaving the bright red imprint of her hand on his cheek. Draco chuckled and winked, as if she'd just complimented him. He captured the hand she'd struck him with and drew it to his lips. He pressed a warm, lingering kiss to the center of her palm and folded her fingers over it, as if capturing the kiss inside.

"I look forward to our next encounter, my love," he vowed. His eyes were fierce now. Smoldering. "And make no mistake...there *will* be a next time, Miranda." His husky voice caressed her name, turning it into the most intimate endearment he'd murmured yet.

Draco glanced around at his men and nodded them to their mounts. Turning back, his steady gaze on Miranda, he drawled, "Are you certain you don't—"

"Draco...a rider comes, just over the east ridge," the approaching sentry shouted his warning from the back of a panting horse.

"Damn it." Draco shot Miranda one last fleeting glance and loped to his horse. "We've got company," he called to his men. "Let's ride."

With that announcement, the group tore off, disappearing in a storm of swirling dust, leaving their victims to stare after them in bemused astonishment. It was then that Miranda realized, aside from that first initial warning shot, not another shot had been fired. She thought of his stolen kiss and shook her head, bemused at Draco's daring.

Miranda shielded her eyes from the afternoon glare and looked to the lone rider who'd crested the hill and was, even now, approaching at a full out gallop. A saddled, riderless horse trailed in his wake. Her heart tripped inside her chest when he leaped from the massive horse's back and turned to face the group. Sable hair curled over his collar from beneath the brim of his dusty cowboy hat. His sharp eyes were the color of quicksilver, piercing clean through her.

He was tall—impossibly so—making her modest height feel puny. Her eyes skated over broad shoulders and settled on his face. He was a handsome devil, all right, in a rugged, angular sort of way. Dark whiskers bristled their way over his strong jaw. The little grooves between his brows deepened his scowl into downright dangerous territory. Her gaze flicked to the riderless gray mare, and she could have moaned aloud.

Oh, merciful Lord, not another bandit...

She blinked, cognizant of the fact he had yet to take his eyes off her. The newcomer stomped straight to her side. She found herself staring in wide-eyed fascination as he glowered down at her, his expression hovering somewhere between grudging compassion and vexed irritation. In addition, unless she missed her mark, there was also a healthy dose of trepidation mixed in there somewhere, and that left her mystified.

Where Draco had held her interest and pricked her curiosity, this man held her very soul enthralled—and *he* hadn't even opened his mouth yet. She shifted from one foot to the other beneath his unwavering gaze, her palms damp. For the first time that she could recall, Miranda didn't know what to say. Heaven help her. First Draco, and now this tall, handsome stranger. All this attention did not bode well for her stay in Texas.

Chapter Three

Garrett couldn't help but stare. She had to be the most stunning creature he'd ever laid eyes on. For one tortured heartbeat—realizing the threat this flame-haired creature posed to his self-control...not to mention his peace of mind—Garrett found himself fervently praying the short, dowdy woman at her side was his assignment.

With the day he'd been having, he knew he couldn't be so lucky.

Too old. Damn it.

He shot one swift, regretful glance at the mouse before settling a resigned gaze once more on the fox. "Miss Thomas, I presume?"

The beauty's flawless brow wrinkled. "I am. And you are?"

Her voice slid through him like hot honey.

"Garrett McCabe." He knuckled the brim of his cowboy hat back on his brow and ran a cool, assessing gaze over her. He flicked a glance at her companions, at the wild disarray around them, and assessed her once more. All things considered, she didn't look any worse for the wear.

Her brows shot up, and she blinked, all but gawking at him. "*Marshal* Garrett McCabe?"

He heaved an aggravated sigh and nodded. She blanched. Garrett took a hasty step closer, ready to grab her should she pitch face-first to the ground.

"Are you all right?" His throat tightened, and a slick ball of unease churned in his gut. "You're not gonna...cry or...or faint or anything, are you?"

Color flooded her cheeks. Her eyes narrowed,

flashing fierce blue fire. "No, I'm not going to cry...or faint." Each word sliced the air between them, each syllable enunciated with precise, offended indignation. "I *never* cry and I never, *ever* faint."

He cleared his throat. Damn, she was a prickly one. All he'd done was ask if she was all right, and here she was, acting as if he'd stomped all over her precious sensibilities. This robbery wasn't his fault. If she'd damned well stayed where she was supposed to have stayed, she could have avoided all this mess. His head was beginning to ache; tension drilled a hole clean through his temples.

Exasperated, Garrett turned to the other travelers. "Was anyone else hurt?"

Chaos descended. A cacophony of information swamped him from every direction. The driver and the driver's assistant commenced arguing about the bandits' descriptions. When the assistant claimed the leader's hair was short and brown, Miss Thomas rolled her eyes and gave an unladylike snort. A slim man in a stuffy suit piped up, giving a very loud, detailed description of the articles the bandits had stolen from him, demanding to know what would be done to recover his property.

Beside Miss Thomas, the mouse joined the melee, demanding the brazen rogues be apprehended with all due haste. One glimpse of Miss Thomas's smug smile set his teeth on edge. She appeared to be taking great pleasure in his predicament. For one delirious moment, he considered mounting up and riding off into the sunset, leaving these screaming, indignant travelers to flounder on their own.

Then his ears perked to attention. His stormy gaze turned to Miss Thomas with icy deliberation, though his question fell to the mouse at her side. "What did you just say?"

The older woman's chest puffed up as she shook

a knobby fist in the air. "That ruffian stole my brooch!"

"No, the part about Miss Thomas," he corrected. His impatient, unwavering gaze pinned his assignment to the spot.

"That blackguard kissed her, bold as brass," the mouse harrumphed. Did she believe Miss Thomas had somehow courted the attention?

His gaze raked over her again, from the top of her fiery head to the dusty, lacy ruffle at the bottom of her skirts, before settling back on her face with palpable displeasure. He had a bad feeling about this.

Somehow…someway…the judge was gonna pin this on him. He just knew it.

Lowering his chin, he stared hard at her. "I thought you said you were all right."

"I am fine." She enunciated each word with careful precision.

"One of the bandits kissed you."

"Hardly a fatal blow," she retorted. The Rio Grande would have frozen solid from the chill in her tone alone.

Unappeased, Garrett launched question after question at her. "Which one? What did he look like? Did you hear his name? Why did he kiss you?"

His charge glared at him in seditious silence. Lifting her skirts, she brushed past him on the way to her trunks. The suit and the mouse began to yammer at him once more, but he paid neither of them any heed as he trailed after his charge, a dog with a bone. She sighed as she surveyed the mess—a great, heaving, put-upon sigh—then bent to pick up what he assumed were her belongings. Vaguely aware the other two passengers had followed, he watched as the frustrating woman shoved her things back into her trunks, ignoring them all.

Garrett towered over her, glowering at the back

of her bent head, willing her to grant him her undivided attention. Meanwhile, the mouse had taken up muttering scripture, and the suit ranted in his ear until Garrett lost his patience at last. He turned to face the man and glared him silent.

"Mister, you and your possessions are *not* my problem. I suggest you gather the rest of your things before they blow back to Coopersville." Dismissing the suit with a cold shoulder, he turned to glower at the judge's niece once more.

Still, she wouldn't look at him, damn her beautiful eyes. Garrett reached out and grasped her by the elbow, dragging her around to face him.

"Get your hands off me. I have had quite enough of being manhandled today."

"Who else '*manhandled*' you?" His tone flashed like gray thunderheads rolling in, but he couldn't seem to get a leash on his temper. "Was it the one that kissed you? Tell me what you remember of him…describe him, damn it!"

"No," she refused, jerking at her arm.

"*No?*" Garrett tugged her back around to face him. How dare she defy him? "What the hell do you mean—*no?*"

Her chin elevated to a haughty angle. "Do you require an explanation of the word, sir, or is it that someone would dare refuse you that has you puzzled?"

"Of all the—" Garrett broke off long enough to drag a deep breath in through flared nostrils. "Why would you refuse to give a description of the bandits? Did they threaten you? Is that it? Because let me assure you—"

"He did not threaten me." Her voice dripped disgust. "As a matter of fact, he was more of a gentleman than some I could name."

Garrett glowered at the stubborn minx. He could have pulled out his hair. No, she was the judge's

37

niece, he reminded himself. He would not lose his temper. He dragged in another deep breath, forced his fists to relax at his sides. No, he would *not* yell.

She crossed her arms over her chest, arched a delicate eyebrow, and set to tapping her toe.

"*Goddamnit, woman!*" He exploded.

"Do you realize, *sir*, that since you rode to our rescue, you've raised your voice repeatedly, used vulgar language in the presence of ladies, grabbed my person, and dismissed concerns of the other passengers on this coach, concerns of which—as a man of the law—you are required to address, I might add." She paused only long enough to drag in a deep breath before she let loose with the rest of her tirade. "Furthermore, you stomp about and have the rude nerve to demand answers after we've all been traumatized enough. You can't expect us to be accommodating, now can you?" Having delivered her scathing set-down, she planted her hands on her hips and waited, obviously expecting abject apologies would now be forthcoming.

Garrett seethed. Hell would freeze over first. He told himself to let it go, but the defiant sparkle in her eyes pushed him beyond his tenuous control. "For your information, *Miss* Thomas, had you stayed in Coopersville, *as instructed*, you could have avoided being yelled at, cussed in front of, grabbed—*and* kissed."

She gasped, sputtering, "Are you implying this is all *my* fault?"

He crossed his arms over his chest and rumbled, "If the boot fits..."

"If you had been on time, I wouldn't have been forced to get back on that bloody coach in the first place." She glared at him, shaking an accusatory finger an inch from his nose.

The mouse's incessant ranting had droned on his final nerve, and he couldn't take it anymore.

Swinging about, he shouted, "Oh, for the love of God, woman, cease your squawking!"

Miss Thomas's mouth fell open and both of her brows shot up. *Oh, hell...* Here we go again, he thought, positive she'd take issue with that slip of his temper as well. However, when the blithering mouse fell silent—if he didn't miss his mark—he was sure he caught a twinkle in Miss Thomas's eyes. He was dead certain her lips twitched before she turned away.

Garrett shook his head at the contrary female's back.

After ordering the driver and his assistant to help gather the trunks and resettle them on the stage, he knelt next to his ungrateful charge and her burgeoning trunk. Without comment, he began retrieving her belongings, stuffing them inside the trunk. He ground his teeth in annoyance, her unwarranted accusations rubbing him raw.

No, he'd keep his opinions to himself if it killed him.

Turning to face her, he waved his hand in her face, a lacy bit of nothing clenched tight in his fist. "I don't see as how you can blame me for this damned mess. My horse threw a shoe, and I had to walk near on to five miles to get to Coopersville. How the hell was I supposed to know you couldn't follow one simple damned order?"

"I'll thank you not to take that tone with me!"

Miss Thomas glared at him. Her eyes widened, locking on what he was waving about in his hand. Twin points of color climbed to her cheeks, and she jumped to her feet. Her hand snaked out, and she grasped one end of the soft material, tugging. Determined to make his point, Garrett tugged right back.

The delicate material gave—with a loud rip. Miranda screeched, wrestling the scrap of thin

39

cotton and lace from him. Puzzled, he frowned at her...until she shook the bit of fabric out, shoving it beneath his nose to display the wide rip down the front.

"Are you happy now, Marshal McCabe?"

Garrett eyed the delicate material. His gaze swung from the torn scrap in her hand to her heaving chest a few feet from his face and back again. In his annoyance, it took a moment to realize what that scrap was...and what he'd just done with it. Wicked images swamped his mind. He was a man, after all, and she was a glorious sight spitting mad. Some of those ideas must have flashed in his quicksilver gaze, for she turned scarlet and rammed the camisole back inside the trunk. She hissed between her teeth, yanking her hand back.

Unthinking, still on his knees, he reached out and grasped her wrist, drawing her resistant hand forward to inspect the injury. Garrett surveyed the scraped knuckle, his brow wrinkling with immediate contrition. Lifting his gaze, he aimed a remorseful stare at her. He still hadn't relinquished his hold on her hand, but his grip eased as his thumb rubbed along her smooth skin, careful to avoid the damaged area.

Knowing full well he was going to have to eat some of his pride where this beauty was concerned, Garrett softened his tone, trying to salvage what was left of the assignment. "Look, I'm sorry. We've all had a...a trying day, and I know we haven't gotten off on the right foot, so to speak. Let's start again, shall we?"

She stared at him with suspicious eyes, and for a moment, he thought she was going to tell him just what he could do with his diplomacy. In the end, her hand still resting in his, some of the tension left her face, and the starch went out of her posture.

"You're right, Marshal McCabe." She offered a

tentative smile, extending her own apology. "I'm sorry for snapping at you. I'm afraid this has all been a bit overwhelming."

"Call me Garrett." He blinked, trying his level best to ignore the shiver her smile sent rippling through his blood. Her skin was so warm. So soft...

"Garrett," she conceded. The sound of his name rolling off her lips was a warm enticement he'd rather not consider.

"Now, Miss Thomas..."

"Miranda," she interrupted.

"Miranda..." Garrett nodded and turned his focus to the mess around them. "I think it would be a good idea if we can get this all packed up and back on the stage as soon as possible. We still have several hours of travel ahead of us before we reach the next town, and by all accounts, the bandits that waylaid you aren't the only band of thieves working this area."

Her eyes widened. Nodding, she turned back to her task then stopped dead in her tracks. He still held her hand.

He didn't know what possessed him, but Garrett drew her hand to his lips and placed a soft kiss on her scraped knuckles before releasing her. Smiling at the bemused expression on her face, he turned away. Together, they gathered the last of her belongings, depositing them back inside the trunk. He tried real hard—honest to God, he did—not to think about the many thin scraps of cotton and lace he gathered from the ground, tried not to think about what they were and exactly what portion of her body they'd covered.

But he *was* a man, after all.

And the vivid red staining her cheeks sure as certain wasn't helping matters any.

The driver and his assistant secured the trunks on top of the stage once again, and the travelers climbed aboard. Garrett tied the reins of both horses to the back of the stage. He ignored the snort of indignation Hades shot him, unsheathed the rifle from his saddle, and climbed up to sit beside the driver, relegating the driver's helper to nest among the trunks.

Garrett laid the rifle across his knees and settled in for a long, uncomfortable ride. His mind wandered to the spirited vixen inside the coach, and he heaved a deep sigh. He considered her dour-faced companion and gritted his teeth.

Damned straight, Judge Thomas was going to owe him for this—and owe him *big*...

Chapter Four

Garrett escorted the coach to Compton, cursing his luck with every rut in the next to non-existent road. More than once, he considered ordering the driver to pull over so he could retrieve his horse, but he was in too much of a hurry to get to the next town.

Garrett heaved a hefty sigh of relief when they pulled into Compton late that night. He climbed down and stretched the stiffness from his muscles before opening the door to hand Miranda and Miss Burns out. Mr. Marks met him at the entrance. Stepping aside, he allowed Marks to descend.

Miss Burns blocked his view when she, too, swept forward. She thrust her knitting bag in his face and demanded assistance. Once on the ground, she stood before him, fists planted on her ample hips, and informed him that Miss Thomas refused to stir herself. That said, she charged off to the nearest boarding house.

Garrett's gaze flew to the coach, and in one, mighty leap, he was inside. Worry gnawed at him, what if she'd struck her head or suffered some unseen injury while at the hands of the bandits? There'd be hell to pay, and it'd be his hide offering the payment.

Miranda was wedged in the corner of the coach, her head tipped at an odd angle. Her chest rose and fell in slow, rhythmic movements, her soft lips parted.

For almost a full minute, he fought the urge to cover her lips with his own. Gritting his teeth, he clasped her shoulder, shaking her. She moaned, soft and low, sliding the tip of her tongue along her lower lip.

His control shook beneath another punch of lust. He gave her another shake, this one more firm than the last. His voice was several degrees less than gentle as he snapped, *"Miranda, wake up!"*

Her eyes drifted open, and she gazed at him. Her smile was soft, her eyes beguiling and hazy with the last dregs of sleep. She murmured his name, saturating his body with a need he could scarce understand. Her hand—so soft, so delicate— caressed his cheek with such tenderness his heart shuddered. The urge to turn his face into her palm and nuzzle was strong, nigh onto impossible to ignore. Her fingers skated over his whiskers, and her brow crinkled. She blinked. Her eyes widened.

She gasped aloud. Her cheeks flamed.

Her breath escaped her in one, horrified word. "Garrett!"

He couldn't fight the smug grin spreading across his face. His gaze dropped to her lips. How would she react if he kissed her?

Her mortified stare dropped to her lap, and she cleared her throat, squirming upright.

Jesus, Mary, and Joseph! What was he thinking? Centering himself, Garrett rocked back on his heels. "We've arrived in Compton."

"Yes, thank you," she murmured, refusing to lift her gaze to his.

A short while later, they stood outside the door to her room in the local boardinghouse. Garrett stole a fleeting glance at her profile. She'd been thinking about him, tender, intimate thoughts judging by her reaction upon waking—regardless of whether it was in the context of a dream or not—and that knowledge affected him more powerfully than he wanted to admit, even to himself.

Clearing his throat—doing his best to keep sight of the fact she was his assignment, his *last* assignment—Garrett eyed her with wary resignation. "We'll be on horseback the rest of the way to Johnston. With a healthy dose of luck, we'll make it in five...maybe six days. You'll need to go through your trunks. Pack essentials in a valise, nothing more. Pack light. I'll make arrangements for your trunks to be delivered to your uncle's house."

He half expected an argument, but she nodded quiet acquiescence. She must be more tired than he'd guessed. Shadows lay heavy beneath her eyes, and guilt niggled at him.

Heaving a sigh, he offered, "I'll have a bath and a tray sent to your room."

"That's very thoughtful of you, Garrett." She tugged a stray lock of hair behind her ear, offering him a wan smile. "Thank you."

He reached past her and opened the door. Oddly reluctant to leave, Garrett leaned a shoulder against her doorframe and observed as she wandered through the room. His thoughts drifted toward the bed, and he marveled at how his mind seemed hell-bent on torturing him. He'd never before had this problem—wanting a woman to the point of distraction.

Damned irritating woman.

What was so special about *her*? Miranda Thomas shouldn't have this kind of hold on him. But she did.

And it worried the hell out of him.

"Miss Burns is in the room next door." Garrett hitched a thumb in his back pocket, unsure if he'd said the last in a bid to offer her comfort, or as a reminder to himself. He pushed away from the doorframe. Best leave now while his pride...and his self-control...were still intact. "If you need anything, I'll be at the end of the hall."

Miranda crossed the room, coming to a stop in front of him. She smiled, and the action lit her features with innocent, albeit sleepy radiance. "Thank you, Garrett. I'm sure I'll be just fine." She studied his face, and a small crease furrowed between her brows. "You should get some rest. You look exhausted...maybe I should be the one ordering *you* a bath and a tray." She eyed his jaw line then, adding, "And a shave."

Garrett blinked down at her, everything inside him had gone strangely still. She was serious. She looked ready to drop—dead on her feet—but the concern she'd just shown him seemed genuine. He shook his head. This side of her was so at odds with the opinion he'd formed of her back in Johnston— back before he'd even met her—the image of a spoiled princess. By the saints, he felt like one of those big catfish he used to catch down at the creek with his brothers, one that'd swallowed the bait...hook, line, and sinker.

Sure enough, that smile of hers was reeling him in, slow and steady.

Ignoring the warmth creeping up his neck and into his cheeks, Garrett offered her an awkward smile. "Don't worry 'bout me. I do just fine takin' care of myself."

"You should trust someone else to take care of you for a change, Garrett. You might find it's worth the risk." Miranda's curious gaze searched his face.

A wide yawn slipped past her guard.

Tenderness swelled in his chest, unexpected. Unsettling. Reaching up, he snagged the soft, wayward curl that refused to remain confined. Savoring every burnished strand, Garrett rubbed the silky tendril between his fingers, marveling that a flame could be so comforting to the touch. Reluctant to break the contact, he tucked the curl behind her ear and traced the contours of her cheek with the backs of his fingers. Her skin was so smooth, so soft.

He tumbled headlong into the beguiling blue of her eyes, and just by the skin of his teeth, did he manage to wrestle his way free. Withdrawing his hand took a supreme effort.

Shaken to the soul, he stepped back and dropped his hand to his side. Still, the urge to sweep her off her feet and slam the door closed on the world was strong. Clearing his throat, desperate to elude those unsettling feelings threatening to set down roots too close to the general area of his heart, Garrett made a mad grab at his wayward wits.

Shaking his head, he spun on his heel and strode down the hall without a backward glance. He paused for a moment just outside his door in a rare moment of indecision, and then disconcerted, he let his feet carry him down the stairs, out the door, and to the saloon at the end of the dusty, rutted street. There wasn't much trouble she could stir up in this hole-in-the-wall town. And she had the stern, holier-than-thou mouse to keep her in line. She'd be fine for a little while without him.

And right now, he needed a little time...and a whole lot of distance...to get his head screwed on straight. Somehow, somewhere along the way, he'd lost perspective.

If he was going to spend the next week with that flame haired hoyden, he was gonna need all the perspective he could get.

A bracing shot of whiskey seemed in order. Remembering the texture of her silky hair as it slid between his fingers, Garrett groaned. He needed something very, *very* badly, indeed.

Unfortunately, it wasn't liquor.

****

Miranda laid her nightgown on the foot of the bed and answered the knock on her door, expecting to see the bath Garrett had promised. Instead, she faced the stern countenance of Miss Burns.

Oh, for pity sake, now what did the wretched harridan want?

Stepping back into her room, Miranda held her door open a bit wider. "Good evening, Miss Burns. I'd thought you'd turned in for the night. Please, come in."

The old wretch stepped just over the threshold but refused to enter any farther. Her mouth pursed. Her beady-eyed gaze darted about the room, as if searching for the slightest indication Miranda had been misbehaving in the least little way.

"Might I help you, Miss Burns?" Fatigued beyond tolerance, Miranda waited for the woman to spew her disapproval and leave her in peace.

Her precious string of pearls came to mind, and Miranda wondered how the woman had come into possession of them. However, at that particular moment, she was too exhausted to delve into that subject. The pearls were gone—along with that infuriating bandit Draco—and arguing the point now seemed moot in any case. Not that it would matter. She was stuck with the woman, whether she liked it or not. She'd just have to keep a closer eye on her belongings.

"Yes, miss." Miss Burns folded her hands before her. Her chin elevated, and she stared at Miranda with cold, self-righteous eyes. "I have come to tender my resignation."

"Really, Miss Burns, there's no need to—"

"No, no," the woman interrupted, holding her hand up as if to discourage Miranda from groveling. "I am determined. I cannot subject myself to any more perils such as I have done today. And, furthermore, I simply cannot countenance such impertinence as I receive from one such as you on a daily basis."

All pretense of obligatory civility vanished in the blink of Miranda's narrowed eyes. She tilted her head to the side, as one would when examining a distasteful bug. "One such as...*me*?"

Miss Burns sighed with dramatic flair. "Yes, miss...one with such obvious loose moral fiber. You ruined a sound engagement in Boston on a whim—don't attempt to deny it, your father told me all about your shameful conduct, you know. Then you saw fit to traipse about the countryside, allowing anyone of a mind to kiss you and lay hands upon your person. You have spoken to me in tones that ought not be heard from a young lady's mouth, and you are impertinent and disrespectful of your elders. Why, it's indecent, I tell you!"

Each inflammatory word set Miranda's teeth on edge. After all this irritating woman had put her through, how dare she criticize? Miranda leveled an accusatory finger and backed the elder woman from the room with each pointed word.

"I believe you've already collected quite more than your severance pay when you took it upon yourself to lay claim to *my* pearls." Miranda glared. "Cast ye not the first stone, Miss Burns..." With that, Miranda slammed the door in the sputtering woman's face. Spinning on her heels, she sagged against the aged wood, exhausted.

What could possibly go wrong next?

Chapter Five

He made his way up the boardinghouse stairs. Miranda met him in the hallway—dressed in a dark blue, curve-hugging riding habit and matching gloves, her fiery hair confined in a severe knot at the back of her head. A jaunty little hat sporting a ridiculous, long white ostrich plume perched on her head.

The valise she carried bulged at the seams. Her step had more bounce than yesterday, but faint shadows lingered beneath her eyes, making her appear vulnerable, ethereal. For a minute, Garrett forgot why he was there. Indeed, he forgot every word in the English language.

"Good morning." A serene smile curled the edges of her lips.

"Ahh..." he sputtered, unable to master his tongue. He blinked, cleared his throat, and tried again. "Good morning. I was on my way to...to—"

"To make sure I wasn't still abed?" Mischief twinkled in her eyes.

Still abed...

He worked—mighty hard—to suppress the vivid images flashing through his mind. What the hell was wrong with him that such innocent statements could lead to such lascivious thoughts? Seeking to turn the conversation, he rumbled, "Is Miss Burns ready? We'll have to stop by the livery this morning and see if we can't find another horse. She can ride, can't she?"

"It doesn't matter if she rides." Miranda grimaced, shifting the valise from one hand to the other. "There will be no need to obtain a mount for her. She quit last night."

"What? Why?" He stared at her, a sinking feeling settled in the pit of his stomach. He could just imagine what Judge Thomas would say when Garrett showed up in Johnston with the judge's niece—without the benefit of the chaperone she apparently was supposed to have with her.

By the saints, what was *he* to do without the tempering effect of that prune-faced old biddy?

"It doesn't matter; she just quit." Miranda clutched the valise before her in a defensive gesture and pushed past him.

No way was he letting that one slide. Grabbing her elbow, he drew her back to face him. "*Now* what did you do?"

Miranda compressed her lips and wrenched her arm free, eyes snapping crystalline fire. "She informed me I was too impertinent. Although, why a common pickpocket should think she was due respect is beyond me. But that doesn't matter to you, does it? It only matters that things aren't running according to *your* plans. Isn't that right, Marshal McCabe?"

He scowled at Miranda, feeling as though he'd landed in the middle of a poker game where the rules had changed without notice, and he was a card short. "A pick-pocket?"

"Yes, a pick-pocket. Though the proof is long gone now, along with that blasted Dra—" She bit the last word off on a groan, rolling her eyes.

Six years of dealing with the criminal element made him fast on the draw, in more ways than one. "Along with whom?"

"I…nothing…"

"Who?"

"I'm hungry," she complained.

"Then I suggest you talk. You're not going

anywhere until you answer my question. You began to say a name..." He glared at her, crossing his arms over his chest. "Now finish."

****

Miranda glared back, furious with herself for slipping. It wasn't as if she felt any loyalty to that scoundrel of a bandit—because she most certainly did not. But Garrett had been rubbing her wrong since the moment she'd met him, with his condescending attitude and his dictatorial commands. She'd had more than her fill of that kind of behavior from her father. She couldn't find it in herself to be forgiving.

Garrett planted his feet, arms crossed over his chest. The glower on his face spoke volumes. Everything about his body language was tantamount to pouring fuel on the fires of malcontent, and yet, she fought her inherent instinct to rebel. Rebellion was what had gotten her here in the first place. Grinding her teeth, Miranda eyed him, wondering how long he'd stand there like that. Could she wait him out? As if reading her thoughts, Garrett lifted an eyebrow and smirked.

Oh yes, he'd wait all day if necessary.

Her stomach growled again, loud and clear, and his smile widened.

Her mother's voice rang in her head. *"Pick your battles, dearest. Men are much easier to manage when they* think *they have the upper hand."*

Heaving a resigned sigh, she snapped, "Fine, the bandit calls himself Draco."

He stared hard at her. "Draco?" A frown wrinkled his brow. "What the hell kind of name is that?"

Her back went ramrod straight, and she lifted her chin. It was just like all those times her father had called her on the carpet for some infraction. He'd always doubted her honesty, though she'd never given him true reason to do so. "If you're going to doubt everything I say, then I suggest you step aside. We're finished here."

"I'll say when we're finished," he growled, stalking forward—towering over her—a move he no doubt used often as a marshal.

His size alone was intimidating in and of itself. When he combined his size with that threatening scowl, many a feared outlaw must have quaked in his respective boots. She, however, was made of sterner stuff. She held her ground, tilting her head back so she could maintain eye contact. Offering him an acerbic smile, she dropped the valise, missing his toe by slim inches.

Damn. She'd have to work on her aim.

"Well then, what do you suggest?" She planted her fists on her hips. "I've told you what I know, and it is more than obvious you have chosen not to believe me. It seems we are at an impasse, Marshal McCabe. Shall we stand here the rest of the day, with my stomach growling and your precious schedule slipping through your fingers? Or do you allow me to pass so we can get on with this bloody trip?"

"I didn't say I didn't believe you. I asked what kind of a name that was, *princess*." He planted his own fists, leaning closer. "If you weren't being so defensive and hot-headed, you'd see there was a difference," he growled between clenched teeth.

She didn't appreciate his tone any more than she appreciated his assessment of her reaction. She wasn't backing down, not for a minute. "I don't know why he calls himself Draco, but I don't believe that's his real name."

Garrett relaxed his stance. Although his scowl was still dark, his nose no longer brushed hers. For the love of all that was holy, trying to get this man to be reasonable was like pulling teeth...from a mule.

"Draco... Draco..." His eyes narrowed and he repeated the name, as if the act of rolling the word off his tongue would loosen some elusive memory into the open.

She watched him mull the name over, aware she'd become, for the nonce, little more than a flicker on the periphery of his awareness. Irritated, she made to step past him, but his hand shot out with the speed of a lightning strike. His grip was gentle, yet unyielding, as he took hold of her elbow. His tone was businesslike, but his eyes gave him away. His mind was already preparing to record every detail. "What else can you tell me about him? What do you remember?"

Heaving a sigh, cursing the man for his stubbornness, she eased back, letting her hands fall to her sides. "He presents himself as a ruffian...dresses like a dusty, down-on-his-luck cowboy. But he seemed very cultured, very...educated. His speech is refined, with a hint of southern drawl...though his accent isn't like most around here. He seemed very self-assured, very arrogant. While the others were careful to keep their faces concealed, he didn't seem to mind that we saw his face. Why, even when I was alone with him in the carriage he—"

The minute the words left her mouth, she knew she'd said too much. Garrett came alive, demanding, "You saw his face?"

Now she'd done it. He wouldn't let up until he had a full description, pumping her for the most minute of details until he was satisfied he could wring no more from her. She thought of Draco's stolen intimacies and cursed her loose tongue.

She pleated the material of her riding skirts between her fingers, then calmed herself with the fact he hadn't picked up on her slip about them being alone. The mere memory of Draco's boldness brought heat to her cheeks. She chewed on her bottom lip, debating how much to offer when her stomach grumbled its complaint again.

Lifting a mutinous brow, she informed him, "I'm not giving you any more information until I've had breakfast."

"Fine." Garrett snarled, the muscle ticking along his jaw. Snatching up her valise, he marched down the hallway and sent a flamboyant wave toward the steps. "At your leisure, *princess.*"

This second use of his insulting nickname grated on her nerves, but before she could let loose her temper, he threw one last comment at her. "One thing you better understand, protect him or not...it'll be a cold day in hell before he's gonna get a chance to kiss you again, so don't get your hopes up."

****

Garrett checked the angle of the sun before stealing a sidelong glance at his stubborn companion. The afternoon bore on, and still she refused to give him more than the most indistinct of descriptions. Long blond hair, blue eyes. Tall. Strong. Handsome.

Handsome, my ass... He was dead certain she'd thrown that last provoking description out there just to spite him.

Hell, the description she'd given him could fit half the men in the damned state. He glanced at her from the corner of his eye again, and grudging admiration displaced his irritation. He'd set a grueling pace, purely out of anger and spite, if he were being honest. Not once had she complained, not once had she lagged behind. To his frustration, the horses showed more wear than she did.

Once the sun crested high in the azure skies, he'd begun to feel guilty, though, and he'd considered slowing the pace. But the more he'd pushed for details, the more she'd refused to bend, and he was determined to wear her down...one way or another. He refused to stop for the noon meal. Instead, he offered her a few tough pieces of jerked beef and a canteen of water. She'd glared her disdain, silent and regal, but she'd eaten.

Her shoulders had begun to droop a bit the last mile or so, and her coloring didn't look at all healthy, but her backbone was ramrod straight. She hadn't glanced in his direction. Not once. He knew, because he hadn't been able to take his eyes off her for long in the last several miles. Gritting his teeth, he tried one more time.

"Look, *princess*. Are you certain there isn't something—some distinguishing mark or distinctive scar—that you might have forgotten? Does he have a nervous tick, a stutter...anything to make him stand out?" She had no one to blame but her hardheaded self if his tone was less than hospitable.

The second he'd called her *princess*, her teeth had snapped together with an audible clack. She dragged in a long, deep breath through flared nostrils and urged the dappled mare to pull ahead of him a few paces.

She turned in the saddle, she called over her shoulder, "You know, now that you mention it..." She tapped a finger against her pursed lips, her eyes narrowed.

Garrett's attention perked. He leaned forward, resting his forearms on the pommel. "Well?" he barked, impatient.

"Although I haven't much experience, he did seem to be a rather talented kisser. Do you suppose you'll be able to find him with that knowledge in mind, Marshal McCabe?"

Her blatant taunt set his teeth on edge. His glare drilled angry holes in her back as he watched her push the gray mare faster. The pace she was setting was beyond stupid. She'd cave in no time at all like this, and that suited him just fine. So what if she got a little wilted. Her condition would only serve to drive his point home. He knew what was best, and the sooner she fell in line, the better it would be for everyone.

He urged Hades forward until the two animals raced side-by-side.

The sun beat down on them, merciless and sweltering. Sweat beaded on his upper lip and forehead. She had to be sweltering beneath all those layers of clothing. Yet she pushed on. Damn her beautiful, stubborn hide. Guilt nipped at him, and he cursed beneath his breath. That damned emotion hadn't bothered him in years, yet it had been sharpening its teeth on his hide with amazing consistency since he'd met the charming Miss Thomas.

What was it about *this* woman? She was no different from any other, except for that cursed mulish streak. How could a woman be so damned...aggravating? She hadn't given him one useful scrap of information. Regardless, he pushed on, unwavering in his conviction she be the one to admit defeat.

Mile passed mile, and still she showed no signs of slowing. Punishing the horses this way was not only stupid, but dangerous. Garrett glanced over to order her to a halt. The words died in his throat. Miranda's expression had gone peculiarly blank. Her pallor flashed from flushed to pale to stark white in the space of a heartbeat. If he hadn't been watching—if he hadn't been so close or hadn't had lightning quick reflexes—she would have toppled from her horse headfirst. Instead, she ended up sprawled across Garrett's lap, unmoving. Hades danced sideways at the sudden additional weight.

Swearing, Garrett tugged the horse back under

control and scowled down at the unconscious woman in his arms, torn between concern and the urge to shake her for pulling a stunt like this. What the hell was wrong with her? She was so pale. He balanced her against his chest and drew rein, swinging his leg back and down, juggling her in his arms. He lowered her to the ground with gentle hands and knelt at her side, holding her slim, soft hand.

"Miranda?"

Nothing.

The sharp bite of fear sank its teeth in deep, far more vicious than the uncomfortable nip of guilt. He patted her cheek. "Miranda!"

Still nothing.

Garrett's heart hammered. He passed a hand over her brow. She didn't feel feverish. If anything, she was a bit clammy. His palm skimmed down the contours of her cheek, registering the satin softness of her skin. His fingers lingered at the base of her throat. Her pulse was racing.

"Hell and damnation," he cursed.

He hesitated, then skimmed his hand lower, hovering over her chest. She was barely breathing. He pressed his hand against the fabric of her bodice and let out an angry hiss.

"Damn fool woman!"

He gave her one short, reproving glare before grasping the upper edges of her bodice in both hands. Garrett yanked with considerable force, venting his anger on the fragile material of her bodice. Buttons sailed through the air, velvet tore, and still Miranda's eyes remained closed, her breathing all but nonexistent. He stared for half a second at the unyielding contraption she wore beneath the velvet, and cursed again. Muttering to himself about women and their infernal ideas about fashion, he unsheathed the large knife from his boot and slipped the honed edge along the length of her corset.

Her chest rose on a sharp, deep breath once the tiny row of catches came loose. Color crept into her cheeks. As her chest continued to rise and fall, he couldn't help but notice, with deep masculine appreciation, what nice breasts she had. Even through the thin chemise she wore, the generous swell of milky white flesh drew his gaze. The shadow of puckered coral pressing against the filmy material made his mouth water. His hands itched with the need to touch, to feel the weight of her breasts in his hands, experience the insistent thrust of her nipples hardening against his palms.

Garrett sucked in a ragged breath and forced his eyes away, but his gaze settled on her narrow waist, and he was confounded. Why on earth would a woman force herself to endure such a restrictive contraption when she plainly had no need for it...whatsoever?

With his rapt attention centered on her midriff, he didn't pay much attention to the muscles tensing in her shoulder. The crack of her hand against his cheek echoed in the sandy, arid patch of plains.

Her breath heaved in and out now. "Get off me you...you *ass!*"

"I'm not on you," Garrett growled back. Nevertheless, he stood and backed away a cautious step, then another. His cheek stung something smart. He had to give her credit. He hadn't even seen it coming. Of course, in all fairness, he'd been more than a little distracted.

Miranda scrambled to a sitting position, clutching at her gaping bodice, cheeks flaming. "What have you done?"

Garrett watched—with more amusement than was probably appropriate—as she wrestled the corset from beneath her clothing without removing the torn bodice. It didn't look to be an easy feat, but she managed just fine. It took everything in him to look away from the jiggle of those magnificent breasts.

She held the slashed corset in her hands for a moment, sheer horror etched in every line of her expression. And then the horror was gone. Replaced by white-hot fury. She waved the damaged corset at him in a furious fist. He'd seen doused cats looking happier than she did right then.

The second time in two days he'd seen her unmentionables brandished about in the air. Even as she scowled, he couldn't help but wonder what tomorrow would hold in store. There was no denying it, with Miranda around life held no hope of ever being dull.

"Oh, would you look what you've done. You've ruined it," she railed, tugging the material open with two hands to examine the sliced edges. "You've cut it clean through."

"It seemed the most expedient way to get it off at the time." He lifted a wry eyebrow, but his gaze had wandered back to her gaping bodice, and he gave a mental shrug—he *was* a man, after all.

How long would it take her to realize her corset hadn't been the only victim?

Following the direction of his absorbed stare, Miranda's gaze dropped to her gaping bodice, and the color in her cheeks deepened. "You've ruined my riding habit, too. Where are all my buttons?"

"Oh, here and there," he drawled, grinning as he gave the area a wide, negligent sweep of his arm.

"Oooh…" she snarled, killing him with her eyes.

Irritation crept up his spine. "You're welcome, *princess.*"

"Welcome? Welcome!" Miranda shrieked. Struggling to her feet, battling to keep the edges of her bodice closed, she glared daggers at him. "How dare you!" She shook the corset at him again, as if to punctuate her point. "You ruin my clothing and expect gratitude? You are impossible!"

Aiming an accusatory finger at her, he snapped, "You passed out."

"You ruined my clothing," she argued.

"You couldn't breathe," Garrett countered, seething.

"A gentleman would have—"

"A gentleman would have what?" Garrett pounced. "No, let me guess. A gentleman would have let you lay there turning blue while he went to find another woman to assist you. Or would he have taken the time to undo all those infernal buttons, so as not to shred your precious wardrobe?"

She hissed, "You rude, overbearing, conceited...*ooooh.*"

His snarl came back, fast as a whip and with every bit as much of a crack to it. "When you start behaving like a lady...instead of some spoiled, pampered princess...then you can condemn me for not being gentleman enough for the likes of you." He leaned closer, his voice dropping an octave. "Be careful of that halo, *princess*. If it slips much farther, you're liable to choke yourself with it."

His hands shook. He wanted, desperately, to shake her...or turn her over his knee. Instead, he stomped off to retrieve the horses.

"Go to hell!" Her voice shot across the distance between them, dripping venom.

He stopped dead in his tracks. It was wrong to let her get under his skin—he knew it—but he couldn't seem to stop himself. He rounded on her with a vengeance, his eyes cold and hard as diamonds, dark as sin. "I've already been there, *princess*...the devil wouldn't let me past the front gate."

Miranda stared, wide-eyed for a moment before turning away. She staggered to her horse and yanked at the valise tied to her saddle, but she must not have been able to get the strap worked free. She gave up and dropped her forehead against the horse's neck, defeated.

Damn it all to hell...

There was that infernal guilt again. Conceding this round as up for grabs, he stomped forward and reached around her, boxing her in, trapping her between his body and the horse. He froze. Her scent writhed around him, a stray wisp of her hair feathered against his neck. His head swam.

Startled, he stepped away and the sensation of drowning receded. She turned to look at him, her inviting lips parted. Her eyes were soft and confused. She was vulnerable, more so than he'd ever seen her. And this side of her triggered emotions he had little experience with. Urges to protect and comfort. Urges to seduce and ravish.

His hungry stare dipped to her gaping bodice. He took a step forward, lifting a hand to smooth the stray lock of hair behind her ear. His fingertips trailed down the delicate line of her jaw. Silk. Her skin was just like perfect, creamy silk. Her lips were plush, smooth, and enticing. His mouth watered for a taste of her. Just one.

She blinked. Once. Then her captivating eyes widened, and she tugged the torn material back together.

It took every bit of his determination, every ounce of his self-control to force the words past the fist desire held clamped on his throat.

His voice sounded gruff, even to his own ears. "Get changed so we can get a move on. At this rate we'll be lucky to make the next town before nightfall."

"Turn your back," she whispered. Her eyes wouldn't meet his anymore.

For a moment, he wasn't sure he could do as

she'd asked. Walking away from her was pure hell, but walk away he did.

Denying himself the warmth of her skin left a hole in him he couldn't even begin to fathom.

Chapter Six

"Don't you ever let up?" Miranda shrugged the tension from her shoulders, glancing over at Garrett. She shifted in the saddle in time with the horse's steady, rolling gait. "You're like a dog with a bone, for pity sake."

"I need to know what you know," he insisted. "Your life could depend on it."

She managed to keep from rolling her eyes, though the unladylike snort escaped her altogether. "That's being a bit dramatic, don't you think?"

"As a matter of fact, I'm very serious. If that bandit begins to worry you're a reliable witness, he could take it into his head to eliminate you. I need to know everything you know if I'm going to protect you." Garrett tugged on Hades' reins, turning his horse into Miranda's path, forcing her mount to a halt. "You could be in danger."

"Protect me from Draco? Don't be ridiculous. He wouldn't hurt me. If he intended to harm me, why would he have—" She broke off mid-sentence, appalled at once again having fallen under the hypnotic spell of those stormy eyes.

Garrett's stare sharpened, turning downright piercing. "Why would he what?"

"Nothing," she muttered, trying to guide her horse around his.

Garrett snatched the reins from her hands and nudged his mount into hers, crowding her. "Why are you protecting him?"

Struggling to keep a leash on her temper, she denied, "I'm not protecting him."

"Then why do you refuse to answer me?" He got right in her face, hammering questions faster than she could hedge, throwing her off-balance. "What did he say to you?"

"What?" Bewildered and defensive, she stared, struggling in vain to keep up with his interrogation. "I'm not protecting him. He said nothing to me, not a thing."

"Did he address any of the other men by name?"

"I don't think so," she stammered.

"Why did he kiss you?"

"Which time?" *Damn it.* She hadn't meant to say that.

"What did he take?"

"He took everything of value, except my money belt."

"Did you have it hidden, then?" His stare was intense as he pumped more questions at her. "How many others were with him?"

"Well, I..." Her head was beginning to spin. "Yes, it was hidden under my bodice. I can't remember—five maybe."

"Did any of the others talk? Did they have accents?"

"No one else spoke..."

He reined his horse to an abrupt halt, his eyes narrowed, as if one of her earlier answers had finally clicked into a certain compartment in his brain, a compartment he didn't like at all. "What do you mean *'which time'*? And if the money belt was hidden *under* your bodice how the hell did he know about it?"

Heat shot up her neck, exploding in her cheeks. Her temples were beginning to ache, her brain to throb. She'd tell him whatever he wanted to know, if he'd just cease his incessant barrage of questions. "Which time implies there was more than one occurrence. Suffice it to say, he knew about my money belt, but chose not to take it. I don't believe he'd harm me. He seemed ruthless, but hurting a woman just didn't seem like it was in his character."

Quicksilver eyes turned stormy gray in the blink of an eye. "Not good enough, *princess*. Explain!"

Heaving a deep sigh, she stared long and hard at him. "If I tell you what happened—all of it—will you just drop it? I want to forget the whole thing ever happened."

"Fine," he consented, then amended, "As long as you'll answer whatever questions I ask, I'll let it go...for now."

Miranda drew a long breath and let the whole story pour out starting with the moment the tall mysterious Draco boarded the stage. As she ended her tale with the odd promise Draco gave her about seeing her again, Garrett stared with shrewd, calculating eyes. She had a good head for details, and she'd given a strong, precise recounting. She gave herself a mental pat on the back, having left no room for him to question or poke holes in her memory.

"How did he know about your money belt?"

Oh, for the love of Pete...

"I'd rather not answer that," she hedged, letting her gaze slide away from his.

"We had an agreement," he barked.

She lifted her chin a notch. "When the other passengers exited the stage, Draco detained me. He said his men would demand to know that they had acquired everything. He said he wanted to spare me the indignity of having them search me."

"Go on," Garrett insisted. His voice was soft, but his knuckles on the hand clenching his reins had turned white.

"He kissed me inside the coach and then he...he put his hands on...on my person," she stumbled through the explanation, never having been so mortified. "I'm sure he felt the money belt. He even hinted at it later when I confronted him. Yet he didn't take it. I don't know why. Please, you can't say anything to Uncle Milton. He'd have apoplexy."

Fretful, Miranda waited, her mount shifted beneath her. Garrett's face was dark red. The lines around his mouth were pinched, grim. His eyes were hard as nails as he stared at her bodice. The muscle in his jaw clenched tight. Then he wheeled his mount around and sent it cantering off, leaving her to follow after, or not.

Miranda blinked after his dust trail, confused. Was that the end of his questions then?

Dear Lord, please…
****

The rest of the day passed in a blur, albeit a silent one. Garrett hadn't uttered a word since their confrontation, and she didn't know whether to be grateful or worried. The outskirts of a small, dust-covered community came into view just as her back began to ache and her thighs to burn. Saunders, the rough plank signpost read. Content to let the silence ride—then again maybe she was just afraid to upset the tenuous balance—she let her mount trail in Garrett's wake as he angled for a hitching post in front of a large, comfortable-looking house.

The crisp, whitewashed structure and its meticulous flowerbeds were incongruous against the rolling tumbleweed and sandy soil. Pots filled to overflowing with bright, cheerful flowers lined the wraparound porch. A slight gust of wind sent the porch swing in the far corner swaying back and forth with a melodic creak.

She could almost hear Garrett grinding his teeth as he vaulted from his saddle and secured his horse to the post before he approached her. He refused to meet her gaze as he reached up and grasped her about the waist. Indeed, he couldn't seem to lift his eyes from her bodice, though the look on his face at that moment was anything but amorous. He set her on the ground with enough force to rattle her teeth, releasing her so quickly she swayed on her feet. Without a backward glance, he spun on his heel and headed for the door.

Miranda blinked after him. *What was eating at him?*

Her shoulders drooped, and her feet dragged as she followed him up the steps through the large door into the front parlor. It didn't occur to her that he hadn't bothered to knock before entering until the door closed behind her.

The parlor was large and cozy. A cheery fire burned in the grate, an inviting grouping of comfortable chairs and a settee flanked the warmth. The brocade covering the seats had faded with time, the wallpaper aged but spotless. Her gaze fell to the gleaming floors, and she wished she'd been sensible enough to wipe the dust from her boots before entering. The enticing aroma of baking bread and roasting fowl filled the air, and she almost groaned aloud.

A large woman, clad from head to toe in starched black, bustled from a doorway at the rear of the house. With a jovial smile, she reached out, clasping Garrett's hands with warm familiarity, tugging him into her plump arms. Her hair, swept back in a tight bun at the nape of her neck, was soft ebony with wings of snowy white at her temples. Her eyes crinkled at the corners in comfortable lines of humor. Her coffee colored skin was weathered and lined with age, but looked soft as silk to the touch.

"Thought I'd surely seen the last of you when I caught word you'd settled over in Johnston, you devil!" She beamed at Garrett. Delight lit her pudgy face, bringing bright, happy color to the apples of her cheeks.

"Pearl..."

Garrett's smile held warmth so deep Miranda felt a twinge of jealousy niggle through her. She watched as he returned the older woman's comfortable embrace. She bussed both his cheeks, then reached up—way up—and patted the top of his head just as she would have a six-year-old boy. Her gaze lit on Miranda, and she turned a wide-eyed smile to Garrett.

"You brought me your young lady!"

Miranda had been sweeping the room in slow, weary perusal. At Pearl's words, her startled gaze swerved back to the woman, and she stuttered, "No, no...I...we aren't...that is I'm not—"

Before Miranda could form a complete denial of Pearl's erroneous assumption, Garrett leapt into the void—albeit with less grace. "She's *not* my *anything*! Miranda is just an assignment."

Her mouth snapped closed. For reasons beyond her understanding, his tone sent a sliver of something akin to hurt spiking into her chest. *Just an assignment...* A frown furrowed her brow, and she caught the inside of her lower lip between her teeth.

"Oh...I see..." Pearl's smile was soft...and unmistakably pleased. Her wispy brows winged up in a study of innocence...too bad the devil still twinkled in her eyes.

"Pearl..." Garrett's tone held a clear warning, but she patted him on the cheek and stepped around him, reaching for Miranda's hands. As soon as she got a firm hold, Pearl hauled Miranda into an affectionate embrace.

"Let me see you, child. My goodness, you're a real looker all right." Pearl grinned approval as she leaned back, her artless smile set Miranda at ease.

Miranda relaxed, taken with the old woman. "Thank you for having me in your home, ma'am. I hope we won't be too much of an imposition."

"Oh, and a sweet one, too," Pearl beamed. Turning back to Garrett, she grinned and crowed, "You picked a right fine one, Garrett, right fine indeed. It's about time, too."

Garrett rolled his eyes, and Miranda gaped, wide-eyed and horrified. Unperturbed, Pearl bustled back through the doorway, calling over her shoulder, "Garrett, you go round up them bags and bring 'em on in. Miss Miranda, you come on with me now, child. We'll have us a cup of tea, and you can tell me how you caught my Garrett."

Miranda looked to Garrett for help, baffled. Embarrassment burned her cheeks. Garrett shook his head as he sauntered to the door, apparently familiar with—or resigned to—Pearl's bossy ways. He shot one last pitying look over his shoulder at Miranda, and then he disappeared outside, leaving her to sink or swim on her own.

Lifting her chin, squaring her shoulders, Miranda set off after Pearl, cursing Garrett to Lucifer and back with each step.

****

By the time Garrett bedded the horses down and carried Miranda's valise inside, Pearl had Miranda ensconced at the table with a steaming cup of tea in hand. Garrett propped a shoulder against the doorframe as Pearl regaled Miranda with the story of how she and Garrett had first met.

"...and in rode Garrett, bold as brass. He chased those scoundrels off and warned 'em never to return or they'd answer to him," Pearl finished on a chuckle, her eyes misty.

From the doorway, Garrett cleared his throat and grinned as Miranda jumped in her seat, rattling teacup against saucer.

Pearl glanced over at him, unabashed, as if she'd known he'd been standing there, listening in the whole time. "There's my hero."

"You're not telling that old story again, are you?" He moved into the room and plucked a sugar cookie from the plate in the middle of the table. Sampling the bit of confection, he winked at Pearl. "I'm gonna have to set something up, so I can sweep in and save the day again. Then you'll have a new story to tell."

Pearl glanced at Miranda, a mysterious smile flirting around the edges of her expressive mouth. "Oh, I'm sure there'll be stories to tell soon enough."

Garrett flicked a gaze over Miranda. An uneasy feeling fluttered in the pit of his stomach. He'd be an idiot not to wonder what his old friend was cooking up now. She glowed with mischief as she floated around her little kitchen.

"You just carry Miss Miranda's things and show her on up to the rose room now. I've got a nice couple staying in the blue room, or I'd give her that one." Turning a crafty glance from Miranda to Garrett, Pearl crooned, "It's the prettiest blue—just like your eyes, child—isn't that right, Garrett?"

When Garrett offered nothing more than a grunt, Pearl shot him an exasperated look. "I sent Josiah and Jude up to get a bath going for her. Miss Miranda, you finish that tea and then you go on up and soak. There's plenty of time 'fore supper's done. The Sherman's have friends in town, so we won't be waitin' on them. That's just fine, gives us a chance to catch up some more. I'll send Garrett up to fetch you down in a bit."

Pearl turned away and lifted the lid off a big black pot. Thick plumes of steam spiraled up, dispersing in tempting fragrances. Garrett polished off another cookie, watching Miranda down the rest of her tea in a few large gulps.

She followed him up the steps in silence. He led her down a long hall with a row of doors on either side. He carried her valise through the third doorway on the right and laid it on the bed. As he straightened, Garrett's gaze brushed the high backed copper tub in the corner. His imagination seized him by the throat and ran away with him.

He fought a valiant battle to keep the taunting images from crowding into his mind. And he failed. Miserably. His teeth ached from gritting them so hard against the lust raking through his guts. "I'll be back in an hour or so," he informed her. By the saints, he had to get out of here. Now...before he did something he'd regret. "Do you need anything else?"

"No, I'll be fine, thank you." Her eager eyes were already on the tub.

Garrett stepped out into the hall and closed the door with a soft click. He dragged in a long, slow breath as he stalked down the hall and thumped his way down the stairs. His feet carried him straight to the kitchen, much as they had dozens of times in the past. He worked to keep his thoughts focused on the woman humming over her bubbling pots. If he didn't, he knew they'd wander to the woman upstairs...and that was *not* acceptable. Leaning against the doorframe, he watched as Pearl added spiced crumble to a pan near to overflowing with plump, juicy peaches.

In some ways, Pearl was very much like his own mother...compassionate, sentimental, and devoted to those she loved. In many ways, they were very different. Mary McCabe was quiet, unassuming, and wouldn't dream of meddling in Garrett's affairs. She was always there, always supportive, but she believed she'd raised her sons to be smart enough to make the right decisions for themselves.

Pearl was another story altogether. She was loud, direct, and saw nothing wrong with pushing and maneuvering, letting the ends justify the means. She'd helped him out a time or two. Hell, she'd even patched up a bullet wound—or three. They had a connection, the two of them. A connection that ran right back to his first week of marshaling. What a mess he'd been back then. It was a small wonder he hadn't gotten himself killed several times over that first week alone.

Pearl's laughing voice broke into his thoughts. "You just gonna stand there all night holding that doorway up, or ya'll gonna come finish this here plate of cookies?"

Garrett grinned, straightened, and ambled across the room. He drew out a chair and reached for a cookie. But the smile of anticipated pleasure died on his lips when Pearl turned shrewd eyes on him.

In typical Pearl fashion, she got right down to business. "Now tell me why you ain't used what common sense the good Lord gave you. Why are you so determined to let that pretty piece upstairs slip right through your fingers?"

****

Before climbing into the tub of steaming bliss, Miranda poured a generous amount of rose scented bath oils into the water. She groaned in sheer relief as the heat of the water cocooned her, easing the ache from her muscles. She made short work of washing the grime from her hair and skin, then leaned back and gave in to the luxury of just soaking, sinking into the blissful elixir, letting the scent relax her body and soothe her soul. Her head tilted back against the edge of the tub, her arms draped along the rim, and she closed her eyes. The events of the last several weeks crowded in on her, and she cringed.

Resolving to push it all aside, she worked to clear her thoughts, but a steady, quicksilver gaze filled her mind. He was a puzzle, Garrett. So by-the-book, so disciplined and focused. Yet, at odd times, she caught flashes of heat, glimpses of something else. Something she couldn't quite put her finger on.

So different from Draco...and yet, strange enough, there was something elementally alike between Garrett and the flirtatious bandit.

Irritating as it may be to her, that quality, too, was illusive. It was as if they both held threads of the same make-up, had been cut from the same cloth. Then she considered Draco's bold flirting and brazen kisses. She fingered her lips for a thoughtful moment, and she snorted.

They weren't so very much alike in that respect. Garrett wouldn't ever lose control long enough to do something so outrageous. But oh, how she wished she could be there to see it when and if he ever did. What a sight that would be, she thought with a faint grin.

****

Garrett stood in front of her door, staring at the wooden panels, grinding his teeth. Even as irritation mixed with worry, he wondered why in the hell she wasn't responding to his knock. Had she decided to take a nap? Patience at an end, he reached out and tried the doorknob. It turned. With a sigh of impatience, he pushed the door inward. He'd just hurry her along and be on his way.

The words died in his throat when he stepped inside her room. The heady scent of roses surrounded him, drawing him farther into the room, speeding his pulse to an irrational, mind-boggling pace.

Like a predator lured by the compelling scent of its prey.

Like prey lulled into an irresistible trap set by the most cunning of predators.

The room was warm, the air damp from the steam pouring from her bath. A toasty fire burned in the grate on the opposite side of the room, emitting a dreamy glow. On the small, round table beside the tub, a cut-glass oil lamp burned low. The flame cast a muted glow, bathing the room and everything in it in golden, rosy hues.

But it was the woman reclining in her bath that stole his very ability to breathe, to move, to think. To resist. Her head rested against the high back of the tub, revealing the delicate curve of her delectable neck and shoulders just above the rim. The sweep of dark lashes fanned her pale cheeks. A slight grin—much as the proverbial cat with the cream—turned the corners of her lush lips up in tempting allure.

Her hair hung down in soaked, fragrant ringlets, the ends swirling in the water around her. The flawless, ivory swell of her breasts, pink now from the heat of her bath, glistened with moisture, taunting him to lick and nibble. Her supple arms rested on the rim of the tub. Her skin gleamed in the soft light. Her trim knees stuck up out of the water. Heaven help him, what he wouldn't give to skim his hands along the delectable line of her thighs. Higher and higher...until he touched her...

His mouth went dry as she lifted one willowy leg into the air, dainty toes pointed, and ran a hand up the length of her calf from ankle to knee. Then she lowered her small foot once more into the water, draping her arm on the rim once more. She sighed, the sound deep and filled with pleasure. His hand tightened on the doorknob, his manhood straining against the buttons of his pants. His heart raced. Every cell in his body centered on the woman in the tub as desire pulsed to life inside him, raw and vicious.

The walls of his resistance trembled.

Gathering his wits—drawing them about him like a desperate, protective cloak—he cleared his throat. Miranda's eyes popped open, and she gasped in startled surprise. For half the space of a heartbeat, she froze as his hungry eyes raked over every inch of exposed flesh. Then she sank down as far as she could, until she'd submerged up to her chin. Water sloshed onto the floor, and he blessed every drop, for that was one less ounce of water to conceal her from his hungry stare. She could do nothing to cover her knees, and his ravenous gaze fell to those delectable limbs.

What would they feel like hooked about his waist as he...

"I knocked—twice," he all but shouted, shaking himself free of those tormenting images. Still he couldn't tear his eyes away from her exposed knees. "Supper's ready."

"Oh...I...I didn't hear you. Thank you, I'll...I'll be right down." Her pointed stare moved from him to the door, then back.

He gawked at her for long moments more. Reluctant, he backed from the room with one last look of longing before he closed the door. Pausing in the hallway, just outside her door, he struggled to regain his wits. The muted sound of water splashing on the other side of the door wrung a tortured groan from his lips, and he clenched his fists at his sides. Gritting his teeth against the demons of lust gnawing at him with vicious glee, he strode out to the back porch and sat down in one of the rockers Pearl loved so much.

Shifting in his seat, he stared at the thick sliver of moon where it nestled in a sky of deep blue velvet, surrounded by twinkling diamonds. He drew one deep breath after another, willing the blood to travel back to other starved parts of his body—like his brain—and leave his throbbing groin the hell alone. Lord knew, only a blood-starved brain would be thinking the things he'd been thinking when he'd been standing there, staring at the princess in her bath.

He groaned aloud and swiped a hand over his eyes, willing the vivid images from his mind. It was no use. They'd been seared upon his mind as permanent as a red-hot branding iron laid to cowhide. He cleared his throat and shifted in his seat again, readjusting the bulge in his pants, glowering at the darkness beyond Pearl's clothesline. The night was quiet. The shadows were still.

Garrett thought of his ranch, just as quiet and still more nights than not. He'd bought it at an estate sale through an agent, and he'd been pleased with the purchase. The spread met all the requirements he'd outlined. He'd designed a new brand for his herd, a four-leaf clover with the letter M in the middle. He'd renamed the spread, christening it the Lucky Clover, in honor of his family, Irish to their bones.

The ranch had given his life new purpose. It had become his haven. A refuge from the memories, both those that had driven him to marshaling...and those that had driven him from it. It had also become his prison as he locked himself in search of the ideal he'd determined his life should be, unable to find the right step to get from point A to point C.

He squared his jaw and rubbed at the knot forming in the curve between his neck and shoulder. It wouldn't be a prison for much longer. As soon as he got back, he'd see about that. He'd stop dragging his damned heels and pick a woman from the gaggle that were forever throwing themselves in his path...someone quiet and obedient with a pretty face.

He'd set up household, and then he wouldn't be alone. So what if he didn't love her—whoever he ended up with—affections grew given sufficient time. Didn't they? And if love never came...well, then he would still respect her. They would have children. Children he could love. A family to replace the one he'd lost. He thought for a moment of Nick and Nora, of the love they'd shared, and he gave a resigned, regretful sigh. A love like theirs just wasn't in the cards for him. The squeak of the springs on the door, the scrape of wood on wood, brought his focus back to the porch.

Pearl pushed the door open and stepped out into the cool evening air with a gusty sigh. He looked up into her warm chocolate-colored eyes as the weight of her knobby hand settled on his shoulder.

"You done good, child. You done real good, makes my old heart proud." She waddled across the porch and lowered herself to the rocker opposite his, drawing a deep breath of flower-scented evening air.

"Now Pearl," Garrett admonished, "I told you. She's not mine."

She pushed his denial aside with no regard whatsoever. "She's a feisty one. I can see it in her eyes—goes with that fiery hair, you know. It's the Irish in her...from her grandmother, she said. Life won't be dull with that one. You'll have your hands full, that's for sure."

Determined to make her understand, Garrett interrupted in a firm, no-nonsense tone, "Miranda— Miss Thomas—is my assignment. She's not my— we're not...involved."

Despite his words to the contrary, the memory of Miranda in her bath brought heat to his cheeks— and his groin—and he was forced to look away from knowing chocolate eyes, forced to consider perhaps he was trying to convince more than just Pearl that there was nothing between him and his princess.

The princess, he corrected himself. *The* princess. She wasn't *his* anything.

"Well, now. I have to say I'm surprised. I expected you to have enough sense to snatch that one right up before someone else comes along and steals her right out from under your nose." Pearl stared at him with pity, heaving a disappointed sigh. "Why are you being so mule-headed?"

"She is *not* what I'm looking for. She's too...volatile." Garrett shook his head and shrugged, struggling to find the right words to make Pearl understand—and perhaps remind himself. "I want peace and quiet."

Pearl tsked. "Aw, now that surely is a shame."

Garrett arched a brow, knowing if he waited long enough, Pearl would give him her take on things. She always did, one way or another.

"They say youth is wasted on the young—well, I say wisdom is. Garrett, life ain't meant for settlin'. Life's meant to be grabbed hold of with both hands and enjoyed. If you're gonna settle, you might as well pick out your headstone, dig a hole out back, and crawl on in." Pearl shook her head, folding her arms across her plump middle.

"She's prickly," he complained.

"You're prickly," Pearl retorted, quick as a flash. "She's just left behind everything she knows. She's movin' to a new town with new faces, and she doesn't have the slightest idea what to expect. Have you considered—jes' once—what she's been through in the last few days alone? Why, my stars! She's traveled halfway 'cross the country through no choice of her own. She was held up in a robbery and kissed by a bandit just yesterday, and by the looks of her, I'd say she was ready to drop on her feet." Pearl turned sharp eyes on Garrett. He squirmed in his seat. "What's your excuse?"

Garrett stared in disbelief as Pearl shook her head one more time and pushed to her feet, her joints creaked as if punctuating her displeasure. He marveled that Pearl had gotten so much out of Miranda in such a short amount of time, but then he snorted in chagrin. He shouldn't be surprised in the least. Pearl was Pearl, after all.

She reached for the squeaky door, her voice floated to him on the cool evening breeze. "Supper's on the table, I'm turnin' in early—storms a comin' and my joints don't treat me kindly when they do. You be sure to let Miss Miranda know I'll see ya'll in the mornin'."

Garrett nodded, and the door slapped closed behind her. Silent and thoughtful, he set the chair to rocking, drawing a measure of comfort from the steady creak of the old wood as he puzzled through Pearl's words. Maybe Pearl was right. Maybe Miranda was just anxious about going to live in Johnston. Maybe, if he tried to ease her way some, she'd be a bit less temperamental.

Then, once he got her to Johnston, she'd be the judge's problem and off his hands.

Nodding his head, satisfied with his course of action, he rose from his chair and went back inside.

Once more—in what was fast becoming a regular occurrence where Miranda was concerned—Garrett was struck speechless. His hands clenched at his sides, and the blood rushed back to his groin, leaving him lightheaded and filled with rampant need. He stood at the foot of the stairs, staring in wonder as a flame-haired angel descended the stairs, and the once solid ground beneath his feet trembled.

Chapter Seven

Garrett stared at Miranda; he couldn't find his voice. Couldn't force his eyes away. She'd brushed her hair back, tied it with a simple ribbon. The fiery tresses bounced and curled down the length of her back, flitting around her waist, glinting in the firelight. She wore a simple cotton dress with full-length sleeves and a modest neckline. There was nothing daring about it, nothing revealing in the least. But it matched her eyes.

His pulses thrummed like a stirred up beehive.

Miranda paused halfway down the steps. Her hand hovered over the polished rail. For one long moment, she stared back. Her lips parted. Then she blinked and glanced away as becoming color flooded her cheeks. When she reached the landing, Garrett took her hand. He drew it to his lips, his bemused stare locked once again with her wide-eyed gaze.

"Pearl turned in, but supper is on the table."

"Oh..." That one word slid over him in a wash of delicious shivers.

Garrett led her to the kitchen and pulled a chair out for her. The scent of roses wafted from her hair, from her skin as she stepped close. He bit down on the inside of his cheek lip to keep from groaning his misery aloud.

Garrett turned his focus to the spread on the table. Pearl had set out her best china. She'd placed a small white vase with an intricate blue floral design in the center of the table and filled it with evening primrose. Covered dishes filled the room with delicious aromas. His mouth watered, and he realized with a shocking jolt that his state of hunger had nothing to do with Pearl's food—and everything to do with the woman at his side. Miranda slid into the chair, drawing the pressed linen cloth across her lap as she waited for Garrett to join her.

"Pearl seems to have gone to quite a bit of trouble. I hope this wasn't all on my account."

Garrett thought it much more plausible that Pearl was trying to *stir up* trouble—and she most certainly *had* done it for Miranda's benefit—but he held his tongue on that point and returned her smile. "I hope you're hungry. If I know Pearl there's enough here to feed a small army."

With that prediction, Garrett uncovered the first of the platters. A mountain of herb-roasted chicken and steamed, seasoned vegetables beckoned them. Garrett moved on down the table, uncovering a heaping plate of golden, fluffy biscuits. Last, he lifted the edge of a towel to reveal Pearl's bubbling, golden peach crumble.

Miranda's eyes rounded as she stared at the food on the table between them. "All this is for us?"

"It is," he drawled, reaching for her plate. "As I said, I hope you're hungry."

He loaded her plate and placed it before her. Then he filled his own plate. The food was every bit as delicious as it looked, and Garrett steered the conversation proficiently. He could be enjoyable company when he set his mind to it.

Somewhere between his description of the mercantile in Johnston, with its nosy proprietress, and his depiction of the skinny, talkative man who ran the telegraph office, Miranda relaxed back against her chair. Laughter rolled from her lips and twinkled in her eyes.

"You'll like Natalia Lewis and Hope Kincaid." He tried to reassure her without being obvious, Pearl's admonishments floating in the back of his mind. "Both women live on ranches just outside of Johnston, but they make it to town quite often. Well, Natalia does. Hope is expecting their first child and her husband doesn't like for her to travel much right now."

"He sounds very...bossy," she commented between bites.

"Over-protective, is more like it...and that's an understatement. They just got married not too long ago," he explained, then added with a grin, "and she has him wrapped around her little finger. So did Matt and Natalia, for that matter...got married, I mean. That's when I met them all—at Matt and Natalia's wedding. I tell you what, that was a day I'll never forget!"

She lifted a curious brow and tilted her head.

"Halfway through the wedding dance, there was a stampede," he began, settling back in his seat. "Ethan and most of the men took off after the herd, but then one of Ethan's stables over at the Circle K was set on fire, and his horses were turned loose. Matt and I went to Ethan's place to help put out the fire and round up the horses. We didn't find out 'til later on that it was all a setup." He fell quiet for a moment, as the darker memories of that night came back. He'd never seen that kind of fear before—the fear in Matt's eyes—and he prayed to God he never would again.

"There was this renegade named Vega plaguing Matt and Ethan. He had killed Ethan's first fiancée, Natalia's daughter, in a similar raid a few years back. Anyway—while we were occupied with the horses, Vega raided Matt's place, the Bar M, and kidnapped Hope. Matt and I didn't find out about it until it was too late for us to do anything."

Miranda's gaze was riveted on his face. Absorbed in his tale, she sat at the edge of her seat and leaned her elbows on the table. "What happened?"

"Natalia came tearing over the hill, a young stable boy holdin' on to her for dear life. She was next thing to hysterical, tellin' us how they'd managed to escape Vega's men, but that one of Matt's men had been shot, and Hope had turned back to help him. By the time we got back to Matt's, Vega's men had killed Manuel and several others. Vega's men were vicious, sadistic bastards—in all my years as a marshal, I've never seen the like. They'd taken Hope up into the mountains. Ethan and Antonio Diaz, Matt's foreman, had gone after her. There was no way for us to get to them in time to be of any help. Matt was half-crazed with fear.

"We headed out after them, all the same, met them as they were coming back down the mountain. Antonio had been shot. He was in pretty rough shape. Ethan was wounded, but they'd saved Hope and killed the bandits." Garrett grinned as he remembered the sight of Matt's relief...and Matt's shock at the incendiary kiss Hope and Ethan shared right there in front of one and all.

"It all sounds very romantic." Miranda smiled at him, her eyes soft and dreamy. "Hope must be very brave, going back to help that man like that. I'm looking forward to meeting her."

"She's one hell of a woman," he said on a grin.

Her brow wrinkled, and she caught the edge of her lower lip between her teeth. Pushing to her feet, she gathered up the dishes in silence. Garrett blinked. What had brought on that swift change? One minute she'd been laughing, her rapt attention encouraging him to continue with his story. The next moment, she looked...disconcerted. What had he said wrong?

"I can get those later," he offered.

"It's all right, I don't mind. Besides, after Pearl went to so much work to provide us with such a fine meal, I just wouldn't feel right leaving a tableful of dirty dishes for her." Miranda carried her plate over to the counter. As she moved back to the table for more dishes, Garrett stepped up and gathered a basin to take it out to the pump. He worked the iron handle until water filled the basin and then carried it back inside, careful not to slosh water all over the floor as he set the tub on Pearl's work counter.

Miranda had already finished clearing the table. She rolled up her sleeves and tied one of Pearl's old aprons around her waist. Garrett leaned a hip against the counter and watched as she bustled about with marked efficiency. She wiped the crumbs from the table and returned to the basin, dipped the rag, and picked up a platter.

God, she was dazzling.

"You look as if you've done that before." He pointed at the dish and the rag in her hands. "At the risk of offending, I didn't figure you'd have much experience with that sort of thing."

Miranda smiled as she tossed him a towel and handed him the dripping plate. "Dry."

Garrett gave in with a shrug. It wasn't as if he'd never done this before either. He motioned with his chin towards the dishwater. "So?"

"My maternal grandmother was from the old country, Irish through and through, a Fitzgerald from County Cork. She believed a woman should take care of her own house. I spent every summer and every holiday from school with her until she died, just after my seventeenth birthday," Miranda explained, her features softened with fond memories.

He couldn't resist teasing, "Irish, huh? That explains the hair...and the temper."

Her eyes narrowed in good-natured threat as she lobbed a handful of soap bubbles in his direction. He let out a bark of laughter and ducked, but her aim was low, and she ended up hitting him in the shoulder all the same. Chuckling, he dabbed at the soap and reached out to smear some on her cheek, astonished at how good this felt, how easy it was to be with her like this.

"My Grandfather's family is from County Cavan." He grinned, meeting her arrested stare.

She tilted her head, smiling as she considered him. "Is that so... I don't know why, but that amazes me."

"That I could be Irish?"

"No...you've got the temper of the Irish, too. I meant that we have that in common, Irish antecedents."

He nodded, drying the next plate. "Granddad used to talk about the old country. He called County Cavan the lake country...with waters so clear you could see clean to the bottom of the lake. In the early days, the flax industry and limestone quarrying thrived, the main means of livelihood where he was from. Granddad worked in a limestone quarry right up until he came to America, 'the land of promise'."

Garrett finished drying the dish and set it aside, reaching for a platter. Miranda continued to watch him, hanging on his words, and so he went on.

"Back in the lake country, he'd dreamed of a house of his own, land of his own. He'd managed to scrimp and save enough to buy the land he'd had his heart set on. But by the fall of 1845, there was no denying the crops were failing. Granddad had wanted that land longer than he'd wanted anything else, but with the change in the wind, as he'd called it, his family came first. He packed up his wife and three small children and spent everything he had for passage to America. They barely escaped the Great Hunger. Nevertheless, he always missed the land of his youth. You could see it in his eyes. You could hear it in his voice and in his stories." Garrett's own voice held a note of sad remembrance.

86

"If he was anything like my Grandmother, he must have told amazing stories," she coaxed.

"Oh, that he did," Garrett drawled, unable to temper the wide grin. "He used to gather us all around the hearth when we were young, my brothers and cousins and I. He'd sit down next to the fire, a mug of tea—tea smelling suspiciously of whiskey, I might add—in one hand, and he'd begin his tales."

Garrett leaned a hip against the counter and flopped the damp dishrag over his shoulder, crossing his arms over his chest. "I remember one story in particular..."

His gaze drifted to that far off time of childhood recollection. The corners of his mouth curved upward. "He told us about his own Grandmother Brigid. She was a well-respected member of a small community near Cormey Castle. Her pies and pastries were the best in the county. To hear Granddad tell it there was none who knew their way around a stew better than Granny Brigid did. So..."

Garrett drew a long, slow breath, drawing the mood out as only a good storyteller can. "When word went round that King James II would be passing through on his way to the Battle of the Boyne, the baron sent for Brigid. He'd hoped to impress King James with his hospitality. For the week leading up to the king's visit, Granny Brigid ruled the kitchens of Cormey Castle. To hear Granddad tell it, she could have been dining with the king rather than serving him, so proud was he." He chuckled, shaking his head as he drew the towel from his shoulder.

"I think you've a bit of storyteller in you, too, Garrett," Miranda complimented him, passing him another dripping platter. "And what of you, Garrett? Do you have family waiting for you to return to Johnston?"

A hollow ache filled his chest. "No, there's no one waiting for me."

His back was rigid, a muscle ticked in his jaw. With infinite care, he laid the towel and platter aside, and stalked from the kitchen, closing the door behind him with a definitive click. The night closed around him as he stepped off the porch. Her question had caught him by surprise, wounding him with the bleakness of his life.

Feeling raw and exposed, Garrett wandered over the yard for a while, kicking at pebbles, cursing himself for picking at old wounds. He bruised a toe on the water pump, then turned and paced back to the steps. There he sat, his shoulders hunched, his elbows resting on his knees, twirling his hat in his hands. The door creaked opened, and his twirling paused. Still, he said nothing. He didn't look up, didn't acknowledge her in any way. Light footsteps crossed the porch, stopping just behind him. Hell, he should have just saddled up and gone for a ride.

The play of moonlight shimmered over the yard, turning inanimate objects to ominous shadows. He waited for her to speak, waited for her to pry. Instead, she sat down next to him and stared at the moon, silent. He wasn't sure how long they sat there like that, drifting on the stillness, shoulder to shoulder. When his voice broke the quiet, she started a little, as if she hadn't expected him to speak.

"I have family back in Oklahoma...my parents, two sisters-in-law, two nieces and a nephew," he elaborated. Guilt weighed heavy in his heart. "I left them all behind."

Still, she waited, silent and patient. Garrett heaved a sigh and turned his head, studying her delicate profile. "My brothers, Nick and Eddie, died in a bank robbery six years ago."

She blinked and lowered her head, but other than that she didn't move, didn't speak. He was grateful she didn't gush sympathy all over him the way others often did. She allowed him his dignity, and for that consideration, a small part of the shield he'd erected around his heart suffered a tiny crack.

Garrett turned back to stare into the dark night. He wasn't sure why he felt compelled to tell her, but he couldn't seem to stem the flow of words. "I see it every time I close my eyes—the blood, the dying. Nick and Eddie were good men. They didn't deserve what happened that day. They had wives. Nick had kids. They shouldn't have had their lives destroyed."

He couldn't stop the bitterness from creeping into his voice. The pain seeped through him like a fresh wound, as it always did anytime he allowed himself to think of his brothers. Surprisingly, inexplicably, the pain eased. It was then that he noticed the warmth against his palm. His startled gaze dropped, and he stared at her hand clasped tight in his, fingers entwined. For the first time since the day he'd lost Nick and Eddie, he allowed himself to open up, allowed himself to talk about his brothers and share their lives with someone else.

Someone who offered comfort, not pity.

"Nick was a marshal...good at his job. He was better at being a husband and father. He loved Nora with everything in him," Garrett said, not bothering to mask his admiration for his eldest brother. "He was steady and strong, by-the-book. There wasn't anything he couldn't handle." Garrett paused, drawing a breath, letting the memories roll through him, bittersweet and cherished.

"Eddie was, by turns, cantankerous and charming, infuriating and amiable." A slight smile curved his lips. "Like as not, he'd spout off at the mouth before he even knew who he was talking to...but he shot straight from the hip. And he wasn't afraid of trouble. He didn't wait to get out of one scuffle before he got into another, but he always had your back. Nick was forever bailing him out of one tussle or another. Eddie was a good husband, too. He thought Moira hung the moon and stars, and he treated her like it."

She pressed his hand, and the gentle pressure eased the weight squeezing his heart. Part of him couldn't believe he was out here, sitting on the porch holding her hand...calmly discussing his brothers. Part of him couldn't imagine not being here, not sharing this with her.

"I couldn't stay in Carlisle. The memories were just too painful. Too fresh. Christ, after six years, it was all still too damned fresh. Sometimes—out on the ranch—the silence haunts me there, too."

He searched her face. Her probing, velvety-blue eyes passed over his face, studying every surface, every nuance of his countenance, as if the answers to life's most vital questions were written there in the lines of his face.

"Family is the very fabric of who you are, Garrett. You take pride in your heritage, that's as it should be. It must be very hard on you to be separated from your loved ones," she observed sagely. "Johnston sounds like a good, solid place to raise children. But Garrett..." She paused, seemed to be weighing her words. When he couldn't stand the silence any longer, he glanced her way. "You can't replace one family with another. It would be a disservice to one and unfair to the other. When you start your own family, Garrett," she laid her free hand on his forearm and squeezed, "do it for the right reasons."

She slipped her hand from his then and lifted a soft palm to cup his cheek as her steady gaze searched his. Garrett couldn't find his voice. She smiled, brushed a lock of his hair from his brow with gentle fingers, and rose. The door closed softly behind her.

At length, the soft glow of lamplight spilled from her window down onto the ground several yards in front of him. He watched, unable to tear his eyes away, as her shadow drifted across the light. The shadow began to undress, tormenting him with what he could not have. His gut clenched tight. Desire he could deal with. It was the sensation of warmth pouring over his icy heart that had him well and truly worried.

Chapter Eight

That uncomfortable sensation—and the tender moment that had passed between them—kept him up a good share of the night. As a result, he was more than a little short-tempered and edgy come sunrise. Miranda had been far too intuitive in her assessment. So much so, that he found himself picking fights just to regain some semblance of distance between them.

A few short miles from town, Garrett drew his horse to a halt and shifted in the saddle. "Did you leave that damned corset off?"

"*Garrett!*"

He stared hard at Miranda's flushed face, let his gaze skim down over her stiff midriff. *Damned stubborn woman.* Swearing beneath his breath, he wheeled his mount around and cantered off, leaving her to follow or get left behind.

They rode in silence. The steady thudding of horses' hooves punctuated the silence. As the morning wore on, he stopped beside a small stream to give the animals a break. Garrett helped Miranda dismount before leading the horses forward. He strained to focus on the gurgling brook and the animals, doing his level best to ignore her as she stretched this way and that to ease her muscles.

She groaned aloud. Before he gave it proper consideration, he glanced her way. His gut tightened. His teeth clenched. She'd locked her hands behind her back, stretching her arms up, straining the material of her bodice. Sweat beaded on his brow. His hands ached to reach out and touch.

With a body like that, why would she ever imagine she'd needed that damned corset? Of course, cutting it off had been a whole new experience. And now that he looked back on it, ripping her bodice open like that... A delicious shudder worked its way through his body as a slow, self-satisfied smile curved his lips upward.

A long moment passed before he realized she was speaking.

"Garrett?" She shielded her eyes from the glare of the late morning sun, waiting for his answer.

"Hmm?"

"I'm sure there must be more important things a marshal should be doing then escorting me?"

"I'm not a marshal." His off-hand comment slipped out before the blood had a chance to make its way back to his brain.

Miranda froze, aimed a sharp frown at him, and demanded, "What?"

Jesus, Mary, and Joseph.

Now she'd start in with the incessant questions, and he sure as certain didn't want to have an extended conversation with her—didn't want to risk watching her work the kinks from her body like that any longer. He was only human, and his control appeared to be in short supply today.

"I'm not a marshal...well, not anymore. I retired a few months back." He forced his gaze from the curves outlined by her snug riding habit and tugged the horses back away from the stream before they bloated themselves.

"You're retired?" She frowned, planting her fists on her hips. "But...you're so young. Why would you retire?"

The muscle in his jaw ticked. Unwilling to answer the jumble of questions flickering in her eyes, he ignored her question and led the horses a short distance away to check their hooves and adjust saddle straps. Then he tied the horses to a lone, scraggly tree and reached for the canteens. He crossed to the stream without meeting her gaze—though he could feel it burning a hole through his hide—and bent to fill the containers.

"So what did he have on you?"

His hands froze in their task. He blinked up at her. "Excuse me?"

"I know Uncle Milton." She shot him an assessing, far-too-perceptive glance. "You're no longer an officer of the law; therefore, he can't just give you indiscriminate assignments. That being said, it stands to reason he's holding something over your head. What is it?"

Garrett stared, nonplussed. The woman was too damned smart for her own good...and meddlesome. Not a safe combination.

She needed a keeper.

"Oh, come now. You won't be hurting my feelings. I know he must have twisted your arm with something," she prompted. "That's his forte, after all. He holds these little debts over your head until he has a use for them."

He shook his head and pushed to his feet. "He bailed me out of a...a tight spot awhile back. I owed him."

Miranda gave a silent, smug nod of the head, but her eyes crowed a loud "I told you so." She waited, her arms crossed over her chest, but when he didn't volunteer any further information, she lifted a brow and tapped a finger against her lips.

He shifted beneath her discerning stare, stifling the urge to flinch when she guessed, "Oh, for him to have saddled you with me...it must have been something bad. Something *really* bad."

Garrett grimaced, all but shoving her toward her horse. "Back in the saddle, *princess*."

Miranda glared her displeasure over the

nickname, but she didn't rise to the bait. Her words floated down from the saddle, promising hours of nagging...unless he caved. "You *know* I'm not going to let this go. I want to know what I'm worth, after all," she goaded. A small smile graced the perfect, delectable curve of her lips.

As he stood there staring up at her—his hand resting on her knee, his eyes sliding to her lips—he wondered what a man wouldn't be willing to sacrifice for just one touch, just one kiss...

"Garrett?" Her head tilted to the side, and her brow crinkled.

Blinking the stars from his eyes, he drew a deep breath and stepped back. Vaulting up onto the saddle, he settled his hat back on his head.

"Colchester," he shot over his shoulder. Then he urged his horse into motion.

As soon as Miranda caught up with him, she demanded, "What's Colchester?"

Garrett sighed, by turns amused and annoyed with Miranda's tenacious curiosity. She wouldn't give up until she'd gotten the truth from him, and he couldn't help but admire her spirit. Still, it wasn't a particularly flattering, high point in his career.

Her voice took on an excited, scandalized tone. "Was it a woman?"

By the saints, the things that went on inside this woman's mind were a true puzzle. "No, it wasn't a woman."

Miranda screwed her face up in a determined frown. At length, her expression brightened. "You lost a prisoner."

Garrett glowered now, offended to the bone. "I have *never* lost a prisoner."

"Well, don't get snippy with me. You won't tell me, so I'm forced to speculate. You could save yourself a lot of irritation if you'd just tell me what the great mystery is," she scolded. In a mercurial shift of expressions, she slanted a furtive grin. "Did you get too drunk to do your job?"

He growled aloud, vexed. "Oh, for the love of... You win, just stop with the stupid questions."

"There's no such thing as a stupid question," she retorted, pointing her pert nose in the air.

He turned in the saddle and lifted a brow, challenging her comment without a word. Then, holding up a hand to forestall any further argument, he snapped, "Do you want to hear this or not?"

She pressed her lips together and nodded, settling back in the saddle.

"The men who killed my brothers called themselves the Chambers Gang." Garrett pushed the brim of his hat back with the curve of a knuckle and turned his face into the sun, letting the warming rays sink into his flesh, even as the memories sent a familiar achy chill bone deep.

Her eyes widened, and she started to shake her head. His hard stare arrested her movements. She'd opened this can of worms with her persistent nagging. She could damned well deal with the mess.

"They were a vicious bunch, robbing banks all throughout Oklahoma and northern Texas. Nick had been working the case with his superior, Merle Colby, and a couple Pinkerton Detectives. The day my brothers died, Nick received word Chambers was in the area. He'd gone to warn the bank. Eddie wasn't supposed to be there at all." His voice dropped to a soft rumble, shades warmer than the ice encasing his heart. "The Chambers Gang got there before expected. There were no survivors."

Garrett paused, the muscle in his jaw jerked as he fought to hold the memories at a safe distance, to look at them with professional, impersonal objectivity. "Long story short, I was the first one into the bank after... It was...bad. It was real bad. Eddie was gone by the time I got there. Nick lasted long enough to confirm the Chambers Gang was responsible. He died in my arms."

His heart throbbed, even after all these years. Tears glittered in Miranda's eyes, but they didn't fall. For that he was grateful. He had a difficult enough time holding on to his own grief as it was.

"I had to tell Nora and Moira and our parents what happened. I didn't realize it at the time, but little Sean—Nick's son—had been hiding in the cupboard. He heard...he heard every word. The look on his face when he came running out of that cupboard, shouting that I was wrong..." Weary, Garrett scrubbed a hand over his face. What he wouldn't give to wipe the guilty anguish from his heart. "I found Colby, gave him Nick's report. Then I took off after the bastards myself before my brothers' bodies were cold in the ground. I tracked a couple of 'em to Colchester. We had a shootout right there in the center of town. That would be where your uncle comes in."

He glanced over at Miranda and smiled, but there was no humor in him. "He was doing the circuit at the time, and none too happy about dead bodies littering Main Street. Lucky for my sorry hide, Colby and a Pinkerton Agent by the name of Damian Morgan followed me. They explained to the judge about the robbery. Turns out Judge Thomas was real fond of my brother, didn't take kindly that he'd been used for target practice.

"Of course—being a man of the law—he didn't take kindly to vigilante justice, either. So he told me he was doing me a favor on account of Colby and Morgan's testimonies...giving me a choice, he said. I could swing from the gallows for taking the law into my own hands and see the rest of my brothers' killers walk free. Or I could *be* the law...or rather an extension of it. I could track the rest of the gang with the backing of the courts, bring 'em to justice."

"So you became a marshal," Miranda whispered.

"So I became a marshal," he repeated, loud and clear, his eyes on the horizon.

What she was thinking? He couldn't tell. Her eyes had clouded; her expression was grave. He didn't want her pity. Hell, he couldn't tolerate sympathy, even now, after all this time. He didn't deserve it. He was still here. He'd survived...though he lived with his shame every day of his life. In the end, he'd made the right choice and become a better man for it.

No, sympathy and pity were not for him.

"I'd have hunted them down, too. They deserved what they got."

Amazed, Garrett stared after her as she nudged her mount into a gallop without another word.

They rode the rest of the day in companionable silence, speaking only when necessary, and that was just fine with Garrett. He wasn't used to this sharing of intimate details of his life. It left him unsettled. By the time they reached the booming cattle town of Sadler, the sun was making its final bow of the day. Breathtaking hues of yellows and oranges, pinks and magentas spilled over the stark landscape.

Garrett assisted Miranda to the ground, his hands lingering at her waist. He just couldn't seem to make himself let go. Their eyes locked and time stopped for a brief moment. She was tired. The shadows beneath her eyes, the pinched lines around her mouth were clear enough. But she hadn't uttered one word of complaint. She had a backbone of steel, and skin like the finest porcelain. Eyes like the deepest summer sky. He couldn't remember a woman ever fascinating him more. Clearing his throat, Garrett released her, but it was a long moment before he could bring himself to look away. A charged silence hung heavy in the air between them as she followed him inside the hotel.

The building was new, smelling of fresh lumber. The inner walls were stark white. A tall, potted plant rested beside the door, an obvious, ineffectual attempt at civilizing the place. The doublewide door on the right led to a dining room of sorts, and the stairwell on the left led to the second floor.

The scarecrow of a clerk behind the counter straightened his stooped shoulders upon their entrance and pushed the wire-rimmed spectacles back up the crook of his beaklike nose. He cleared his throat and smiled, his balding head gleaming in the soft light cast by the wall sconces behind him.

"Good evening," he greeted them, his voice as thin and reedy as his body.

"We need two rooms—close together." Garrett dropped their baggage at his feet and rested an elbow on the counter as he glanced around the room.

The clerk eyed them, his gaze ripe with speculation. To his credit, he kept his curiosity to himself. He told Garrett the going rate for rooms as he reached behind him and snagged two keys from the hook on the wall. Handing them to Garrett, he remarked, "End of the hall, second floor. Last two on the right."

Garrett nodded to the clerk. He picked Miranda's valise up and his saddlebags, and made his way to the steps. His eyes scanned the shadows as she fell into step behind him.

For the better part of the day, he'd had the strangest feeling, as if they'd picked up a tail. The fine hairs on the back of his neck had been standing at attention, warning him something wasn't quite as it seemed. Still, no matter how cautious he was, no matter how he'd backtracked and kept his attention on high alert, he hadn't been able to detect anyone. Maybe he was just being paranoid. Maybe it was just more of those old habits.

Then again, that sixth sense had never been wrong before.

He stopped at the last door at the end of the hall. After ducking his head inside the room and scanning the shadows, Garrett stepped out into the hall and motioned Miranda ahead. He followed her in, dropped his saddlebags by the door, and settled her valise on the bed.

A bed, a nightstand, and a short chest of drawers were the only pieces of furniture. A large pitcher and bowl rested on the dresser. A small oval mirror hung on the wall just above the chest of drawers. A generous window graced the far wall. The lock on the window was broken, but the window itself was too high above the street to breach from the outside. The room was plain...far less than she was used to, he was sure...but it was serviceable and easy to protect should the need arise.

To Garrett's way of thinking, that was all that mattered.

Miranda approached the mirror and leaned forward, staring at her reflection. He caught sight of her wince as she rubbed at the bridge of her nose.

Though he knew he shouldn't, he couldn't help himself. "What's wrong?"

She turned soulful eyes to him. Her tone was plaintive. "Look at my face, Garrett! It's horrible!"

Garrett stepped closer, peering hard at every flawless feature, unable to see what it was she found so distressing. Her skin was smooth as satin. Ivory...sprinkled with tiny cinnamon flecks across the crests of her cheeks and over her nose. There was just no way around it. She looked perfect to him...downright stunning, though he'd happily have every tooth in his head pulled—without the benefit of whiskey—before he told *her* so.

He gave a clueless shrug. "What?"

With a disdainful snort, she pointed at the nose

on her face, as if the answer were so obvious. When he continued to stare at her, baffled, she sighed with dramatic disgust.

"Freckles, Garrett... My face is ruined!"

She closed her eyes, and her lips compressed. Dear Lord, don't let her cry...anything but that. He floundered, torn between the urge to sooth her and the need to laugh at her groundless worries. How in the hell was he to do either without admitting he'd never seen a more beautiful face in his life, freckles and all?

And so he did what any intelligent man of strategy would do when faced with insurmountable odds.

He retreated.

"You, ah, you look—fine, you look fine," he choked out as he backed toward the door, bumping into the frame. He grappled with his saddlebags, snatching them up with a complete lack of grace.

Then his mind zeroed in on strategy, clinging to it like a lifeline. *Cover your flank, lay down cover fire, confuse the opponent...distract her.* "I have to go to the telegraph office to send word to the judge. Stay in your room and don't open the door for anyone but me. I'll see if they'll send up a tub or something for you. I bet you'd like a bath...not that you stink or anything..." He rolled his eyes at his own stupidity. *You didn't address a lady's personal needs...did you? And you sure as certain didn't tell her she stunk.* "Are you hungry? I'll be back soon to take you to the dining room for supper." He'd called the last bit of information over his shoulder and closed the door in her bewildered face.

Mentally patting himself on the back for escaping in the nick of time, he went to his room, tossed his saddlebags on the bed, and locked the door behind him on his way out. He pounded down the steps, proud of himself for dodging the bullet

Brenda Huber

with Miranda, so to speak...

Great big, wet, tear-shaped bullets, to be exact.

A short while later Garrett stepped onto the boardwalk in front of the telegraph office where he'd sent off his dutiful update to the judge. He scanned the streets as he made his way back to the hotel. Once inside the lobby, he strode past the clerk without glancing in the thin man's direction. On the stairs, he stepped to the side to allow a tall man in a long, black duster to pass.

The man tipped his black hat to Garrett, concealing more of his face than he'd revealed, flashing silver studs on the hatband, before he continued on his way. The man's blond hair hung half-way down his back and fluttered with his momentum. An odd sensation of recognition tickled the back of his neck as Garrett watched the man bound down the steps.

Frowning, his mind shuffling and discarding mental images of faces, Garrett paced down the hallway. He knocked on Miranda's door. His frown deepened to a scowl when she opened the door without verifying who was standing on the other side.

"I told you not to open the door for anyone but me," he growled.

She pierced him with an annoyed stare. "It *was* you."

"You had no way of knowing that unless you asked...which you *didn't*."

"I knew it was you." She rolled her eyes, turning away.

"How? You sure as hell didn't *ask*."

"You're the only one I know that stomps everywhere he goes," she bit out, lifting a brow as if waiting for him to try to dispute her logic.

Would it even do any good to point out he was hardly the only man in the state to stomp? Taking a page from her book, he rolled his eyes, tossing in a snort of aggravation for good measure. Arguing with her while his stomach growled was as good as telling the wind not to blow. Pointless, to be sure.

"Are you ready to go down to the dining room?"

Miranda nodded, accepting his arm.

As with the night before, the meal with Miranda was pleasant. He told her anecdotes from his childhood, and he told her another of his grandfather's stories. Her laughter was relaxed and genuine. Husky and sensual. Her eyes sparkled and rosy color tinged her cheeks. After they'd finished the last of their meal, Garrett pushed back from the table and rose. He drew her chair out, held his arm out to her, and escorted her back upstairs. He couldn't remember having spent such an enjoyable evening in longer than he cared to consider.

Garrett opened the door to her room, and then he stood back, waiting for her to enter. The temptation to draw her into his arms and seal his lips to hers was great. And so, instead, he drew back a step and offered, "Get a good night's rest. Morning will come soon enough."

Her brow furrowed, and she gnawed on the edge of her bottom lip as she stared up at him. Frowning, he waited for her to speak, wishing she'd hurry before he gave in to those unwise urges riddling his conscience with faulty holes.

****

The inquiring, quicksilver depths of Garrett's eyes were mesmerizing. Her thoughts, a jumbled mass of confusion, careened toward some conclusion she couldn't or wouldn't yet face. She could feel the pull between them—had felt it from the first, but she'd fought to deny it. Yet it remained, undeniable and confusing. Garrett felt it. She saw it in his eyes whenever he thought she wasn't watching.

If her uncle had anything to say about it, he'd

see her married off to some stodgy old rancher before the year's end. Her soul cried mutiny, desperate to experience life before it was over. Before she was trapped beneath a husband's overbearing thumb. Throwing caution to the wind, she firmed her resolve and stepped closer, until her skirts brushed at his legs.

"Kiss me, Garrett." She hated the heat rising in her cheeks. She was trying to be a confident woman, but she felt more like a ridiculous, naïve schoolgirl.

"What?" Garrett squawked, his mouth falling open. He dragged in a huge gulp of air, then another and blinked owlishly at her.

"Kiss me...*please.*" She softened her tone, batting her lashes. She'd never had trouble plying her feminine wiles on other men before, bending them to her will before they had any inkling of what she was about. Why, then, was this one simple request so difficult.

Because she'd never wanted anything so badly before, a little voice whispered in the back of her mind.

Too, she'd never practiced at *this* particular game, either...this game of seduction.

Garrett jerked back a step. Wounded, but determined nonetheless, she followed. She might not be doing the best job at acting the coy flirt, but she was hell-bent on getting her way. His panicked gaze flew down the length of the hallway and back to her. The indomitable, arrogant marshal's indecisive retreat sparked her temper. Draco hadn't suffered any qualms about kissing her. It didn't seem right that it should be so difficult to get Garrett to comply with such a simple request. She held her chin up and squared her shoulders.

"Kiss me, Garrett." An order this time. A demand.

"Miranda..." Warning flickered in his wary gaze.

He took another step back, and she advanced again. He swallowed, hard, and pressed up against the wall, trapped. A sliver of panic glimmered in his eyes. "Stop that!" he barked, his tone sharp. "You don't know what you're asking for."

"Yes, Garrett, I do," she argued. "I want you to kiss me. I want to experience a little bit of life before I'm trapped in a marriage someone else deems acceptable."

"Miranda," he stalled. "You shouldn't—"

"I shouldn't what, Garrett?" She lifted a hand, settling it on his chest, just over his pounding heart. "Shouldn't I wonder what it would be like to be held in your arms?" Her bold stare lifted to his. "I do." She forced a swallow, fighting to hide the sudden crack in her self-confidence. Was she doing this right? She'd never before played the wanton. "Shouldn't I wonder what it would be like to be kissed by you?" Her gaze lowered to trace Garrett's lips. "I find myself thinking about it quite a bit of late. Shouldn't I wonder why your heart is pounding so hard beneath my hand? My heart is pounding just as hard—" She met his gaze, brazening it out to the end. "Or shouldn't I tell you that either?"

She eased closer to him, and this time he didn't step away—he couldn't as his back was to the wall— and she let a small, sanguine smile curve her lips. She knew she was goading him, knew her next words might not get quite the exact reaction she wanted from him—might gall him into turning away from her—but she needed this...needed his kiss like she'd never needed anything else in her life.

"I'm curious, Garrett," she murmured. "I want to know...I *need* to know. Does every man kiss like Draco does? Do all men taste the same?"

His stormy eyes flashed, like lightning just before it reaches down to scorch the earth. He cursed beneath his breath, vehemently, and heat soared in her cheeks. A tiny tendril of uneasiness coiled deep in the pit of her stomach. She'd pushed him too far. She'd challenged him—prodded his temper—and his pride wouldn't allow him to back down.

Damn it, she hadn't wanted it like this. She'd wanted him willing, not coerced, but he'd left her no choice.

Garrett's heated stare locked on her mouth, and an animal growl rumbled through him as he snaked an arm around her waist, hauling her hard against him. Her eyes flew wide, and she gasped. His hand tangled, fisting in her hair, dislodging pins, rough and demanding. Their gazes connected for a heartbeat, and with a tiny flare of fear, she realized she hadn't just pushed his limits. She'd broken his control. Comprehension—apprehension—registered a split second before his lips swooped down to seize hers.

Uncertainty, regret, any chance for second thoughts disappeared in the blink of an eye...vanquished with the press of his lips.

Raw heat. Scorching need.

Hunger, primitive and disturbing. Erotic.

An onslaught of sensations swirled through her melting her bones, fusing her to him.

More. She needed...*more.*

****

Garrett angled his head, delving deep. The taste of her, the scent of her skin was intoxicating, went straight to his head. Driving him to taste more, to take more. His tongue tangled with hers, and she shuddered in his arms. Her hands clasped his biceps, skated across his broad shoulders, questing until they settled at the nape of his neck, her fingers entwining in the hair curling over his collar. The feel of her hands upon him sent greedy shivers of desire racing through his body.

She opened to him like a moonflower opening its

petals to the first silvery caresses of the night. Her unfettered response touched him, drew him in, tempting him to stake his claim. For a heartbeat, he struggled to remember she was an innocent, untouched. He worked to gentle the kiss, battled to tame his strength.

In that heartbeat, she pressed against him and fisted her hands in his hair. Her kiss turned demanding, unleashing something primitive, something feral inside him. His head angled again, his mouth slanted over hers, plundering the sweetness within. She tasted of cinnamon and vanilla, and he gladly drowned in her. Miranda's awakening and evolving responses to his kiss, to his touch drove him beyond any thoughts of control or self-denial. He threw away his lifeline, tossed away all good sense, sinking beneath the waves of desire washing over him without a fight.

Greed consumed him—whole. In one large, voracious bite. All too soon that simple contact wasn't enough, instead it fueled the addiction. His hands burned to touch her silken skin; his body ached to quench the unbearable thirst she incited deep in his soul. The taste of her was driving him crazy, and he wanted more—craved more. His hands found their way to her hips, the sides of her breasts, her waist. He clamped his arm around her lithe body. Fitting her snug against his hard angles, Garrett ground the fully aroused evidence of his desire against her.

She moaned, low and deep, but the sound was enough to jolt Garrett back to awareness. When he realized his arm had banded around her—that one hand cupped the curve of her bottom, pressing her full length against his painful arousal while the other kneaded her breast, his thumb rubbing at the pebbled nipple buried beneath layers of restrictive clothing—he dragged in a ragged breath and prayed for the strength to release her.

It took a moment, but he managed to move his hands to her shoulders. He pushed her away from him, tearing his lips from hers at last. Her breathing was harsh in his ears, but then so was his. He had to make a conscious effort to gather his control, to snap it into place, despite his raging need.

The slow burn of attraction he'd been fighting so hard to ignore, had more than flashed, it had exploded—right in his face.

Miranda stared up at him, her eyes glazed with passion, her lips swollen from his kisses. She'd gotten what she'd wanted all right—and far more than she'd bargained for in the process by the looks of her. Garrett pressed against the wall once more, battling the urge to haul her up against him and finish what she'd started. Miranda drew herself up, dragging in deep gulps of air. She stepped back, wide-eyed.

Desperate to recover his equilibrium, anxious to ignore the rush of desire thrumming through his veins like liquid lightning, Garrett grasped for something to say. And so, unwise as often is the case, he said the first thing that came to mind.

"Be ready to go in the morning, *princess*, I don't want to have to wait for you. And don't wear one of those damned corsets tomorrow, I'd hate like hell to have to cut another one off," he ordered. Then, ridden mercilessly by the demons of desire she'd stirred to raging life, he gave her the most wolfish grin he could muster and added, "Then again..."

He would have liked to blame his thoughtless comments on the lust fogging his brain. He wanted to blame them on the blatant haze of desire she still wore on her face. He would have loved to blame them on the lack of blood flow to his brain...or on the fact he hadn't had a woman in longer than he cared to think about. He had no excuse for teasing her the way he had, but the urge had been irresistible.

Maybe if she thought him less than a gentleman, she'd use more caution around him and would think twice before tempting him like this again.

The good Lord knew, after tasting her like this he was going to need all the help he could get in keeping his hands off her...as if it wasn't bad enough before.

The answering flames in her cheeks and the dangerous spark in her eyes seemed to justify his suggestive innuendo. Unfortunately, it also stirred his already boiling blood, and Garrett couldn't help but wonder what it was about a riled up woman that made a man incapable of thought. Then again, maybe it was this particular woman, and no other, who held that power over him.

God help him.

Miranda's eyes flared, and her cheeks flushed. "It's hardly your concern what I do or do not choose to wear, Garrett. I'll thank you not to ruin anymore of my clothing, ripping it and shredding it right and left as you've been doing. I can't even repair my riding habit since I couldn't find all the buttons after you ripped my bodice open."

An older couple chose that exact moment to step into the hallway from the room next door. By the shocked expression on the woman's disapproving face, it was a pretty safe bet she'd heard at least a good portion of Miranda's last comments.

Her cheeks went up in flames, and she closed her eyes, dropping her chin to her chest.

Garrett chuckled with wicked delight. He leaned toward her and effected a stage whisper, "You're right, darlin', I'm sorry. But I just can't seem to help myself when I'm around you." Then, letting his eyes skim down her figure, as if intimately familiar with what lay beneath the layers of her clothing, he drawled with warm approval, "But, sweetheart, you don't need those god-awful corsets, and they just keep gettin' in the way."

He winked as her mouth fell open in stunned incredulity. His grin widened when the dour woman gasped at them from the top of the steps. "Well! I never..." Then she grumbled beneath her breath and hauled the gaunt man down the stairs behind her.

Miranda glared at Garrett, opening and closing her mouth as if she couldn't determine what to say to him that would be scathing and insulting enough. At last, when words failed her, she hissed a disgusted harrumph, stepped back into her room, and slammed the door in his face.

The fire in her eyes had kindled another, equally scorching blaze deep in his gut. For one insane moment, he considered forcing the door open and giving her a taste of her own medicine. She'd started the inferno, by God, she wasn't going to walk away unscathed.

Opening that door would be a mistake, though. If he went anywhere near her right now any confrontation between them would end one of two ways. Either they would kill each other, or he would make love to her. If he had to lay odds, he'd bet on the latter of the two.

Either way, he'd end up in a whole heap of trouble with the judge—and probably swinging from those gallows yet. He drew a deep breath and stared at the panels of her door, his fists clenched and unclenched at his sides. Unbidden, a flashback of Antonio as he sat in the Busted Wheel the night Garrett received his summons came to mind. Antonio patting the scarred tabletop and claiming he'd every intention of staying right there and drinking himself under the table.

Garrett was beginning to think Antonio had had the right of it.

Chapter Nine

The next morning, Garrett woke to a battalion of blacksmiths waging war between his ears. The pain hammered away at his skull. His stomach lurched. Groaning, he rolled over, shielding his eyes from the brutal sting of sunlight pouring in through the uncovered window. The sound of his own muted voice stabbed at his brain like ice picks, and he winced as a fresh wave of agony sliced through him. His tongue was heavy, thick against the dry roof of his mouth. His eyes were gritty, his vision blurred.

He lay still for a moment, praying the pounding would recede to a dull roar, but instead it intensified, growing more deafening by the minute. Then he realized Miranda was calling his name from the other side of his door. Recollection hit him like a bolt of lightning—where he was and what he was *supposed* to be doing. He swore, bolting upright in bed. Garrett gasped in agony—his hands flew to his temples—and he fell back against the flat pillow where he groaned like the mortally wounded.

At his sudden movement, an empty whiskey bottle rolled from the bed and clattered onto the floor. The pounding on the door ceased. Nothing more than a momentary reprieve, as the banging resumed with renewed vigor.

"Garrett? Garrett, are you in there?" Bang, bang, bang. "Garrett, are you hurt?" Bang, bang, bang. "Damn it, answer me, Garrett!" Bang, bang.

He wanted nothing more than to crawl through the cracks in the floorboards and disappear, but his guilty conscience responded to the note of rising

111

panic in her voice.

"Yeah, just a minute," he croaked, but she must not have heard him over the din she was making, because she continued to pound with relentless determination.

"Garrett? Garrett, hold on—I'm going to go for help."

Garrett muttered an oath, wincing at the sound of his own voice. He cringed in anticipated pain, pressed the palm of his hand to his temple, and bellowed, "Wait!"

"Garrett?"

"Yeah," he croaked again, winded and hoarse. "Give me a minute."

Bracing a forearm against the chest of drawers, Garrett forced himself to his feet. Scrunching his eyes closed, he willed the room to stop spinning long enough for him to get his bearings again. Served him right for going to bed with a bottle instead of a woman.

Then again, if he'd gone to bed with the particular, flame-haired vixen he'd wanted last night, he'd probably be feeling a whole lot worse this morning. A hangover wasn't as debilitating as an attack of conscience. For a man like Garrett, that particular weakness was far worse punishment than a mere hangover—any day of the week and twice on Sunday.

Drawing a bracing breath, Garrett squeezed one eye open with extreme caution and was pleased to see the room had righted itself. Too bad he still felt like he had a wad of raw cotton in his mouth and a hammer pounding away on the inside of his skull. He raked an unsteady hand through his hair and began the arduous journey from the chest to the door some five steps away—five steps that felt like five miles.

Garrett would have shaken his head in

disappointment at himself, if the mere thought of doing so hadn't all but crossed his eyes in pain. He could drink with the best of them when the occasion warranted it, but he couldn't remember ever having drunk to the point of sheer idiocy before. He'd *never* soaked his liver with so much liquor, not even the day they'd buried his brothers...and that day had been a study in true gluttony.

Then again, he'd never known a beautiful enchantress like Miranda Thomas before either.

He should have known better than to try to drink away a memory. No matter how much he drank, he couldn't remove the taste of Miranda from his lips, or the feel of her from his arms. Instead, the drink had served to make the memory of that ill-advised kiss all the sweeter. He was amazed he'd managed to curb his impulse to go to her after he'd left the saloon, proud he'd managed to crawl into his own room rather than hers given the salacious content of his thoughts during the height of his foolhardy bender last night.

He dragged in a deep breath and reached for the lock, every minute movement a study in agony. Miranda must have grown impatient, because just as Garrett's fingers connected with the cold metal, she gave the door one more forceful bang and shouted, "Garrett!"

He almost went to his knees in agony. At that particular moment, he couldn't say which idea held more appeal—wringing her beautiful neck, or simply passing out from the pain.

A sharp oath from the other side of the door pried one blurry, burning eye open. His mouth gaped open.

Where had she learned that *kind of language?*

Pulling himself together, fearful of more banging, Garrett moved faster than he'd thought possible given his present condition, yanking the door open so fast he startled a gasp from her. Panting, Garrett sagged against the doorjamb when the room began to tilt precariously once more. Garrett squeezed his eyes closed and fisted his hand in his hair to keep his head from rolling from his shoulders.

****

Startled, Miranda jerked back a step as the door swung open without warning. She stared in disbelief, her mouth hanging open as she took in his disheveled appearance. For a moment, torn between alarm at the state he was in and amusement that he looked so miserable—and so obviously hung over— she couldn't speak.

His sable locks stuck out every which way. His pallor was sickly, and a thick layer of stubble covered the strong line of his jaw. Garrett glowered at her through bloodshot eyes, the effect ruined by the fact that he swayed on his feet, squinting like a myopic old man. He stood clutching the doorframe in a white-knuckled grip, as if he were afraid to let go, lest he fall on his face. His feet were bare, as was his chest, and Miranda stared, dry-mouthed, at the wide expanse of smooth, golden, *male* skin stretched taut over well-defined, rippling muscles. His arms were long and powerful, as was his torso. His shoulders filled the doorway. A short, white scar snaked across his left bicep.

His chest tapered to a narrow waist. Another scar, an obvious bullet wound, marred the perfection of his chest just below his left collarbone. Low on his left side, just above his waistband, an angry-pink, jagged scar snaked its way across his flesh. Those imperfections made him all the more...*perfect*. All the more dangerous.

All the more desirable.

Miranda's gaze traveled over his lean, muscled abdomen and lower. His trousers were unbuttoned,

114

gaping wide to reveal the silky smooth skin just below his navel. Her cheeks flamed when she realized she stared at his trousers, trying to discern the only thing that had been left to her imagination, and she forced her gaze back to his face.

Then she remembered how he'd left her last night, throwing orders at her like some self-important general—specific orders to be ready on time—*after* he'd deliberately embarrassed her in front of that older couple from down the hall.

Her temper ignited.

"Excuse me, but weren't *you* the one who warned *me* to be ready this morning," she asked, letting her voice crack in the silence, taking great satisfaction from his pained wince.

"You don't have to yell at me," he whispered. His eyelids snapped closed, his face a study in misery. "I'm not deaf, you know."

Though she was irritated, she took sympathy on him and lowered her voice. "No, I'd say you're just suffering from a stiff case of brown bottle flu."

Her witty remark proved well beyond his cognitive abilities at that point. He squinted and frowned. "I'm not sick."

She rolled her eyes, praying for patience. "You are suffering from a hangover, Garrett."

"I know that," he scoffed, and flinched.

Miranda lifted her hands to his chest and pushed him back into the room. The foreign sensation of warm, male skin—naked beneath her fingers—was thrilling, tempting her to explore further, but she pushed that urge aside, determined to be compassionate and sensible.

"Let's get you back in bed," she suggested in a gentle, hushed voice.

His startled gaze flew to her face, and a surprised, almost hopeful expression arrested his countenance.

"There's no help for it. You're just going to have to sleep it off, I'm afraid," she sighed, frowning when his face fell. He looked so disappointed, so crestfallen, she had to wonder at what he'd been thinking.

"I don't have time to sleep it off," he grumbled, even as she pressed him back against the pillow.

She stopped her ministrations long enough to scowl at him. "Do you mean to tell me you feel well enough to get on a horse, let alone ride one for the rest of the day?"

His expression was eloquent, and she gave an unladylike snort as she reached for the blanket that lay bunched and tangled at the foot of the bed. She gave it an efficient tug and a snap, then pulled it up and tucked it around him.

"I have to—"

"Rest," she ordered, cutting him off mid-sentence.

Her palms cupped his bristled cheeks, and she searched his face to make sure there wasn't anything else wrong with him—anything other than poor judgment. Satisfied, Miranda went to the dresser and picked up a cloth, splashed water over it, and wrung out the excess. Pouring a small splash of tepid water into a glass, Miranda carried it, and the washcloth, back to his side.

Sitting down on the edge of the bed, hip to hip, Miranda cupped the back of his head, holding the glass steady against his lips, stopping him after the smallest of sips. She laid the washcloth on his brow. Pleased with his compliancy, she smoothed the hair back from his brow and gave him a slow nod and a soft smile. It was rather nice taking care of him like this, even if he had been an idiot. She felt useful.

Useful...she hadn't felt useful in a good long while.

"I'll tell the clerk we'll be staying one more

night. I trust you won't be indulging again this evening?" She raised a sarcastic eyebrow as she lifted the empty bottle from the floor with her fingertips and waved it at him. She set it on the dresser with a thump that made him flinch, then turned back to place a palm against his cheek. "I'll check in on you later and bring you something to eat. Sleep now."

At the mention of food, Garrett paled. She couldn't help the small, vindictive smile that curved the edges of her mouth as she rose and turned away.

"Miranda," he called as she headed for the door.

She turned back to face him, both brows raised. She half expected him to offer an apology for his condition, or perhaps a thank you for her consideration, and so she waited with a benevolent smile.

"Don't leave the hotel," he ordered.

"What?" Her smile faded, replaced by a confused frown.

"Don't leave the hotel," he repeated. He turned his head and considered her for a moment. "In fact, it'd be best if you didn't leave your room."

She stared at him in disbelief. He was the one who'd overindulged. He was the one too ill to ride, not her. Yet he had the nerve to try to confine her like some naughty child...or some reprobate prisoner. She drew herself up to her full five foot seven inches, and her back stiffened, ironing board straight. She ground her teeth together, annoyed by his autocratic attitude.

His eyes swept down to her chest and waist, and he pounded the final nail into his coffin. "You're not wearing one of those damned corsets again, are you?"

Miranda's eyes narrowed, her lips compressed, and her fists clenched at her sides. She'd stay in her room all right—just as soon as pigs sprouted wings and took to the skies. Elevating her chin, she pivoted on her heel, gliding to the door with regal disdain. In the doorway, she turned back and smiled, sweet and innocent.

Then she slammed the door with all her might, hard enough to make the wall sconces in the hallway dance in their holders.

A ripe curse burst through the closed door, followed by a muffled groan.

A vindicated smile curved her lips as she tugged on her gloves and made her way down the stairs. *Stay in the hotel? Stay in her room?*

Garrett McCabe was just going to have to learn—and apparently learn the hard way—that Miranda Thomas took orders from no one.

****

Draco sat at a table in the far corner, watching the door. He'd sat in the hotel restaurant for over two hours, waiting for her. He'd decided to check the livery to make sure he hadn't missed them, when Miranda stepped inside the room. He settled back in his chair, lifting the paper he'd been reading to shield his face. He needn't have bothered. She didn't seem to take notice of him or anyone else in the room.

Miranda seated herself at a table in the middle of the room and gave her order to the waiter. She stared out the window, lost deep in thought, and when her breakfast came, she toyed with the food on her plate. What was troubling her?

He waited for her escort to join her, but none came. He was, by turns, pleased and puzzled. He knew the old chaperone had quit. That hadn't surprised him. He'd overheard the whole conversation from behind his door just across the hall, and he'd silently cheered Miranda on when she'd given the old bat what for. He'd briefly considered stealing into her room in the dead of night, but he'd heard the exhaustion in her voice. The marshal was pushing her too hard. She'd needed her rest.

He was glad she'd gotten rid of the old biddy though. The woman had been a con, and from the look on Miranda's face when he'd demanded the old woman's possessions, the dour Miss Burns had stolen from Miranda herself. He slipped a hand into his pocket and fingered the strand of pearls he'd held back from his band of thieves, and he smiled.

She traveled with a U.S. Marshal now, but that didn't worry him...not in the least. He hadn't been able to get a good look at the man just yet. He'd passed the marshal on the stairs, but Draco had been trying too hard to keep his own face from being seen to have the opportunity to risk even a glimpse of the man, although, something about the marshal was vaguely familiar. He hadn't been able to put his thumb on where he'd seen the man before, but it would come to him. He had a very good memory for such things.

Where was the man now? Whoever he was, he was doing a damn poor job at keeping an eye on her. He studied Miranda as she sipped her tea. His gaze skimmed over her hair, across the delicate features of her face, and down the graceful column of her neck. He hadn't imagined it possible, but for the first time since that long ago day his world had burned to cinder and ash, he considered a change in lifestyle.

He recalled how she'd flirted with him on the stage, remembered the taste of her, so innocent and curious, and considered that some of his associates might have had the right idea after all when choosing a woman over the thrill of the job. He caught himself nodding, and reflected that, given the right woman, it just might be worth it.

Miranda Thomas, late of Boston, would be just such a woman.

It was true, in recent months he'd grown tired of the job. Dealing day in and day out with cutthroat thieves and slippery bandits—men who could and would turn on you in the blink of an eye—had become tiresome, to say the least. He'd become disillusioned with the profession he'd chosen. That attitude was dangerous. Complacency could get a man like him killed. Yes, maybe it was time for him to move on to a new phase in his life, find a less hazardous career—and the love of a good woman.

That last thought brought a slow, illicit smile to his lips.

He observed Miranda as she finished with her breakfast, dabbing at the corners of her mouth with a napkin before she stood up. She gathered her reticule, secured the ribbons around her wrist, and made for the front door of the hotel. The gentle sway of her hips drew his gaze.

He rose, tossed a few bills on the table, and trailed her at a discreet distance. All the while, his mind began cementing his plans for his future. He had this one last job to finish, one last obligation to meet, and then he'd be free. He'd retire. He had more than enough money put by to live quite comfortably the rest of his days. He'd made sure of that. It would be a simple matter of relocating some place where no one would see his face and recognize him as the bandit Draco. He could live a respectable life after all these long years of living in the shadows.

Across the way, she stepped inside the telegraph office, and he waited for her to emerge. She wasn't inside long, and soon she was on her way once more. Her next stop was the small mercantile at the end of the dusty street. He lounged against the side of the building, watching her through the dingy window. His gaze roamed down her delicate frame as she stretched up to pull a book down from a high shelf.

She studied the volume for a few moments. Then, nodding to herself, Miranda carried it to the counter. Her movements were graceful, mesmerizing.

She spoke to the clerk, who nodded eager enthusiasm, and reached below the counter. A few moments later, Miranda shuffled through the contents of the box, selecting a small pile of...were those buttons? She spent several moments conversing with the woman behind the counter before digging in her reticule and withdrawing some coins.

Miranda passed a flash of silver to the beaming store clerk. She scooped the pile of buttons up and deposited them inside her reticule. Draco ducked to the side, out of sight, as she stepped out into the bright sunlight, a satisfied smile on her lips, her new book tucked under her arm. He couldn't help but smile, she seemed so pleased with herself. He noted with mild interest that she must enjoy reading. A pastime, it seemed, they both shared. He watched as she paused for a moment on the boardwalk, as if trying to determine what project to take on next.

In the blink of an eye, she turned, bustling along the boardwalk...her obvious destination the livery. She was a bundle of efficient energy this morning, and he found it amusing and endearing, even if he was annoyed she flitted about town unescorted, oblivious to the dangers lurking nearby.

Draco was just about to fall into step behind her, when something odd caught his eye. In the last several years, he'd become an expert at moving through a town, blending enough to not draw any undue notice. He'd perfected following a mark without having that mark be any the wiser—until it was too late, at least.

He also became expert enough to realize when someone else was doing the same.

He hung back, sticking to the shadows. A few

moments later, a tall, slim man with unremarkable, light brown hair and dull brown eyes fell in behind her. The man wore a dusty brown cowboy hat and a brown leather vest. Draco eyed him for a moment, remembered seeing him in the hotel dining room, outside the telegraph office, and just now, coming out of the mercantile.

His old mentor used to say, there's no such thing as coincidence. Draco had a tendency to agree with him. With an ominous, predatory growl, Draco stepped off the boardwalk, keeping a watchful eye on Miranda, and a wary eye on Slim.

****

Satisfied the horses were being looked after, Miranda stepped outside through the wide double doors of the livery. She'd taken care of all her errands for the day already, and it wasn't yet noon.

That left the better part of the day with not much to do. On the other hand, she'd found some nice buttons to replace those now missing from her riding habit. There would be no saving the corset. In addition to that, she'd found a book, a collection of stories by Hawthorne. At least she'd have something to look forward to this evening.

Her mind filled with the small details of repairing her damaged wardrobe, she stepped down off the boardwalk and began the trek back to the hotel. Absorbed in her thoughts, Miranda didn't notice the shadows shifting between two closely situated buildings until it was too late.

Without the slightest warning, a long, powerful arm yanked her off her feet, pulling her into the snug space between the buildings. A large, strong hand clamped over her mouth before she managed to scream. Her heart hammering, her eyes wide with fear, she scrambled to keep her head. Her assailant snaked an arm around her waist—an arm as unforgiving as an iron band—and pulled her back,

122

flush against a tall, powerful form. Panic threatened to consume her. She had to escape somehow.

If she could get her mouth free, perhaps...

Miranda bared her teeth and sank them into flesh. At the same time, she let loose a sharp elbow and planted it in her assailant's midsection with a satisfying thud. Wrestling, squirming like a wildcat, she managed to wiggle some room between them as a stifled oath hit her ears.

Without warning, her abductor spun her about and pressed her up against the wall. Before she could scream for help, he covered her lips once more. However, this time it wasn't a strong hand, but firm, warm lips that did the covering. Lips she recognized. Her eyes widened, connecting with clear, irritated, wintery blue. Long, golden locks floated about the edges of her vision, and the solid rock wall of male chest filled the space before her, pressing against her. She gasped in surprise, and froze.

Draco took swift advantage, pressing against her, deepening the kiss.

The heat of his kiss sizzled through her, clear to her toes. But it didn't stagger her, not like Garrett's kiss had. She pushed at Draco's chest, insisting on her freedom. Draco lifted his head, his lips hovering close to hers—too close. Determination glinted in his eyes. He made no effort to move any farther away from her, his eyebrow cocked, his grin wolfish.

"Draco!" Miranda hissed. "What are *you* doing here?"

"What can I say? I just couldn't stay away from you, my love." His warm gaze fastened on her lips. Intent glowed heavy in his eyes.

She squirmed, thumping a fist against his shoulder. "Let go of me."

Sighing, he allowed a slim bit of distance between them. She brushed at her bodice and skirts, glaring at him, miffed. The corner of his mouth curled upward as his eyes followed her hands.

"Now..." She took a breath and leveled an irritated scowl at him. "Why *are* you here?"

"You wound me, darlin'," he murmured, dazzling her with a charming smile. "Why won't you believe I desire nothing more than to be near you?"

She retorted, "I don't believe that for one moment. There must be something..." Then her eyes rounded in amazement, and she gasped at him. "Please tell me you're not going to try to rob the bank!"

Draco's eyes danced. His smile grew. "Be careful, sweetheart. I might start thinking that you care for me—even the tiniest bit."

"Oh, don't be ridiculous, you dope." But she bit her lower lip, frowning. Irritating as he may be, he was amusing—likable even—and she didn't like to think he might do something so risky.

"You needn't worry, sweetheart, I'm *very* good at what I do," he murmured, wagging a suggestive eyebrow as he brushed a loose curl over her shoulder. "I won't get hurt."

"It would serve you right to swing from the gallows. You might hurt someone innocent..." she trailed off, her thoughts filled with the tale Garrett had told her of his brothers, and her stomach clenched tight. Even if he knew what he was about, sometimes things went wrong. Horribly, tragically wrong. "Don't do it, Draco. It's not worth it."

Draco was quiet for a moment, then he changed the subject. "Where's that fool escort of yours?"

"Garrett?"

"Garrett..." Draco tested the name with a frown and something, some glimmer of recognition flickered in his eyes.

"He's...he's not feeling well." Miranda shifted, edging closer to the boardwalk.

"He should be shot for being so irresponsible,"

Draco growled. "He shouldn't have let you wander around town unescorted. There are all manner of men here who wouldn't think twice about snatching up a delectable piece like you."

Miranda arched a wry brow at him, calling his own actions into question. "You mean like thieves and *bandits*?"

"That reminds me," he drawled, brushing her insult aside as he dug in his pocket. "I have something for you."

Miranda meant to shake her head in refusal, but froze when he let the string of pearls slip through his fingers like a cascade of shimmering silk until it dangled from two fingers. "A token of my affections," he drawled, his eyes hooded.

"My pearls," she breathed, reaching out to take them. But at the last moment, he lifted them up out of her reach.

"I believe this is where you express a bit of appreciation for my having recovered your necklace," he invited.

"You stole them." She glared at him, making another fruitless snatch for the item in question.

"Now, if you want to be technical," he drawled, humor lighting his eyes. "Miss Burns stole them. I'm just returning them. I would think such a selfless act would warrant a reward."

Miranda frowned, drawing her hand back, wary. "What kind of reward?"

His sanguine smile was immediate...and devious. "A kiss for a bauble, my pet."

"That's... That's... That's *not* funny," she stammered. "Give me my pearls, Draco!"

"Give me my kiss, Miranda," he shot back, stepping closer, crowding her again.

"You've stolen more than enough kisses from me." Miranda backed away, her retreat impeded by the rough plank wall behind her. But she eyed the pearls, biting her bottom lip. "Please, Draco. They are very important to me," she pleaded. "They were my grandmother's."

He paused then, graced her with a gentle smile, and inclined his head like a knight of old bestowing a token of his devotion. "Then I give them back to you, along with my heart."

Draco leaned closer, reached for her neck. She blinked, staring up at him in disbelief as he fastened the clasp at her nape with long, nimble fingers. He cleared his throat and stepped back. Just when she'd judged him a lascivious cad, he had to go and do something so sweet. She couldn't hold on to her irritation.

If Garrett had made such a gesture—if he'd been the one asking for a kiss—she wouldn't have thought twice about it. She would have kissed him, in a heartbeat...

Shocked, Miranda sliced that line of thought off and focused on the man before her.

"Thank you, Draco." She fingered the delicate necklace, blinking unexpected moisture from her eyes.

"You're not off the hook just yet, my sweet," he murmured. "I still expect a kiss for returning them to you, but I'll wait for it—for now."

Draco's gaze flicked over to the street. She frowned as he tensed. Swearing, he tugged her farther into the shadows. She opened her mouth to protest, but he silenced her by laying a gentle finger across her lips. He pulled her to his side and pointed to a tall, slim man across the street. The man seemed to be searching for someone, his puzzled gaze sliding from one end of the street to the other.

Draco's lips hovered near her ear. "Do you know him?"

She shook her head, a frown puckering her brow. "No, I don't believe so."

"He's been following you all day."

Miranda turned to stare at him. "What?"

He nodded, slipping an arm around her waist. He toyed with a button at her midriff. "He's been following you...the dining room, the telegraph office, the mercantile. You need to inform that idiot marshal of yours that you're being followed."

Miranda pushed at his hand, squirming away from his embrace.

"Why would he be...wait a second. How do you know he was following me?" She scowled at him as understanding dawned. "You were there, too, at all of those places. You wouldn't have known he was there if you hadn't been there yourself!"

He grinned down at her, brazen and unrepentant.

She glared right back, hissing, "I don't like to be spied on."

Unconcerned, he leaned close and murmured a seductive invitation against her ear. "You could leave your door unlocked tonight, my pet..."

"I wouldn't plan on it, were I you," she snapped.

His grin widened, as if exhilarated by the challenge. "You know, I'm very good with locks."

Her eyes narrowed, and she growled between clenched teeth, "Don't even think about it."

"Of course, I could just do this the easy way and take you with me now." He smoothed the back of his knuckles along her jaw.

"You wouldn't."

He leered down at her, caressing the backs of his long fingers over her cheek. "I would... Unfortunately, I have an obligation to meet, and now a mystery to solve as well. I want to find out why someone is tailing you." His fingertips fluttered down the side of her neck, the gentlest of caresses. "Don't worry, my darling. You'll see me again...very soon."

She opened her mouth to protest, but he moved in...fast as a lethal predator closing in for the kill...sealing his lips over hers in a fast, hard kiss. His tongue thrust into her mouth and swirled around hers before she could do little more than gasp. When he pulled back, she shook her head, vexed and—despite herself—flattered.

"Will you *stop* doing that?" she demanded.

"I must, it seems—for now, at least. I'll see you to your hotel," he informed her, holding up a hand before she could protest. "Since your escort doesn't seem to be able to stir himself to offer you protection, I feel it my duty to do so." Then his expression turned serious. "I will see you back to the hotel, Miranda—whether you want me to or not."

It would be pointless to argue. The look on his face frightened her a little, so determined and ruthless was he. She nodded, wary, and accepted his arm.

Draco walked with her back to the hotel, as the lanky man in brown blinked in confusion and hurried to fall in behind them. In the hotel lobby, Draco drew her hand to her lips, pressed a lingering kiss to the tender skin on the inside of her wrist, and bowed with elegant flair.

When he straightened, his eyes were hard, brooking no argument. "Go to your room. Lock the door. Don't go out alone again. I might not be the one to catch you next time."

She blinked, nodded silent understanding, and she watched him stride back out into the sunlight. His long golden hair flowed about his broad shoulders. The silver studs on his hatband gleamed against the black of his hat, his black duster slapped against his long legs. She stood there for a moment longer, bewildered. Squaring her shoulders, Miranda ascended the stairs. It was about time to check in on the patient again.

Chapter Ten

Garrett angled his head toward the window, moody and groggy. Scowling, he squinted down through the bright sunshine at the woman as she walked across the street toward the hotel, her hand resting on the crook of a strange man's arm. He ought to just shoot the hardheaded little minx and have it over with, damn her beautiful hide.

The way she moved, the way she gestured with her free hand, set his teeth on edge. She'd averted her face from the sun—and from him. A fashionable hat covered her head, but that unmistakable shade of red hair could only belong to one woman. Couldn't she listen just one time? Was that asking for too much? Edgy and restless, he growled, prowling from the window to the door and back again. He should race down stairs and give her—and her newfound escort—hell.

No, no he needed to get his temper back under control before he spoke to Miranda again. There was no telling what might happen if he came face to face with her, as angry as he was right now. Bracing a forearm against the window frame, hands fisted, he peered harder at Miranda's companion.

Now that he looked closer, there *was* something familiar about the man. Then, Garrett placed the tall stranger in black on the stairwell last night—the man in the black hat and duster. He wracked his aching brain, trying to remember the man's face. Garrett scrutinized the man with the flowing blond hair until he and Miranda disappeared beneath the hotel awning below him. That flowing blond hair...

He'd only ever seen hair like that before on one man. A man to whom Garrett owed his very life. However, reliable sources had confirmed that Damian Morgan had been killed in the line of duty several years back.

Damn fuzzy brain.

He just couldn't get things to add up straight to save his hide today. Damning himself once more for letting her get to him last night, Garrett dragged on a shirt. As he worked each small button through its designated hole, he glanced out the window once more. The tall man in black emerged from beneath the awning once more, alone, to stride across the street as if he owned the town. With any luck, the bounder—whoever the hell he was—would saddle up and ride out, and Garrett wouldn't have to worry about him anymore. Still, that odd sense of recognition nagged at Garrett again with irritating persistency.

Shaking his head, he started to turn away from the window, and another detail caught his attention. He'd been so focused on Miranda and her companion, he'd let everything else that was going on down there slip right by him. He knew better. That's how a man got shot in the back, by not paying proper attention to what went on around him. At the corner of the mercantile, two men conversed in heated motions. One was tall and slim, with a brown vest and hat. However, he wasn't the one that had drawn Garrett's attention. It was his companion.

The second man was brawny—a hulking bull of a man. He wore a spotless, white cowboy hat, tugged low on his brow, and a tailored suit—much like the garb of a banker. From this distance, Garrett was unable to see the brawny man's features at all.

The burly man shook his head. He appeared to bark a few curt words before stalking back inside the building. The door slammed behind him hard enough to shatter one of the panes of glass. The slim man scurried away, a nervous man on a mission.

Garrett cursed the fog clinging to his brain like a raincloud. He'd recognized that man, though his slim companion held no recognition for Garrett whatsoever. Where had he seen that man before? Then his fingers froze, his mind blanked in disbelief. He had to be mistaken. He blinked the sunspots from his vision and ground the palms of both hands against his gritty eyes. When he opened his eyes, his vision cleared some, and he stared at the empty street, shaking his head in self-disgust.

No way. It was...impossible.

His brain must still be pickled. He was seeing not one but *two* dead men from his past.

Jesus, Mary, and Joseph!

Crossing the room on legs that had gone wooden, Garrett sank to the edge of the bed. He finished buttoning his shirt as his mind wandered. The face of the man who'd made his life a living hell—that smile of pure, malicious evil—came to mind. Garrett shuddered with residual anger and frustration. Clint Chambers, the infamous leader of the Chambers Gang. The very same man he'd spent six long years of his life tracking—then to watch him elude the hangman's noose by succumbing to the flames of a fire he'd set by his own hand.

Garrett could only pray—if justice extended to the afterlife—that the bastard continued roasting in the flames of hell. He shook his head again at the unfeasibility of that man across the street being Clint Chambers. Garrett had seen the fire with his own eyes. He'd seen the flames lick at the outlaw's clothing, seen the man's features twisted in outrage and pain. No one could have survived that inferno. *No one.* It just wasn't possible. Satan himself would have needed burn salve.

With a self-deprecating snort, he raked a tense

hand through his hair. He just needed to get back to the ranch, back to peace and solitude, he told himself. His imagination had run away with him, aided by the lingering traces of alcohol no doubt still steeping his system. First he'd thought he'd seen Morgan...and now Chambers.

He'd never touch another bottle again.

He wondered at what else his strained mind would come up with next. It seemed he'd already lost his professional morals, kissing Miranda last night. Moreover, if kissing her hadn't been bad enough, he'd gone and gotten whopping drunk, like some green field agent on his first assignment. Next, he'd be doing something beyond stupid. Like dragging Miranda off to bed...or worse still, dragging her to the nearest preacher.

God forbid...

His head pounded like Comanche war drums as he leaned down to tug on his boots. He took a spare moment as he straightened, pressing his eyes closed as he waited for the throbbing to recede. Garrett pushed to his feet, strapped his gun belt around his hips, and headed for the door.

That little hoyden had better have enough sense in her head to hide in her room the rest of the day...at least until he'd had sufficient time to cool off. His skull felt shattered, his brain sorely abused. Garrett yanked the door open with enough force to tear it from its hinges, then paused midstride when he came face to face with the hat he'd seen on the street.

Damn her sweet, irresistible hide.
****

Miranda stopped in the hallway to dig in her reticule for her key, her head bent to her search, when the door beside her swung inward. She gave a jolt of surprise. A slow smile of greeting spread over her face...until she recognized the fury burning in

Garrett's glare.

Oh, for Pete's sake, now what?

Rolling her own eyes, she shuffled her book to the other arm and pulled her key free. Without a word to Garrett, she took two unhurried steps and paused outside her door long enough to insert the key and twist. She'd no more than pushed the door inward, when she felt Garrett's presence behind her. He was like a dark storm cloud just waiting to hurl bolts of lightning at her head.

She turned to face him, gritting her teeth. If he thought, for one minute, that she'd stand here and let him chastise her for disobeying his absurd orders, he had another thing coming.

His hands descended to her shoulders, and he propelled her backwards into her room ahead of him, stalking her step for step. Miranda gasped aloud. Once he'd cleared the threshold, he kicked the door closed with a booted heel.

"What do you think you're doing, Garrett?" Miranda demanded. "This is *my* room, get out."

Garrett didn't stop steering her until she stood firm in the middle of the room and pushed back. Her efforts seemed paltry when compared to his, but they succeeded in gaining his attentions. He dropped his hands to his sides, fisted them, and glared at her.

"Where have you been? Who was that man walking with you?"

Miranda stared at him in silence, seething. Then she turned aside, laid the book on the foot of the bed, and tugged the ribbons of her reticule from her wrists. Without offering a word of explanation, she reached up to yank the long hatpin from her hair, removed the hat, and jammed the pin onto the felt. Tossing the hat onto the bed beside the book, Miranda drew a deep breath. She would not respond to his surly, autocratic attitude.

"Miranda..." His voice held an unmistakable

note of warning.

She whirled to face him, fists planted on her hips. "Get out of my room."

"Who was he, Miranda?"

"He's just a...a good Samaritan," she replied, scowling. "He walked me back to the hotel."

Garrett's eyes narrowed. Leaning forward—towering over her—Garrett frowned, his voice deadly calm. "Where were you that you needed an escort, *princess*?"

"I had a few errands that needed seeing to," she replied, poking at his chest with a pointed finger. "Stop towering over me, you're not intimidating anyone here."

Garrett's eyes flashed. "Errands? I told you not to leave the hotel, damn it woman—"

"Yes, you did," she interrupted with a sticky-sweet smile. "And I'll thank you not to swear at me." Furious, Miranda turned away and stomped to the chest of drawers where she drew the gloves from her hands, one finger at a time. How dare he act as though she were some common criminal? How dare he glare at her, much less swear at her?

How dare he look so handsome?

"Then why the hell didn't you listen?"

She slapped the gloves against her palm with an angry crack. "Because I am not some...some obedient hound that falls all over herself, eager to please. Because *you* were the one too *ill* to travel...not me. Because *you* were the one that saw fit to drink himself into oblivion, *not me*. Maybe I didn't see the logic in confining myself to my room when there were a number of things that needed to be dealt with. I didn't think there was any reason for me to stay inside, until... Well, I just didn't."

His eyes narrowed, and he advanced an ominous step, demanding, "Until what?"

She grimaced and tried to push past him, but he

grabbed her wrist and tugged her back to face him. Though his grip wasn't tight enough to hurt her, his hold was that of an iron manacle. Unbreakable. She jerked at her arm anyway.

His voice was low and dangerous, his eyes turbulent gray. "What aren't you telling me, Miranda?"

"Somebody followed me around town today," she relented, thrusting her chin up defiantly.

"Someone followed you?"

She wanted to squirm beneath the intensity of his stare. She could already see it coming, the interrogation, the endless questions, and she sighed in defeat when he began. "Do you know who followed you? Did you get a look at him? Would you recognize him again?"

"As a matter of fact, I did get a good look," she said on a sigh, tugging at her arm again.

Garrett released her wrist, but kept her trapped in his steady regard.

"The man was tall, thin—sort of gangly. He had light brown hair, a brown vest, and a brown hat," she outlined. The only way to get the interrogation over faster was to cooperate. She'd learned that the last time around.

Garrett's eyes narrowed when he recalled the man on the corner. "How did you figure out he was following you?"

She shifted, biting her lip. "Well, I didn't..."

He tilted his head and arched a brow.

Heaving a sigh, she hissed, "Someone else told me."

"Who? Your good Samaritan?"

Miranda braced herself for the explosion and nodded.

"God*damn* it, woman! What the hell were you thinking? I want his name, Miranda. I want his name, and I want it now."

Something undefined coursed through her, something anxious...something fearful. He'd never before looked like this, not even after the stagecoach robbery. He was cold, determined. Dangerous.

She forced a swallow, and whispered, "Draco."

The second explosion was worse than the first. "Draco? *Draco!*" He stomped to the door, then he stomped right back. One hand raked through his hair, the other clenched and unclenched at his side. "He was here—he strolled with you through town—and you didn't think it was important enough to mention?"

"He was a perfect gentleman...for the most part," she hemmed, edging back a cautious step as she fingered the pearls at her throat.

"Gentleman, was he? He's a damned *criminal*," Garrett snarled. His eyes narrowed on her, and she clamped down on the urge to shrink away. Instead, she held her chin up and met him glare for glare...until his next question made her wince. "Did that bastard kiss you again?"

She flinched, and Garrett let out a long string of curses that made her face burn. He growled, a low frightful sound, his face turning red.

Miranda's eyes widened. Her mouth fell open. She backed up another step despite herself. She'd expected him to be angry, but she'd never expected this strong of a reaction.

The mention of the kiss had thrown her a bit, as well. She hadn't given all that much thought to Draco kissing her again. He was good at kissing...very good. There was no doubt about that, not in the least. But Draco's kisses didn't leave stars in her eyes. Not the way Garrett's kiss had. In truth, it had almost struck her as funny, the way Draco insisted on trying to kiss her. And the way he spoke to her—as if he were trying to woo her with flowery words and affectionate pet names—was rather...well, endearing.

She sighed, exasperated, while Garrett muttered beneath his breath. Garrett swung about midstride and marched over to tower above her. She tensed, expecting him to blast her with questions again, or to blister her once more with vulgar language.

Instead, he reached for her.

Nothing could have prepared her for the shock of his touch.

One strong hand grasped her by the back of her neck. The other snaked around her waist. Before she had time to do little more than squeak in surprise, he hauled her up against the hard length of his body. His eyes, storm cloud gray, locked on hers for one breath-stealing, heart-stopping moment.

His head dipped, and his mouth covered hers with ferocious need. As if he were trying to brand himself upon her. Mark her as his own. Erase the taste and the memory of Draco.

He was doing a damned fine job.

His lips moved over hers for a moment, hard and angry. His tongue thrust over the rim of her lips, hot and questing—demanding a response from her. Her head began to spin, her pulses to hammer, and the world rocked beneath her feet while their tongues tangled and danced in a wild, erotic mating. She grasped at his shirt, frantic to hold on to something solid. It wasn't enough.

His muscles bunched and rippled beneath her touch, but the fabric of his shirt thwarted her. Her fingers itched to touch his skin, yearned to explore the secrets of his flesh. Garrett's passionate kisses stirred something deep in her, something Draco's most ardent kisses just couldn't touch.

Driving, elemental desire coursed through her. She wanted to fill her arms with him, and so she gave in to the urge. Circling her arms around him, she pressed herself against his body, reveling in the hard planes and firm angles, savoring how well they fit together. Garrett's arms tightened around her, sweeping her beyond the realm of restraint. He slanted his head and deepened the kiss, growling pure, unmistakable male satisfaction as she melted against him. Passion, raw and unleashed, roared free, ravenous and untamable.

Miranda barely registered the bed pressing against the backs of her legs. The man in her arms overwhelmed her, working magic with his skillful lips. Then those delectable lips moved away from hers. Whimpering, she bemoaned the loss, until his hot mouth slid to the pulse-point just below her ear. A delicate shiver coursed through her as his teeth nibbled and grazed the sensitive skin.

Fire soon replaced that delicate shiver when his tongue licked and lapped down the side of her neck, and his large, hard palm kneaded her breast. His knee pressed between her thighs. Pleasure, liquid and golden, pooled deep in her center. She arched against him, breathless and wanting.

With a low growl, he lifted her against him, crushed her to him. The breath trapped in her lungs. Their lips broke apart for a split second, their breathing ragged as he lowered her to the bed. Then his lips claimed hers again with a raging fever before she had a chance to gather her scrambled wits into any form of good sense. His hands tugged at her bodice. His weight pressed her hips into the mattress. The rumble of pleasure deep in his chest sparked a wildfire of need within her. Her greedy hands ran over his back, his arms.

Garrett's nimble fingers had already loosened the fastenings spilling down the length of her bodice by the time she'd even thought to tangle with the buttons on his shirt. His warm, hard hands pushed the material open, and he lifted her off the mattress, rolling with her, pulling her on top of him, wrestling the material from her shoulders. His hot lips devoured every inch of skin he managed to bare, scorching her with his passion. Gasping, she shivered against him, pulling and yanking at his shirt.

More.

She needed...*more*. She had to have her hands on him, had to touch his skin. The need clawed through her, stronger than anything she'd ever experienced. What was this ravaging need? It seemed the only way to appease it, the only way to ease the ache was to yield, surrender completely. She ripped at his shirt, tugging and pulling until her palms skated over bare flesh.

More...

****

Garrett rolled to the side, freeing an arm from his shirt. Her skin was finer than silk beneath his fingers. Sweeter than honey on his tongue. His mind held no reason now, no thoughts of restraint or common sense. His body ruled, filled with desperate, aching need. A need only Miranda could quench. She was so warm, so willing in his arms. So eager. Her kisses were driving him out of his mind. The feel of her hands on his body urged him onward. Her thighs parted, cradling him, and he grasped the curve of her bottom, pressing her closer. By the saints, if he didn't bury himself inside her soon he'd explode—

The sharp corner of a book gouged into the side of his neck. An unmistakable crumpling sound followed that initial, painful call to attention. It wasn't much.

But it was enough.

Garrett froze. The heady fullness of her breast filled his hand, nothing more than a thin scrap of chemise separating their skin. The other hand clutched the back of her bodice while she straddled him, struggling against his shirt, her soft lips devouring his burning flesh. His parted lips hovered over the smooth skin of her chest, and the sound of her ragged breathing caressed his ears, sweeter than the celestial music from a choir of angels.

With a groan, he dropped his head back against the mattress and closed his eyes, a man tormented with the touch and taste and scent of the one woman he wanted above all else. The one woman he could not have. He forced his hands to move when he felt her fingers connect with the bared skin of his abdomen and dip inside his waistband. He caged her wrists between them. She whimpered against the bristled edge of his jaw, straining to free her hands. Garrett moaned, gritting his teeth, wanting nothing more than to turn his head and capture her lips with his own.

Some selfish, hedonistic part of him urged him onward, cajoled him to take what she so enthusiastically offered. Surely the fires of damnation couldn't burn any hotter than the rivers of need boiling through his veins.

Calling forth near superhuman restraint, Garrett rasped her name aloud.

She lifted her head and stared, her beautiful eyes cloudy with desire. She blinked in confusion, once—twice. Her eyes shot wide open, and her face flooded with the rosy hue of mortification. Her lips parted, shock and horror etched on every striking feature of her flawless face. With a tiny gasp, she scooted off him, tugging her clothing back in place.

Garrett sat up. His body vibrated with unquenched desire, his conscience racked with guilt. He should offer her some sort of apology, but he hadn't a clue where to begin. He didn't have the foggiest idea what to say. And so he sat in miserable silence, watching as she scrambled to button her bodice back up once more. Drawing a ragged breath as the last button slipped into place, he hoisted himself to his feet and turned to face her. How had he managed to let things get this far out of hand?

"I'm sorry, I shouldn't have—"

"Oh no," Miranda cried, reaching for her hat. The flimsy straw and felt concoction dangled from her fingers, mangled beyond redemption. She lifted it with a small piteous moan and ran a hand over the flattened crown, her expression mournful.

"Miranda," Garrett persisted, glowering now. "I'm trying to apologize here."

She turned wrathful eyes to him, and Garrett began to wish he'd ducked out of the room while he'd had the chance. At the same time, something inside of him reacted—violently—to the sight of her sitting there on the bed, mussed, glaring at him with fire in her eyes. Her hair tumbled about her, wanton and wild. Her cheeks bloomed with furious color.

"Look, I—"

She cut him off with a furious hiss as she shot from the bed and waved the ruined hat in his face. He backed away, his hands held up between them, palms outward, in a bid for mercy. Miranda stalked him, steam all but rolling from her ears.

"Are you happy now?" she railed. "I won't have anything left to wear at this rate."

Garrett gaped at her. Her words weren't helping his already raging desire. The picture of her, standing there naked before him, flashed through his mind with a cruel jab. He blinked and sputtered, shoving those images aside, focusing on her angry sapphire glare.

"It's just a damned hat."

The moment the words left his mouth, he knew he'd said something wrong. Something terribly wrong. For the life of him, he just couldn't figure out what. Her eyes narrowed, her chin dipped, and she advanced with mayhem glowing in her eyes. Once more, he found himself standing on the threshold of her doorway, looking in.

Clearing his throat, he attempted to placate her. "Look, I'm sorry, all right?"

She didn't look the slightest bit mollified.

The hell with it, he thought, throwing common sense to the wind. "Next time I tell you to stay put— stay put! I don't know who's following you, but it's not safe to stay here any longer, so we're leaving. Be downstairs in fifteen minutes."

Her teeth snapped together with a loud clack. Her narrowed eyes were little more than slits now, and she drew a deep, deep breath through flared nostrils. Then, without warning, she slammed the door in his face hard enough to knock one of the glass globes from a nearby wall sconce. It fell to the floor and shattered, the sound echoed in the hallway around him.

Garrett stared at the door, mere inches from his nose. The snarl slipped out before he could stop it, not that he particularly cared right now. Angry enough to chew the hide off a seasoned bull, he shouted, "Fifteen minutes, Miranda!"

Dead silence met his straining ears, and the fight went right out of him. He dropped his chin to his chest, closing his eyes in weary resignation. She hadn't uttered a sound, and yet she'd still managed to get in the last word.

Chapter Eleven

Clint Chambers drew the imported lace curtains aside. His narrow-eyed stare followed McCabe as he paced on the boardwalk in front of the hotel. Every few minutes, Garrett glanced at the doorway, his lips would move, he'd kick at some inconspicuous pebble in his path, and then he'd resume his pacing. He'd been out there going well on to half an hour. The corner of Chambers' mouth quirked up, and he chuckled—amused at anything that could irk his nemesis so.

And McCabe was angry, there was no doubt of that. Even from this hidden vantage point across the street, it was unmistakable.

Chambers pulled a chair closer to the window and sat down. Leaning an elbow on the armrest, he dropped his cheek against his fist and settled in for the duration. This latest development was...fascinating. Sheer, dumb luck had thrown McCabe into his path once more. Luck was a fickle thing indeed. After all, if it hadn't been for a stroke of said luck, he wouldn't be sitting here now. Luck had sent that fiery wall crashing to the ground, allowing the space for him to crawl free of the wreckage of the burning building. Of course, an unfortunate stroke of luck had also trapped him instead of McCabe inside the building, in the first place.

Unfortunate bad luck...and a brilliant plan that had backfired—quite literally.

After spending close to six years existing like a hunted animal, always looking over his shoulder, sleeping with one eye open, forever on the watch for the determined marshal, he'd grown weary of living on the run. He'd had enough. He'd determined it was time to fight back, and so he had turned the tables, setting the stage with painstaking care. The plan had been to lure McCabe in, trap him inside, and set fire to the farmhouse. But McCabe had come too soon, and a stray bullet had ignited the blaze before Chambers could escape.

On the other hand, his plan had worked, in a roundabout way. McCabe had been watching when his clothes caught fire. He'd seen the wall collapse— and McCabe had assumed he'd died in the flames. Meanwhile, Chambers had managed to squeeze through the hole in the wall. He'd rolled through the dirt to extinguish the flames, then crawled to a ravine and lay low until McCabe and his men rode out. The pain, and the ensuing infection, had almost killed him, but he'd gotten McCabe off his trail, true enough.

He'd paid a high price for his freedom.

Turning away from the window, he glanced into the mirror across the way and fingered his disfigured cheek. Tilting his head into the light, he studied his marred reflection, bitter resentment seething in his heart. The flames of his freedom had seared the flesh of his right cheek and the side of his neck. In fact, the angry red scarring stretched from just below his eye all the way down over his shoulder and across his torso.

The disfigurement reached forward to pucker the edge of his mouth and back to his mangled ear. A good portion of his body still held scar tissue, a reminder of McCabe that Chambers would carry to his dying day. His palms had also suffered extensive blistering, and although those blemishes weren't quite so obvious at first glance, he'd lost a good deal of sensation in those appendages. He lived every day with the bitter reminder that McCabe had eluded his trap, and he'd been the one to suffer. Well, that was behind him. He'd recovered. He'd rebuilt his gang, replacing the men McCabe had hunted and turned over to that cursed Hangin' Judge Thomas.

He'd lain low, focusing his attention on the rail line and the money chests the army sent through for the forts in the state. He'd also taken on a partner. A formidable man with a good head for business...a brilliant man with a lot to lose should his illegal dealings ever come to light.

Periodic shipments of cash bound to the treasury for exchange were easy pickings, intercepted with little difficulty from trains that had pitiful defenses. As far as Chambers was concerned, old money padded the pockets just as well as new could. The only problems to arise from his latest enterprise were those damned Pinkertons.

Chambers turned his gaze back to the view from his window and shifted in his seat as he mulled over the latest wrench in his well-oiled plans. They were becoming a big pain in the ass.

They could be damned near as tenacious as McCabe had been.

All that aside, he had McCabe back in the crosshairs at last. He'd be damned if he'd let him slip away again. Chambers almost rubbed his hands together in hungry anticipation of the revenge he would exact. Oh, it wouldn't be quick and easy, not by a long shot. But in the end, the great Marshal Garrett McCabe would die knowing he'd failed in avenging his brothers' deaths. Chambers longed to see that realization in McCabe's eyes—just before the light of life faded and died behind a wall of flames and smoke.

Revenge might be a dish best served cold, but Clint Chambers preferred his hot—inferno hot.

Chambers picked a tattered copy of a

newspaper, twisting it in his unfeeling hands. When he was done with McCabe, he'd turn his attention to that bastard Thomas. He'd get a little bit of his own justice out of that crooked arm of the law. That vindictive, old son of a bitch had hung Chambers' best men without batting an eye. Well, as far as Chambers was concerned, what goes around comes around. He'd see Thomas dancing from the end of his own rope before too long.

That thought brought a small, satisfied smile to the unruined side of his mouth, and he turned back to the window in time to see a flame-haired beauty step through the doorway of the hotel. McCabe moved to intercept her but backpedaled as she turned an unmistakable, malicious stare his way. Chambers' eye narrowed, and he leaned forward in his chair, thoughtful now. The lady in question seemed to be putting McCabe through his paces.

My, my...what a beauty.

How sad. He hated wasting beauty. Chambers gave an apathetic shrug. His man, Griggs, had informed him of the woman's presence and tailed her throughout the morning. He'd reported back with baffling information about a tall stranger with long blond hair who'd appeared out of nowhere and escorted her back inside the hotel. Had it not been for that stranger, the redhead would already be in his keeping.

He chewed on the end of his cigar as he watched McCabe shake his head and point at the saddled horses. The woman snapped something at him, putting a dark scowl on his face, but she allowed him to assist her into the saddle nonetheless. McCabe's hands lingered on the woman, and Chambers' smile grew wide in speculative interest at how proprietary—how possessive and *telling* McCabe's touch was.

In that instant, as McCabe's hand lingered

overlong on the woman's knee, his face turned up to her, the woman's fate was sealed. She would be the instrument with which Chambers would bring about the great Marshal Garrett McCabe's downfall.

Chambers settled back in his chair, pulled a watch fob from his vest pocket and checked the time. Smiling, he tucked the timepiece away.

Revenge was at hand.

****

Garrett glanced at her from the corner of his eye and muttered a soft oath. Miranda held herself rigid in the saddle, gripping the reins in her fists. She stared forward, unblinking, her mouth pursed in angry displeasure. She refused to participate in any kind of conversation. Apparently, she wasn't about to let him off the hook. Even now, guilt gnawed at his insides like a rabid rat.

She sat so stiff, so rigid. She had one of those damned corsets on again. He knew it as sure as the sun would set in the west tonight. Shaking his head, he could see how it would all play out. Just like last time, she'd pass out and he'd have to catch her. He'd lay her on the ground and have to tear open her bodice again. Then he'd have to slice the corset free. When she woke up, she'd smile at him and draw him down into her arms. She'd press her lips to his and he would...

What in the name of God was he thinking?

Shifting in the saddle, Garrett pushed the brim of his hat up with the edge of his knuckle. He had no damned business having daydreams about ravishing her.

He'd had no business ravishing her right there in her hotel room either, but he hadn't let that stop him.

Squashing that line of thought, he turned his attention to the trail. They rode in tense silence for several miles, until his irritation got the better of him. The words flew from his mouth before he gave it reasonable thought. "Why the hell didn't you tell me right away that the bandit had been following us?"

Miranda continued to ride, looking straight ahead, as though she hadn't heard a word he'd said.

"Damn it, woman," he swore, losing what little patience he'd had left. "You owe me an answer."

At last, she looked at him...a slow turn of the head, a cold and distant stare, a delicate, arched eyebrow. Her lush lips pressed together in a flat line of displeasure. Three, precise heartbeats ticked by, and she turned back to face the trail, chin elevated, silent as the grave.

"Why couldn't you just stay in the damned room like I told you," he growled.

Her words, when they came, were biting, acerbic. "I wouldn't have been expected—unreasonably so—to remain in the room had *someone* not drunk himself to the point of lunacy."

"So this is all *my* fault, now?"

"No," she snarled. "This is my father's fault!"

"What?" Garrett gaped in sheer confusion. He couldn't help but marvel—and cringe—at how the female mind worked. Miranda's in particular. He should just let it go, shouldn't poke the snake with a stick so to speak, but he couldn't resist. "How do you figure that?"

"It's very simple. If my father hadn't decided to marry me off to that...that *monster*, I wouldn't have been forced to take extreme measures. I wouldn't have been exiled to this God forsaken state to live with my meddlesome uncle. I wouldn't have been on that stagecoach. I wouldn't have met that blasted bandit—who, it seems, has nothing better to do than follow me around stealing kisses. My wardrobe wouldn't suffer mishap at every turn—at your hands, I might add—and I wouldn't be manhandled and kissed every time Draco...or *you*...get a whim."

Fuming, he rode for a time in silence before turning in the saddle to face her. "Are you ever going to take responsibility for your own actions?"

That whipped her head around. Fury burned away the ice crystals in her eyes. "What did you just say?"

"You heard me, *princess*," he drawled. "Did it ever occur to you that if you'd used common sense, rather than going to extremes as you put it, you might have been able to avoid all this?"

"Common sense...as in I should have put up and shut up?" She glared at him, color rising to her cheeks. "You mean, if I'd just fallen in line—bowed my head and been a good little girl, and obediently marrying whomever my father chose, settling down to be a good submissive little wife, and raise half a dozen babies—that I wouldn't be in this mess? If I'd married that tyrant and pretended to be happy...and *ignorant*, then I wouldn't have been sent away in shame. Is that what you're saying?"

Her logic gave him pause. He sensed the conversation was spiraling out of hand, heading in a direction he didn't want to go, but he was helpless to stop it. A feeling he neither enjoyed, nor was he accustomed to experiencing.

"It would never have worked, Garrett," she snapped, not waiting for his response. Her eyes flashed with the anger of betrayal. "That's just not me. I'm not made that way, and if you believe that of me—then you're no better than my father."

Sensing the insult, Garrett's eyes narrowed. More importantly, the hurt behind the insult was tangible, and that knowledge diffused some of his anger. "I just meant you could've found a better way to get out of the engagement."

"Like what, Garrett?" Her gaze searched his. "Should I have talked to my father...tried to reason with him? I tried that. He told me the marriage was for my own good. He advised me it was a suitable, profitable arrangement, and I should be happy anyone of such prestige would consent to have me...all things considered. I was also told to leave the important decisions to the men folk."

Garrett was at a loss for words. The coldness of the situation was beyond his ability to understand—or approve.

"I tried begging him, Garrett," she admitted on little more than a whisper.

A hint of her shame glowed on her cheeks. Her admission floored him. His insides twisted. He couldn't imagine his proud, headstrong Miranda...*begging*.

"I tried pleading with my father to give me a chance to find someone more suitable to me. He told me I'd been given sufficient time, and I had failed him. I tried arguing that I couldn't have settled for someone with no backbone, someone I didn't, at the very least, care for. Would you like to hear his reassurance?"

His brow puckered. Garrett stared at her, silent, waiting.

"He said affections grow with time," she spat at him. "And if they don't...well then, I'd have no one to blame but myself."

Garrett stiffened, furious on her behalf. How could a father be so cold, so callous to his own child? Miranda deserved better than to be bartered off like some commodity. Then it occurred to him that he'd been willing to put some other woman in the same situation. Facing the future with nothing more than the hope that affection might grow in time.

"Miranda—"

"No, Garrett," she interrupted, holding her hand up in the space between them, forestalling his argument. "You don't know the man my father intended for me to marry. Conrad Covington the Third is a horrible man—autocratic and snobbish, little more than a thief. Head of one of the major shipping lines based out of the Boston ports."

Miranda fell silent for a moment, twisting the reins in her fingers as though imagining the esteemed Covington's neck there within her grip instead. Her eyes were distant, the lush line of her mouth flattened. Garrett waited, positive there was more to come.

He wasn't disappointed.

"The working conditions he allowed for his employees were abominable. He paid low wages across the board, and the other shippers fell in line. The men working the waterfront, with no other options available, had no choice but to accept the terms...and suffer for it," she railed. "Meanwhile, he drove the prices of cargos up, reaping a nice and tidy profit for himself."

"So he was some stingy old codger with questionable business ethics," Garrett murmured, understanding how Miranda might find marriage to such a man undesirable.

"Oh, he wasn't old," she hissed through gritted teeth.

Garrett swung her a questioning gaze.

"He's twenty-seven and hideously attractive. He has the face of an angel—and the disposition of a cheating, insensitive bounder," she informed him. "He had the nerve to flaunt not one, but *two* of his mistresses in my face. Then, when I'd made my objections known, he had the gall to inform me I'd better get used to the idea, because he had no intention of changing his ways because he was getting saddled with a prudish wife."

Garrett couldn't help it—he stared in open-mouthed, wide-eyed disbelief. The man must have never kissed Miranda...or never in a million years would he have called her prudish. Any man who had a woman like Miranda for a wife would be insane to consider looking elsewhere for entertainment. She'd be more than enough of a handful all on her own.

Covington was an idiot, plain and simple.

"Okay, I'll allow that this Covington sounds like a snake," he admitted, and Miranda nodded in vindicated satisfaction. Still, knowing her as he did, remembering the judge's comments about the obvious attempts on her life, he couldn't help but add, "That aside, you should have been more cautious of your actions. You should've realized causing a man like Covington social embarrassment wouldn't have been forgiven lightly."

Miranda gave an annoyed sniff, muttering, "Men and their infernal pride."

"What about *your* pride?"

She arched a suspicious brow.

"What was the real reason you went out of your way to cause him so much embarrassment?" Garrett eyed her, speculative. "Was it to spare his workers? Was that why you wanted to avoid marriage to such an attractive, wealthy man? After all, how many other women look past their husband's business practices in the interest of family? How many women turn a blind eye to their husband's mistresses?"

Miranda's eyes flared, and she huffed an outraged gasp.

Before she could let loose another tirade, Garrett rushed to interrupt. "Now, hold on. I'm not saying I approve of such actions—in business or in marriage. And I think it's pretty safe to say, given the fondness in your voice when you speak of your family—father aside—you'd like to have one of your own someday." Her blush answered his question, but before she could reply, he forged on. "Was it your sense of moral obligation, or your own pride that got in the way?"

"My pride?" she sputtered.

"Your pride," Garrett repeated. "I'm sure it must have taken a considerable blow when your intended taunted you with his mistresses."

"I have no intention of settling for—"

The crack of a rifle cut the rest of her words off, shattering the quiet sounds of nature around them. Garrett's body jerked with the bright flash of pain. Instinct kicked in before he had time to register his wound, and he launched himself from his saddle.

Straight at Miranda.

****

She'd only just begun a scathing retort, when, without warning, a loud noise rent the air. And then Garrett threw himself at her, knocking the wind from her sails. He wrapped his arms around her as his momentum carried them both over the side of the horse, sending them sailing through the air. Mid-flight, he twisted to take the brunt of the impact. Even so, the impact jarred every bone in her body, snapping her teeth together. But Garrett didn't pause, rolling until his body covered hers, his arm curled around her head. A gun materialized in his palm in the blink of an eye.

Miranda stared up at him, her head spinning. Garrett kept his head down and scanned the surrounding area with sharp eyes. His hat had tumbled off when he threw himself at her, and now his glossy, sable hair tangled about his head in wild disarray. His face was tense, the lines around his mouth grim.

His body, rigid and alert, pressed against the length of her. Pointy little pebbles dug into her back, and the sharp edges of his belt buckle pressed into her hip. His strength surrounded her—protecting her—and she'd never felt so safe.

Then she saw the blood, and she panicked.

"Garrett! You're hurt—"

"Shhh," he hissed, scanning the landscape.

She pushed at his chest, desperate to see his injury. As she shifted, the crack of a rifle rang out again, and a small spray of dirt kicked up some ten yards to their left.

"Lay still," he growled, using his weight to press her down. He readjusted the arm surrounding her head, and he tucked his cheek close to hers, blocking the sunlight.

"Your bleeding," she whispered, slipping her hands to his waist. "Just let me—"

Garrett shifted. Rather than allowing her to move, he clamped his free hand over her mouth. She grunted her displeasure, shook her head, and squirmed again, unable to shake his hand free. The muscle in his jaw leaped, but he didn't release her. Her angry stare drifted to the crimson stain flowering on his shoulder, and she stilled beneath him.

Without lowering his eyes, he whispered, "Are you hurt?"

"Mmmph," she mumbled against his palm, glaring daggers at him.

He looked down. Garrett blinked, as if just realizing he'd been covering her mouth, and he released her.

"Sorry," he muttered. "Are you hurt?"

"Only my pride," she snarled. "Can you see anyone?"

Garrett shifted his eyes back to the east, shook his head. "No, there are too many places back there where he could be hiding."

"How long do you suppose we need to lie here like this?" Miranda asked, wiggling a leg free.

She bent her knee, using her foot to shift beneath him, unaware, at least until it was too late, that in doing so she'd settle him more firmly between her thighs. Startling. Intimate. She peered at the bloody tear in his shirt, and she chewed on her bottom lip. Unable to see enough to be reassured, Miranda turned a worried gaze to Garrett's face.

His expression was pained, strained, and it hit her just when the last time was he'd looked at her thus. He was giving her the same look—or a very close likeness of it—as when he'd been pacing in her room, just before he'd crossed to her and kissed her senseless. Her mouth went dry, and her eyes locked on his lips, bullets and pebbles forgotten.

Garrett drew a deep breath and jerked his head, gazing off into the distance. "I'm going to move off you. When I do, I want you to run to that ravine over there. Stay as low to the ground as you can."

Miranda blinked. "What about you?"

"I'll be right behind you," he assured her.

She peered up at him, forced a swallow, and nodded. Garrett stared back for a long moment, then he lowered his head to hers. His lips claimed hers in a kiss so soft, so tender, her eyes misted and her heart wept.

When Garrett broke the kiss, she murmured protest. He stared at her, a puzzled frown wrinkling his brow. He opened his mouth, as if he were about to say something, but the crack of the rifle kicked dirt up again, missing them by the narrowest of margins.

Garrett shot her one last grim smile, and nodded. In a heartbeat, he rolled to the side and opened fire, aiming the bulk of his ammunition into a small grove of trees to the north of the trail they'd just traversed. Miranda winced at the deafening roar of his gun, but she scurried to do as he'd instructed. She ran, crouched low to the ground, diving for cover behind the wash in the ravine. Miranda held her breath, fighting the urge to peer over the rim of the bank. Garrett would burn her ears if he saw her do something so foolish, and so she waited.

The answering crack of the rifle echoed in the clearing, and for a few heart-stopping seconds, Garrett's gun went silent. Miranda's heart slammed against her ribs and plummeted to the soles of her feet. Fear clawed at her throat, choking her. Her hands fisted in her skirts, and she prepared to peek over the embankment, when Garrett's gun began firing again. Her breath escaped her lungs in a relieved whoosh, and she sank back down on trembling knees.

A moment later, a shadow flew over her head, and Garrett landed with a thud at her side. Dirt from a ricocheting bullet showered down over them. He shot to his knees, crouching to stay beneath the edge of the ravine, tensed to move. He laid his finger to his lips and motioned for her to stay put. Then he edged his way down the dried up riverbed, creeping onward until he came alongside the copse of trees a few hundred yards away.

She watched, terrified, as he slipped back over the rim and disappeared from her sight with fluid, deadly grace. The report of the rifle cracked now and again. The soft spray of dirt showered over her whenever a bullet chanced close enough to the ravine. Her own safety was the farthest thing from her mind.

Where had Garrett gone? Would he be safe?

Then, an abrupt and echoing silence descended. She waited and worried, chewing on her lip until it was raw. When no more sound broke the silence, she began to fret. Despite Garrett's silent admonishments to stay where she was, Miranda crept down the ravine, just as Garrett had done. When she got to the approximate point at which she guessed Garrett had crawled out, she peeped over the rim.

Oh no. No, no, no...

Garrett rolled on the ground with the slim man dressed all in brown who'd been following her, locked in a tug of war with a revolver as the prize. A rifle lay in the dust several feet away. The men grappled and punched. Grunted and cursed. Blood and buttons flew. Then Miranda squeaked, ducking for cover as the gun fired and a small puff of dust shot into the air only a few short feet from her hiding place. She drew a quick gasp of air and then, with more daring than common sense, she peered over the rim once more, tense and ready to dive for cover should the need arise.

Garrett and the skinny man had rolled a few feet from where they were the last time she'd looked. Still they fought like furious, grunting, hissing demons. Garrett was strong, she'd felt the power of those muscles herself. But his opponent was wiry and agile. The tussle was vicious, and Miranda winced when the skinny man rammed a knee in Garrett's middle.

Not to be outdone, Garrett planted a solid punch in the skinny man's chest, followed by a stiff uppercut to the jaw. Their attacker's head snapped back and rebounded off the packed dirt. He appeared stunned for a split second, but he didn't relinquish his hold on the gun, though Garrett looked to be twisting it with all his might. Then their bodies tangled close, rolling in a blur until Miranda had difficulty distinguishing whose fist was whose, whose grunt was whose.

Just when she couldn't stand it anymore, a loud explosion rent the air. She watched in stunned horror as both men balanced, motionless in the short tufts of grass. Then they both toppled over sideways, lying motionless on the blood-splattered ground.

Miranda shot to her feet, her heart lodged in her throat. Fear for Garrett drove her up over the rim of the ravine, scrabbling across the ground until she managed to get her feet beneath her again. Once she gained her legs, she flew to Garrett's side.

Panic clogged her throat.

He was silent, motionless. Her eyes flew over his body, searching for a second bullet wound, even as she fell to her knees beside him. Her hands grasped at him, patting his cheeks, prodding at his chest, poking at his arms.

"Garrett! Garrett! Oh, God—please don't be dead! Please, please, Garrett!" she exclaimed, hysterical, and gave his chest a good solid thump. Moisture welled in her eyes. She squeezed them closed and fought against the hot torrent of tears raining down her cheeks.

Oh God, please no...

Chapter Twelve

Garrett blinked, his body too exhausted, too sore to move. The shock from his earlier gunshot wound and the steady loss of blood, combined with the after effects of the brutal struggle for the weapon, had left him shaky and weak. She'd been babbling nonstop from the moment he had become aware she was beside him, and he hadn't been able to get a word in edgewise. When she thumped him on the chest, he couldn't stifle the grunt. She apparently hadn't heard it, for she continued to blather.

"So help me Garrett, I'll never forgive you for dying on me—" She sobbed, her eyes scrunched closed, cheeks damp. "This is all my fault!"

Unable to stand the sight of her misery any longer—unable to insert a word to save his life—he reached up with both hands, clamped one on each of her glistening cheeks, and drew her face down, sealing his lips to hers.

As a method of silencing her, kissing proved quite effective. It might serve him well to keep that little bit of leverage in his arsenal. Miranda's eyes flew open as she leaned over him, motionless and stunned. After a minute or two of savoring her lips, he released her and grinned, unapologetic. She leaned back, sputtering, as he sat up.

Her stunned smile all but blinded him. "You're alive..."

"Yep," he said with a cocky grin.

In a mercurial flash, her smile transitioned to a fierce frown, her eyes narrowed, and she hissed, "You're alive."

"I think we've already established that, sweetheart." He grinned, flirting with danger. "But if you'd like to kiss me again, just to make sure..."

"You just lay there and let me babble like... Knowing full well that I thought... And then you... *Oooh*," she snarled.

Without warning, she doubled up her fist and swung with all her might. She caught him smack in the middle of his chest. Garrett fell back on the ground, the wind knocked from him. His chest and shoulder throbbed. Garrett stared up at her, amazed, as he rubbed his hand over the spot she'd hit.

By the saints, she was glorious.

Twin points of angry color rode high on her cheeks. Pushing to her feet, she stomped away to stand over the dead body some yards away, nudging him with the toe of her shoe.

"Is he—is he dead?"

"Lord, I hope so," Garrett muttered.

Gaining his feet, he stood next to Miranda, staring down at the dead man without a flicker of emotion. Their assailant lay sprawled on his back, his dull, sightless eyes staring at the thin wisps of clouds drifting overhead. The gruesome hole in his chest had seeped dark crimson.

Garrett was about to lean over him in order to search his pockets when Miranda gasped. He palmed his gun, his alert gaze scanning the immediate area. He demanded, "What?"

"Your arm," she whispered, her face pale.

He glanced down. Blood soaked his sleeve from shoulder to elbow. Miranda pushed and tugged at him until Garrett sat on a fallen log a short distance from the body.

"Take your shirt off," she ordered, eyes wide and worried.

He frowned, but complied without argument. As

soon as the material slid from his shoulder, she sucked in a sharp breath and leaned close. The soft scent of roses surrounded him, and he forgot the searing pain in his shoulder. Then she prodded the wound, and the pain came back. He hissed between his teeth, flinching away.

"Hold still," she snapped as she probed his wound, sending another wave of fire over his injured flesh. He scowled, but remained motionless, gritting his teeth against the pain. Stepping back, she informed him, "You got lucky. It doesn't look all that bad."

"You get shot and see how lucky you feel," he grumped.

"You don't even need stitches," she murmured, ignoring his comment. "But you're going to have another scar. We need to get that cleaned out."

"I need to catch the horses," he countered, pulling his shirt back up and fastening the buttons.

Please God, don't let them have run far.

Miranda nodded and moved out of his way. Though she didn't approach the body again, she stared in that direction. "He's the man that was following me today," she said at length.

"Are you sure?"

She nodded, and his frown deepened. He'd recognized the man as they'd wrestled for the gun, identifying him as one of the two men he'd seen talking on the street across from the hotel. An uneasy feeling settled in the pit of his stomach. He could feel her gaze on him, but he wasn't ready to deal with questions yet.

"What's wrong, Garrett?"

Damn it. He knelt down next to the body, silent. He should have searched the man's pockets for identification. Instead, he reached for the man's left hand, dread eating a hole in his gut. Flicking the cuff buttons on the dead man's shirt open, he rolled the sleeve back.

Garrett swore, loud and sharp enough to peel the hide from a three-day old carcass.

A small tattoo in the shape of a snake, coiled and poised to strike, glared at him from the inside of the man's forearm. The serpent's well-defined pupils were in the unmistakable shape of the letter C. Staggering beneath the weight of shock, Garrett's ass hit the ground beside the dead body, and he smacked a hand against his forehead. He could feel the blood drain from his face, one drop at a time.

Oh, God...how?

"Garrett?" Miranda edged closer.

"Oh damn it," he muttered beneath his breath. His stomach churned. "It can't be. It just can't be...son of a bitch. Shit... Aw, hell!"

"Garrett." Soft hands cradled his face, tilting his head until his horrified gaze met hers. "Tell me what's wrong," she demanded.

Her scent and heat surrounded him, centered him. Drawing a ragged breath, he fought for control, fought for logic.

"I'm okay," he muttered, pushing to his feet.

Her hands fell to her sides, and she stepped back, allowing him room to stand.

"Stay here, I'm going to go round up the horses," he ordered over his shoulder as he stalked away.

Fighting the waves of nausea roiling through his system, he pushed himself faster, until he broke from the small copse of trees at a jog. His mind raced, even as the world wrenched to a screeching halt. He lurched to a stop, gasping for air. Right before his very eyes, the landscape around him faded into memories—vivid with blood spatters and the stench of death. Bodies littered the ground at his feet, and his brothers' lifeless, accusing eyes stared up at him, demanding retribution.

Swiping a trembling hand across his face,

Garrett clenched his teeth. He opened his eyes again, and the blood and gore were gone, replaced with the verdant oasis surrounded by harsh, arid tan. The scent of Miranda lingered on his skin, driving back the stench of death enveloping his soul.

Still his mind reeled, stuck on one endless loop of questions. How could this be possible? He knew he'd captured or killed every last man riding with the group that fateful day in Carlisle.

To the best of Pinkerton intelligence, the entire gang.

How then could he explain away the tattoo, the coiled serpent, with fangs bared and the unmistakable, telltale letter C in the eyes? Each member of the gang sported that exact same tattoo, in the exact same location. It had been their mark...their brand.

A soft whickering drew his wary gaze.

At least the horses hadn't gone far. He wasted no time before calming the skittish mare, and then he gathered Hades' reins. He took several minutes longer than necessary with the animals before he returned to Miranda, using those stolen moments to steady his hands and his mind.

As he led the horses into the tree line, it hit him that he'd gone off and left her with a dead body. Alone. Jesus God, what had he been thinking? He hurried his steps. Grimacing, he leveled apologetic eyes at her as he looped the horses' reins over a low branch.

"Miranda, I'm sorry," he murmured as he approached her, keeping his voice low and easy, his movements unrushed as he'd done with the mare. He cupped her elbow, drawing her a few steps away from the corpse. His fingers trailed over her forearm until he clasped her hand. The differences in their hands were marked—soft to calloused, small to large, fair to tan. "I shouldn't have left you alone with—"

"Don't." She reached up to silence him, pressing the tips of her fingers against his lips. Her eyes held shadows of concern, but her smile was calm, coaxing. "Someone had to go after the horses and let's face it, in this dress, I'm not much of a match for them, I'm afraid."

Garrett tilted his head, regarding her with a strange mixture of awe and confusion. It would've served him right if he'd returned to histrionics...incoherent babbling at the very least. Yet here she stood, composed and stoic, concerned enough about him to banter in an obvious attempt to get him to set his guilt aside. Her fingers against his lips tempted him to kiss and nibble. He stood motionless, afraid to move. The way his body was behaving around her—and the shock he'd just received compliments of that distinctive tattoo—he didn't know what would happen.

Miranda gave his hand a comforting squeeze and insisted, "Let me look at your shoulder again, you've lost a lot of blood."

"I have some supplies in my saddlebags." Did his voice sound as unsteady as he thought it did?

He let go of her hand, as one would a hot branding iron, and he moved away to dig in his saddlebag for the small kit he kept there for times such as these. What the hell was wrong with him? Where had his levelheaded, unshakable courage under fire gone?

His fingers brushed against the small pouch, and he snatched it. The last time he'd gone to Pearl with a piece of his hide missing, she'd clucked and tsked, but she'd patched him up and mothered him all the same. Then she'd given him the kit, insisting he take it with him—for the next time he wasn't fast enough to get his sorry hide out of the way. This was the third time he'd had cause to use it. It was almost eerie, the way that woman could foresee things.

Turning back, he handed the kit to Miranda, unhooked the canteen from his pommel, and then sat down on the fallen log once more. Garrett glanced at his shoulder and winced. His shirt—his favorite shirt, at that—had a nice, jagged tear across the shoulder. Almost the entire sleeve was stained dark red. The rest of the fabric hadn't held up well during his tussle with the unknown assailant either. Tiny tears and grass stains covered the front of the shirt. He'd lay odds, the back didn't look much better. Heaving a deep sigh, he began working on the buttons.

Miranda set the linen bag down at Garrett's hip as he fumbled with the buttons. He shrugged the damaged material from his shoulders, and her fingers froze on the lacings of the pouch.

Her wide-eyed stare locked on his chest, burning him, as sure as if she'd laid hands on him instead. The effect was instantaneous, stimulating, and just as sensual as skin sliding over bare skin. His manhood swelled, and he cursed his trousers as they became unbearably tight. He stole a glance from beneath the long sweep of his lashes, and the healthy color in her cheeks intrigued him. Her eyes glittered.

Then, male that he was, he brought the injured arm forward and flexed his muscles, sending them bunching and rippling. He peered at his arm, as if inspecting the damaged flesh, but his gaze skidded sideways to gauge her reaction. She snagged her lower lip between her teeth, and her hands bobbled the kit. He didn't even try to hide his smug smile when her eyes followed the ripples with greedy fascination.

****

She was being ridiculous. After all, she'd seen a male without his shirt before. Three of them, in fact.

They'd been swimming in the river while she and a group of her friends had huddled behind the corner of a building, spying, giggling behind their hands. True, those males had been little more than boys when compared to all that lean, sculpted muscle Garrett bore. Their physiques had made her giggle. His sent weird flutters through her, deep inside. He made her blood warm and her mouth water.

After a long moment, exerting great effort, Miranda wrenched her hungry gaze away. She focused on the contents pouring from the bag, snatching up a tin of ointment and a sliver of carbolic soap. Then she looked about for a moment. She needed a rag, a scrap of cloth to cleanse the wound. Nothing. Heaving a sigh, she turned away from him and lifted the edge of her skirts. She twisted and tugged on the hem of her split petticoat until she managed to tear a long strip free. She repeated the process several times over on both sides.

She dropped her skirts and faced him, long strips of white cotton in hand. Miranda paused, then frowned at the tender smile softening Garrett's rugged features. His eyes were gentle and warm, and disturbing to her state of mind when set against the framework of his muscular male body. Unsettling feelings overwhelmed her—sensations she'd never before experienced until she'd met this particular man. The butterflies that fluttered in her belly seemed to double in size.

Desperate to fight her way to familiar ground, she tried to be snippy. He had to stop looking at her like that. He made her feel things she had no business feeling. "I should keep a running list of all the pieces of my attire that have been ruined because of you, you know."

Garrett grinned, unrepentant.

But the soft emotion still lingered in his eyes.

She approached him with caution, uncertain of herself, uncertain of the need swelling inside her at the sight of his smile, and at the sight of his bare chest. She focused on his wound. Or tried to. Her mind whirled. How had they come to this point in their relationship so quickly, and with so little effort? As if she'd known him forever, bantering with him, touching him. It felt...right. He was like a magnet for her. When turned one way, she bounced away from him, pushed in opposite directions by different goals and beliefs. Yet when turned just so, she was drawn to him, like a missing half that needed the other to be a whole.

No...no, that was wrong. She couldn't allow herself to feel anything for him.

Falling in love with him was out of the question. She was *not* falling for him, and that was all there was to it.

Or was she?

Her hands trembled, and she almost dropped the tin of salve. Her mind raced.

Oh, merciful heavens. What had she done?

****

He caught an occasional word here and there as she bent to her task, though, for the most part, it all sounded like muttered gibberish. Among them, pigheaded, arrogant, and autocratic seemed to factor at the top of her list as she repeated each of them, several times. Though her words were fierce, her touch was gentle. Careful compassion softened her face, and he couldn't help feeling more than a bit smug, flattered that she would show such concern for him. No one these last several years, aside from Pearl, had dared show him tenderness. He hadn't allowed it, pushing all aside, including his mother and his sisters-in-law, in his quest for vengeance.

None had been able to touch him. None had been able to reach his heart. Somehow, marvel that she was, Miranda melted the ice shielding his heart. And oh, could she touch him. Her baby-soft fingers sent flames of need shooting through his blood.

That last thought brought him out of his reverie with a rude jolt. He recoiled as if she'd slapped him. What in the name of all that was holy was he thinking? He'd been off the job for too long, lost his professional objectivity. That was it. It had to be.

Hell, maybe he was just getting soft in the head, because Garrett McCabe was *not* the type to wear his damned heart on his sleeve. He just needed to get this assignment over and done. Then he could go back to his life, go back to working on his future.

At the same time, a little voice nagged at the back of his mind. He needed a woman to complete the picture he'd formed in his mind. And yet, whenever he tried to call that particular picture to mind of late, the woman at his side had feisty red hair and spirited blue eyes. Yes, he needed a woman, his little voice prodded. Miranda *was* a woman, it argued. A very delectable, very appealing woman, it taunted.

No, he reminded himself, frowning now. He had requirements, though it took a long moment to remember the list of expectations he'd selected with such care. He needed someone that wouldn't judge him, someone that wouldn't have expectations he couldn't or wouldn't fulfill. He wanted someone that didn't make him feel like he was constantly in the eye of a tornado. He wanted someone with red hair and blue eyes and a laugh that...

Garrett shook his head, trying to dislodge that troubling voice that just wouldn't leave well enough alone. It took more than beautiful eyes the color of a clear spring sky and the body of a goddess to turn his head. It took spirit, and intelligence, and grace. His gaze fell to the top of her head, and he narrowed his eyes in thought.

"Garrett, what upset you so much?"

Her question caught him off guard, and he blinked down at her in surprise. Then it all came rushing back to him, and he shook his head. He couldn't believe, that for those few short moments beneath her gaze—beneath her tender ministrations—he'd become so wrapped up in her that he'd forgotten about the Chambers Gang, forgotten about his pledge for vengeance.

Forgot about a damned dead body not ten feet away.

Lord, he was going soft in the head.

"Nothing," he rumbled, forcing himself to stare at some blurry point beyond her shoulder.

Her voice was patient and gentle, coaxing, pulling his gaze down until he got lost in her eyes. "I saw your face, Garrett. Who was he?"

"No one," Garrett snapped, looking away. "He's probably one of Draco's buddies."

Miranda jerked back.

"Don't be ridiculous." Her eyes spit impatient, offended fire at him. "Why would Draco send him after us? For that matter, if he intended something like this," she argued, waving her arm in the general direction of the body. "Why would he have pointed this man out to me from the alley? Why wouldn't Draco have just gotten rid of me himself if he felt so threatened, as you keep presuming." She lifted a caustic brow and barbed him, "After all, he's had sufficient opportunity."

"And whose fault is that, I wonder? Maybe if you'd just for once follow orders, he wouldn't find it so easy to get to you. Maybe he was just trying to throw you off the trail." Garrett knew he was grasping at straws by casting the blame on the elusive Draco, but the alternative meant he'd failed his brothers—and that was more difficult to deal with.

"What an asinine thing to say," she snapped. "Draco wouldn't do anything so dangerous that it might cause me harm." She glared at Garrett, jerking the knot in the long strip of material tight. He hissed between his teeth, and she rocked back on her heels, glaring.

"So loyal to your precious bandit," he snarled, jealousy and hurt grinding his control thin. Reaching for his torn and soiled shirt, Garrett balled the material in angry fists. "He's nothing but a common criminal, Miranda."

"No, he's not. He's..." Miranda trailed off, then shook her head, as if struggling to find the right words. Her unwavering, unreasonable defense of the outlaw grated on Garrett's last nerve.

Jealousy chewed a vicious hole in his pride, and he spat, "He is a stagecoach robber, a thief...a criminal, for God's sake. I don't understand why you take it upon yourself to defend him."

"It seems someone must, since you're so willing to condemn a man you've never even met," she accused.

"Then let him get a lawyer," Garrett growled.

"I'm not defending him—not like you're implying, anyway. Common sense tells me I'm right." She glowered at him, crossing her arms over her chest. "Throughout the entire robbery, Draco never once fired his weapon."

Garrett stared at her, hard. He couldn't believe she'd chosen to base her entire argument on that one, flimsy point. "You think that gun strapped to his hip is a showpiece?"

His question gave her a moment's pause. "I saw the mark on that dead man's arm, Garrett. I think you're keeping something from me, and you're using Draco to start an argument to sidetrack me. It's not going to work. I want the truth."

Garrett blinked, swearing beneath his breath.

Just once, he'd like the upper hand with her. He shrugged her argument aside without a word, retrieved Pearl's kit, and stalked away. Garrett jammed the damaged shirt and the kit into his saddlebag, then stomped around the horse to dig a fresh shirt from the other saddlebag.

He refused to meet her gaze, though he could feel it drilling frosty holes in his hide. Thrusting his arms into the clean shirt, he set to work doing up the buttons, muttering beneath his breath all the while about senseless, irritating females. Then, when his fingers reached the last button, he rammed the shirttail into the waistband of his denims. Halfway through, his movements stilled, and his wide-eyed, horrified gaze swung to her once more.

The brutal realization shot through him with the force of a mule kick to the midsection. If it was the Chambers Gang, albeit a resurrected one after him—and he wasn't sure he was ready to face that fact just yet—then it stood to reason, because of him, she had become a target herself.

"What?" She took a cautious step away from him. Tilting her head, she regarded him with anxious, wary eyes. "Why are you looking at me like that?"

Rage filled him, searing through his veins. How dare those bastards have the nerve to go after her? How dare they think to harm so much as a single hair on her beautiful head? Then an icy torrent of fear washed the flames away. What if he couldn't protect her? What if she died because of him? That last thought, a blow to his steadfast confidence, left him reeling. His mouth went dry, and his breath left him in one short burst. Panic—the likes of which he'd never before experienced—consumed him.

Miranda's eyes flared, and concern replaced wary suspicion in her eyes. She leaped forward, placing a gentle hand on his chest and peering up into his face. His heart slammed in his chest beneath her hand.

"Garrett?"

He stared, kicking himself. She deserved to know the truth of her situation. She was strong. She could handle it...even if he couldn't. He captured her hand and drew her back to the log. He urged her to sit and perched beside her, still holding her hand, unwilling—unable—to break the contact.

"The truth is...I'm pretty sure I know who sent him."

Miranda stiffened, and she looked as if she were about to speak, but he squeezed her hand to forestall her. She frowned but closed her mouth.

"I have reason to believe he's a member of the Chambers Gang." Garrett paused, studying the confusion on her face.

"Chambers...but I thought...I thought you said..." she stammered, staring through wide, confused eyes.

"Yeah..." Garrett rubbed the back of his neck with his free hand. "I was wrong."

"But, Garrett, how can that be possible?" She bit her lip, lacing her fingers through his. "I thought you retired because they were all dead."

"I did. I don't know what's going on. I just...I don't know."

She sat in silence for a moment, absorbing his words.

"Garret, what makes you think that this man is...was one of them?"

Garrett stood, tugging her to her feet. He led her to the body, then released her hand and bent down. Once more, he rolled the man's sleeve up, only this time he held the arm up for her inspection. Miranda stiffened at his side. She took a step back, then another. Garrett stood and turned away from the body, settling his hands on her shoulders, steadying her. His heart twisted at the confusion in her eyes. Her body trembled beneath his hands.

Unable to resist, he drew her to him, wrapping her in a gentle embrace. He smoothed his hands up and down her back, soothing her. His lips brushed against the crown of her head as he breathed her in, taking comfort in her even as he gave comfort. Miranda rested her cheek against his chest, her arms slipped around his waist.

"Every member of the Chambers Gang has one just like that, in just the same place," he explained. "Chambers branded all his men the way a rancher brands his herd."

Miranda was silent for several heartbeats. She tipped her head back to look at his face, her eyes filled with bewildered panic.

"But, Garrett, he was following *me* today."

Her words twisted in his gut like a rusty blade. He could hear it in her voice, hear the fear—saw the understanding in her eyes, and he cursed himself for having put her in this position.

"Shhh," he murmured, urging her head back against his chest. He kissed her hair again, drew the scent of it in deep, and held her tighter. "It's going to be all right, sweetheart. Trust me. I'll keep you safe, I swear I will."

"I do, Garrett. I trust you." Her quiet admission humbled him. Once again, as he stood there cradling her in his arms, those warm, sweet feelings swelled inside him, melting another layer of that precious ice around his heart.

Chapter Thirteen

Garrett glanced up, gauging the angle of the sun. He ran a tired hand over the back of his neck and turned to his companion. Overall, Miranda was holding up rather well, considering the day's events. Impressive. He'd known some men who'd cracked under less pressure. They'd come to a tentative truce there in that small copse of trees, as he stood beside a dead body, holding her in his arms. He couldn't help but marvel at that—the timing, the circumstances.

Then she'd gone and surprised him, again.

He'd figured she'd balk when he told her they were going to sling the dead man over his saddle and send the horse off in the general direction of town. Garrett assumed she'd put up a mighty stink about the impropriety of it, at the very least. He'd been quick to explain it would be almost a full three days ride before they came to the next town, and taking a dead body with them in order to turn it over to the law was not feasible. He'd also rushed to explain that at least one member of the Chambers Gang—in all likelihood, more than one—was still in the town they'd just left behind.

Going back was tempting fate beyond good sense.

Instead of arguing, as he'd anticipated, Miranda had agreed. She'd even gone so far as to hold the skittish animal's bridle while Garrett deposited the body across the horse's back. The one thing he hadn't told her, hadn't wanted to explain, was that he was sending a message to whoever had sent their attacker. A very loud, very unmistakable message.

Anyone coming after her would meet the same fate.

After several hours in the saddle with little more than an hour's rest in the late afternoon, Garrett glanced over at Miranda. He had to give her credit. She'd proven to be an exemplary rider, despite the grueling pace he'd set. She'd been quiet for this leg of the journey, but he'd been caught up in his own musings, and until now, he'd paid her silence little heed. He peered closer, noting the strained line of her mouth and the shadows beneath her eyes. The sight weighed heavy on him.

Maybe he was pushing her too hard, expecting too much? Experienced as she may be in the saddle, she wasn't used to this kind of riding. Still, if they could push on just a little farther—put a few more miles behind them—he'd be a lot happier. He considered striking up a conversation but drew a blank.

As if sensing his change of mood, Miranda regarded him with the tilt of her chin and soft, considering eyes. "Garrett?"

He lifted both brows. "Hmm?"

"Why did you stop being a marshal? You're young, but I'm guessing you're very good at marshaling. At least, I'd like to think Uncle Milton wouldn't have sent just anyone to escort me."

Garrett smiled at her half-teasing assumption, shrugging the rest off. She sighed, aiming a look at him designed to make anything male cringe in fear.

"Okay, okay," he groaned, as if exasperated by incessant nagging. Although he tried hard, he couldn't quite keep the note of laughter from his voice. "I give. Stop carping."

Her mouth fell open, then she laughed aloud, the sound pure music to his ears. The sound of her throaty laughter had shaken something loose inside him, something that longed to drag the temptress down off that saddle and claim a kiss...claim a whole lot more. He shook free of those disturbing images, and considered his words for a while.

"The main reason I became a marshal was for revenge," he began his tale. "I resigned because I'd fulfilled my promise to my brothers." He grimaced, adding, "Or I thought I had."

"Come on, you can't just stop there."

He turned wide, innocent eyes her way and asked, "What?"

"I know there's more to it than that, Garrett," she prompted. "Tell me the rest."

"What makes you think there's more?"

"The way that you helped Pearl tells me you were good at being a marshal. I'm sure somewhere along the road of vengeance you've helped others like her. That's just the kind of person you are. Why would you give that up?"

He shook his head. A small smile flirted with the corners of his mouth, but his gaze grew serious.

"I decided I wanted more for myself." Her expression demanded a better explanation, and so he continued on, "I wanted a family—a wife and kids—but I refused to risk their future the way I've seen so many of the other marshals do with their own families...the way Nick did with his. I want stability for my family. I want to see my kids grow up. I want to be there every night for my wife, not just in between assignments. I want to be able to tell my grandkids the stories my granddad told me..." he trailed off, feeling foolish.

****

Miranda stared at him, startled to find herself filled with longing. The picture Garrett painted with his words touched her. It sounded so romantic, so content. That had been one of the reasons she'd resisted marriage back in Boston—the desire for a real family.

Miranda hadn't wanted one of those marriages of conveniences. She hadn't wanted some cold union, where an heir was required, but she and her husband led separate lives, lives that brushed against each other at social functions and never a meeting of the hearts. She didn't want a marriage like her parents shared. Miranda wanted hearth and home.

She wanted...devotion.

"But you're still not married. Slacking off a bit, aren't you?"

He grinned over at her. "I'm working on it."

A spear of jealousy shot through her, sharp and unexpected. She knew she had no right to feel jealous where Garrett was concerned. But jealous she was. Determined to push her tangled emotions aside until she could sort them all out later, she looked to the distant landscape and rode in silence for several long moments.

She must be a glutton for punishment, considering what she was about to suggest. "I could help you."

Garrett stared, his expression riddled with alarm, and he demanded, "How?"

"I can help you find a wife," she insisted, warming to her subject, ignoring the almost painful tug of emotion that threatened to close her throat. "I could help find a woman to meet your expectations. Being a woman, I can see through the affectations other women put on in order to impress a man to the altar. I could help you sift through the chaff, so to speak."

Her idea held merit. Heavens knew, he wasn't getting anywhere on his own. Nevertheless, it just felt plain odd—wrong even—talking to him about this. Yet here she was...tormenting herself with things that could never be. Just because she couldn't have a happily ever after, why couldn't he? But why, then, did offering to help him seem to twist a knife somewhere deep inside herself?

"I would've figured you'd have had your fill of meddling back in Boston."

Miranda sniffed in disdain but refused to take the bait. Pushing his snide comment aside with careless disregard, she pressed, "What are your requirements?"

He gawked at her and stammered, "My requirements?"

"Yes, Garrett, your requirements," she said on a knowing sigh. "A man like you must have a neat and tidy list of requirements. You know what I'm talking about, expectations for the woman you intend to take to wife. Tall or short, smart or obedient..."

"Don't you think a woman can be both smart *and* obedient?"

"No," she huffed. "An obedient woman follows blindly, though not necessarily for her own good. A smart woman questions whether or not something is in her best interest, and then acts accordingly."

Garrett stared at her for what seemed an eternity, until she fidgeted in the saddle. Oh, he had a list all right. And he wasn't happy she'd called him on it.

"Okay, *princess*," he drawled. His tone warned that she wouldn't like what she was about to hear. "I'll tell you what I want. I want someone soft-spoken and sweet-tempered, sensible, unassuming, loyal, and *obedient*. I want a wife who won't be nagging at me or harping on about something or other. Someone who knows when to keep her mouth shut, and when to mind her own business. In short, I want a woman who will compliment my life, not disrupt it."

"Is that all?"

"It wouldn't hurt if she was easy on the eyes."

Miranda glared at him with undisguised hostility. "Are there any physical attributes you would prefer?"

Garrett glanced at her hair, then at her face, and he shifted in his saddle. His expression was troubled. When he responded, the distinctive note of desperation lay thick in his voice. "Blonde. Definitely blonde—a short, plump blonde."

Miranda blinked askance at him, battling the pangs of disappointment clenching her stomach tight. Everything he'd just described was the exact opposite of what she was, what she had to offer, and that knowledge stung her pride.

Not that she was offering, of course.

Still, she couldn't help wondering when a man would look at her—get to know her—and want her for her. Not just be taken in by her face, find out she was opinionated, and then judge her lacking.

She longed to tell Garrett the woman he'd just described didn't exist, or if she did, she would bore him to tears. She considered telling him that if those were the requirements he was set on, he'd be better off getting a dog. Instead, she pasted on a cheery smile. "I will endeavor to do my very best to find you a suitable female."

Garrett stared at her for a long while. Then he shook his head, turning away. "Don't worry about it. I don't need help finding a wife."

"Nonsense," she replied, waving his refusal away. "It's the least I can do. I am giving you my promise, Garrett. I will find a suitable wife for you."

Garrett's sharp gaze swerved to her. He frowned but changed the subject. "Come on," he called, nudging Hades into a gallop. "I want to put a few more miles behind us before we make camp tonight."

Equal to the challenge, Miranda urged her horse forward until they were racing neck and neck, anxious to put their unsettling conversation miles behind her. She tossed her head back as the wind whipped the pins from her hair, and let the long tresses stream behind her. Freedom coursed in her veins, heady and exhilarating.

All too soon, Miranda followed Garrett's lead as he pulled rein beside the steep slope of a gully. She dismounted as the sun crested the horizon, casting the evening sky into flaming glory. A narrow river shushed by on one side, the sheer wall of an eroded hill towered over them on the other. A tall oak grew at the edge of the hill, affording a dense canopy of foliage overhead. Lush green grass formed a fresh carpet beneath the tree, tempting her to kick off her shoes so she could wiggle her toes in the verdant luxuriance. The little nook was inviting, giving the impression of privacy and safety.

She stepped back, watching Garrett hobble the horses for the night. She crossed her arms over her chest and ran her hands up and down, from shoulder to elbow, chilled as night crept toward them.

Seeking a diversion, she asked, "Can I help?"

Garrett glanced over at her, surprise evident on his face. He nodded and indicated the tree behind her. "You can gather wood for a fire. It's an old tree, so there should be a lot of sticks and bark on the ground that will work. You can pile it over here."

Miranda set to work. By the time Garrett had the horses bedded down for the night, she had a sizable stack of kindling piled where he'd specified.

"I'm going to see if I can't scare something up for supper," Garrett told her. "Don't worry if you hear a shot or two."

Miranda nodded and turned back to her task. She wasn't sure how much they'd use, but it gave her something to do, and keeping busy calmed her nerves. She'd almost talked herself into believing that sleeping out in the open, beneath the stars— vulnerable to whatever creatures lurked out there in the dark—wouldn't be all that unpleasant. Then the report of gunfire echoed in the eerie silence, and she almost dropped the thick log she'd managed to wrestle into her arms. She stifled the startled scream before it slipped through her lips.

She waited, frozen, heart pounding against her ribs.

It's just Garrett, it's just Garrett...

Giving herself a stern mental shake, she squared her shoulders and forced her feet to move. Adding more wood to the pile, she turned back to approach the tree, and another crack of gunfire made her jump.

She froze again, her eyes darting about the shadows, half expecting some wild renegade to come riding out of the darkness and gun her down. She cursed Garrett beneath her breath for not sticking around long enough to start the fire, at least. Before hysteria set in with full force, Garrett came striding into the small encampment, two wild hares dangled from his hand by their ears. He tossed them on the ground beside the woodpile and glanced at her.

"Why didn't you start the fire?"

Frazzled, her tone was sharp when she snipped, "Sorry, I must have slept in and missed the morning Sister Mary Catherine taught us how to start campfires."

Garrett blinked at her and frowned. Muttering beneath his breath, he rolled up his sleeves and set about starting the fire. She crossed her arms and watched every move he made. She wouldn't be caught out here again unprepared. That finished, he drew a wicked looking knife from a sheath on his belt, glancing her way.

"I suppose you missed the course on cleaning wild game as well," he teased with a wry twist of his lips.

"Indeed," she shot back, smiling with obvious,

false sweetness.

Garrett made short work of the hares and had a cozy little campsite set up in a matter of minutes. He went to the stream once to wash the blood from his hands, and then he returned to fill the canteens. Miranda stood on the edges of camp and surveyed Garrett's handiwork, noting every detail.

He roasted the hares on a whittled spit over the crackling fire. A small tin of beans, the jagged lid pried open, sat nestled in the rocks at the base of the fire. Garrett spread two bedrolls out near the inviting warmth of the golden, cheerful blaze. The horses nickered and shuffled beneath the tree. The ebb and flow of a soft breeze stirred the leaves overhead and the grass underfoot. Somewhere in the darkness that surrounded them, insects chirped and clicked. The gentle hoot of an owl cooed through the breeze, charming her—relaxing her.

Shooting one last glance about the homey campsite, Miranda smiled at Garrett when he returned to camp and teased, "You know, you don't make a half bad wife yourself."

Tilting his head, Garrett grinned, "You think so now, just wait 'til you get a taste of my cooking."

She laughed despite herself and stepped forward, accepting the canteen he offered. "If it's half as good as Pearl's, you'd better go catch another rabbit or two—I'm starving."

They sat beside the fire. Garrett turned the spit and checked the progress of their meal.

Garrett took a long draw from the canteen and passed it to her. "Do you cook?"

"I used to when I visited my grandmother," she admitted. She took a drink and handed the canteen back. "I haven't had much call to do so in quite some time. I'm a bit rusty, I'm afraid."

"Well, then, you'll just have to see how much you remember. You can have the honors of cooking tomorrow night."

She offered a wide smile, tickled by the challenge she saw in his eyes. "You're on—but if it's horrible, consider yourself forewarned."

At length, Garrett removed the spit from the fire and slid the fare onto a small tin plate at his side. He smiled, handing her a fork with great flourish. Taking a rag in hand, he lifted the can from the rocks and set it next to her.

"Dig in," he invited.

Miranda picked up a forkful of meat. She tasted it, and her eyes widened in surprised delight. It was very good. So good, in fact, that she reached for another bite.

"I was right," she said between mouthfuls. "You will make someone an excellent wife someday."

Garrett chuckled at her good-natured ribbing. She watched as he pulled a leg from the platter and devoured it with gusto. When the final scraps of the hare were gone, and the last bean polished off, Miranda leaned back on her palms and tilted her face to the silvery moonlight. Despite her earlier nervousness, she was content. Her belly was full, her body exhausted, her mind beginning to slow down. Garrett was beside her, and she felt safe.

Just as she began to release the tension she'd been carrying with her for longer than she could remember, an eerie yipping broke the hush that had descended on the land around them. Miranda gave a nervous start and tensed. Garrett leaned up a bit and studied her face. Another shrill yip broke the stillness, and Miranda shivered.

Garrett stood and shook out his bedroll. She watched in wide-eyed curiosity, too nervous to ask what he was doing. Her mouth fell open when he proceeded to lay the bedroll down—right next to hers.

"Garrett..." she protested, but her voice was

much too nervous to hold a proper warning.

"Shhh," he drawled.

He sank down beside her, wrapped his arm around her waist, and pulled her back until she lay full length against him. Pulled off balance, she landed with her head cradled in the crook of his shoulder and her thigh nestled between his. Indignant, Miranda gasped, the coyote forgotten, and put her hand on his chest, pushing up and away from him.

Garrett, however, had other ideas and, being much larger and much stronger than she was, he got his way. He kept one arm anchored around her back, caging her to him. His other hand came up to cover hers as it lay over the steady thud of his heart. "My granddad used to tell us a tale when we were young..."

Oddly enough, it wasn't the undeniable physical strength of his body, but the velvety tenor of his voice that held her immobile, captivated, enticing her to give up the fight before it even began.

He was telling her a bedtime story. She relaxed against him.

He let go of her hand long enough to reach over and draw his blankets up and over them both. His hand slid back beneath the covers to close over hers once more, and her heart trembled.

Miranda shifted her head back to look up at him. She shouldn't be here, lying with him like this. Something like this would ruin a lady's reputation. Miranda opened her mouth to protest, but he shushed her and pushed her head back onto his shoulder until her forehead pressed against the side of his neck. Her breath feathered across the bare skin of his chest where his shirt lay open. It wasn't appropriate for her to lie here like this with him. But just now, with that bone-chilling yipping in the distance, the warmth of the fire crackling at her back, and Garrett's soothing, silky voice rumbling in her ear, she couldn't have cared less if every disapproving Boston matriarch came striding through camp to turn their nose up at her once more.

"He called it the story of the White Trout," Garrett began, his voice low and relaxing. "Long ago, in County Mayo, there lived a beautiful, young woman. She'd been promised in marriage to a king's son. He was a handsome and charming young man, and she loved him very much. He loved her in return, and the couple had a bright and happy future ahead of them. Then one day the king's son was killed, and the woman fell deep into mourning. Everyone in the village felt sorry for her. They knew how much she had loved her handsome prince and been loved in return. Then, without warning, the beautiful woman disappeared. The villagers thought that the good people had come and taken her away to ease her pain."

"The fairies," Miranda murmured, recalling her grandmother's stories.

"The fairies," Garrett confirmed. "Now, some time later a white trout was noticed in the lake and that was curious, for white trout had never been seen in that area before. The villagers watched the white trout for many, many years, but it never changed how it looked or where it swam. The people thought the trout must be a magical fish, and so they never bothered it and always treated it with respect. Many, many years later, an arrogant soldier went fishing in that same lake. He caught the white trout, and he laughed as he taunted the people of the village that he'd caught their precious, magical trout and intended to cook it and eat it."

In the distance, the yipping faded, and the chirp of crickets hummed low. Miranda snuggled closer to Garrett's warmth and closed her eyes.

"So he built a fire and began frying the fish. However, no matter how long he cooked it, it refused to brown. After a while, the soldier gave up trying to brown the fish and took his knife out. He began to cut the fish, but stopped when he heard a loud scream. He dropped the knife and jumped back when the fish changed into a beautiful woman who stood before him holding her bleeding arm."

Garrett paused in his story, his fingers stroking the back of her hand and her forearm. She shifted against him, enthralled by his story. When he didn't resume his story, Miranda tipped her head back and blinked up at him through the dark, soft and sleepy. Garrett grinned down at her. An odd, mischievous smile. Miranda shifted again, impatient, and Garrett picked up the threads of the story once more.

"The woman told the soldier that she was waiting for her true love to return to her and demanded that he take her back to the lake. Now, the soldier was frightened, but she was so beautiful he didn't want to return her to the lake. And so she threatened him that if he didn't do as she asked, she would haunt him forever. With that dire warning, she changed back into a fish. The frightened soldier scooped her up and returned her to the water.

"As the fish slipped back into the lake, there was a stain of red in the water for a few minutes from where the soldier had cut her. To this day, all trout have a red mark on their sides. As for the soldier, he never again made fun of other people's beliefs. And he never, never again ate another fish!"

Miranda yawned, but she made no further effort to move away. Garrett waited, staring at the stars. He considered rising to add another log to the fire, but the feel of her—lying there half-asleep in his arms—just felt too good to deny. And so he stayed where he was, listening to the night sounds, savoring the feel of Miranda pressed against his side.

Her breathing evened out. Her body relaxed. He should move away now—put as much space between them as possible. But if he moved, he would wake her, and then his efforts—his suffering—would have been in vain.

Garrett shifted, checking to make sure he had easy access to his gun should he need it, and he settled in for a long, sleepless night, reminding himself that he would soon be rid of her, and that he shouldn't allow himself to grow attached. After all, she was *not* what he was looking for.

Be damned if his heart didn't seem to whisper...*So what?*

Chapter Fourteen

Garrett heard her stirring, but he resisted the urge to look. Truth be told, he'd spent more than a fair amount of time looking already, both last night and this morning. In the golden light of the fire, he'd lain there—wide awake—long after she'd drifted to sleep in his arms. Her head had fallen back against his shoulder, and he'd studied the fine details of her face at great length, right down to the tiny, almost unnoticeable scar at the edge of her left eyebrow.

Her face was the last thing he'd seen when he'd closed his eyes last night, and the first thing to greet his eyes when he'd opened them this morning. To his utter chagrin, one frightening, longing-filled thought flickered across his mind, and then stuck— stubbornly refusing to budge. He wouldn't be objectionable, not in the least, to seeing her face every time he closed his eyes at night and every time he opened them in the morning—for the rest of his life.

As it was, he had but to close his eyes, and her face was there in his mind's eye, with startling clarity. Every last ounce of perfection, from her fine brow and stubborn chin to the light dusting of freckles across the bridge of her nose, right down to that tiny little scar.

Groaning, he picked at the frying fish and gave the coffee pot a rattle. Fishing that morning had proven to be both relaxing as well as productive. He'd used a small hunk of dried beef and been surprised with the results. He'd managed to procure several fish for their breakfast in no time at all.

Silent as a wraith, Garrett had moved around the campsite rekindling the fire, cleaning the fish, and setting the coffee to boil. Now and again, he'd caught himself staring at her as if in a trance, enchanted beyond measure. He'd shake his head at his own odd behavior, and then go on about his business, only to stop and stare once more. Again and again.

He could have woken her—he should have, daylight was burning. But he'd seen how tired she'd been last night, and she looked so peaceful this morning, that he hadn't had the heart to disturb her. That aside, he was still trying to master his own odd responses to her without the sounds of her honeyed voice dripping temptation every time it caressed his ears.

"Please tell me you're not cooking a white trout." Her voice was husky and warm, and the sound of it rippled through him, stretching his nerves taut.

Turning a bit, damning himself for being ten kinds of a fool, Garrett let his eyes roam over her. His hungry gaze drank in her sleepy eyes, her tousled hair, and her soft expression. To his amazement, he realized that if he lived to be a hundred, he'd never again see such a beautiful, tempting sight.

"Nope, I threw her back while you were still sleeping. I'm afraid you'll have to settle for plain old Crappie, unless Bluegill is more to your liking." His tone was a little gruffer than he intended, but he couldn't seem to help himself.

Stifling a drowsy yawn, she replied, "I wouldn't know, I've never tried either."

That gave Garrett pause, and he echoed in disbelief, "Really? Don't you like fish?"

"I've never tried it." She shook her head, shrugging.

Her hair fell about her shoulders, pooling about

her, making his mouth water as he hungered for a taste—and the fish frying in the pan was the last thing on his mind. He had to struggle to focus on her words when she continued speaking.

"My father didn't like the taste of fish, or any kind of seafood for that matter, and so we never had fish at our table."

Her words puzzled him. The picture she'd been unwittingly painting of her father was so at odds with Garrett's very idea of what a father should be. In his mind, a father should be what his own father was—what Nick had been—a man who put his children first, a man who showered his children with unconditional love and would do anything—sacrifice everything—to see them happy. A father should be a man who opened a world of possibilities to his children, not placed such severe restrictions on them.

The picture he'd formed of Miranda's father, however, was that of an autocratic, self-righteous, self-centered cad. He thought of the fond tone the judge had used when he'd been speaking of his brother, and Garrett was baffled.

Frowning to himself, he probed, "How long has it been since your uncle was in Boston? When was the last time he saw your father?"

Pushing herself into a sitting position, Miranda stared off into the distance for a moment as she folded her legs beneath her. Her brow wrinkled. Her lips pursed.

"Oh, well," she hesitated. "It must have been—hmm...maybe fifteen years ago, I believe. I couldn't have been more than five or six. That was about the time the twins were born."

"The twins?"

"My brothers," she clarified.

She'd rarely spoken of them, and he wondered why...though he didn't think it his place to meddle.

As if sensing his curiosity, she eyed him for a moment. "What's troubling you, Garrett?"

He blinked in surprise. She'd read him so easily. Most had a difficult time telling what was on his mind—he must be slipping. Then, considering she'd given him an opening, he asked, "Your family seems so distant, so impersonal."

"I suppose to someone who grew up in a close-knit family, it would." Miranda paused as she pulled the heavy length of her hair over her shoulder. Running her fingers through the thick tresses in a vain effort to untangle the wild mass, she explained, "Mother told me once, a long time ago, that my father hadn't always been so concerned with social standing. When my brothers were little, our family was—much closer. Then, as the boys got older, my father became more and more obsessed with attaining a certain position in society. He determined that my...*beliefs* were too unnatural, too liberal, that I was a bad influence on my young and impressionable brothers, and so he took steps to limit my time with them. As a result, the boys and I grew apart."

Garrett could see the effort it cost her to present a cool and untouched façade. Her eyes reflected the sadness within. He fought the urge to go to her, to draw her into his arms, and offer her comfort. He knew it wasn't his place, but that didn't make it any easier to resist. It was baffling how she stirred those protective, possessive instincts in him with little to no effort on her part.

Instincts no other woman had ever touched.

"Breakfast is almost finished, if you want to change or get cleaned up you should hurry. We'll be getting a late start as it is." Unsettled, he turned back to poke at the fish.

Garrett ate breakfast in silence, preoccupied with the trail ahead. The rest of his day passed in relative silence as well, as Miranda, too, seemed lost in thought. Garrett led the horses to a small stream mid-afternoon for a short break, then pushed them onward, driven by some unknown force. He was anxious to get to Johnston and turn her over to her uncle—anxious to put as much distance between them as possible for his own sanity.

He knew the pace he set was unrealistic and grueling. There was no rational reason to press on so hard, but he couldn't shake a vexing sense of foreboding that hung over him like a raincloud. The afternoon sun hung low in the sky, the day had proven to be cloudless and temperate. Miranda had been pleasant company, and still he pushed onward, wanting nothing more than to be safely back at the Lucky Clover before the other boot dropped—wanted nothing more, except maybe Miranda herself.

"We ought to reach Johnston sometime late tomorrow," he called out. Garrett glanced over at her when she made no reply.

Miranda smiled at him, drawn and pale, her shoulders drooping. He was a horse's ass. She couldn't keep to this grueling pace. He should never have pushed her so hard. Filled with contrition, he reined Hades in and guided him close to Miranda's mount.

Reaching out to snag a stray lock of her hair, he tucked it behind her ear. "Why didn't you tell me you were tired?"

She pinned him with a knowing look. "Would it have mattered?"

Properly chastised, he grimaced. "There's a pond up ahead, maybe two or three miles away. Think you can make it that far?"

"I've made it this far," she quipped.

True to his word, Garrett led them into a small, secluded glade nestled on the edge of a small, clear pond. He helped her dismount and released her, only to have to make a second, quick grab at her when her legs wobbled a bit beneath her.

"Miranda…"

She scowled and pushed away from him. Stalking away, she stretched her arms and back, her gaze skimming across the picturesque little piece of paradise. Then she stopped and stared at the pond. The evening sunlight glittered on the smooth, still surface like molten gold. She heaved a deep sigh, rolled her shoulders, and turned to her horse.

Garrett hurried to take the reins from her hands. She looked ready to drop where she stood. He should never have pushed her so hard. Leading their mounts a short distance away, Garrett settled the horses in for the evening. From the corner of his eye, he spied Miranda as she approached the small copse of trees at the water's edge.

Bending at the waist, she began gathering up kindling and slightly larger, broken branches for their fire. Once she had a decent sized pile, she knelt next to it and began assembling the wood and dried bark as he'd done the previous evening.

He considered telling her to leave the fire for his return, but the grim determination on her face held him silent. Pride was, most likely, the only thing that was keeping her going at this point, and he'd pushed her far enough today.

Garrett returned to camp carrying a large, plump pheasant. He quirked an eyebrow at the tidy camp set up around a blazing fire in the circle of stones. A tidy pile of spare sticks and small branches rested nearby. She'd spread out the bedrolls near the fire as well. Her industriousness was impressive, all things considered, but she refrained from speaking the thought aloud. Garrett set to work cleaning the pheasant, then fashioned a spit, and propped the fowl over the fire. He stoked the blaze she'd so carefully arranged, and then went to dig in his saddlebags.

Maintaining the awkward silence, Miranda sat beside the fire and began turning the bird. Her hungry gaze turned to the pond, time and again. He could all but read her mind. She imagined that water, cool and refreshing, surrounding her—enveloping her. Sliding over her hot skin the way he wished he could slide his hands over—

Jesus, Mary and Joseph...pull yourself together, Garrett. Quit torturing yourself.

Garrett watched Miranda as she stared at the pond. He would have had to have been blind to miss the stark longing on her face. He considered the long day she'd spent in the saddle, and he, too, looked at the pond. It would be the gentlemanly thing to do—allowing her to swim and relax—after the day he'd forced her to endure. It would be pure hell on him to stand guard while she had a few moments of pampering...but she'd more than earned it. It would be such a simple matter, the honorable thing to do, to offer her the chance to take that rose scented soap of hers and...

No, he shook his head, appalled—horrified—at the very idea of what he'd been about to offer. The mere idea of her stripping down to nothing and slipping into that glittering, golden water sent shivers of scalding desire coursing through his veins, and a torrent of icy prickles of apprehension skittering down his spine.

It was more temptation than he'd be able to withstand.

Gentlemanly. Honorable. Hell, it would be sheer insanity! What had he been thinking? He'd seen her in her bath once before. The simple memory of that night still haunted him every bloody time he closed his eyes. He groaned to himself as he fought the images, ruthlessly denying them. It was his duty to protect her, his duty to deliver her to Johnston safe and sound—not to seduce her.

Duty was a cold bed-partner. He'd learned that cruel fact of life the hard way.

And duty was hell on dreams.

Try as he might, he couldn't shake the temptation of her enjoying that pond. As they sat in silence and ate their meal, Garrett noticed the furtive glances she kept shooting at the pond, kept hearing her wistful, resigned little sighs. Seriously doubted she was even aware she was making them. Those sighs were tying him in knots. Even as he called himself ten kinds of fool, he heard his own voice echoing out in the silence that surrounded them like a dark, sensuous blanket of need.

"Would you like to go for a swim?"

For a full two minutes, Miranda blinked up at him, wide-eyed. Eve and the forbidden fruit.

Her quiet glance skated around their little sanctuary, so reminiscent of that far off garden paradise. Her gaze slid back to Garrett, and his mind began to whirl. It would be so easy, too easy, to imagine that Miranda and he were the only two people in the world tonight.

Too easy, indeed.

"Are you sure it would be all right?" She frowned, nibbling at her lip.

"I'm sure," he replied, his gaze lingering on her lips. "I'm willing to bet it would be more than worth it…"

His voice trailed away, and he suddenly blinked at her, unsure if he'd been speaking of swimming in the pond—or something else altogether.

Miranda's gaze slid to the water again, and like Eve, Miranda gave in to temptation that was greater than she could resist. She stood and walked to the pond's edge. Bending, she trailed her fingers through the clear water. Ripples broke the placid surface. Her stare darted to the shadows beyond the campfire's glow.

The look of longing on her beautiful face made him willing to jump through rings of fire to please her.

"Are you sure it's safe? Last night those coyotes seemed so close..."

Garrett stood by the fire, restless and tormented. Torn, he stared hard at her. Didn't she realize there was a far greater threat to her safety than the pack of coyote she seemed to be obsessing over? He narrowly managed to bite back the retort that she should be more worried about the hungry beast prowling around her campfire.

"I'll keep you safe," he managed to assure her. "Go ahead, I'll keep watch."

But what would he be protecting her from—an outside threat...or himself? Garrett sat down, back to the pond, and set himself to the task of cleaning his guns.

Clothing rustled behind his back, thudding softly as it hit the ground, and he gritted his teeth. How had he managed to get himself into this? No, he would not think about what she was doing, standing there, shedding layer after layer of clothing. All those fragile, nearly see-through undergarments he'd once held in his hands. Until she stood absolutely naked with the fading sunset at her back...

The sound of water splashing blurred his vision.

A moment later, Miranda's laughter cascaded through the campsite. The husky sound washed through him with tormented pleasure. His body stiffened, and he battled the urge to turn around and watch. His hands went through the motions of cleaning and checking his guns, mindlessly guided by years of routine.

Long minutes stretched on, and Garrett sat motionless, rigid with need. Was she ever going to get out of that damned pond? Having finished cleaning his guns, he rose and crossed the campsite to root through his saddlebags. He ground his teeth in vexation, feeling hot and prickly as a cactus.

Full moon tonight. Desperate for a distraction, he tried to latch his mind onto something other than the provocative temptation swimming in the pond. A hunter's moon. A raider's moon, the old men called it.

A lover's moon...

Shaking his head at that fanciful thought, he cursed his luck. She was taking her own sweet time, and he didn't know how much more he could stand. Before he realized his mistake, Garrett's gaze involuntarily drifted to Miranda. His warning not to stay in the water too long died a soundless death on the tip of his tongue, and his lungs seized. His body locked in stunned disbelief at the ethereal vision of splendor.

She looked like a mermaid—a siren in her own little sea—fueling him with unquenchable fires of lust, beckoning him to his doom, tempting him. The tension, the desire, built inside him until he felt like he was suffocating beneath the weight of it—ready to explode with it.

Breathe, Garrett...breathe...

That desperate drag of air made him uncomfortably aware of how much he needed other things.

Carnal things.

Garrett sucked in another deep pull of air, praying it would clear his mind of thoughts best left for the dark of night. He looked around and realized—it was the dark of night—the dark of night with a lover's moon. His body throbbed with need. As if in a trance, he prowled across the campsite, silent and lithe as a mountain lion on the hunt, until he came to stand a few short feet away from the edge of

197

the water.

"If you stay in there much longer, you're going to freeze," he drawled in a low voice, his eyes flashing heat over her skin.

Miranda gasped, unaware he'd come near. Self-conscious, she sank down into the water until it lapped at her chin. "You startled me."

Garrett said nothing, only quirked one side of his mouth up in a wry smile.

Recalling his words of earlier, she smiled bashfully. "This feels wonderful."

In that moment, good intentions fell by the wayside. In that moment, things like duty and honor were as candles in a twister, snuffed out beneath the scorching, gale-force winds of his desires.

In that moment, all he wanted to do was slip into that pond, and slide inside her.

"Garrett?"

Grasping desperately at self-control, Garrett croaked, "What?"

"I forgot to grab my soap before I got in. Would you mind getting it for me?"

Wordlessly, Garrett turned and strode across the campsite. Opening her bag, he lifted aside a handful of frothy lace and delicate silk. A fleeting, wicked smile crossed Garrett's lips when the thought came to him that he was, once again, on intimate terms with Miranda's wardrobe. A few minutes of searching produced a bar of rose scented soap. He couldn't resist letting the fine silk slide through his fingers as he replaced her clothing. Miranda's soft, alluring scent tormented him. He closed his eyes, imagining...

Drawing a deep breath, the muscle leaping along his jaw, Garrett closed her valise and dropped it back onto her bedroll.

He knelt at the pond's edge and held the fragrant bar in his hand, extending his arm out to her. Miranda eyed the soap, then the short distance between them.

"Toss it to me, please."

"Come and get it," he countered, the corner of his lips curled up in the blatant challenge of temptation.

Miranda's eyes widened, then narrowed. A small, mischievous grin flirted around the corner of her lips as she edged forward. She rose a bit from the water, and Garrett's gaze dipped to the waterline in greedy anticipation.

However, instead of reaching for the soap, as he'd guessed she'd do, she skimmed the flat of her hand and the length of her arm along the top of the water sending the liquid crystal droplets showering down over him.

Cold and shocking.

Garrett sputtered in surprise and shrank back from the water, taken completely off guard, amazed by her audacity. Miranda turned and swam away. Her laughter trailed behind her.

A siren's call—undeniable.

Garrett stood, shirt and hair drenched. The little voice of duty and honor shouted inside his head that he should just turn around and walk away, warning him that he was treading too close to the edge of something neither of them might be ready to face. That voice of reason screamed at him to slow down, take a breath, and examine the ramifications of what he was about to do—very, very carefully.

Then something else, something dark and dangerous, reared its head. It rattled its cage and taunted him, reminding him that this particular little voice, who lectured so self-righteously, was what had gotten him into this mess in the first place.

Duty, it scoffed. *Honor*, it sneered.

What had those noble ideas gotten him? More than one hole in his hide and a lonely, cold bed, it mocked.

Before Garrett even realized what he was doing, he shed his clothes—stripped right down to the skin—and took a deep breath. Right or wrong, *this* was his choice. He would stand by his decision, and by his actions, come what may. Clutching Miranda's soap in a tight fist, throwing lists of expectations and hopes for a calm and peaceful domestic life to the wind, Garrett dove in headfirst.

Chapter Fifteen

Miranda's laughter stuck in her throat at the loud splash. She whipped her gaze toward the bank, staring into the darkness, searching for Garrett's shape. Her heart pounded with fear and excitement.

The bank was empty.

Garrett was nowhere in sight. A pile of discarded clothing scattered across the ground where he had stood moments before.

Miranda's anxious gaze skimmed the water, searching the wake his body had created. The moon glowed, full and luminous, overhead in a sky of rich, dark velvet sprinkled with millions of tiny sparkling diamonds, casting the water around her to shimmering iridescent and silver. Quicksilver, just like Garrett's eyes. Her feet found purchase on a deep ledge close to the pond's edge, and she stood. The water, cool yet so very inviting, lapped at the curve of her breasts, her thin chemise almost transparent in the clear waters. Her wet hair flowed down her back and pooled in the water around her as she searched the rippling surface of the water.

Where had he gone?

A full minute passed, and still she couldn't find Garrett. Her breath caught in her throat in a momentary surge of panic. What if he'd struck his head on something when he'd dove in? What if...

The sound of splashing behind her made her whirl around and gawk in awe. Rising out of the water like some celestial god, Garrett shook sparkling droplets from his hair and swiped one powerful hand over his face. Water streamed down his smooth chest, tracing the hard plains and firm, defined bulge of muscle. The white strip of bandage covering his wound made his godlike presence seem more earthy...more attainable. Despite her distraction, that bandage called his injury to mind. But he moved with sensual grace, not a flicker of pain darkening his hungry features.

Golden skin glistened in the water and moonlight, and she hungered for a taste. His nipples puckered tight against the shock of the cold water, and her eyes locked for half a second on those tiny male nubbins, before her voracious gaze slid over the rest of his sinewy torso, drinking him in like a potent aphrodisiac. The mere sight of him went straight to her head.

Garrett's clouded stormy-gray gaze, lit on her face. Miranda was speechless, stunned by the intense, considering look in his eyes, as if he were staring at his future, rather than just her face.

Miranda took a cautious half-step back, then another, shying away from Garrett's scrutiny. Away from the heat in his stare. She sank to her chin again—uncomfortably aware that with the water as clear as it was—as close as he now was, Garrett would have an unhindered view.

"Garrett, what are you doing?"

"If the mountain won't come to Mohammed..." He shot her a wily grin and lifted her soap free of the water, holding it out to her. The wicked, sinful look he gave her belied his innocent words. He glided closer, steadily bringing her within easy reaching distance. "I bring your soap, princess."

"Oh," she murmured, her wits set adrift by the gleam in his eyes.

For the first time since he'd come up with that irritating nickname, she didn't mind. How could she when he used such a warm, caressing tone? His husky voice sent shivers racing through her, shivers that had nothing to do with the temperature of the water.

She reached out to take the soap. Her stare locked with his, as if she could hold him at bay with that simple contact. Nevertheless, their fingers brushed, and a jolt of lightning swept through her from the inside out.

Miranda surged back a wary step, her probing stare searched Garrett's face, unsure of what she might find—uncertain of what she *wanted* to find. Instead of pursuing her, as she half hoped he would do, he turned away without warning and dove beneath the surface. Miranda stared after him, bemused and inexplicably frustrated.

Drawing a deep, steadying breath, she set to work washing her body, cursing the chemise that clung to her and got in her way, more hindrance now than help. That done, she focused on her long, thick hair. She shoved thoughts of Garrett from her mind, working hard to ignore him as he cut through the water, breaking the surface here and there, agile as a fish. Miranda worked the soap into a thick, perfumed lather, humming to herself.

Strong, capable fingers sank into the suds and began massaging her scalp. Miranda jolted in surprise.

"Allow me," Garrett drawled smooth and easy near her ear. His hands moved over her scalp and down through her hair in caressing, seductive strokes.

She hadn't realized he was right behind her, but now he was so close she could feel the heat radiating from him. Her initial reaction had been fright, sparked by the undeniable attraction that connected the two of them like an invisible cord. Each time they fought the attraction and tried to pull away from each other, it only snapped them back, closer to a catastrophic collision.

At first, she fought the urge to move away from him, feeling like a coward. Then, as his nimble fingers worked through her hair, and his breath feathered across her damp skin at her temple, she had to fight the urge to sink back against him and revel in his heat and raw masculine strength. She tilted her head back, closed her eyes, and gave herself over to the pleasure of his hands working through her hair.

A low moan of pleasure rippled from deep in her throat. Garrett's hands stilled. With palpable reluctance, Garrett withdrew his hands from her hair. He stepped back, allowing her to turn and dip her head back into the pond to rinse the soap from her curls. The weight of his hungry gaze set a swarm of butterflies loose in the pit of her stomach.

"That was wonderful," she admitted, closing her eyes, her voice a purr of raw pleasure. "You're talents are endless, Garrett. Thank you."

"I aim to please."

Garrett's voice was husky, strained. When she turned to look up at him the lines of his face were grim, as if he suffered from great pain. And his eyes...his gaze was so intense, so strange and...needful. Miranda's brow wrinkled in concern. She straightened and stepped closer. Lifting her hand, she laid it against his chest—over his pounding heart.

"Garrett?" She peered up into his steady stare, bemused.

The heat of his skin scorched her. The erratic pounding beneath her palm seemed to accelerate. His stare seared her. Miranda felt that gaze clear to her soul, branding her as his. The feel of his skin, so hot and smooth beneath her fingertips, sent unexpected little shockwaves pulsing through her nerve endings, and her eyes flared wide with awareness.

****

The touch of her hand on his flesh arrowed straight to Garrett's heart. For a moment he couldn't breathe, the sensations shooting through his body were so delicious, so consuming, that he wanted to savor them, savor this moment for a little while longer. She was a fever in his blood, one he couldn't deny—one he couldn't resist.

Miranda, her expression soft and accepting, opened her mouth to speak, but in a mercurial shift, she screeched and launched herself, trembling, against Garrett's chest.

The instinctive urge to protect her swamped him, and he wrapped his arms around her, his gaze devouring the area around them. Where was the danger? Had he, consumed as he'd been with his desire for her, missed something harmful?

Nevertheless, the feel of her lush body pressed so tight against his—with nothing more than her thin, wet chemise to shield him from her curves—was more than he could withstand, and he froze. His limbs felt like granite, weighted and unable to move. His tongue seemed to have gone numb, and the power of speech evaded him completely.

"What was that?" Miranda demanded.

"Ahh…" He managed to croak, lost to coherent thought, focused on the sensation of her warm body wrapped around him.

"Something swam by me, something slippery. It *touched* my leg, Garrett," she whispered, expression horrified, and squirmed closer still, plainly terrified of the unknown entity lurking in the waters around her.

How long would it take her to notice he was naked?

And aroused.

Painfully so.

Her wiggling jerked Garrett out of the land of

shock and thrust him into the land of sensual abandon. Where previously his body had been frozen in surprise, it now stood ready and alert, and drenched with need.

His hands began moving of their own accord, sliding over her body in a languid caress. His lips brushed against her temple, her cheek, her ear—whispering soothing, unintelligible sounds. His body curved into hers, curved around hers, molding itself to her. He could feel the abbreviated little bursts of her hot breath against the side of his neck, her heart hammered against his chest. Her skin burned him.

He drank it all in, reveled in it.

"Garrett," Miranda whispered. "What *was* that?"

"Maybe it was the white trout," he whispered back, his tone a strangled mix of desire and poorly attempted humor.

Miranda puffed out a breath. Her body relaxed against him. Her hands pressed against his chest, and she pushed out of his embrace. She stared up at him for a long, long moment. Without warning, her eyes shot wide, and she jumped into his arms once more, wrapping her arms around his neck, all but strangling him.

"Oh," she cried, burying her face in the side of his neck. "There it was again. Garrett, do something!"

"It's just a fish, Miranda," he murmured, enthralled by the feel of her in his arms. Dimly, he wondered how in the world she didn't notice the hot length of his erection, hard as tempered steel, pressing against her soft stomach. He grimaced. She should be far more worried about that than some paltry little fish.

"It was slimy," she cried out in alarm. "What if it was a snake?"

"It's probably more afraid of you than you are of it."

"I sincerely doubt that," she hissed against his skin, shaking like a leaf. Her nails dug into his skin. "*Please*, Garrett."

Hearing the fear in her voice, cringing at the bite of her nails, Garrett forced his feet to move. He tried his best to sound reassuring, not an easy feat considering his knees shook with the force of his desire, and he could think of little else than kissing her into submission. "It's all right, sweetheart. Trust me, I'll keep you safe."

Doing his damnedest to ignore the throbbing ache in his loins, Garrett shifted against her. The cool water lapped at his body, restoring some sense of control in his over-heated body. He swept an arm beneath her knees, scooped her up, high against his chest, and waded to the side of the pond, intent on setting her on her feet in shallower waters.

His words of comfort didn't seem to ease her anxiety. Miranda clutched at him with a strength that surprised him. Her breasts pressed against his chest, wringing a low growl from him. Drawing a steadying breath, unmindful of his own state of undress, Garrett carried her up the gradual slope. He strode to his bedroll and lowered her legs.

As he straightened, her arms still around his neck, he told himself to let her go, to no avail. Garrett's painful arousal nestled snug against the silken curls at the juncture of her thighs. Her shift provided no barrier for all that heat.

Her stunned gaze locked with Garrett's, and her eyes flared in shock. Now that she didn't have the distraction of the fish swimming around her, she'd understood he was naked—and that he wanted her. More than he wanted his next breath. Her jaw dropped open, but she couldn't find her voice.

An odd fire simmered to life low in his stomach, its glow reflected in her eyes.

Her stare held Garrett spellbound, and he didn't

have a snowball's chance in hell of fighting his way free. Despite his intentions to release her—of their own volition—his arms tightened. The pink tip of her tongue shot out to moisten her lip. Garrett's stare locked on the motion, and he groaned, stiffening.

It would take a greater man than he to walk away from a woman like this.

He was certain, beyond all doubt. This was meant to be.

This was right.

This decision would change his life, irrevocably. Everything he'd decided he wanted in a wife...none of it mattered anymore. He wanted Miranda. Right now, and forevermore. As the woman in his bed.

As the woman he would build his future around.

He would claim her tonight...and, as soon as was possible, he'd make her his wife.

****

She knew Garrett didn't love her. He might want her right now, but he had his precious list all worked out, and she had none of the qualities he'd so meticulously listed. His list didn't matter anymore. She wasn't expecting a proposal of marriage. She only needed here and now. Garrett might not be what she'd expected to want—or need, but that didn't change the fact that want him she did.

She needed *him*. But it was more than that. He'd touched her heart. Miranda had come to know Garrett better than she'd ever expected. And in a strange way, he'd come to know her. Right or wrong, there was a connection between them. A connection she couldn't ignore any longer.

Making love with Garrett wasn't logical. Lord knew the complications she might face. When her future husband-to-be somehow figured out she was no longer pure. He would be able to tell, wouldn't he? What might his reaction might be?

No, this wasn't logical, not at all. It was impetuous, and emotional.

A disaster waiting to happen...

But Garrett was her last chance to taste a bit of her own personal heaven before she was leg-shackled to some anonymous marriage made in hell.

She'd just have to do a better job of shielding her heart. If she weren't careful, he'd worm his way inside her heart...and do serious damage. After all, she couldn't keep him. She had to remember there would be no happily ever after for them. This was her chance to experience life and that was enough.

It had to be.

Miranda glanced up at him from beneath the dark fringe of her lashes. The transparent yearning in his eyes stole her breath, and she made up her mind. Her head tilted up, and her lips parted expectant, inviting. Garrett's eyes narrowed; his answering stare was hotter than the sun, feral with primitive need.

A sudden, albeit brief stab of uncertainty lanced through her. She pushed it aside, determined to experience this moment as if it were her last. She snagged her lip between teeth.

How did one go about seducing a man?

No, Miranda. You're over-thinking this. You're a woman, damn it. Use your instincts...not your head.

Miranda pressed closer against the rock hard planes of his chest, gliding her palms over his shoulders. Her fingers toyed with the soft curls at the nape of his neck.

"Kiss me, Garrett," she breathed.

A low growl rumbled deep in his chest, shooting a thrill through her. His head swooped down, and his lips closed over hers with savage force, sealing their fate. His hands were less than gentle as they swept down her sides, trailing fire in their wake. His fingers searched for and found the hem of her wet shift. Miranda shuddered at the abrupt loss of his heat, trembled when Garrett stripped the last barrier of modesty from her. In one swift move, startling a gasp from her, he lifted the soaked material up and away from her body, leaving her completely vulnerable. Heat stole into her cheeks, but she made no move to cover herself. She'd made this choice. She wouldn't hide now.

Her lips felt bruised from his fevered kisses, swollen, and she ached in places she hadn't known existed.

She'd never felt more alive.

His greedy stare devoured her bare flesh.

Her curious gaze lowered, roaming over the brawny expanse of his chest, his muscled abdomen, and lower. Her gaze locked on to that heretofore-mysterious part of his anatomy, and her eyes widened in apprehension. His member stood proud, thick and pulsing, rigid in its bed of dark, wiry curls, and Miranda couldn't catch her breath. Her heart threatened to explode inside her chest. Her hands shook, and her head swam.

He was so very large...*too* large. There was no way this would work, no way it *could* work. This was a mistake. She'd been crazy to think this could work.

She took a hesitant step back. Quick, shallow spurts of breath puffed in and out as she shook her head. Garrett closed the distance between them before she could lend voice to her fears. His hands closed over her hips with firm insistence, drawing her flush against him, pressing the blistering, steely length of his arousal against her skin.

"It's too late to turn back now," he murmured as his hot lips skimmed up the side of her neck. He nibbled at the sensitive spot behind her earlobe, sending delicious shivers streaking through her. "Trust me."

Miranda had stopped trying to draw away the

moment he touched her. His coaxing words feathered over her skin, and some of the fear began to ebb. Garrett's lips claimed hers once more, and she melted into him. Slow and easy, he lowered them to the bedroll.

Garrett leaned over her, systematically wrapping her in thick, warm layers of need and hunger. His lips stole her breath. His hand stole her will, sweeping over her in unrushed, questing caresses. One powerful, muscled thigh came to rest intimately between hers, the thick shaft of his manhood pulsed against her hip. His tongue plunged into her mouth, over and over, sliding against hers in erotic abandon. Garrett's fingers found all her most sensitive spots, mastering them as his eager mouth captured her cries of astonished delight.

Need, swift and consuming, swelled inside her. She turned her body into his and returned his kisses with all her heart. She trembled when he slid his splayed palm down her ribs and over her navel. Her body jerked in surprise when his fingers delved into the soft curls below. He traced her sensitive folds, swirling slow, languid circles against her scalding, damp flesh. Garrett angled his head and deepened the kiss, slipping first one finger, then two into her tight sheath. He stroked her, thumbing at the tiny nub of her desire, drinking in her gasps of delight like the nectar of life. Miranda rode the crests of pleasure, straining against him, shocked by the sensations rocketing through her.

Just when she'd thought the experience couldn't get any better—any more powerful—he pushed her higher and higher, until the pleasure consumed her, and she shattered in his arms. She cried out, unable to prevent the sobs from slipping free.

"God, Miranda," he growled against her ear, hoarse, panting. "I need to be inside you, *now*."

She'd just experienced the most shocking, most

delicious sensations of her life, and yet she sensed there was more in store for her. His words sank through her, inciting the fires of desire to rage once more.

Miranda pulled at his shoulders, urging him closer, pushing him to take all she offered. Take all he needed. He moved so fast her breath trapped deliciously in her throat. Garrett's chest brushed against her tingling breasts as he positioned himself between her thighs. His arm slid beneath her shoulders. His body shook as he settled himself above her.

Garrett slipped his free hand beneath her bottom, cradling her—holding her firmly—lifting her to meet him. He paused, dropping his forehead to hers. Tense lines tightened around his mouth and dug deep grooves between his brows. His gaze burned her. Then he slipped the tip of his manhood inside her, and his gasp mingled with her own. He lifted his head and stared at her in the flickering firelight, his face tense, and she could all but see the last shreds of his conscience lick at him. His jaw flexed, tightened with the effort of restraining his desire. His stare pierced hers.

"I'll make this right, Miranda, I swear it," he rasped, his voice husky with raw need. "Trust me?"

"I'll always trust you, Garrett." She smiled tremulously at him, drawing his head down and kissing him like there was no tomorrow. She didn't want words now. She wanted him to touch her, and kiss her, and make her forget there was a tomorrow.

Garrett quivered in her arms, but he tore his lips from hers and still he pressed on. His gun-metal-gray eyes probing, his touch possessive, he growled, "You're sure? There'll be no changing your mind."

Miranda was lost in the maelstrom of awakened desire. This serious look in Garrett's eyes made her unaccountably nervous, and she was anxious to lose herself in those overwhelming pleasures once more.

"Yes, I'm certain," she insisted. "Please, Garrett..."

She floated on a heady cloud of need. At that point in time, Miranda would have agreed to almost anything. That Garrett asked for nothing more than what she gave him already—her trust—made her answer all the easier to give. That he would take the time to reassure her that he would do his best not to hurt her and offer her words he thought she needed—despite the effort it clearly cost him to hold back—made his vow all the sweeter.

"Please, Garrett," she repeated again, desperate to make him set this conversation aside and get on with loving her. She rocked her hips against him in deliberate demand.

He groaned aloud, but continued to peer down at her, his expression an odd mix of awe and lust.

"Now, Garrett, please," she pleaded.

Her plea snapped the last tenuous strands of Garrett's shredded control. She could see it in his eyes. His lips sealed over hers, his body tensed, his hands anchored her. Miranda moaned as he pushed deeper inside her, filling her. Stretching her. And the fullness pulsed. Throbbed.

Her nails dug into his muscled shoulders when that stretching became an uncomfortable burn. The broad head of his erection butted against her maidenhead. Her breath clogged in her throat. Panic hit her full force, and her body instinctively strained to get away from him, but his hand and his body held her firm. Garrett's hips pulled back the tiniest bit, and their eyes connected and held—his gaze filled with determination and desire.

Though he spoke through clenched teeth, his breathing ragged, Garrett's tone was an odd mixture of tender reassurance and brutal restraint. "Hold still, sweetheart. Just one…moment more…"

With that, he thrust into her, hard, rocking her back, burying himself to the hilt. Miranda's nails scored his back, and she cried out in shock as pain, sharp and burning, lanced through her. Garrett held her caged, immobile beneath him. Remorseful lips sought her face, raining kisses across her brow and over her damp cheeks. His lips were salty as they captured hers once more.

"Shhh," he murmured against her brow between kisses. "Just hold still, sweetheart. It will get better, you'll see."

Demonstrating the proof of his words, Garrett flexed his hips, sliding slowly out before reseating himself deep inside her. She tensed, holding herself absolutely still. Expecting more pain. But there was none. Only the slide of his powerful body and the promise of pleasures untold.

Miranda shifted experimentally beneath him. She pushed her hips up against him, embedding him deeper inside her, and Garrett sucked in a sharp breath. Pleasure, sharp and warm, coursed through her. Garrett groaned aloud. Yet he held himself motionless above her, his face grim, as if determined to give her as much time as she needed.

Miranda's fingers eased from his back and lifted to cup Garrett's cheeks. She drew his head down until their lips brushed, met, and clung. Tears burned the backs of her eyelids. Garrett muffled a groan and began to move. He cradled her against his body. His strokes were long and forceful. Instinct contracted her inner muscles and, above her, his large body jerked. He groaned, skimming his hand down the length of her thigh, caressing and guiding, lifting her knee higher as he thrust deeper. Faster.

All around, the breeze shushed, whisper soft against the grass. Nocturnal creatures chirped and hooted, muted by the pounding of her heart raging in her ears. Ragged breath tore from her lips, interspersed with soft cries and moans of passion, urging him onward. She opened her eyes, and the brilliant twinkling of stars glittered bright above them. The moon bathed him in silver. His gaze locked on hers, and everything else fell away, nothing else mattered.

The coils of release tightened inside her, and, as if sensing the state she was in, Garrett pumped harder, deeper, pushing her closer to the edge. It was a bittersweet agony, reaching relentlessly for that final, blissful moment—yet desperate to prolong the journey.

She'd never before felt this raging, consuming fire, and she didn't want to give it up. She wrapped herself around him, holding on to him for dear life. Nevertheless, the sensations were too big, too bright, and she couldn't contain them, couldn't hold on to it any longer. He leaned back, thrusting harder and faster—driving them higher, lifting himself away from her as he stared into her eyes in that final, binding moment.

"Stay with me, Miranda. Good, sweetheart, that's right. Look at me." Garrett gasped, his breathing ragged. "I want to see you melt for me, princess."

Miranda's stare locked with his. The world began to tremble, and everything exploded into millions of tiny bursts of light. Her body trembled, and she screamed his name into the darkness. Garrett tensed, thrust twice more, hard enough to rattle her teeth, and then he threw back his head and shouted, shuddering atop her. Deep inside her, he pulsed, gushing liquid heat straight into her very core.

****

A long while later, Garrett lay on his back, running his hand through Miranda's silky tresseš.

215

His breathing finally returned to normal. His heartbeat still pounded in his ears. Miranda lay curled against his side, her head snuggled in the crook of his shoulder.

He grinned like a fool at the velvet sky, stunned by what had passed between them. He'd never before lost control like that. Then again, he'd never had a woman respond to him that way, either. Garrett was exhausted, exhilarated, and contented in a way he'd never imagined possible. In short, he'd never felt better in his life.

Miranda was asleep at his side. She continued to amaze him at every turn. Every time he thought he had her all figured out, she caught him off guard. She'd been so responsive, so uninhibited, and in the end, it had driven him out of his mind. Life with her was going to be anything but mundane. Stranger still, he found himself looking forward to whatever life held in store for him, as long as this incredible woman was beside him—in his arms—he could face anything.

He considered the wedding. Undoubtedly, she'd want a large and lavish wedding. He gave a small sigh, girding himself for war. He would bow to her wishes where the wedding was concerned—but only so far. He'd be damned if he'd be the main attraction at some three ring circus. She'd just have to compromise. Then he considered both Natalia's and Hope's weddings and almost groaned in despair. Once those two got involved, he wouldn't stand a chance at keeping things under control.

Like the proverbial domino effect, Garrett's thoughts of the wedding invariably led to thoughts of the judge. Garrett grimaced. He'd be lucky if Miranda's uncle didn't string him up from the nearest tree when he found out Garrett had been less than honorable where his niece was concerned. Well, Judge Thomas would just have to get the hell over it. Miranda was his now.

His.

Nothing and no one was going to take her away from him.

Miranda shifted in her sleep, her head fell back against Garrett's shoulder, and her damp, fiery locks spilled down over his arm. Bright moonlight shone down on her, illuminating her features in the softest of silver. Garrett's gaze traveled over her face, his eyes caressing every feature, committing every freckle to memory.

She was his now. Because of that fact, he realized with a roguish grin, it was an added bonus that he got to kiss her whenever, *wherever* he wanted—just because he could. He leaned down and feathered whisper soft kisses over her delectable lips. His grin widened against her mouth as the idea stole over him that he could do a whole lot more than just kissing.

Lord, what had gotten into him? He'd never been this insatiable before.

Miranda stirred, responding to his kiss—coming alive at his touch. She arched against him, and he moved to cover her lithe form. Even that little voice of duty and honor seemed to have been placated. Miranda gave a little purr when Garrett slipped into her heat. He gave an echoing sigh of bliss.

All thought and plans of the future fled when Miranda wrapped her arms around his neck and her legs around his waist and began moving to the tempo Garrett's body set. He became the rhythm, and she the melody. Together they drifted into the night, wrapped up in the loving.

Brenda Huber

Chapter Sixteen

Outraged, Garrett glowered at Miranda. "What the hell do you mean, you won't marry me?"

His voice echoed throughout their little Eden, seething and insulted. He scowled at her as she dug into her valise and began pulling articles out haphazardly, morning sunlight made the highlights in her hair shine like liquid fire.

"I said no, Garrett, just leave it at that," Miranda hissed, yanking her chemise on so fast one of the seams tore. She muttered a curse beneath her breath and turned to glare at him, as though her torn clothing were somehow his fault—again. "And I will thank you not to raise your voice to me."

"Then start making sense, woman," he growled, yanking on his trousers. "Last night we—"

"Don't go there—" She tried to cut him off, glaring over her shoulder, but he plowed on as if she hadn't uttered a sound.

"*Made love,*" he enunciated each word loud enough to be heard in the next county. "We *made love,* Miranda. *Several times.* You can't just pretend it didn't happen. I won't let you."

At his last comment, she swung about to glare at him.

"To what purpose, Garrett?" Miranda asked in a subdued voice, throwing him off kilter with her change in tone.

His eyes narrowed. "What do you mean?"

"What good would come of us getting married? Your sense of honor would be satisfied, true. What of the rest it, Garrett?" Miranda stomped around the

218

campsite, half clothed. The mere sight of her was enough to make Garrett have to work twice as hard to focus on her words. "We would make each other miserable."

"Miranda, listen to me—"

"No, Garrett." She sliced the air with her hand to punctuate her denial. "*You* listen. You have your precious list. You've told me all about it, or have you forgotten? You want soft-spoken and sweet-tempered, unassuming and *obedient*. You want a woman who knows when to keep her mouth shut and when to mind her own business. I am none of those things. *None* of them, do you hear me?"

Her lips compressed, and for one aching moment, she looked miserable. Then she thrust her shoulders back, lifted her chin, and turned away to rummage for her dress. "I want my freedom, Garrett. I don't want to be reined in and put through my paces."

"I wouldn't treat you like some broodmare, Miranda," Garrett snarled, offended to the tips of his toes.

"Be reasonable. You want pliable and safe. I know who I am. I know *what* I am, Garrett. I have a tendency to get into trouble. It's my nature. I can't pretend to be something I'm not." Her words were matter-of-fact, but her tone—and the look in her eyes—told him of the pain her nature had caused her on countless occasions.

"I'm not asking you to pretend anything," Garrett argued. "You have to admit, these last few days we've gotten on well together."

"Marriage is more than 'getting on well together'," she snapped. "I refuse to be a convenient fill-in for you. I am not some woman you can just toss into the role of wife so you can get on with your bigger picture." She turned away from him with that last jab, blatantly ignoring his indignant sputtering.

She finished dressing, her body language speaking eloquent volumes.

Garrett's head felt ready to explode. There was an odd, hollow ache in the middle of his chest. Why did she insist on making more out of this than necessary? Every hissed word muttered beneath her breath only made him dig his heels in farther and refuse to accept defeat.

"I promised you I'd make this right, damn it, and I intend to stand by my word," Garrett growled at her back as she hopped from one foot to the other jerking at a recalcitrant stocking. The dying campfire smoldered between them.

She slowly straightened and, just as slowly, turned to stare at him, her narrowed eyes glittered. "You think I would accept this—this *benevolent offer*—knowing it was made out of guilt—or from some twisted, superior sense of moral obligation?" Her voice was so calm, so even, he almost didn't see the fury building behind her eyes.

Almost.

Garrett stared at her, baffled by her unreasonable attitude. "I'm trying to do the right thing here, Miranda—"

"If you think that changes anything, that I'll meekly fall in line because you or anyone else dictates it's the right thing to do...or because you're trying to fix *your* mistake...then you don't know me at all, Garrett. I will not be another one of your *duties*," she snapped, then spun around and stomped away.

Garrett couldn't believe he was hearing this. How could she be so...so...

"Woman!" he bellowed, striding after her, his long legs eating up the distance between them.

She refused to stop, refused to look over her shoulder or glance at him in any way.

"Damn it, Miranda, stop," Garrett snarled.

When she refused to acknowledge him, Garrett grabbed her arm and yanked her around to face him, determined that this time—when it counted the most—he *would* have the final word. He caged her shoulders in an iron grip, not tight enough to cause her pain, but tight enough to let her know he would not be denied. His stormy stare pinned her to the spot.

"Last night, you gave yourself to me," Garrett growled. "You agreed to be mine. It's too late to change your mind. I won't let you. *You will be my wife.* Get used to it."

Miranda opened her mouth, then snapped it closed without uttering a sound. Her expression changed. She was no longer furious. Instead, she wore a patient, placating expression. "You can't hold me to—"

Garrett cut in, "The hell I can't." She looked so shocked, so at a loss that he relented. His gaze softened and lowered to her lips. "Look at it this way, *princess*, you're just keeping your promise."

She scowled. "What are you talking about? What promise?"

"You promised to help me find a wife," he reminded her, smiling grim satisfaction.

She gasped aloud. "I didn't mean *me*! I will *not* marry you, Garrett. I won't do it."

"Yes, you will," Garrett enunciated each word, slow and deliberate, staring her down.

Then, before she could utter another denial, before she could shake her beautiful head in refusal, Garrett sealed his lips to hers in a bruising, uncompromising demand. Failure had never been an option for Garrett, and this seemed to be a test of sorts—a life altering one, at that. One he would not even consider backing away from, no matter how much she resisted.

Her every word of refusal cemented his resolve.

The fact she was melting in his arms even now, as vehemently as she'd denied him, convinced him he was right. Whether she wanted to see and accept the truth of it or not—there would be no changing his mind now, no denying that this would happen. One way or another, they would marry.

She'd just have to get used to the idea.

As his lips left hers, his gaze roamed over her face. He was more than pleased to find her gaze vague, hazy with passion. Even if it only lasted for a heartbeat.

She jerked back, pushing out of his arms, as though he'd slapped her. "That didn't change anything, Garrett. The answer is still no. I won't marry you."

"I believe your uncle will disagree when I tell him about last night," Garrett snapped, his temper pricked.

"You would do that?" He could all but see the blood drain from her face. "You'd take my choice away from me?"

Her tone, the look in her eyes, twisted his insides with guilt. Garrett almost wavered.

Almost.

"On this—yes, I would." His tone was softer, his expression more sympathetic, but he meant every word.

He thought she was done then. That she'd finally given up the fight. Without warning, a malicious smile crept across her sensuous mouth. "I got out of one engagement. I can get out of another."

Her stubborn little chin lifted into the air, and she pivoted on her heel, gliding away with the grace of a vengeful queen.

"True—but then again, you weren't engaged to *me* before, were you?" Garrett called, stopping her dead in her tracks.

After firing that parting shot, he dismissed her

and turned back to dismantle camp, smiling because—miracle of miracles—he'd finally gotten the last word.

****

They arrived in Johnston late that afternoon. Miranda had kept her own counsel for the majority of the day, and Garrett began to worry. His anxiety had nothing to do with the brooding woman at his side. He could swear someone followed them. He'd tried backtracking. Nonetheless, to his everlasting annoyance, whoever followed them continued to elude him.

Dusty and tired, Garrett rode straight through town, not stopping until he drew rein in front of the judge's house. He dismounted and tossed Hades' reins over the hitching post. Turning to face Miranda, he couldn't miss how the lines of her mouth compressed, or the shadows of fatigue beneath her angry eyes as she gazed past him, staring at the whitewashed house. He didn't wait for her to dismount; instead, he reached up and gripped her waist. He lifted her from the saddle and lowered her directly in front of him. Her skirts swished around his pant legs, her bodice brushed his shirt. Blood surged to places he didn't have time to entertain just now.

Watching her face, Garrett caught her apprehensive glance at her uncle's door. He wanted to reassure her that the judge wouldn't be too harsh, but knowing her uncle as he did, he just couldn't offer her the guarantee she seemed to need. He used the tip of his finger to nudge her chin up until their eyes met.

"Everything will work out fine, you'll see," he offered instead, tightening his fingers on her waist. This vulnerability, this apprehension was so unlike the Miranda that he knew...his Miranda...that it left him baffled. Feeling helpless. Not something he was accustomed to.

For a moment, she looked as though she wanted nothing more than to lay her head on his shoulder and accept the comfort of his embrace. He felt the weight of her anxious stare. Guilt weighed heavy for holding the threat of her uncle over her head in order to force the issue of them getting married.

As fast as that emotion pulsed through him, he pushed it aside. He'd known what the consequences of their actions would be last night. He'd known, and he'd accepted them. He was a man who shouldered his responsibilities, and he wouldn't—couldn't—take what had passed between them lightly. If she hadn't realized at the time what it would mean…

Well, she *should* have.

He'd warned her, damn it.

Miranda blinked at him with guarded eyes, as if she could read his thoughts and waged a silent battle of wills with him. He could feel her spine stiffen beneath his hand and let out a resigned sigh. Stepping back, waiting for her to move ahead of him up the walk, he drew a deep breath, preparing himself for battle.

Miranda didn't wait for Garrett to proceed her. She marched down the well-tended gravel path. Her small boots clicked up the three steps and across the porch. Without a moment's hesitation, Miranda reached up and rapped on the panel of wood. Tucking her hands in the folds of her skirts, she squared her shoulders and lifted her chin a solid two inches.

Garrett had followed her up the steps and set her valise down on the ground by his. Miranda rapped her knuckles against the door a second time. She was as stiff as a pine board. His hands itched to reach out to touch her, ached to sooth the tension from her rigid shoulders. Her obvious anxiety, her uncertainty—no matter how she tried to disguise it behind a brave front—wrenched at his heart.

In the blink of an eye, he recalled how she'd writhed beneath him in the pale moonlight, sure of herself and filled with the newfound knowledge of the power she held over his body. He lifted his hands, intent on drawing her back against him. The door opened, and he dropped his hands to his sides, empty...bereft.

The judge's elderly butler, stooped at the shoulders and sporting a long set of shaggy, gray sideburns, eyed them with no visible expression and waited.

"I am Miss Miranda Thomas," Miranda announced, her voice echoed in the dimness behind the butler. "I believe my uncle is expecting me."

"Yes, miss." The butler bowed, stepping back to allow them entrance.

Garrett picked Miranda's valise up and followed her into the small foyer. He watched with a puzzled frown as the butler reached inside his vest and withdrew a small square of folded parchment, rather than retreating into the house to inform his employer of their arrival.

"Marshal McCabe." The butler handed the missive to Garrett.

Garrett allowed his frown to deepen, but he held his hand out to accept the butler's offering. Garrett ignored Miranda's curious stare and unfolded the paper to read its contents.

Marshal McCabe,

I have been detained in Washington longer than expected. It is hard to say how long it will take to settle this matter to my satisfaction, and so I must impose on you a while longer.

I do not trust the bandit you wired me about, this Draco, and I fear for my niece's safety. Despite the loyalty of my staff, she will not be safe residing here alone. I must insist that you continue to give her your protection until my return. I realize you have a ranch to run, and I understand if Miranda must stay there with you, rather than you here with her. Her escort should provide sufficient protection against gossip. Look after her well.

M. T.

Garrett stared at the missive in his hands, helpless but to shake his head in bemusement. With all the excitement that had surrounded their trip, he'd forgotten to notify the judge that Miranda's companion had resigned. He handed the parchment to Miranda, watching her face as her eyes scanned the contents for herself.

When she finished, she frowned and flipped the paper over, as if looking for something more. Lifting troubled eyes to Garrett, her frown darkened before her stare shot to the butler.

"When will my uncle return?"

"Don't know, miss," he drawled, his face impassive.

"When did you receive this letter?" His tone was much more tolerant than Miranda's—or maybe just more resigned.

"Last week, sir." The old man's voice was bland. Garrett wouldn't want to face this man across a poker table.

"I see," Garrett murmured, chewing on the inside of his cheek. By his best estimate, the judge wouldn't have even made it to Washington yet—if that was where he'd even gone. He turned to address Miranda. "Let's go."

"Go where?"

"You read the note. We're going to the Lucky Clover."

"I'm not going anywhere with you," she hissed, forgetting the servant who melted into the shadows and disappeared.

"Yes, you are." Garrett took her by the elbow

and pulled her to the door.

She wrenched her arm free, glaring daggers at him. "I most certainly will not. It wouldn't be proper."

"We can do this one of two ways, *princess*," Garrett snapped. "Either you walk out of here on your own and preserve your dignity, or I carry you out and toss you over that saddle like a sack of feed. One way or the other, you *will* come with me."

Miranda's eyes narrowed. "You wouldn't dare!"

Garrett set the valise down and took a meaningful step toward her, his hands outstretched. Miranda shrieked and lurched sideways, scowling her fury at him.

"Garrett, be reasonable," she squawked, doing her best to evade his hands.

"I am being reasonable. I'm following your uncle's wishes. I'm taking you with me." He reached for her once more.

Her voice took on a definitive note of desperation as she dodged sideways yet again. "He thinks I have an escort with me. He doesn't know—"

"It makes no difference," Garrett cut in taking another step, reaching. "He was right—I have a ranch to run. Besides, I can't protect you here in town. It's just too easy to get to you while you gallivant all over the place. And I'll be damned if I'm going to spend the foreseeable future trailing you like some tamed doggie."

This predatory game of pursuit and evasion had begun to stir primal instincts. Miranda must have seen it in his eyes, for she threw her hands up in supplication. "Okay. You win. I'll go, just stop chasing me."

Her abrupt acquiescence drew Garrett up short. For a moment, he almost shrugged it aside and continued his pursuit, tempted beyond belief by the idea of tossing her over his shoulder and making off with her like some medieval conqueror.

Drawing a disappointed breath, he stepped back and waited for her to walk back through the door. He gathered her valise and glanced around, not surprised to find himself alone in the foyer. His eyes narrowed on the letter in his hand, and then he glanced at the door through which the butler had disappeared.

What in the hell was going on here?

Shaking his head, feeling as though he'd just played dupe in a very elaborate, very nasty, game of chance, Garrett stepped back out onto the porch. What got his goat was the fact he couldn't decide if he'd just lost the hand or won the whole pot.

****

Garrett ushered Miranda inside the ranch house on the Lucky Clover. He stood near the door for a moment as she surveyed the living area. Not a single feminine touch was evident anywhere, save for a delicate bit of stitched lace hanging above the mantel. Didn't that just figure. At length, Miranda turned her weary gaze back to Garrett. His smile was an odd mixture of anxiety and satisfaction. Without a word, he nodded toward a door on her left and proceeded her through the house.

Miranda stepped inside the room, overwhelmed by Garrett's scent. The furnishings in this room—obviously Garrett's bedroom—were much the same as those in his living room. Spartan. Masculine. She knew it even before he confirmed her suspicions. Sturdy, rugged and all male. Just like Garrett.

"This is my room." Garrett dropped her valise on the foot of the bed. "You'll sleep here."

Miranda's eyes flew to Garrett's steady gaze. "I couldn't—"

He scoffed, "Don't be ridiculous, where else do you plan to sleep, the sofa?"

"Well, it's not fair to make you sleep there,

228

either," she demurred, but she was already drifting toward the bed, fatigue weighing heavy on her. She ran a hand over the blankets covering his bed.

"I'll go see if I can't dig something up to eat," he said, turning away.

"That sounds...delicious," she muttered archly.

He shot her one last, narrow-eyed look over his shoulder, then stepped out into the hallway and closed the door behind him. His footsteps paused for a moment, and she thought she heard a slight thump against the door, then his footsteps receded down the hallway. Stifling a weary groan, Miranda ground the palms of her hands against her eyes and sank down on the edge of the bed. Soft. Hmm. Sliding back, she nestled her head against his pillow, turning her nose into the scent. Sighing, she pulled the pillow closer and closed her eyes.

Just for a minute...

****

Garrett sat in front of the fire, his feet propped up on the scarred edge of the small table in front of the sofa, nursing a bottle of whiskey. He consoled himself with the fact he was taking it slow with the bottle tonight...very slow. No way was he drinking to excess like he did the last time Miranda had driven him beyond reason. He'd learned his lesson well.

Greedy flames lapped at the dry bark of the log he'd just thrown on the blaze. A hush hung over the house, but it was a different kind of silence now.

Now there was a woman in the house. A woman in his bed. That fact, which should have brought him warm, pleased sensations, was, at this moment, killing him via a painful ache in his loins because the woman in his bed was so tired he hadn't been able to rouse her even to eat. She was exhausted, and if he joined her, sleep would be the last thing on his mind. She needed her rest, and as much as he wanted her, he wouldn't put his wants above her needs.

Her comment earlier came back to him and he snorted aloud. Him, sleeping on the couch.

Ha!

Not in this bloody lifetime...

That, however, didn't make the night move any faster or the ache any easier to bear. He sighed and tipped the bottle to his lips once more. It was then that he heard the scuff of boots crossing the porch, soft as the whisper of a breeze through the scrub oak on the side of the great mountain range in the distance. Garrett was out of the chair in a shot, silent as the night. His gun palmed in a flash, primed and ready to dispense justice. He stood next to the door, drawing a deep, centering breath.

Garrett's thoughts flew to Miranda, cursing the Fates that had placed her anywhere near his dangerous ghosts, especially since they seemed so hell-bent on tracking him down with such vindictive glee. The window in his room, low to the ground and large enough for a man to slip through, had been cracked open. He swore beneath his breath. He'd been so besotted by the sight of a sleeping Miranda curled against his pillow, he hadn't thought twice about that window.

Garrett glanced down, watching the door handle turn. Slow. Quiet. He tightened his grip on the gun and pushed Miranda from his thoughts. His body tensed, coiling to spring. The barrel of a Colt slid through the sliver of an opening, and the toe of a scuffed leather boot edged into the room.

Garrett waited until a black gloved hand cleared the doorway, and he pounced. Moving faster than a lightning strike, he grabbed hold of the hand, jerking the intruder into the room. He used the intruder's momentum to propel the man through the door and all the way into the room. Garrett let out a vicious curse, leveling his gun in fury. The intruder sprawled face down on the floor, but only for the space of half a heartbeat. In a flash, he rolled and sprang to his feet, leveling his gun with lethal intent.

Chapter Seventeen

"*Madre de Dios!*" The intruder uttered the hoarse exclamation, shifting his grip so the barrel pointed at the ceiling.

Garrett glowered as his nighttime prowler brushed the long, silky curtain of dark hair out of his eyes and rose to his feet with the agile grace of a panther, dropping the Colt back in its holster. Garrett, too, tipped his weapon, though it seemed to take him a moment longer to recover from the near fatal confrontation.

"Jesus, Mary, and Joseph," Garrett snapped, his heart thumping against his breastbone. "Are you trying to get yourself another hole in your hide?"

"Welcome back." With a negligent grin, Antonio swaggered across the room and settled into the chair Garrett had vacated.

He picked up the bottle of rotgut Garrett had set down and tipped it to his own lips with a steady hand. Garrett closed the door with a gentle click, his pulse seemed to take forever to return to normal. He joined Antonio by the fire, dropping onto the matching chair on the opposite side of the hearth. Antonio passed him the bottle and turned his gaze back to the fire.

"I was passin' by, saw light in the window," Antonio drawled. "Thought I should do the neighborly thing and check in—make sure your place wasn't gettin' picked over while you were gone."

"Mighty obliged," Garrett replied, savoring the burn of the alcohol as it raced from his throat to his gut.

"Wasn't expecting you back just yet."

"Made decent time," Garrett said, glancing over to meet his friend's dark, steady gaze. "Thanks for keeping an eye on the place. I know you're busy enough over at the Bar M just now."

Antonio gave a slight shrug, as though the extra responsibility had been of no particular burden. He eyed the bottle in Garrett's hand instead and remarked, "Never known you to be the kind to sit in the dark and drink alone."

Garrett thought of the woman in his bed and gave an inarticulate, enigmatic grunt.

"The assignment didn't go quite as smooth as you were hoping?" Antonio eyed Garrett, waiting for the answers to fall into place. He accepted the offered bottle and took a long draw.

Garrett stared at the dancing flames, uncomfortably reminded of Miranda's hair, feathering over his skin as he'd driven himself deep inside her, over and over—

Clearing his throat, Garrett took the bottle back, relishing the burn. After long moments passed in silent reflection, he cleared his throat again, startling himself as the sound pierced the silence. He knew Antonio wouldn't pry, he just wasn't that kind of man, but he also knew that Antonio's prolonged silence was the same as an offering of a companionable shoulder and a sympathetic ear.

Garrett tipped his head back against the chair and closed his eyes. The words began tumbling past his lips, unvarnished in their honesty. However, when he came to the night he'd spent in Miranda's arms, he stated, "Needless to say, things—got out of hand."

Antonio nodded acceptance of his friend's words, his eyes free of judgment and condemnation. Nevertheless, Garrett's next words managed to startle a spark of surprise in the otherwise unshakable foreman of the Bar M.

"...damnable woman got mad when I reminded her that I intended to do the right thing. She refuses to marry me. Obstinate, prickly, bull-headed, stubborn..." Garrett's voice trailed away on a note of disbelief and wounded pride.

Antonio sat quietly as Garrett grumbled beneath his breath before chasing the words down with a long shot of amber liquid. Antonio's dark brown eyes were filled with sympathy, and that, too, grated on Garrett's nerves.

"Did you ask her—or did you tell her?"

Garrett paused for a moment then replied, "She should have known what it meant when—"

"Did you *ask* her?" Antonio pressed the question, cutting Garrett off before he got a decent head of steam built up. "Did you actually say the words? Did you ask her for her hand? Or did you just assume she'd fall in line?"

Garrett's chagrined silence was, apparently, all the answer his friend needed. Antonio inclined his head and took a long draw off the bottle. He took his time, before responding. "She's a woman, Garrett. Not some subordinate you can order around," Antonio explained.

Garrett muttered under his breath, "As if she'd bloody well listen."

Antonio continued as though Garrett hadn't uttered a sound. "A woman doesn't want to feel like a man is marrying her out of a sense of obligation or duty. She wants to be wooed. She needs to feel wanted."

Garrett eyed Antonio with equal parts vexation and worry. Then, unmindful of the knife he was digging into his friend's still-bruised pride, he growled, "Aw, Hell! What do you know about women? You haven't exactly been successful in the area of courtin'."

As soon as the words left Garrett's lips, he could have kicked himself for the fleeting shot of self-deprecating irony that flickered in the depths of Antonio's velvety, dark gaze. Garrett cursed himself for letting the bottle do his talking for him, and he set the liquid demon down on the table between them with a definitive thud.

Garrett leaned forward in his chair, his face twisted with contrition. "Jesus, Antonio, I'm sorry. I shouldn't have…"

Antonio waved his apology aside with a wry snort. "You're right. I haven't been successful in that particular corral, my friend. However, I have learned something as I've picked myself up and dusted my own backside a time or two. A woman has every bit as much pride as a man, maybe more so. If you want to keep her, you'd better be willing to let her into more than just your bed. What's more, you'd better be ready to say those three little words, Garrett. Say them to *her*."

Antonio swiped the bottle from the table and settled back in his chair. He stared into the flames with a distracted, far-off gaze as Garrett stewed over that last bit of advice. Garrett eyed Antonio. Antonio's words seemed to have hit the mark as far as Miranda was concerned, closer than Garrett wanted to admit. He considered his friend and the dark, almost sad expression on his face, and he wondered if Antonio thought about Hope.

"So, tell me about this bandit," Antonio inquired, breaking the silence, his question chasing all thoughts of woman troubles from Garrett's mind. Mostly.

Garrett's spine stiffened, and his fingers dug into the arms of his chair at the mention of the man who'd become the bane of his existence. "He goes by the name Draco," Garrett informed Antonio with enough venom in his voice to take down a seasoned bull. "The rotten bastard."

Antonio blinked. Surprise lit his expression over Garrett's immediate, hostile reaction. Jesus, what was happening to him? As a marshal, he'd been near legend, known for his icy patience and single-minded level-headedness. The waves of fury roiling through him stunned him as he laid out the bandit's heretofore-mysterious dealings and the vague description he'd gotten from Miranda for Antonio. But, damn it, the bandit had laid hands—and lips—on Miranda.

On more than one occasion.

Antonio grinned, but made no comment.

"But the most irritating thing of all," Garrett spit out. "I swear I've seen him before. I haven't been able to get a good look at him, but somewhere, somehow, I know I've met him. I just can't, for the life of me, remember where or when. And from what I have seen, he looks so damned much like someone else I used to know, they could be brothers."

He'd tried in vain to convince himself his irritation had nothing to do with Miranda—or the fact that this bandit had taken liberties with her Garrett had designated solely his privilege. He told himself he was just irritated because he couldn't quite put his thumb on the man's identity. But he couldn't deny the truth any longer. This malady of his—this inability to think with a level head—had only come upon him with the introduction of a certain flame haired vixen into his life.

Jealousy was a real bitch to live with.

Antonio seemed to be weighing his words carefully then, as he was about to speak, he tensed at the slight scrape of a door opening down the hall. His amused gaze drifted to Garrett, and he drawled, "So, I take it you didn't leave her in town with the judge?"

"I couldn't," Garrett answered, sighing. He dropped his chin to his chest and shook his head. "Thomas isn't back from Washington yet. I couldn't leave her there alone."

"Of course not," Antonio drawled.

Garrett's head shot up at Antonio's tone, but he was spared having to reply when Miranda stepped inside the room.

****

"Oh," Miranda murmured, stifling a yawn. "I'm sorry. I didn't mean to intrude."

In that moment, two sets of eyes turned her way. One set steely-gray, the other set dark and velvety-brown.

Her eyes settled on Garrett's companion, and she couldn't help but stare in feminine appreciation. The two men were as different as night and day. Garrett was rugged—blatantly, powerfully muscular. His looks held the power to knock the breath from a woman like a jolt of lightning.

Miranda blinked owlishly at Garrett's friend. He appeared every bit as powerful, yet that power came in a sinewy, whipcord strong package reminding her of one of those dangerous, predatory cats that belonged in some mysterious tropical locale. His hair was long and sleek, falling well past his strong shoulders in lustrous hues of the darkest, silky chocolate. His profile was strong, his skin seemed to glow a burnished gold in the firelight. His features were sharp, and a fine line bracketed his mouth on both sides when he smiled. His was the kind of charm that wound its silky way around a woman, enthralling her body and soul, and once coiled would refuse to relinquish its claim.

What gave Miranda pause was the distance in that velvety-brown gaze. He was wary. Charming, yet carefully aloof. So guarded, she couldn't help wonder what woman would have broken this beautiful man's heart.

Miranda gave a slight start at her own thoughts and cleared her throat. Imagine, someone breaking this gorgeous man's heart, she scoffed to herself. Impossible. No woman in her right mind would be so stupid. In the same vein, she pitied the woman who gave her heart to this man. Whoever she was, she would have her work cut out for her. He was just too good looking.

He unwound his lean length, stood, and inclined his head in Miranda's direction with a polite, if albeit cool smile. He drawled, "Ma'am."

Miranda stepped farther into the room, into the pool of light, conscious of the cool boards against her stocking covered feet. She cursed herself for being so careless as to tread down the hall without stopping to don her shoes. But in her own defense, she hadn't been expecting to find visitors at this time of night either. Color flooded her cheeks when she caught Garrett staring at her toes.

"Miranda, this is my good friend, Antonio Diaz," Garrett addressed her, not bothering to rise. "Antonio, this is my *fiancée*, Miss Miranda Thomas."

Miranda had been about to greet Antonio politely when Garrett's words caused her teeth to snap shut in mortification. Her livid, sapphire gaze burned Garrett to a cinder with one well-aimed glare.

Garrett glared right back, refusing to budge an inch on his claim. Miranda crossed her arms over her chest, embarrassed that Garrett should behave so, friend or no friend. How could he embarrass her like this?

"We'll discuss *that* later," she informed him, wrinkling her brow as he reached for the bottle on the table.

Conscious that Antonio was following every furious exchange between her and Garrett with avid fascination, Miranda gritted her teeth.

"It's nice to meet you," she told Garrett's friend. She refused to lower herself to squabbling like two year olds in front of their guest...regardless of Garrett's apathy. From the corner of her eye, she caught the slow, warm grin creeping over Garrett's face.

Flustered, Miranda's eyes fell to the bottle in Garrett's hand—the almost empty bottle—and she rolled her eyes in mock despair. Turning to face Antonio, she offered him a smile, remarking with exaggerated patience, "You'll have to forgive Garrett for his manners—and his delusions—he's obviously been at the bottle again."

Antonio's brows shot up in undisguised interest. Devilment glittered in his eyes. "Again?"

"Oh, yes," Miranda replied with a conspiratorial nod. "Dear me, he seems quite prone to over-imbibing."

Garrett sputtered, and Antonio's laughter broke loose. He motioned Miranda to join them. As soon as she took a seat on the couch, Antonio prompted her to clarify her claim. All the while, his amused gaze was riveted on Garrett's outraged scowl. Miranda half expected him to rub his hands together in anticipation at any moment.

"Well," Miranda drew out as if uncertain. However, the look she shot Garrett was vindictive. "I shouldn't—"

"That's enough, Miranda," Garrett warned. Then he aimed a quelling look at Antonio. "We wouldn't want to hold Antonio up any longer, it *is* getting quite late."

"Nonsense," Antonio drawled, settling back in his chair. "I wouldn't dream of missing this."

Pleased by Antonio's willingness to allow her some vindication, she drew her feet up, tucking them beneath her. Leaning forward, her cheeks still warm from her nap, she smiled at Garrett's friend.

"Why, one morning, he gave me quite a start. I was so worried I almost summoned help. You see, we were *supposed* to leave at first light, but Garrett had spent the night *carousing*," she dramatically whispered the last word on a scandalized note. "By the time I found him that morning, why, he was barely able to stand, weak as a babe, and so *terribly* fussy. In fact, I felt so sorry for him I tucked him right back into bed and—"

Garrett interrupted her story with a loud, pointed cough.

She blinked at Antonio in feigned innocence and finished with, "But I'm sure, being his friend, you know all about Garrett's little—*weakness.*"

Great gales of laughter burst from Antonio, leaving him teary-eyed and holding his sides.

"You'll have to excuse my intended, the lack of sleep seems to have gone to her head," Garrett growled as soon as he could be heard over Antonio's guffaws.

"There, you see. He says the strangest things when he's been drinking." Miranda waved toward Garrett, as if he'd just proven her point.

Garrett glared at her, clearly at the end of his patience. Sensing retreat was now in order—living to fight again another day and all that, Miranda stood with regal aplomb.

"You will have to excuse me, Mr. Diaz," Miranda said. "I find dealing with Garrett when he's in this condition rather exhausting."

"Antonio," he corrected, standing as she made her excuses. Warm humor had vanquished the cool distance in his eyes.

"Antonio. I fear I am more tired than I thought. Undoubtedly all that riding to make up for lost time." She shot an arch glance at the still-seated Garrett for a moment before turning back to their guest. "I think I shall retire for the evening, but I look forward to seeing you again. It was a pleasure to meet you."

"Believe me, the pleasure was all mine." Laughter rumbled in Antonio's voice.

****

Grimacing, Garrett reached for the bottle once more and settled back in his seat as Antonio turned a measuring look on him and shook his head in a thin mockery of sympathy.

"You, my friend, are in over your head." Antonio glanced to the door Miranda had disappeared through, and grinned. "*Way* over your head. I think, on that happy note, I'd better head out. Gotta head up to the north range for one last swipe at the strays before we start branding in the morning." Antonio ambled to the door.

Garrett followed close on his heels.

Antonio shot a telling look toward the back portion of the house and commented with deceptive casualness, "You might want to think about hiring on a ramrod. Looks like you're gonna have your hands full 'round here."

Garrett shot Antonio a long-suffering glare and asked, "Any suggestions?"

Antonio paused, thrusting his hands into his back pockets. He rocked back on his heels and suggested, "Xavier's doing a right fine job over to the Circle K for Ethan, can't say that surprises me none. Enrique, now—he stepped up, that's for sure. I'm real impressed with him. I'll be put out to lose him, but he'd make a fine foreman."

"I'll take that under advisement," Garrett said by way of thanks.

However, Antonio wasn't done with him just yet. "As long as you're taking things under advisement..."

Heaving a put-upon sigh, Garrett tossed back

Brenda Huber

another swig of whiskey. "Go ahead...get it out of your system."

Antonio's grin widened, and he drawled, "Seems to me whenever Hope is in a snit over something, the fastest way Ethan talks her round is to just admit he was wrong. Then he kisses her senseless before she gets a chance to gloat. Seems like the way to go for Matt, too. Course, if that don't work, you could always try the alternative."

"That alternative being?"

Antonio stepped out on the porch, turned his face into the slight breeze, and drew a deep breath. His hair ruffled as he turned back to eye Garrett with a grin of shameless enjoyment.

"Get down on your knees and grovel," he crowed.

With that parting comment, Antonio strode across the porch and disappeared into the night, his warm, rich laughter trailing behind him. Garrett stared after him, irritated beyond belief. He stepped back into the house and closed the door, careful to secure the locks—something he'd never done in his own home—not before Miranda came along.

Heaving a weary sigh, Garrett went back to his seat and his bottle, trying his best to put Antonio's helpful suggestions out of his mind. His mind refused to let well-enough alone, though. No, it kept dragging forth visions of Miranda, perched on the sofa with her feet tucked beneath her like an eager child, a mischievous twinkle in her beautiful eyes.

Woo her...

"Damn it," Garrett whispered beneath his breath. "I am *not* wrong."

Nevertheless, the silence in the room refuted his claim.

Then he considered Antonio's words, and he allowed that Ethan might very well have the right of it—at least in regards to kissing her senseless. That idea held merit. Then he scoffed at his own lurid imagination. All that stuff only worked because Ethan and Hope were so in love. Matt and Natalia, too, for that matter. He wondered what Antonio was thinking, offering advice like that.

As if he were some moonstruck fool in love, desperate to win his lady's hand...

The moment that little four-letter word crossed his mind, he froze. Garrett stared in dismay at the bottle dangling from his fingers, as that stunning word circled in his head like a swarm of angry bees. With a sinking feeling in the pit of his stomach, he shifted in his seat. The very idea seemed to come to life and leap from his mind to coil at his feet like a hissing, writhing viper. He mentally recoiled, staggering back one subconscious step after another, reeling as the realization—the truth—hit him right between the eyes.

He'd gone and fallen in love with Miranda Thomas.

He loved her. Plain and simple.

The problem was...there wasn't anything plain or simple about her, or the way she made him feel. Garrett leaned forward in his seat, placed his elbows on knees, lowered his head to hands, and groaned to the unsympathetic floor. Somewhere along the way, he'd stopped looking at her as his duty and started looking at her as the woman who held his heart in the palm of her hand.

That understanding left him shaken—and terrified.

Chapter Eighteen

Garrett stomped away. She stared after his rigid back, bemused and irritated. Even a man with an ego the size of a mountain should find it hard to stomach that much refusal, she thought with a frown. How many more times would she be forced to tell him *no* before he accepted her answer? Why wouldn't he just accept her refusal and move on?

Why couldn't he just let it go? Why did he keep torturing her with things that could never be?

The feelings he'd awakened inside her were more than she wanted to think about. Yet, she'd been able to do nothing else—all night long. As the soft glow of the sunrise crept across the windowsill, Miranda faced the undeniable truth. She loved Garrett—and because she loved him, she had to let him go. He would never be hers. She'd lain awake into the wee hours of the morning, grappling with the truth, but now she knew what must be done.

He saw her as an obligation and nothing more, she reminded herself, doing her best to look at things from a realistic point of view. He'd never deceived her, never tried to convince her otherwise. He'd never gone out of his way to pretend a devotion to her that she knew he did not feel.

Though it didn't make facing the truth any easier, it did cement her course of action. For his kindness in not trying to woo her with false words and pretended emotion, she was grateful. Nonetheless, because she loved him, she couldn't be the shackle and chain around his neck. It may not be today—or even the next year, for that matter—but someday Garrett would come to resent being forced into a union with her, and her heart would die a bitter, withered death. Just as her mother's had in the face of her father's careless—sometimes contemptuous—disregard.

No, she wanted no part of a loveless marriage—and even less of one where the love was only one-sided. One way or another, she had to make him understand. This would never work between them. Only heartache and resentment lay in their future if she allowed a marriage between them. If she let herself give in to the one dream she'd clung so stubbornly to, marrying and raising a family with the man she loved, they would both suffer. Shaking her head with abject determination, squaring her shoulders, she lifted the hem of her skirts and tramped across the yard after him, dogging his steps.

"I don't care what my uncle wrote in that letter, I want you to take me back to town," Miranda demanded, trying her best to mimic petulant tones guaranteed to set a man's teeth on edge.

"No," he growled over his shoulder, changing course and heading for the stables.

"Oh, so when *you* say no I'm supposed to just accept it, but when I say it, you refuse to bend." Her eyes drilled angry holes in the back of his neck.

"Yes," Garrett snapped, ducking into the dim shadows of the stable.

"Garrett!" Miranda stomped her foot in frustrated fury. "Why won't you be reasonable about this? This is ridiculous! You don't want to marry me. I am nothing more than an obligation, a mistake in your eyes. I don't want to marry you. You can't fix one mistake with another."

Her words stopped him, but his reaction was one she couldn't understand—one she wasn't prepared for. Garrett whipped around to stare hard at her.

The look in his eyes froze her breath in her lungs. His stormy-gray eyes glinted with anger, and something infinitely more vulnerable.

Was that pain? No, no it couldn't be pain. He'd have to really care for her to be hurt. No, it was just his wounded pride, nothing more than wounded pride.

"Garrett, think about this logically. I would make you miserable," she began, but given the steely glint of determination in his eyes, she decided to change tact. "Give me one sound reason, Garrett, one sound reason that has *nothing* to do with obligation or society dictates and duty."

There, she thought. She had him now. He'd have to concede her point.

Garrett stood immobile before her, looking for all the world as if she'd just struck him. Then his eyes narrowed with unmistakable intent, and one corner of his mouth curled up.

"I'll give you a reason even you can't deny," he growled.

Before she could back away, before she could put up even a token resistance, he snaked one arm around her waist. His other hand clamped on the nape of her neck, and he hauled her resistant form flush against his rigid length. His lips locked over hers, fierce and demanding.

Miranda pushed against his broad shoulders. She twisted her head, trying in vain to tear her lips from his. The harder Miranda pushed, the harder Garrett pulled, until he crushed her against him, and she was in danger of having her ribs cracked beneath the force of his onslaught.

Miranda gritted her teeth against the invasion of his tongue, but she couldn't fight the quiver of longing that coursed through her at the feel of him licking and probing at her lips. He ground his hips against her, surging his arousal against her soft stomach.

And then he softened his touch, gentling his kisses, devastating her defenses.

She shuddered, and then melted into him. Yielding with a soft moan. He'd won this round, but, just now, as he angled his head and swept her along on his kisses, she just couldn't find it in her to care. Despite the softening of his lips, his embrace left no room for escape, the unyielding, steel cage of his arms became bonds of desire that pulsed and writhed around her. His body, a rock-hard bulwark of dominance that refused to accept nothing short of surrender, became sensual temptation personified, curving around her—pressing against her in all the right places until she wanted nothing more than to wrap herself around him. His lips turned persuasive and alluring, enticing her to relax into him.

Miranda was helpless to resist. She lost herself in his embrace, hungry and aching, meeting him kiss for kiss until she was breathing as ragged as Garrett. His hands roamed and caressed, leaving her breathless and begging for more. He surged his hips against hers, once again providing her with the undeniable, unmistakable evidence of his desire for her. Rhyme or reason fell away, and the only thing that mattered to her was that Garrett kept right on kissing her.

Garrett's lips left hers to skim her cheek. His voice whispered at her ear, as elusive and as tangible as a puff of smoke. "Say yes, sweetheart."

Miranda very nearly did. In fact, she'd already drawn breath, and the "yes" was halfway out of her mouth. All it was missing was the S at the end. Then the full force of his words sank through her like a razor-sharp knife of betrayal. She stiffened and shoved away from him, fighting like a wildcat, until she managed to break out of his hold.

"No! I refuse to marry for anything less than

love, Garrett McCabe," Miranda cried, covering her swollen lips with the back of her hands.

"You may not love me, but you sure as hell want me—and that'll have to be enough for now," Garrett snarled. Fury glowed in his eyes, drew the lines of his face taut. He swung up onto his horse's back and, crouching low in the saddle, he tore off as though the hounds of hell were after him.

****

Miranda stood in front of the bookshelves, staring blindly at the titles before her, her mind wrapped up in what had transpired between her and Garrett a short while ago in the stables. One hand lifted to knead the knot of tension that had taken up permanent residence at the nape of her neck.

Her fingers fluttered over her lips, and she wondered how it was possible that every time Garrett touched her—every time he kissed her—she melted into him and became a mindless puddle of longing. Giving an unladylike snort of self-disgust, she tilted her head, this way and that, trying in vain to ease the stiffness. Heaving a frustrated sigh, Miranda made up her mind to put Garrett and his maddening obtuseness from her mind. She refocused on the books that graced Garrett's shelves and was surprised at the diversity.

Just as she reached up to trace the leather binding on a book, strong hands claimed her hips, drawing her back against an unforgiving chest. She tensed, but, worn down by her own confusion, she didn't put up a fight. Why had Garrett doubled back to press his suit? Why couldn't he just leave her this time to herself to straighten out her own mind...firm her quaking resolve again?

"I thought you left," she grumbled.

A velvety voice crooned close to her ear, "Oh, now, I could never leave my heart for long. Did you miss me, my love?"

When that all-too-familiar, seductive baritone whispered against her skin and a smooth-shaven cheek nuzzled her neck, she leaped forward, almost crashing into the bookshelves. As Miranda bolted in surprise, her mind raced in disbelief. How could *he* be here—*inside* Garrett's house? Her mind screamed that it wasn't possible, even as she whirled around to see with her own eyes that not only was it possible—it was actually so.

"Draco!"

He smiled, oozing charm and the sinful promise of pleasures of the flesh. He held his arms open in invitation, as though fully expecting Miranda to throw herself at him at any moment.

"Come on, angel. Give me a kiss," he drawled. "You know *I* missed *you*, my heart."

Miranda stammered, backing away until her spine pressed against the bookshelves, "What are you doing here? You need to go. Right now. This very instant. This is Garrett's home. He'll be back any second, and he'll arrest you the minute he sees you."

"Oh, I doubt that very much, my love," Draco murmured stepping closer. "I saw him tearing off over the hill. He looked as if he had a whole passel of burrs under his saddle. I doubt he'll be back any time soon."

Draco lifted a gentle hand to cradle her cheek. His icy-blue eyes settled on her mouth with such a serious, meaningful expression that unease slithered through her. He lowered his head, his intent unmistakable. However, he overestimated her willingness to participate, and his lips skated along her jaw as she sidestepped out of his loose embrace.

Draco exhaled a long, slow breath, the light of the chase flickering to life in his determined, sky-blue eyes. Miranda saw it for what it was and began shaking her head as she backed away. No, damn it. She didn't need this right now.

"Stop that, Draco, stop that this instant." She pointed at him, trying to use her most logical of tones—though of late it hadn't proven to be effective with any man she'd used it on. "You don't really want me, you just think you do because I'm probably the only woman that's ever told you no."

Draco tilted his head to the side, as if considering the validity of her words. He gave a negligent shrug, but his footsteps never faltered as he stalked her around Garrett's living room.

"Why are you here—really?" She bumped into the sofa before sidling away to find a new escape route.

As though in disbelief at her low opinion of her own self-worth, Draco scoffed, "You don't believe you are enticement enough?"

"Not for one cursed minute." She edged past the table.

If she could just make it to the door...

As if reading her thoughts, Draco lunged for her at the same moment she scrambled for the door. He missed her.

However, she missed the door as well, because he was now blocking it, so they both got the raw end of the deal. Miranda leaped back out of his reach once more and edged her way around the room. Draco pursued her, as if he had all the time in the world, a cat—a great big, predatory cat—toying with a mouse.

Maybe she could make it to the bedroom, her mind raced. She couldn't remember if there was a lock on the door, but maybe she could barricade herself in until Garrett returned. Then, she remembered how fast Draco could move—and the fact there was a bed in that room—and she changed her mind. No way was she giving him that kind of temptation. Instead, she planned escape through the kitchen.

"Why are you here? Tell the truth."

Draco grimaced, his guilty gaze sliding away from hers. "I will admit I do have other business in town." His gaze returned to her with renewed determination. "However, that's just an added bonus when cast in the shadow of your charms."

"Stuff and nonsense," she snorted, refraining from rolling her eyes at his romantic drivel. "Tell me, do women fall for that rubbish?"

Draco gave a dramatic gasp of pain and slapped his hand to his chest, as if she'd wounded him. She bit her lip to keep from laughing aloud. Rake that he was, his wounds healed quickly, and he once again locked her in the crosshairs.

"I have come to plead my case and beg you to take pity on me," he said with mock seriousness. Then his eyes skated down over her body, and a wicked smile curved his sensual lips. "Come away with me and let me devote my life to your every pleasure."

Now Miranda couldn't resist giving in to the urge to roll her eyes to the heavens. Shaking her head, unable to hide the slight grin that flirted around her lips, she asked, "Will you be serious? Why do you do the things you do, Draco? The life you've chosen for yourself is dangerous."

"Like many a man before me, and, I dare say, many that will follow after, when given the choice of two evils, I always try to take the lesser of the two. That is—unless the devil's offer is just too tempting to refuse," he drawled, grinning at her with unrepentant glee.

"You speak in riddles, how am I to take you seriously." Miranda frowned.

Draco leveled a look at her that was too serious by half. Miranda's heart skipped a beat, and she drew a panicked breath, pulling back out of his reach once more. Draco let his arms fall to his sides, and he stopped walking. Miranda was thrown too far off kilter by his new change in tact, and she didn't realize when he'd stopped moving, so had she.

"Miranda, I may have had other pressing reasons for being here, but that doesn't belittle how much you have affected me. I come to you, not as what you perceive me to be, but simply as a man. I am prepared to set aside my—profession. I am willing and able, prepared even, to settle into any respectable life that you desire." His words, the earnestness of his tone, were no longer those of a devil-may-care rogue, but those of a man laying his heart at a woman's feet.

She froze, stunned.

"I would give you the moon and the stars. I would give you my very heart. I would give up everything I've worked for and believed in for the last ten years if you would consent to be my bride. Just say the word, Miranda. I'd give you anything. I'll give you *everything*." He stole her breath with words she'd dreamed of hearing...from another man.

Miranda stood rooted to the spot, staring wide-eyed, gaping in shock at Draco. He closed the distance between them in two long-legged strides. His arms slid around her, and he drew her into his embrace with a stunning tenderness that almost brought tears to her eyes.

Damn you Garrett, why couldn't you be saying these things to me?

"Darling," Draco whispered, his voice, his eyes filled with longing as he lowered his mouth to hers.

The contact was silky smooth, holding a tenderness Draco's kisses had never before held. She curled her fingers into his shoulders, and for a moment she closed her eyes and wondered what it might be like if she allowed this man to sweep her away as he seemed so intent on doing.

Then her heart wrenched inside her chest,

spoiling it all. Draco didn't even know her. He didn't want her any more than Garrett did. Oh, granted, maybe he had different motives, but in the end, it all boiled down to one thing. They'd both painted neat little pictures in their fool heads—pictures that they were trying to force her to fit into—never mind that neither one of them had never bothered to ask what her own little picture of her future looked like.

Twisting her head away, breaking the kiss, she pushed at his shoulders until she held him at arm's length. "Draco, you need to listen to me…"

Her tone should have warned him that he wasn't going to like the answer, but he must have thought a little more gentle persuasion might tip the scales in his favor.

His eyes locked on her lips, and he smiled ever the slightest bit. His arms began to tighten around her, drawing her back into his embrace. He was far stronger than she. Her arms began to give. Panic descended, lightning swift, and her arms trembled, straining against him as she fought to make her objections known.

"Draco, stop!" Miranda exclaimed. "I need you to listen to me. *Stop kissing me, damn it…*"

"Well now, at least I'm not the only one you hold at arm's length," Garrett drawled from the open doorway. Miranda whipped her head around to gape at him, cursing her luck. His voice may have been deadly soft, but his body was rigid and ready for battle.

And his steely-gray eyes promised mayhem.

****

Fury boiled through Garrett. The sight of Miranda in another man's arms—in *this* man's arms in particular—drove him too close to the edge of mindless rage to consider. This had to be her bandit. Draco… The name stung his soul like salt on an open wound. She hadn't even waited for his dust to

253

settle.

In a flash of blinding speed, Draco positioned himself to shield Miranda, one arm anchored her to his side...the other held a long-barreled gun leveled, unflinchingly, at Garrett's chest. The bandit kept his head tilted down so that his face remained shielded by the wide black brim of his hat and the curtain of his long, golden hair. Once again, recognition niggled...just beyond his grasp. Damnation, who was this bastard? He moved like lightning, and the glint in his eyes declared he knew what to do with that hogleg.

He was dangerous.

And familiar.

"Get your hands off my woman." Garrett snarled, filled with the rage of savage possessiveness, fighting the urge to unload his weapon into the man who'd become a thorn in his side. He didn't doubt his own aim—the only thing that stopped him was the fact Miranda was too close. A slight miscalculation, a subtle shift, and she could be harmed—something Garrett wasn't prepared to gamble on.

"So the brave lawman returns," Draco drawled softly, inching his way toward the middle of the room, drawing Miranda along with him.

The blatant insolence the man used in addressing his former profession grated on Garrett. He cocked his head to the side as a glimmer of something flickered.

Try as he might, he couldn't put his thumb on whatever it was that called to him, unable to focus on anything other than Draco's impassioned plea for Miranda's affections, and the sight of her standing in his arms, kissing him. Jealousy gnawed at Garrett's insides—a rabid beast waiting for the chance to break free and wreak destruction.

"Let her go," Garrett demanded yet again, his

tone hard and uncompromising. "She belongs to me."

Draco smiled cold denial, and even though the only thing Garrett could see was the flash of white teeth and the shadow of Draco's icy stare, a chill raced down Garrett's spine. He strained to hear the words the bandit murmured into Miranda's ear.

"Come away with me, Miranda. Be mine," Draco urged, his tone soft and sincere.

Her gaze locked on Garrett, and she hesitated. Emotions flickered over her expressive face, one after another, so fleeting he could scarce track them. Sorrow, confusion, longing. Those emotions ate a hole in his gut.

Oh, God...she couldn't love the bandit. She couldn't.

Could she?

Her troubled gaze slid to Draco, and she bit her lip.

Garrett's blood ran cold. Jesus, she wasn't actually considering going away with this man...was she?

Over his dead body.

Panic knifed through him when he recalled the inexplicable soft spot she exhibited for this lawless scoundrel. How many times had she defended him? Yet, her eyes held *his*, searching for something—needing something from *him*.

Garrett shook his head. His steady gaze bore into hers, pleading—wordlessly demanding—that she stay with him. He stood motionless, silent, telling her with his eyes if not his lips what, he hoped, she longed to hear.

Miranda raised her hand and laid it on Draco's forearm. The bottom of Garrett's world fell away. Was this, then, her choice?

Draco blinked down at her, surprise etched on his face, but he lowered his weapon, though he didn't holster it. Garrett watched in jealous fascination as

Brenda Huber

this wild bandit responded with tame submissiveness to Miranda's gentle touch.

With careful movements, as though anxious not to upset the delicate balance that held the room enthralled, Miranda faced Draco. Ignoring Garrett's low growl of warning, her smile was tender and genuine when she laid a hand upon Draco's chest.

"I'm deeply touched, and I know you are sincere," she assured him, her words obviously meant for the bandit's ears alone. "You are a very special man, and I'm sorry if I'm hurting you, but I can't go with you, Draco. My place is here." Then, whisper soft, her eyes pleading with the bandit, she implored, "My heart is here...please understand."

Her heart was here? Was she saying these things solely for Draco's benefit...or did she really mean them? Hope surged in his chest, making it difficult to breathe.

Something glinted in the bandit's eyes, something fierce and heretofore unchallenged. His hand lifted to cup her chin, then, with the reflexes of a predator, he planted a fast, hard kiss on her lips. It was over before Garrett had time to do little more than curse. If he'd had a clear shot, he would have dropped the twice-bedamned bandit where he stood.

Draco devoured her with his eyes before he winked at her with wicked promise. "I'll change your mind yet."

Garret stiffened.

Not if he had anything to say about it, damn it.

Catching Garrett by surprise, Draco faced him, depositing his gun in its holster. With deliberate, unrushed movements, the bandit reached up and removed his hat, then lifted his face into the light, giving Garrett a complete, unhampered view of his visage.

Recognition settled upon Garrett, like an icy fist clenching his heart. His eyes widened, and he caught his breath.

"You..." Stunned, Garrett could barely find his voice. "We were told you were dead. Killed in..."

In the line of duty, he'd been about to finish and caught himself just in the nick of time.

"That's the story, anyway," the would-be bandit muttered.

Dimly aware of Miranda staring at him, Garrett schooled his features. Undercover. All this time, he'd been undercover. But Garrett's mind raced in a hundred different directions. Why was he here? And he was going by the name of Draco now. What did this all mean?

"Your old friend turned up a few months back," Draco announced. "Apparently he had some unfinished business that didn't allow him to cross over after the fire. It seems the afterlife has been quite lucrative for him."

The blood drained from Garrett's head. The room lurched around him sickeningly. No...it wasn't possible. *Chambers... Alive...* He'd been there, seen the fire catch Chambers' clothing. No one could have lived through that. No one. Not even the devil himself.

A muscle ticked along Garrett's jaw. "Where is he?"

"I'm still working on that, but it shouldn't matter to you. You're not a marshal anymore, McCabe. It's time for you to step aside," Draco warned.

"I finish what I start," he hissed between clenched teeth.

"Not this time, my friend." Shaking his head, Draco's eyes issued warning. "It's in my hands now."

Garrett flexed his hands at his sides in frustration. Long moments passed in tense silence as he glared at the *bandit*. Heaving a sigh that was anything but resigned, Garrett stepped to the side and allowed Draco to amble from the room without as much as a by your leave. Draco cleared the porch, and Miranda came scurrying forward. Garrett closed the door before she could step out into the sunshine to watch her bandit ride away.

"You had your chance to leave," Garrett snarled. "You aren't going anywhere now."

"I didn't..." Miranda trailed off. Her expression shifted from shock to confusion to indignant outrage. "How could you... You can't seriously think for one moment that I would have gone with him, do you?"

Garrett mumbled beneath his breath as he stalked away from her. He should have known better. She'd never just let it go at that. She hurried forward and grabbed him by the elbow. She dug her heels in, tugging until he finally stopped and faced her, lest he drag her in the dust behind him.

Miranda's face was pale, her features pinched. "Answer me, Garrett."

Garrett stared hard at her, filled with dread. If Miranda learned who Draco was—who he *really* was—would she be so quick to discount Draco's affections? Garrett's back stiffened, the muscle ticked to life on his jaw once again. It didn't matter, he told himself. Miranda belonged to him. He'd see her in Draco's arms again—over his dead body.

"I know you wouldn't have gone with him," Garrett relented, silently adding that he wouldn't have allowed it. He'd have killed the man first— regardless of who he was. Garrett's answer seemed to pacify her. He reached out and tucked a loose tendril of flame behind her ear. His gaze searched her face for a moment, and then he turned and started to walk away.

"You know who he is, don't you?" Miranda's voice—her words—froze him in his tracks. A long slow breath eased out of him. He resumed walking again, determined not to answer. "Who is he,

Garrett?"

He stared at the door ahead of him, lost in the great debate—tell the truth and risk losing her, or pretend ignorance and skulk away with his tail between his legs like the coward he was. In the end, he knew he could do neither. Cursing his luck and hardheaded, inquisitive women, he spun around to face her.

"Just drop it, Miranda," he urged. "Drop it and forget you ever met the man."

Then, before she could voice protest, he strode from the room, closing the door behind him.

Chapter Nineteen

Garrett was on edge. His brothers' killer was still out there, alive and prospering. That knowledge grated on him. The realization he'd failed to avenge his brothers was a cross he was ill-equipped to bear. Garrett's dour mood spilled over to Miranda. She'd managed to poke and pry until she'd loosed the name of this *"old friend who'd turned up a few months back"* from his lips, and he'd finally admitted his failure aloud.

Clint Chambers still lived and breathed, walking the earth a free man.

He had no choice. He had to go after Chambers. Never mind the fact that his quest for vengeance had almost cost him his life the last time around. Resolved, Garrett began packing his saddlebags in preparation of his impending trip. Miranda hovered nearby, arguing vehemently, but to no avail. He'd made Nick and Eddie a vow. He had to see it through.

Miranda clutched the back of the sofa in a white-knuckled grip. "You're not even a marshal anymore, Garrett."

"That doesn't matter." He stepped around her as he headed down the hall, grim with resolve. "I need to finish this."

Trailing him into the bedroom, Miranda probed, "Even if it kills you?"

"Don't be ridiculous," Garrett quipped, though he couldn't quite meet her eyes. "I'll be fine. I'll be back before you even notice I'm gone. And then we'll send out the invitations."

"Invitations?" That brought her up short. Good grief, did she think he could just forget the vow he'd made to her, too? He'd told her they would be getting married. He had no intention of changing his mind—or letting her weasel out of it, either.

"You didn't think I forgot about the wedding, did you, sweetheart?" Garrett shot her a shameless grin over his shoulder as he rummaged in a drawer of his bureau.

For a moment, something flashed in her eyes. Longing. Raw and unmistakable. Plain as the nose on her beautiful little face. The emotion flickering in her eyes shot straight to his heart. He froze in surprised disbelief, his hand suspended over the now forgotten items in his drawer.

She felt something for him, too.

She blinked, turning away to stare out the window. But it was too late for evasion. He'd seen the proof with his own eyes. It was time to push the issue. He wouldn't let her deny her feelings—or him—any longer.

Miranda jolted when his hands settled on her shoulders. Refusing to allow her to squirm away yet again, he turned her to face him. Garrett squeezed her shoulders. "Look at me."

Miranda stared adamantly at the buttons on his shirt.

"Sweetheart, look at me," Garrett insisted, keeping his voice gentle and coaxing.

Her miserable stare lifted to his throat, and then his chin. He waited. At last, Miranda's reluctant gaze lifted to his.

Garrett gazed into her eyes for a long moment. So many things poured through his mind, only to slip away like water through his fingers. The only solid thought that remained was that he loved this woman, and she felt...*something*...for him.

That was enough.

For now...

Without a word between them, he lifted his hand to cup her cheek. His thumb smoothed across her lower lip, his free hand dropped to cradle her hip. Miranda lifted her hands to Garrett's chest, sliding up to his shoulders. Her touch fired his blood.

She didn't pull him closer—but she didn't push him away either. He took that as a good sign. Garrett searched her face, probing the clear blue depths of her eyes for the slightest sign of denial. All he found was shining acceptance. Satisfied with the ground he'd gained, he tipped his head down until his lips hovered mere inches from hers.

And he waited.

Drawing a deep, steadying breath, Miranda went up on tiptoe, reaching for his lips like a rose stretching for the sun. As their lips met, brushed, and met again, Garrett slid his hand around her waist, drawing her against him. His hand moved from her cheek, his fingers sank into her hair.

Garrett's lips moved over hers with exquisite care, his tongue stroking hers slow and deep. She clung to him, melting in his arms. And as only seemed to happen in her arms, he was complete. He was indestructible. His fingers went to work on the row of tiny buttons spilling down her bodice, and her dress sagged to the floor pooling around her ankles. His hands burned to caress her naked flesh, and he swept the thin cotton of her chemise aside with unrushed reverence.

The hunger in him, restrained with ruthless determination, seethed and boiled. She rubbed against him, arching her body and purring deep in her throat. She wasn't making it easy to go slowly. Nonetheless, no matter how she provoked him, Garrett refused to be rushed. Instead, he controlled the pace, holding them on the path of languorous seduction.

Her hands skated down Garrett's chest, his buttons giving way in her nimble quest. His mouth branded the side of her neck as he peeled away the last barriers of clothing that stood between his flesh and hers.

Garrett broke the kiss for a heartbeat, stepping back to stare at her. His ravenous gaze devoured her. Dear God, she was beautiful. Then he surged against her, sweeping her into his arms, sealing his lips to hers once more. He clung to the last shreds of his control like a drowning man clinging to his last lifeline. Miranda pressed against him, from knee to chest, and moaned. With calculated movements, Garrett reached down and swept an arm beneath her knees, sweeping her off her feet.

He kept his eyes locked with hers as he carried her across the room and laid her down upon the bed. Inch by slow, tormenting inch, he stripped away the rest of his clothing, excited by her rapt gaze following his every move.

****

Miranda gasped in surprise and stared into storm cloud gray eyes, amazed, captivated. Holding her arms open, beckoning him to her, she waited with bated breath. Still, to her everlasting frustration—and her reluctant joy—Garrett wouldn't be hurried.

Finally, with a predatory gleam in his eyes, Garrett very slowly crawled up the length of her body, his hands and knees braced on either side of her, caging her in, licking and nibbling every inch of her skin. He nuzzled the sensitive flesh of her stomach, scraping his prickly cheek across her tender skin. His stare locked with hers as he aimed higher, setting his lips and tongue and teeth to torment her aching breasts.

She moaned, arching against him as he drew her puckered nipple deep into his mouth and suckled, all the while he watched her with blatant carnal possessiveness. Then he licked his way across the upper swells of her breasts and across her chest to nibble at the hammering pulse at the base of her throat. Garrett lowered his weight onto her until every one of her pulse points throbbed for him.

His calloused hands slid over flesh that was already too hot, too sensitive. Garrett's agile fingers sought and found all her most vulnerable places, wringing cries of passion from her lips. Driving her out of her mind. How could he go so slow? How could he torment her like this?

Couldn't he see how she wanted him?

Couldn't he feel it?

"Please, Garrett," she pleaded breathless against his nibbling lips, straining against him, unable to bear this sweet torture one moment longer.

Garrett angled his head and deepened the kiss, sliding his tongue against hers, tangling, taunting her with its seductive motion. At the same time, he settled himself in the cradle of her soft thighs. His hands splayed on her hips, skating up her sides. His hands shook, relaying just how tenuous his control had become.

Finally.

Thank God...

His greedy fingers skimmed past her breasts, pushing her arms up above her head until his hands covered hers, palm to palm, fingers entwined, pinning her hands to the mattress. As soon as their hands linked, Garrett lifted his head and gazed at her. The unmistakable pressure of his rigid arousal pressed against her—pressed into her. Slow and easy. Oh Lord, so slow. In that heady moment that his flesh filled hers, Miranda's vision blurred, and she let out one long gasp of pure delight.

He lowered his head and peppered butterfly

kisses along her jaw and down the side of her neck, his hands pressed hers against the mattress, the sinewy length of his body caressing her from shoulder to hip with every powerful surge of his manhood deep in her core. Garrett's lips burned her sensitized skin as he nuzzled into the crook of her shoulder. She wanted to touch him so bad, needed to run her hands over his body and make him lose control.

But, as if sensing her desire, he anchored her hands, refusing to budge.

She wrapped her legs around his waist, locking her ankles, desperate to hold on to him any way she could. Garrett's grip on her hands tightened. She was at his mercy. Miranda flexed her inner muscles, squirming beneath him.

Groaning against her throat, he continued to thrust deep and slow, grinding against her, driving her closer to the ragged edge of release. His lips seared their way back up to her ear.

"No other man will ever touch you like this," he growled against her ear.

His words enflamed her—thrilled her every bit as much as his masterful touch. Every thrust of his hips surged pleasure through her body, even as his words surged emotion through her heart.

"No other man will ever love you like this, Miranda. I will *never* let you go."

Then his thrust went deeper still, more purposeful with each successive word. "You. Are. *Mine.*"

Sensations coiled tight, deep in the pit of her stomach, and she cried out, desperate, mindless, "Please, Garrett, let me hold you…"

He surged into her once more, seating himself to the hilt, grinding his manhood into her with a deep-throated growl, then he released her hands and slipped his arms around and beneath her, cradling her.

The second her hands were free, Miranda wrapped her arms around Garrett, holding him tight. Something was different. She could sense it in the restrained urgency of his touch and in the quiet hunger of his kisses. Something had changed inside Garrett since that night by the pond, and it stirred an echoing response deep inside of her. She reveled in the sensations spiraling through her as his powerful body laid indisputable claim to hers.

They moved together as one, breathed as one...hearts pounding to the same elemental rhythm...and she'd never felt such a sense of belonging. Such a sense of *rightness*. All too soon, she was there, hanging precariously over the jagged cliff of ecstasy. Wave after wave of bliss began to build, buffeting them. Gathering her close, Garrett swept her up the crest, cradled her close, and leaped over the edge—dragging her with him.

At length, Garrett gathered her in his arms and rolled, bringing her with him. He lay back against his pillow, and Miranda savored the intimacy of the moment. What she wouldn't give for a lifetime of moments just like this.

But she couldn't turn a blind eye, either. How could she deny, even for a moment, that if Garrett stayed the course he'd set for himself—if he went after this Clint Chambers again—he could be forfeiting everything he claimed he wanted. She wasn't stupid. She could see the determination on his face, in his eyes...even now. He'd focused on fulfilling his promise to his dead brothers for so long that he couldn't look beyond it any longer. Miranda—the family they might have had together—were not his priority. She couldn't live like that. Always knowing that something, or someone else, was more important than the commitment he'd made to her.

She wouldn't.

But her heart broke all the same.

Miranda lay in the warm comfort of Garrett's arms, taking what she could...for who knew what tomorrow might bring. His heartbeat throbbed against her ear. His skin was smooth and damp beneath her cheek. Had he been able to understand what had driven her to give herself to him? Did he understand how much he'd come to mean to her? Did he understand she'd given him her heart...even if she hadn't been able to bring herself to say the words?

She longed to give him the words, she did. But they refused to pass her lips. It wouldn't make any difference anyway. He'd still go after Chambers, and she'd be left with nothing but a hole where her heart should be.

But she'd felt the emotion in him as he'd made love to her. Even now, he held her with undeniable tenderness. Maybe...if she told him—if she gave him the words she feared to speak aloud—maybe it would make a difference after all. She called herself a coward, and yet the fear he didn't return her love with equal measure stayed her tongue. Every time she tried to throw caution to the wind and blurt out her love, that cautious, scared little voice in the back of her mind warned her to tread lightly. After all, it reasoned, if she kept her feelings—and those three, binding words—to herself, then Garrett wouldn't feel pressured to make declarations he didn't mean and promises he would regret.

What they had between them right now was enough, she told herself. It would have to be.

Still, it wouldn't hurt to tell him one more time. After all, didn't actions speak louder than words?

Miranda feathered her hand down his chest and across his abdomen. Her smile widened when his muscles bunched and tensed beneath her fingertips.

Turning her head on his shoulder, she gazed at him from beneath lowered eyelashes. Garrett sucked in a sharp breath as her hand closed over his already hardening arousal.

He groaned deep in his throat when her hand began to move, experimenting with motion and pressure and touch. His skin was like the finest velvet encasing unforgiving steel, and she took her time, exploring, delighting in the soft gasps and slow sighs she wrung from his lips. She skated kisses over his chest and up the side of his neck, but when he shifted, clearly intent on moving to cover her once more, she sat up and pushed him back down onto the mattress. He leaned back without a fight and watched her with curious, eager eyes, as if waiting to see what she would do next.

Emboldened by his compliance, she slipped her thigh between his, sliding her foot up his calf. Miranda leaned over him and nipped her way across his chest, taking encouragement from the low growl that escaped him. She shifted, sliding lower against him, running her tongue over the defined ridges on his stomach, scooting lower—and lower.

Garrett groaned as she took him into her mouth, his body jerked. He sank his fingers deep in her hair, guiding her head until she picked up the rhythm. She tasted him and explored for a few more minutes, swirling her tongue around his satiny skin before he pulled her up until she sprawled across him. He must have thought he had her off balance and at his mercy, but he couldn't have been farther from the truth. Once again, he tried to roll over, tried to pin her beneath him, but Miranda was ready this time.

She pushed at his shoulders, bracing her knees on the bed on either side of him until she sat astride him, his throbbing manhood nestled at the juncture of her thighs. Smiling down at him, she rubbed herself against him and watched as his eyes drifted closed on an expression of tormented bliss, and his body went still in expectation.

Her rubbing, however, proved to be a double-edged sword. A gnawing, hungry need pooled deep in her belly, empty and aching to be filled. Miranda guided his hands to her hip as she impaled herself on his rigid length, savoring every last inch of him. His fingers flexed, tightening around her, as she began to ride him slow and deep.

She gasped in delight, savoring the sensation of being in control. She set the pace, changing it as she liked. Angling her hips, she used her body to drive him wild. By the grit of his teeth and the ticking muscle in his jaw, she'd say it was a safe bet that she was succeeding.

Garrett's hands roamed over her, exacting equal retribution. Everything outside the walls of Garrett's bedroom ceased to exist, and her world narrowed to a time of touch and taste, laughter and loving.

Her world shifted, and her center of gravity now revolved around Garrett.

As the sun peeked high in the cloudless cerulean sky, Garrett stirred. Miranda lifted her head from his shoulder and peered up at him. Every muscle in her body was replete, weak with satisfaction. Not a word had been spoken between the two of them for hours, and yet there was a comfortable peace between them.

"We need to get dressed." Garrett dropped a light kiss on her lips. "We're going for a ride. There are some people I'd like you to meet."

Incredulous, she blinked at him. "Now?"

"Now," he confirmed, sliding out of her arms.

Lifting a curious brow, Miranda scooted from the bed. She washed in a rush and began pulling on her scattered clothing. Questions filled her, but every time she tried to sneak one by him, he shook his head and kept his mouth shut.

Frustrated, she crossed to a nightstand and picked up her brush, taming the unruly, fiery red tresses with a few deft strokes. By the time she finished restraining her hair in a loose chignon, Garrett had already dressed, stolen a fleeting kiss, and told her he would be waiting in the stables. Miranda finished with her primping, puzzling over Garrett's odd, secretive behavior, and then she scurried outside.

Garrett was just tightening the cinch on Miranda's dappled mare, when she stepped inside the stables. As soon as her eyes adjusted to the dimness and she approached him, Garrett reached for her. The fleeting kiss he bestowed upon her spun out of control, shocking her. Where had this sudden desperation come from? Her fingers tangled in his hair. Lips mashed, and tongues dueled. Garrett pinned Miranda between his hard body and the rough planking of the stable door. Angling his head, he deepened the kiss until she gave up trying to think at all.

With a groan, he dropped his hands to his sides. But he'd already sent her head spinning by then. He dragged her back to the horse and all but tossed her onto the saddle. Garrett swung up onto Hades and set off without a word. Bemused, she urged her horse alongside Garrett's as they rode away from the Lucky Clover.

As always, the stark beauty of the land awed Miranda, and she asked endless questions about the landscape, the cattle, and the nearby town. Garrett answered her questions, appearing both amused and pleased that she was so enthusiastic and curious.

They arrived at another ranch just before dinner.

Garrett reached up to lift Miranda to the ground. He must have caught the nervous glance Miranda shot at the main house. He ran the backs of his fingers down her cheek and slid his hand around to grasp the back of neck. Tugging her forward, he caught her startled lips in a kiss that sent warmth tingling through her system. As he drew back, he winked at her and took her by the hand.

A tall man stepped from of the bunkhouse and walked across the yard toward them.

"Howdy," he hailed them from across the yard, a welcoming grin on his weathered face.

"Matt," Garrett exclaimed, grinning like a rooster in the hen house.

Taking possession of her hand, Garrett tugged Miranda along behind him, not stopping until they stood before the larger than life owner of the Bar M. She'd thought Garrett was big. She had to crane her neck to look up to Garrett's friend—great mountain of a man that he was.

Salt and pepper gray liberally sprinkled Matt's auburn locks. His face was lined and care-worn. His eyes were the most brilliant shade of green she'd ever seen. They sparkled like jewels in the sun, inviting and warm.

"'Bout time you came around. Antonio said you made it back." He turned a dazzling smile on Miranda. "Welcome to the Bar M, darlin'."

"Matt, this is Miss Miranda Thomas." Garrett drew her forward into the circle of his arms, and heat climbed in her cheeks. She tensed, but Garrett gave her waist a squeeze—the only warning she had before he announced, "My fiancée. Miranda, this is my good friend, Matt Hughes."

"Your fiancée, huh?" Matt grinned from ear to ear. He beamed at Miranda, as though she were the answer to his prayers.

She wanted nothing more than to squirm beneath the weight of his smile. The warm press of Garrett's lips against the side of her neck startled her, and she bit back an embarrassed gasp. A rush of intense heat flooded her cheeks at Garrett's boldness, but Matt's smile was so enthusiastic and warm, she was helpless to do anything but smile back.

"It's nice to meet you, Mr. Hughes."

"Oh, now, we'll have none of that formality here on the Bar M—not between friends. You'll call me Matt." It was an order, not a request. Then Matt pinned Garrett with a stern glance. "It's about damned time, boy. Now maybe my wife will give me some rest and stop frettin' about you over there, all alone." Then his gaze turned shrewd, and he cocked his head to the side. "You wouldn't happen to be relation to that polecat judge in town, now would you?"

"Yes, sir—I mean, yes, Matt," she replied, uneasy. Would this man's welcome be rescinded now?

"Ah, well," Matt clucked. "You can choose your friends, but you surely can't choose your relatives...and I wouldn't be any kind of gentleman to hold *him* against you."

Miranda blinked, at a loss. But the merry twinkle in Matt's eye put her at ease once more.

Garrett's warm laughter teased her ears. He pressed another kiss to her temple and released her. Before she could bolt, he snagged her hand and dragged her along once more. Matt and Garrett talked of ranching on the way into the house. Garrett gave her hand a reassuring squeeze, then released her as soon as they'd entered the house so she was able to trail behind them at her own pace.

Miranda was content to fade into the background, gazing around her in wide-eyed interest. She took in every detail of Matt's home, noting with enthusiastic approval the southwestern flair. She'd never seen this type of décor before, and Garrett's place was stark, devoid of any feminine touches, but she found the more she looked around, the more she liked it.

She followed them at a distance down a long hallway, past the kitchen and through a dining room, their voices muted. As she walked along, she became absorbed with a beautiful work of mosaic tiles, so delicate and intricate that she couldn't resist examining it. The detail was fascinating. As a result of her absorption, she lost track of Matt and Garrett. She looked up, a series of questions heavy on her tongue, and found herself all alone in the hallway.

Glancing around, she strained to hear masculine voices, trying to discern which way they'd gone. She thought she heard murmuring in one of the rooms close by, and so she wandered forward, peering through the open doorway.

She froze in her tracks at the sight that met her eyes as she rounded the corner. Wide-eyed, she whispered in surprise, "Oh, my..."

Her cheeks flamed with embarrassment. She'd stumbled upon a young couple, standing in the middle of one of the many rooms off the hallway, locked in a very passionate, very intimate embrace. In fact, they appeared to be so involved with each other, that they didn't even notice her standing there, staring in open-mouthed shock.

The man was tall, rivaling Matt in height, though not quite as bulky. His wild, sun-kissed hair brushed at his shoulders in disarray. The petite woman in his arms had her fingers sunk deep in the golden mass. From what she could see of his face—buried as it was against the woman's throat—Miranda felt it safe to say he could, by far, be one of the most striking men she'd ever seen.

She couldn't see much of the woman—so wrapped around her the man was—but she seemed small in stature, delicate. Her glossy black hair hung in long, curly waves down her back, reaching all the way to her waistline.

Her very pregnant waistline.

"Let me take you home." The tormented, pleading note in the man's deep, husky voice was unmistakable. His lips cruised up the side of the woman's neck to nuzzle her ear. His hands roved over the curve of her hips, pausing to caress her burgeoning stomach with unmistakable adoration, before moving on to knead her full breasts.

The woman laughed, a light tinkling sound. "You know we can't leave yet. Natalia and Matt are expecting us to stay for dinner."

"God, I'm starving *now*," the brawny sun god growled. "Let me take you upstairs, sweetheart. They won't even notice we're gone. Please, Hope, I need to—"

His heated words disappeared into the petite woman's ear, and Miranda backed from the room as fast as she could. She clapped her hand over her mouth, fighting the urge to laugh aloud. She had a pretty good idea, courtesy of Garrett, what the golden haired Adonis *needed* to do. When she heard the sudden feminine giggle, and the sound of the young couple fumbling their way closer to the door, Miranda scurried down the hall, heat suffusing her cheeks, as she darted through the first door that she came to.

Chapter Twenty

"There you are." Garrett motioned her forward.

Miranda glanced behind her in time to catch a fleeting glimpse of the couple from the other room sneaking past the door like naughty children hoping to escape detection. The golden Adonis was leading his petite, very-pregnant pixie toward the stairs at the end of the hallway with single-minded determination.

Stifling a knowing smile, Miranda turned to face Garrett. He occupied a leather chair, his long legs stretched out before him. The heat in his eyes deepened the color in her cheeks. How could he still look at her that way—as if he'd like to nibble on her from head to toe—after the way they'd spent the better part of the day? Snagging a stray lock, Miranda tucked it back with a loose pin, stopping just shy of fanning her flaming cheeks. When had it gotten so hot?

Movement at the opposite side of the fireplace drew her startled gaze. Matt sat in one of the matching leather, wing chairs flanking the wide fireplace. A dark-haired beauty with soft brown eyes and big dimples perched on the arm of his chair. Matt's arm encircled her waist.

Miranda crossed the room and stood at Garrett's side. She bit back a soft gasp when his arm snaked out, and his hand settled with startling familiarity on her hip, drawing her down, forcing her to either perch on the arm of his chair or sprawl across his lap. The devilish look in his eye said he would welcome either. Shooting him a narrow-eyed warning, she conceded and settled against his side with as much grace as possible. His arm slid around her waist, and he toyed with one of the buttons at her waist, sending butterflies fluttering low in the pit of her stomach.

"Miranda," Matt addressed her. "This little tyrant is my wife, Natalia."

Natalia smiled at Miranda, warm and welcoming. "I'm pleased to meet you, Miranda. Welcome to the Bar M."

"Thank you," Miranda replied, charmed by the warmth in Natalia's gaze. "You have a beautiful home."

The next few moments passed in companionable conversation between the two women, then Matt interrupted, worry clear in his voice as he asked his wife, "I wonder where Ethan and Hope are? I thought they were staying to eat with us. You don't think Hope started feeling poorly, do you?"

Miranda bit her lip and wondered if she should mention the couple she saw sneaking down the hall, then thought better of it. Without a doubt, they'd had other things besides socializing on their minds. And if that dark haired woman felt anything nearly as potent for her golden Adonis as Miranda did for Garrett, the last thing she would appreciate was an interruption.

"Don't fret so," Natalia murmured, tweaking Matt's cheek. "I'm sure they will be along when they are good and ready."

"Speaking of where people are—where's Antonio? I needed to speak with him," Garrett asked, diverting their focus.

"You just missed him." Matt frowned at Garrett. "He left this morning. Ethan sent him up to Harper's Gulch to meet the train. I'm not expecting him back for a good two weeks."

Garrett frowned, puzzled, and asked, "Why did

he go all the way to Harper's Gulch to meet a train? What's wrong with the train in Johnston?"

"You must not have stuck around town long when you came through. Bandits blew up the rail line over to Cranston Gap last week. They've been hittin' the rail lines pretty hard around the area. They're targeting the trains that are running deliveries for the Treasury Department, and the ones carrying payrolls for the forts. Anyway, Ethan sent Antonio up to collect a friend of Hope's—some girl she went to school with. Ethan didn't want to leave Hope for that long, especially now that her time is getting so close."

"Damn," Garrett muttered, a troubled frown settled on his face.

Matt tilted his head, concern wrinkled his brow. "Something I can help you with?"

Garrett hesitated. Taking some unspoken cue, Natalia stood. "I better get dinner on the table." She began to walk toward the door. "Would you like to join me in the kitchen, Miranda? I can make you a cup of tea."

Miranda glanced at Garrett. He smiled at her, giving her a little squeeze and then released her. She followed Natalia back to the kitchen, taking a seat at the large, well-worn table in the middle of the room. Smiling her thanks, she accepted the steaming cup Natalia set before her, and asked, "Can I help you with anything?"

"Thank you, but no. You just enjoy your tea." Natalia poured herself a cup of tea. She peeked beneath the lids of two of the pots that bubbled on the stovetop, and then took a seat across the table from Miranda.

"I was so pleased to hear you and Garrett are engaged," Natalia offered, beaming at Miranda. "I've been so worried about him. He has been so lonely."

Unsure of how to respond, Miranda took a

cautious sip of the steaming liquid. She weighed her words. Sensing that Natalia was a practical woman, she ventured cautiously, "To be honest, I'm not sure that Garrett and I getting married is such a good idea."

Natalia's brows drew together, her brown eyes curious. "Why do you say that? I know you haven't known him long. Is that the reason for your hesitation? Because, I can assure you that Garrett is a fine, honorable man."

"Oh, no," Miranda rushed to explain. "I know he is, believe me, I do. It's not that..."

Natalia waited, her eyes friendly and free of judgment.

"You see... Garrett has very *definite* ideas of what he is looking for in a wife. I am none of those things. That's why I don't understand why he is so determined to marry me," Miranda explained, hoping Natalia could help her make sense of Garrett's irrational behavior.

Natalia stared at Miranda for a moment. She let out a loud, unladylike snort. Smiling, she reached across the table and patted Miranda's hand in sympathy.

"Miranda, I have found that what a man *thinks* he wants, and what a man *needs* are sometimes two very different things, indeed."

She blinked in surprise. Hope flared, wild and unbidden, in her chest.

"You love him."

It was a simple statement of fact. Natalia's voice rang with an unsettling note of certainty, and Miranda felt heat flood her cheeks. She ducked her head, trying desperately to marshal her wits, chagrined that the other woman had been able to see through her so easily.

"Please, do not be embarrassed." Natalia patted her hand. "This is wonderful—"

"Oh, no it's not!" Miranda blurted, then immediately wanted nothing more than to slink off into a corner somewhere and disappear.

Natalia frowned. "But why?"

Miranda hesitated indecisive for a moment, and then she shrugged. The cat was out of the bag, she couldn't very well stuff it back in, now could she. "When love is one-sided it becomes a burden until the one who loves becomes resentful of not having that emotion returned, and the one who is loved sees it as a noose—or worse yet—a weapon."

Natalia stared at Miranda, shaking her head, her gaze sympathetic. "You are too young to be so cynical. I can only imagine at how you came by such a sad opinion. All I can say is that a man who sees love as a noose or a weapon is not man enough to deserve it. Garrett is not such a man."

Miranda sat in silence, sipping tea and contemplating Natalia's words, while Natalia busied herself around the kitchen. She considered her feelings for Garrett, feelings she'd kept hidden away. She took them out now and examined them, then considered the man himself. The tenderness Garrett had shown her, the consideration, and the trust...all were so foreign to what she'd been raised with. Garrett was not like her father—Garrett *wasn't* her father.

Garrett would never be so careless, or as ruthlessly indifferent, if she were to lay her heart at his feet. Duty-bound jerk that he could be sometimes, he was still an honest man, and that's what made all the difference. She had to believe that. She stared at her cup in silence, a small smile curving her lips.

A short while later, a slight, muffled sound came from the doorway, and Miranda turned in her seat to glance behind her. The couple she'd seen locked in that torrid embrace now stood in the doorway, smiling at her. The woman's long inky tresses were mussed, as was the man's golden mane. Her cheeks were flushed with a healthy, radiant glow that Miranda suspected had little to do with her pregnancy.

"You must be Miranda," the beautiful sprite said as she glided forward, welcome glowing in her emerald eyes—eyes identical to Matt's.

She held one hand out to Miranda, the other rested lovingly on her prominent belly. The golden Adonis wasn't far behind. His arms snaked around the sprite's burgeoning waistline, cradling her tenderly from behind. From the twinkle in his eye and the satisfied smile curving his lips, Miranda felt it safe to assume he'd gotten exactly what he'd been *needing*.

For perhaps the first time, Miranda let herself hope. She began to wonder what it would feel like to have Garrett hold her like that—to have Garrett wrap his arms around her very pregnant belly just like that—so in love and acting as if he were holding the world in his arms.

The Adonis smiled his welcome over the woman's shoulder as she continued speaking. "I'm Hope Kincaid—and the man groping me is my husband, Ethan." Hope grinned. "It's nice to meet you."

Standing, Miranda clasped Hope's hand and smiled, intrigued by the couple before her.

Ethan's assessing gaze locked on her face, and he addressed her in a deep, husky voice as he engulfed her hand in his. "I hear congratulations are in order."

A bit more confident after Natalia's bolstering words, Miranda's smile widened. "Thank you. Garrett has told me so much about you both—I feel I already know you."

At that precise moment, Garrett and Matt

joined them. The group fell into companionable conversation. Miranda marveled at how easily Garrett's friends accepted her. As the conversation wound down and the plates were cleared away, Garrett nodded to Matt before he stood, drawing Miranda up beside him.

"Thank you, Natalia. As always, it was a wonderful meal," Garrett praised Matt's wife before excusing them. Turning to Miranda, he took her by the hand and led her outside.

As they wandered across the yard in silence, Miranda absorbed the raw beauty of the land around her. He led her to stand beneath the shade of a tree growing near the meandering, blue-ribbon of a stream. Once there, he tugged her around to face him, slipping his hands around her waist.

Garrett stared into her eyes, a frown shadowing his brow. His quicksilver gaze was troubled. She opened her mouth to ask him what was wrong, but he sealed his lips over hers. The kiss was slow, and incredibly sweet, as he molded her against him, lips to lips—body to body. After several breathless moments, Garrett pulled back, his gaze tender yet determined.

Apprehension settled over her like a blanket of ice. "Garrett, what's wrong?"

He stared long and hard at her. "I'm going after Chambers."

She shook her head, intentionally misunderstanding. "I know you believe you need to. But we can talk about this later when we get back to the—"

Garrett shook his head. His arms locked around her when she made to draw away. "I want you to stay here with Matt and Natalia until I come back. It'll be safer for you here."

"Garrett—"

"They are good people, Miranda. I want you to

trust them, you'll be safe here." His gaze pleaded with her, begging her to trust in him as well. "They will take good care of you, and I'll be back before you know it."

"You're leaving *now*." She pushed the whispered accusation past the lump in her throat.

His expression turned grim, the light in his eyes anguished.

Damn him...if it hurt him so badly to leave her, then why was he going?

"Listen to me, sweetheart," he pleaded, his hands running over her rigid back in long, soothing strokes. "If...if something happens to me—"

"No, Garrett!" Miranda's heart lurched, and she fought to free herself from his embrace, shaking her head. "I won't hear this—"

"Miranda," Garrett barked, refusing to let her out of his arms. Once her struggles waned, and she stared up at him through tears that refused to fall, he spoke again. "If something happens, I left specific orders—papers—I left papers with Matt. Everything is legal and binding. The Lucky Clover, everything I have will all be yours."

"No! No, I don't want it, Garrett, I, I only want..." She shook her head again, thumping his chest with her small fist.

Garrett gripped her shoulders, forcing her to look at him. "I need to know you'll be all right. I need to know that if..." He paused, then lifted a hand to smooth a stray lock of hair behind her ear. Trailing the backs of his fingers over her cheek with immeasurable tenderness, he drew a deep breath. "You could be carrying my child inside you even now. I need to know you'll both be taken care of."

His words gave her pause, and she stilled in his arms. The possibility of a child had never crossed her mind.

Until now.

"If you're so worried about me—or a...a baby— then stay here. Stay! Take care of us yourself, Garrett," she railed at him. "Don't foist me off on strangers. Don't do this, damn you."

Miranda beat her fists against him again. But she knew it was useless. He wouldn't change his mind. She sagged against him for a moment, closing her eyes, and bowing her head in defeat. In despair.

Damn him. Damn him to hell and back for doing this to her.

And damn her own sorry hide for giving her heart away so stupidly.

****

It killed Garrett to leave her like this, but it had to be done. He had no choice. It was the only way to make sure she stayed safe. As long as Chambers was out there, a free man, Garrett and all he held dear would be at risk. He couldn't raise a family that way. He couldn't put Miranda at such risk. But there was more than anger in her eyes. There was fear as well. Garrett could see it, and he knew she wasn't afraid for herself—she was afraid for him. Even if she couldn't say the words, he could see them in her eyes. It meant the world to him. *She* meant the world to him. Garrett's heart swelled.

And his resolve firmed.

He would do everything in his power to make sure she would never have to fear like this again. If he had anything to say about it, she would never be touched by the evil that was out there, lurking in the shadows—waiting for him. He didn't want to live his life worrying about that evil getting anywhere near her, or their children—using them against him...hurting them to hurt him.

"I have to do this, Miranda," he whispered against her temple. "Please, sweetheart, don't cry."

Her back stiffened, and she hissed against his throat, "I never cry."

Tears had begun coursing down her cheeks.

Smiling with grim tenacity, he squeezed her again and nuzzled his nose in her fragrant locks. Then, with unexplainable need, his fingers rose to her hair, and he plucked the pins free, releasing the mass to bounce and unfurl down her back. He groaned with tortured pleasure and let the silk of it smooth against his cheek and flow through his fingers like liquid flames...ethereal, but necessary to his survival.

"Garrett." She pulled back, peering hard into his eyes, her cheeks drenched. "You have to let this go. Do you think your brothers would want you to throw your life away for the sake of vengeance? Do you really think they'd approve of you turning your back on your family because of this need to absolve yourself? They are gone, Garrett. Chasing Chambers down and killing him won't bring your brothers back. They are the ones that died, Garrett. You are still alive—stop refusing to live."

Her words were harsh, deliberate, and they hit their mark with startling accuracy. Yet Garrett refused to be goaded—and he refused to bend. He'd made up his mind. The only way to keep her safe was to eliminate the threat that Chambers presented. To keep Miranda safe, he would do anything—anything at all—including bearding the devil in his own den, and if need be, give up his own life in the process.

Garrett feathered a hand over her cheek, his eyes searching hers for understanding.

"Please, Garrett... Please don't leave me," she whispered, clutching his shirt in frantic fists. Her sapphire eyes glistened with tears, both shed and unshed, in the dying sunlight.

Garrett's breath left him in a long, ragged sigh. Sorrow filled his heart, and yet her plea made no difference. Her fists pounded against his chest in futile fury one last time. He stood firm, unmoving beneath her anger, accepting it as his due.

"Damn you, Garrett. Damn you for the stubborn, mule-headed fool that you are. How could you put revenge before—" She bit her lip. Her eyes flashed bitter cobalt fire, and she shoved at his chest, hitting him with her fists. "I won't wait for you, do you hear me? I won't sit here, pining for you like some moonstruck fool while you chase after ghosts. I'll go out and marry the first man that comes along. I'll...I'll marry Draco. I swear I will! I'll have Draco's babies, and I'll—"

Those last words garnered a reaction out of him, at last—but not quite the reaction she wanted, he was sure. He drew her hard against him and sealed his lips to hers before she could dig the knife in any deeper. He kissed her hard and long, shredding her resistance until she clung to him and returned his kisses with equal fervor. Finally, when he couldn't take any more or run the risk of ravishing her right there in broad daylight by the stream, he tore his mouth from hers and nipped kisses along her jaw until his teeth snagged her earlobe with a slight sting.

"You will *never* marry Draco, do you hear me? You'll never marry anyone but me. The only babies that you will grow round with are *mine*," Garrett growled into her ear. "You marry another man, and you will forfeit his life. I swear I will come back for you—and *no* man will stand in my way."

His lips found hers once more, but the kiss was tender, so contrary to the tensile strength in his body as his arms held her caged against him. Garrett released her and stepped back. His gaze swept boldly, proprietarily down the length of her, then settled on her fiery tresses as they fluttered in the slight breeze, committing every detail to memory—just in case.

Without another word, he turned on his heel and strode away.

****

Miranda stared after him, wide-eyed and shaking. She reached out a trembling hand, groping behind her until she felt the rough bark of the tree trunk beneath her palm. On knees that had turned liquid, Miranda backed up until she could lean against the tree, her arms wrapped around her middle, trying desperately to contain the grief that threatened to spill out of her.

She could go after him and tell him then—tell him that she loved him. She could beg him not to go, plead with him not to leave her.

In the end, she couldn't do it. After all, where had pleading gotten her in the past? She wouldn't beg, she'd never lower herself like that again. She couldn't tell him she loved him and give him the power those words held. She refused to use those words to try to hold on to him when she knew it wouldn't be enough to make him stay. The steady thud of a horse's hooves drew her attention.

When she realized Garrett had returned to her side, she forced her body to move until she stood, proud and tall before him. Her chin tilted in defiance, her teeth gritted against the urge to plead once more. Her eyes were gritty, burning with restrained tears.

Garrett stared, his expression filled with longing and regret. But he didn't dismount. Instead, he remained in the saddle, tightened his hands on the reins, holding himself rigid and unyielding. "Miranda…"

She lifted her chin and narrowed her eyes. No, she wouldn't plead. She might never be whole again, but she wouldn't beg.

"Before I go…there's one more thing you need to know." He drew a deep breath, the look on his face suddenly intense and penetrating. "I love you."

His words wrung a startled gasp from her lips.

Not giving her a chance to respond, Garrett wheeled Hades around and urged his horse into a full out gallop, leaving Miranda to stare after him in slack-jawed, wide-eyed wonder.

Chapter Twenty-One

Miranda stepped from the dim interior of the mercantile out into the warm, late afternoon sunshine and drew a deep breath. Matt's booming voice echoed throughout the interior of the building as he haggled good-naturedly with Mrs. Weston, the proprietress. She could still hear Natalia, coaxing and benevolent, as she interceded with a compromise, and Miranda smiled. Garrett had been gone almost a full week, and in that time she'd grown accustomed to—and more than a little fond of—Matt and Natalia. Ethan and Hope, as well.

Yet there was still a gaping hole in her life—the hole where Garrett should be.

She missed him.

She could admit that to herself at least, if to no one else. However, she was also very upset with him. What a horrible thing to do to her. To blurt out that he loved her—to throw it at her like that, and then ride away—was reprehensible. He hadn't given her a chance to respond.

He'd just...ridden away.

Oh yes, she'd tell him what she thought of his timing for such a profound announcement...as well as his delivery. Just as soon as he came back.

Fear pushed up, choking her. *Where was he? Was he safe? Was he hurt? Was he—*

No! She couldn't go there, couldn't face that possibility.

Instead, she squared her shoulders and let her gaze skate down the street. The town was quite lovely, and thriving. Her eyes skimmed over the tidy face of the bank, the clean brick façade of the hotel, the front of the busy telegram office. Her wide-eyed stare swerved back to the hotel—and the dark figure lounging with insolent negligence against one of the hitching posts in front of the building.

The sun glinted off the silver studs on his hatband. His black duster was thrust back over his hips, revealing a dangerous array of weaponry. Long golden hair lifted in the breeze behind him, and icy-blue eyes rested solely on her.

Darting a swift glance behind her, she inclined her head at Draco and hurried across the boardwalk. She cleared the side of the building, ducking into the small space between the mercantile and the livery. Miranda peered around the corner before pressing back against the wall, relieved to see Draco had understood her silent request.

A few moments later, he joined her in the narrow alleyway. Taking her by the hand, he tugged her farther into the shadows, motioning her to silence until they were far enough from the street for his comfort. He turned to face her, his eyes lit on her face with hungry interest.

"Have you come to your senses, my love?" His voice was a low rumble. He pressed her knuckles to his lips for a brief kiss, then he released her hand to caress her face, the backs of his fingers skimmed her cheek in a gentle, affectionate caress.

She captured his wrist and, gently but firmly, pushed his hand away. "No, Draco. I have not changed my mind. I'm not the woman for you. But I do need to talk to you."

Draco grinned and continued to toy with her hand, waiting patiently for her to go on.

"I need to ask you some questions." She tried her best to ignore the tiny circles he traced on her palm. "I want you to tell me how you know Garrett."

Her question took Draco by surprise. The

delicate circles ceased, his body tensed, and his eyes darted down both ends of the alley. Then his gaze settled back on her face, and his eyes were shuttered, his expression guarded.

"What makes you think I know McCabe?"

"Give me some credit," she said, lifting a brow as she waited.

His expression grew shuttered. "What did he tell you?"

"I'm asking you."

Giving a slight smile, Draco leaned closer. "Is McCabe keeping secrets from you, my love? Because if you were mine…" He ducked his head, his gaze intent on her lips.

She was ready for him this time, swiftly inserting her hand between their faces. His lips met her palm.

"Stop it, Draco." She cut him off, pushing at his face while wriggling out of his grasp.

Undaunted, Draco captured her wrist and covered her palm with hot little licks and tiny nips. Miranda yanked her hand away, glaring her displeasure. The man was incorrigible.

"I want the truth, Draco. There's more to you than this," Miranda waved carelessly from the top of his black hat to the tip of his black boots, "this persona you're trying so hard to wear. You know Garrett…somehow, and I *know* you're not nearly so heartless and criminal as you would have others believe. You're more than a simple outlaw—"

Draco's large hand covered her mouth, muffling her words. His eyes darted to the street yet again, as though he feared discovery. He glared at her, hissing between clenched teeth, "Shhh."

She narrowed her eyes at him, shaking his hand loose, demanding, "Who are you?"

"Woman, keep your voice down. I've worked too long and too hard to have you stir up trouble now," he cautioned. "You just need to back off. Let McCabe and—"

Draco's body jerked, his eyes rolled back in his head, and he crumpled to a heap at her feet.

She let out a startled gasp, trying her best to break his fall. Nevertheless, Draco was a large man, and he dropped like a ton of bricks. She did her best to cradle him, her hands bracing his head until it rested on the ground. When she lifted her hand away from the back of Draco's head, her confused eyes rounded in shock as she stared at the smear of blood on her palm. Lifting her startled eyes, she came face to face with the business end of a Colt.

"That's right, missy. Stand up and step over here. Nice and easy like," a sinister voice addressed her from the shadows.

Her worried gaze flicked back to Draco's pale face. For a split second, she considered the gun on Draco's hip. Could she get it clear of his holster in time?

What would she do with it if she did?

As if reading her thoughts, the dark voice drawled. "Don't even think about it. I'd just have to shoot you, and that'd make my employer real upset. You see, missy, he has something extra special planned for you..."

That promise sent a chill skating down her spine. The only chance she had was to get back to the street. Miranda hesitated for a moment, guilt-ridden. Leaving Draco, unconscious and injured, at the mercy of this man felt heartless, but she couldn't help him like this. She had to try to get help.

Glancing one last time at Draco, praying he'd be okay, she bolted.

Miranda managed to take four long strides down the alley, sucked in a deep breath to shout for help, and then the veil of darkness descended before her eyes on a blast of pain against the back of her skull.

Her scream died away in a soundless whoosh as she, too, crumpled to the ground in a haze of darkness.

****

Garrett cursed a vicious streak as he tore away from the Bar M. Hades hooves stirred up a storm cloud of dust behind them. Dread, cold and hard, fisted in his gut as he headed toward town. Something was horribly wrong. He just knew it. Enrique said Matt, Natalia, and Miranda should have been back hours ago. What was keeping them?

Jesus, Mary, and Joseph...please, please let her be all right...

He'd ridden for close to a week, tracking and backtracking Chambers' long and winding trail—a trail that had led, unerringly, straight back to Johnston. The trail would grow cold, only to resurface—more than once. Words he'd heard long ago floated in his mind, something Nick's superior was fond of saying—*When it comes to thieves and outlaws, there's no such thing as coincidence.* That was the bottom line.

All these conveniently placed clues were just too much of a coincidence.

The last clue had set his teeth on edge. He'd cornered one of Chambers' hirelings and managed to extract a tidbit of information that, at first, hadn't made much sense. The hireling had made reference to a crooked 'hanging judge' getting his due—doing a jig at the end of his own rope.

Chambers had been leading him on a wild goose chase, the same as Chambers had done countless times before with Nick. He finally realized his mistake. He'd left everything that mattered to him back at the Bar M, and he wasn't there to protect her.

He'd ridden off and left her because he felt he had to satisfy some twisted need for vengeance and absolution. Miranda had been right in accusing him of that, as well as not truly living. He'd been too afraid to live, too afraid of having it all taken away again. Guilt had also been a motivating factor. He was alive, and his brothers were dead.

Yes, Miranda had been right about so many things, including the fact that Nick and Eddie wouldn't have wanted this half-life for him.

Miranda was more important than some vendetta, and he intended to tell her that...just as soon as he found her. He'd never leave her side again. He'd woo her, as Antonio suggested. He'd win her heart and make her love him. He'd be the most devoted husband a woman could ever ask for. He just prayed that his instincts were wrong.

He prayed with all his heart that Chambers hadn't gotten to her first.

Garrett spied Matt and Natalia standing in the middle of the boardwalk, in front of the jail, deep in conversation with the sheriff. His heart dropped to his stomach when he realized Miranda was nowhere in sight. He urged his mount down the street, so focused on the couple speaking to the sheriff that he almost missed the shadow weaving drunkenly from the alley beside the mercantile.

He vaulted from the saddle and hit the ground running. Before his quarry could blink, he had Draco by the throat, shoving him back against the side of the building.

Garrett growled, "Where is she?"

Draco shoved him back, but his efforts were less forceful than Garrett expected, giving Garrett his first solid clue something was wrong. Easing up on his grip, but not his tone, Garrett demanded once more, "Where the hell is she—*Damian*?"

"I don't know, damn it. And don't call me that," Draco began, only to have Garrett shove him up against the building once again.

Draco's head bounced against the wooden

planks. He swore, viciously, giving Garrett a more forceful shove than he'd been able to muster before, and he snarled, "Damn it, I don't know. I was talking to her—and then someone must have snuck up on me and hit me from behind. The next thing I know, I'm waking up with a mouthful of dirt, Miranda's gone, and it's dark. I just came to a few minutes ago."

Garrett eased up on his hold a bit more, but he pressed the questions, "How long have you been out?"

"Jesus, I don't know—a couple hours, maybe." Draco let out a sharp hiss as he tested the back of his head.

Garrett's hands tightened on Draco's duster. "What the hell were you doing back there with *my woman* in the first place?"

"Man, I realize you're upset—but you better think twice about slamming me up against that building again. I've had about all I'm gonna take, even from you, McCabe," Draco warned, his voice suddenly soft and deadly menacing. "You want to point fingers—where the hell were you? Because you sure as hell weren't taking care of her, now were you? Maybe you deserve to have her stolen away."

Garrett snarled a deep, guttural sound, and his fists tightened on Draco's duster for a tense moment, then guilt flashed through him, poisonous and razor sharp, and he closed his eyes in self-condemnation. He heaved a weary sigh, released Draco, and stepped back.

"We'll get her back, but now is not the time to let jealousy take over," Draco lectured him.

Garrett turned a tormented stare to Draco. "He has her, doesn't he?"

"Yeah, that's my guess." Grim, Draco frowned and pushed away from the building. "But he wants you. As long as he thinks he can use her as leverage, she's safe—or as safe as she can be, given the circumstances."

"He has to be holed up around here, someplace close by," Garrett thought aloud.

"From what little I've been able to learn, he's got a real grudge against you for the way you took his gang out. He's bent on revenge—the more painful the better," Draco informed him. "Aside from Miranda, how else could he hurt you? He's fixated on making you suffer as much as possible before he finishes you off."

Garrett's face paled, and he staggered back a step, as if Draco had punched him. "Oh, hell..."

Without another word, without waiting to see whether Draco would follow or not, Garrett wheeled around and raced back to Hades. In a flash, he was back in the saddle and racing out of town once more.

****

When Miranda came to, she was lying on the sofa in Garrett's house. The scent of Garrett surrounded her and helped to ease the ache that pounded in her temples. Warmth rushed through her, stirring the shadow of a smile on her lips.

Wait...how had she gotten here? She was staying with Matt and Natalia...

Draco... The alley...

Then the rest of it came rushing back.

Panic, bitter and merciless, swamped her. Miranda squinted one eye open, and then the other, blinking away the blurry edges of her vision. The delicate needlepoint still hung with such loving care over Garrett's mantel. The books were still on the shelf. Everything was as it had been the day Garrett had taken her to Matt's place...the day he'd *left* her there.

A bull of a man sat in Garrett's chair beside the cold fireplace.

He must have been considered handsome at one

point in time. But now—with his hideously scarred face, and the chilling malice in his eyes—the very sight of him sent apprehensive tremors racing through her. Inch by inch, she wiggled herself up into a sitting position, cursing the abrasive rope that bound her wrists and ankles. She took one look at the wintery detachment in his eyes, and Miranda knew she was in serious trouble.

Stiffening her spine, lifting her chin in rebellion, she feigned confidence she did not feel, refusing to let him see how terrified she was. "Who are you? What do you want?"

She didn't need him to answer. She already knew who he was, or could well guess. And she couldn't care less what excuses he came up with. But she did need time to regroup. Time to work her bindings loose.

Time to figure out how to get herself out of this mess.

"Cut right to the chase, don't you, my dear?" He grinned—a grin that did not reach his eyes—and nodded, a flash of reluctant approval flickered in his steady regard as he let his gaze sweep over the open defiance in her face. "That's just as well. I have neither the time nor the patience for female histrionics."

Miranda's eyes narrowed in anger at his provoking comment, but she bit the inside of her lip, refusing to rise to the bait. She was, however, determined to get him talking, to keep him talking. Maybe she could get him to reveal something— anything. Most important, she needed to know if he'd harmed Garrett somehow.

If so, she had to figure out a way to get free and help him. At the very least, she told herself, if she kept this villain talking long enough, maybe someone would come along and help *her*. Thin and uncertain as those hopes were, they seemed to be pinned on Draco. He was the only one who would have any clue as to what had happened to her. That was—if whoever had abducted her hadn't finished him off already.

Lord, what a pickle.

Part of her cursed Garrett for leaving her to face this alone. And yet, she was wildly thankful he was nowhere near here. She prayed he was out of harm's way—at least for the time being. Unfortunately, her only hope lay unconscious and bleeding in the back of an alley. She glanced ruefully at the ceiling for a moment. Someone up there must be having a real good laugh about her and her infernal curiosity right now.

"I suppose it won't hurt to answer your questions." He eyed her restraints, and a flash of something evil lurked in his eyes, some macabre secret he couldn't wait to share. "I'm Clint Chambers, my dear." He nodded at her, dripping sophistication and charm. "And as to what I want..." His cool façade melted away, and he snarled, "I want McCabe *dead.*"

"Garrett's not here." Miranda tried to sound as rational and as calm as she could—all things considered. "I don't have any idea how long he'll be gone. He could be gone weeks..."

Chambers' chilly, knowing smile sent ice coursing through her veins. "Oh, something tells me he won't be all that long."

Changing tactics, she stared at him like a bug, like a speck of dust beneath her fingernail. "You're wasting your time if you think to use me as bait. I'm nothing more than a burden to Garrett—an assignment. He'd be glad to be rid of me."

Her last conversation with Garrett came back to her, all the horrid things she'd said to him. She had to fight to keep her lower lip from trembling, ashamed of herself for making those baseless threats, and even more ashamed for being a coward. How could she have kept the truth of her feelings from him?

More than likely, he'd reconsidered his brash declaration and was already regretting asking her to marry him even now.

"You underestimate your charms, my dear," Chambers praised her, cutting into her thoughts with an all-too-knowing grin that left her feeling exposed and revolted. "Oh, yes. Garrett will come for *you*. The fact that you are who you are simply makes my revenge all the sweeter."

Miranda's eyes narrowed in confusion. "What are you talking about?"

"I am talking about the fact that not only will Garrett suffer—so will that crooked judge you call an uncle. That bastard hung every one of my men, at least the ones Garrett didn't shoot outright. Now it's time he got a little of his own," he growled, his eyes sparkling with far more glee than Miranda felt sane. A person this far-gone in seeking vengeance was simply too far gone to reason with.

She desperately wanted to ask what Chambers was planning, wanted to know what fate she faced, but the words stuck in her throat. Whether he'd read the fearful curiosity in her eyes, or he just took pleasure in torturing a helpless female, Chambers leaned forward, bracing his elbows on his knees.

"You think me crazy, I can see it in your eyes," he drawled, seeming to regain the cold aloofness he'd displayed earlier. Leaning back in his chair, he leveled calculating, emotionless eyes on her and let the corners of his mouth twist up in a hideous imitation of a smile.

Miranda caught herself drawing back, pushing back against the cushions of the sofa, in a bid to put as much space as possible between her and the hulking madman before her. She drew a steadying breath as she forced herself to remain motionless.

"These scars you see all over my face were compliments of your precious Marshal McCabe," Chambers hissed. His hatred for Garrett cracked the calm façade he tried to hide his insanity behind. "He'll come for you. When he does, he's going to have to choose. Either he saves you and loses his chance to see justice for his brothers, or he gets the chance he's been waiting for—the chance to capture me— and he loses you in the process."

Miranda couldn't bite back the shocked gasp. Chambers' grin grew until he leered at her, evil to the bone, giving her another glimpse of the madness within.

His cold gaze ran over her once more. "I wonder which he'll choose?" He gave an indifferent shrug, adding, "Not that it matters all that much. Either way, you both die."

As if tired of their discussion, he stood and approached her, drawing a length of material from his pocket. This time Miranda couldn't fight the urge to scoot away.

"You're wrong," she denied. "He won't come."

Even as she spoke the words, she knew them for the lie that they were. Garrett would come, if for no other reason than that was who Garrett was, honorable to the last. Whether it was the catalyst of Chambers being here—within reach at last—or the threat to her own life, Garrett would come. He'd said he loved her.

God help her—God help them both—he would come for her.

Her gaze darted around the room, searching for something—anything—to help her stop this lunatic before he could do any more damage. Bound as she was, there was nothing she could do. The last thing Miranda saw before he drew the rolled material across her eyes was the satisfied, confident smile on

Chambers' deformed face.

Miranda wasn't sure how long she sat on the sofa, but the minutes stretched into an eternity as she waited for she knew not what. It was true what they say. When one of your senses is taken away, the others heighten. Unable to see, she strained with every other part of her body, trying to determine what was going on around her. At first eerie silence met her ears, the familiar scent of Garrett lingered on the sofa, and the cool evening air brushed her skin.

Then something pricked at her ears, something peculiar and unnatural, a gurgling, like liquid being poured from a container, liquid splashed and splattered somewhere in the distance, Garrett's bedroom perhaps. The sound seemed to move down the hall and into the kitchen. As the sound drew closer, a strange and unpleasant odor assaulted her nose, cloying and oily. It hit her in the back of the throat and made terror coil deep in her stomach.

Kerosene.

Panic closed her throat.

No, this couldn't be happening. She was mistaken—it had to be something else. She desperately tried to convince herself she was wrong, even as the fumes made her gag.

He couldn't mean to...

Like the crack of thunder, an evil chuckle from somewhere near the door jolted her. Then the faint scratch, the quiet whoosh, and the unmistakable crackle and hiss as the flames took hold, chilled her to the bone.

Chapter Twenty-Two

Miranda leaned back and then rolled to the floor, landing on her side with a small grunt. She fought with her restraints until the warm trickle of blood dampened her wrists. But the rough rope wouldn't loosen. She wiggled and shimmed around the edge of the low table in front of the couch, striking her head hard on the leg in the process. Still she kept moving, trying to get to the door.

If she could just make it to the door, she might be able to get free. As she cleared the end of the sofa, she scooted on her hands and bottom, cursing Chambers for binding her hands behind her back. The noxious cloud of smoke descended, sucking the air from the room. She dragged in panicked gulps of air while she still could.

In just a few short minutes, the slow and steady crackle had risen to a hungry roar. Even beneath the blindfold, the acrid smoke stung her eyes, causing tears to well. Smoke burned her nose and seared her throat, making the simple effort of breathing a monumental task in and of itself. Knowing there would be no more furniture between her and the doorway, she lay back and began rolling toward the door.

Then that other sense kicked in—the sense of touch. Miranda stopped rolling. A solid wall of heat intensified the closer she got to the door.

Cursing the blindfold, she rubbed the side of her face on the floor, trying in vain to loosen the material enough to gain even the tiniest sliver of sight. It wouldn't budge, and all she succeeded in

301

doing was giving herself a streak of floor-burn on her cheek. Frustrated, she rolled back until she bumped into the couch. Her mind raced. What now?

****

Garrett drew rein and prepared to vault from Hades' back. Draco drew up beside him and grabbed his arm, his warning stare locked on the treacherous shadows near the house. Garrett lashed out, batting Draco's hand away. Nothing would keep him from going to Miranda. Damn it, she needed him. How dare Draco try to stop him?

Draco palmed his gun, turning his icy, discerning stare to the shadows near the stables. "It's a trap."

"She's in there, damn it," Garrett hissed. "I know it. I can feel it."

A low string of curses tumbled from the undercover agent's lips. "Keep low, I'll cover you."

They leaped to the ground in unison. Garrett crouched and made a fast beeline to the front door, leaving Draco hunkered down in a small grove of trees near the stables, swearing beneath his breath.

****

To her left, the front door crashed in, and Garrett's frantic voice called out, "Miranda…"

She twisted around at the sound, straining to find her voice in her raw throat.

"Garrett," she croaked, swallowed, and forced the sound louder. Though she reeled beneath the weight of the fear for her own safety, an even greater fear for Garrett pushed her, desperate to make him hear and obey. "Garrett, no…a trap… Get out of here…"

Those first, unmistakable cracks of gunfire from somewhere outside made Miranda yelp and jump. Terror hit her like a fist, knocking the wind from her burning lungs. Fearing the worst, she screamed, "*Garrett…*"

Nearby, Garrett let out a vicious curse. The sound of scuffling wafted to her over the crackle of the fire. A loud thud echoed in the room. She cursed the blindfold.

Where was he?

What had happened?

Locked in a sightless world of sound and smell and touch, Miranda whipped her head back and forth, her heart lodged in her throat making it impossible to find her voice. Smoke choked the air around her. The hiss and crackle of the flames hurt her ears, the intense heat made the sweat dry before it could roll down her skin.

Another shot rang out, closer this time—inside the room—and Miranda jumped again, whimpering, frightened beyond a more substantial sound. The world exploded with sound. A hail of gunfire erupted, and Miranda plastered herself against the back of the sofa, trapped between the blistering, greedy blaze surrounding her and the promise of cold oblivion via a shower of bullets should she manage to escape the fire.

****

Garrett cleared the doorway. A dark shadow hurtled out of the night, crashing into him, driving him into the blaze. He rolled through the flames, grappling with the shadow, grunting at the impact of an elbow in his midsection. The skin on his arm sizzled as the fire took hold of his shirt, only to be snuffed out on the next roll.

Garrett managed to wrestle his arm free, drew his gun, and thrust the barrel into the soft midsection of his assailant, firing before either of them had a chance to draw another breath. Pushing the now motionless shadow off him, he struggled to his knees, blinking aside the moisture the acrid smoke wrung from his eyes. His frantic gaze swept over the hazy room until he found her, huddled in a small ball on the floor beside the sofa.

A rush of wild emotion swelled within him at the sight of her—his woman—terrified, and in so much danger. Sucking in a deep, burning breath, Garrett surged to his feet, and hurled himself through the flames to her side.

Driven by the urge to feel her against him—needing to reassure himself she was still alive—he wrapped his arms around her and crushed her to his chest. Sobbing, Miranda stiffened and tried to pull away, gasping great, labored gusts of breath.

"Garrett! *Garrett...*" Miranda screamed, struggling like a madwoman.

"Miranda, sweetheart," Garrett crooned against her ear. "Shhh, it's me."

She collapsed against him, mumbling unintelligible words against his chest, sobbing. Garrett squeezed her shoulders, offering a brief moment of comfort, then he pushed her back. Loosening the blindfold, he drew it away from her face, flinging it behind him into the flames. He locked her face between his hands and lowered his mouth to hers in a grateful kiss filled with everything in his heart. Breaking the kiss, drawing his knife, he sliced through her restraints. As soon as her hands and feet were free, Garrett helped her to stand up.

Her legs wobbled beneath her, and he braced an arm around her waist. His heart lodged in his throat. *Dear God, what had that bastard done to her?*

"Come on, sweetheart," he urged, his voice hoarse from smoke and emotion. "We have to get out of here."

Outside the walls, the steady barrage of gunfire still cracked through the night. Miranda's breathing was ragged, labored. Her gaze scanned the room. Her terror must have increased tenfold as she saw the magnitude of the blaze. She'd begun to shake like a leaf. Maybe he should have left her blindfolded, at least until he'd gotten her outside.

Reaching back, Garrett grabbed the throw from the back of the sofa and tossed it over Miranda's head and shoulders in an attempt to protect her from the worst of the flames. The thick beams supporting the roof creaked and groaned. Tossing her over his shoulder, he dashed for the door, ignoring the flames swirling around his boots, licking at his legs. Garrett's smoking boots had no more than cleared the front porch, when the roof collapsed, sending sparks shooting into the air to rain down on them. The flames reached high into the midnight sky, and an eerie glow lit the yard.

Garrett set her on her feet and pushed her down to crouch on the ground behind him, protecting her with his body as bullets flew around them, kicking up dust and smashing into the destruction of Garrett's home. She tugged the blanket from her head, panting. In the shadows in the distance, a figure that blended all too well with the night, clad head to toe in black—an angel of death—crouched low to the ground half-concealed behind a tree.

The glare of the fire reflected on the barrel of a gun moments before another crack rent the air. Miranda whipped her head around in time to see a man near the stables clutch his chest and fall to the ground where he lay motionless. Swearing, Garrett urged her up once again. Using his body as her shield, he pushed her across the yard into the shadows near Draco, gunfire punctuating each step.

Suddenly, Miranda cried out, staggering a step to the side. His blood turned to ice in his veins. Had she been hit? Yanking her ahead of him, he swung her around the trunk of a huge oak and pinned her there against the bark with his body. Her arms crept around his waist, and she buried her face in his shirt, trembling and unnaturally silent. Even as he squeezed off another shot around the side of the tree, his free hand slid up along her nape. His fingers dove into her hair. His palm cupped the back of her head, pressing her against him.

"Are you all right?"

As he asked the question, his hand skimmed back down the side of her neck. She flinched and his hand came away, sticky with blood. The bottom of his stomach dropped away.

"Miranda," Garrett exclaimed, grabbing her roughly by the shoulders, his gun dangled uselessly from his fingers. "Are you all right? Sweet Christ, you're bleeding, damn it. Talk to me!"

"I'm all right. It's just a scratch."

A form emerged from the darkness nearby. Draco prowled closer, his steady gaze on the now silent shadows near the barn. Ignoring him, Garrett stared into her eyes for a moment, then he lowered his head. His lips settled on hers, his tongue plunged into her mouth urgently at first, but then the kiss became a slow, savoring caress. Longing and fear choked him. He knew what he had to do. He also knew he might not survive.

How could he walk away from the only thing in his life that mattered...again. But, to protect her, how could he not?

His happiness. Or her safety.

There was no choice. Absolutely none.

With regret weighing heavily upon him, he straightened and softly caressed her cheek. He offered her a sad smile, already mourning what could have been.

Miranda's eyes flared with understanding, and she reached up to cradle his face in her hands. "No! Garrett, no! Please, don't—"

"I have to, Miranda. I have to see this finished."

A fresh barrage of shots exploded in the night,

ricocheting off trees, kicking up dirt. Men were out there, beyond the darkness, wounded and dying...dead, and the only thing he could hear was the plea in her voice, the only thing he could see was the fear and the pain in her beautiful eyes.

"I love you, Garrett." Miranda blinked the glassy sheen from her eyes.

His eyes widened, his nostrils flared with a savagely indrawn breath. His surprise quickly turned grim, and his resolve hardened. "I love you, too."

Garrett pressed his lips to hers in one last, hard kiss before he called over his shoulder, "Damian."

Miranda blinked up at Garrett, clearly confused.

In a flash, the tall, handsome bandit was at Garrett's side, firing his weapon into the darkness, seemingly unaffected by the bodies dropping beneath his effortless, deadly accuracy.

"Take her—get her out of here." Garrett pushed Miranda's resistant form into the bandit's arms. He met Draco's stare through the darkness. Stormy-gray to icy-blue. An unspoken message passed between them.

Miranda's heart froze in her chest.

"Keep her safe." Garrett growled. His voice was raw and miserable. "Deserve her."

With that, he disappeared into the night, fading into the shadows.

"No!" Miranda struggled in Draco's gentle but unyielding grip, fighting to follow Garrett. When she realized Draco intended to carry out Garrett's order, she turned wide, pleading eyes to him. "Don't leave him, Draco. He needs your help—you know he does!"

Draco let out a foul curse, his gaze shifting to the darkness where Garrett had disappeared. Fear roiled through her. Not fear for herself. It was all for Garrett. She stood before Draco, tall and proud, soot-covered blistered by fire, and bloodied...and she

307

pleaded with him to go after Garrett—to save Garrett. "Please, Draco...go after him. Please..."

"Aw, hell," he hissed, and Miranda gripped his hands, grateful to the marrow of her bones.

Resigned, he nodded, and she launched herself into his arms. Wrapping her arms around his neck, Miranda squeezed him tight in a desperate hug. She heard him grumbling to himself about having left his common sense back in that damned alley, and she knew she'd won. Drawing back, she paused long enough to drop a chaste, thankful kiss on his cheek.

"Go," she urged. "Please, Draco..."

"You're gonna owe me a better kiss than that, darlin'." Then he narrowed his eyes at her and replied in a stern tone, "I'll go...only if you swear to me you'll stay right here. Don't even think about following. Stay down and stay out of sight. I don't want to have to watch over my shoulder to make sure you're safe. If anything happens to you..." he paused, staring down at her with an odd expression on his face, and he then finished, "McCabe will kill me."

"I swear," she vowed, nodding agreement as he pushed her back to crouch in the shadow of the tree. She'd agree to just about anything right now to secure aid for Garrett.

Draco reached behind him, beneath his black duster, and pulled another gun from his waistband. Even distracted by her fear for Garrett's safety, she couldn't help marvel at the walking arsenal that was Draco. Handing the weapon to her, Draco advised, "Don't shoot us when we come back."

She accepted the gun, though she had serious reservations about how much good it would do her, having never fired one before. She'd never even held one in her hand. But she wasn't about to confide that to him. He might change his mind. "Hurry, Draco. Help him."

Then, as he was turning away, she called out, "Draco..."

He paused, glancing down at her, and she smiled up at him, cautioning tremulously, "You be careful, too. I don't want anything to happen to you, either."

One corner of Draco's mouth curled up in a cocky, self-assured grin, and he tapped the brim of his black hat. In less than a moment, he, too, disappeared into the shadows, leaving her behind, gripping his gun for dear life and praying for all she was worth.

Time spun out, a hideous torture of tense waiting while the distant sound of gunfire shattered the night. Then, worse than the gunfire, eerie silence descended in the darkness, and her already tense body went rigid as a bowstring, waiting for Garrett and Draco to return.

The crack of a twig nearby made her jump. Her heart hammered at the rustle of the grass. Even the wind blowing through the branches above her head frazzled her nerves. She drew her skirts close, tucking them around her before she turned to the side and peered around the side of the tree.

The glow of the fire washing the night sky in hues of orange and gold brought tears to her eyes. *Garrett's home...* The yard—empty now but for the dark mounds of fallen, lifeless bodies that littered the ground—was silent as a cemetery. The shadows around the stables were motionless—lifeless. She couldn't find Garrett. She couldn't see Draco.

Where were they? Had they been shot?

Were they...

No, she couldn't think that way. They were both fine.

They had to be.

She couldn't even begin to imagine the energetic, irreverent Draco injured, or—heaven forbid—dead. And the mere thought of Garrett, lying out there in the dark, bleeding, or maybe even...

Icy panic clutched her heart, and a wave of dizzy nausea washed over her. Life without Garrett...well, she wasn't even willing to consider it.

Drawing a steadying breath, she turned back around to lean against the tree trunk, and her eyes widened in shock. She sucked in a sharp breath of horror and stared up into the disfigured, leering face of Clint Chambers.

Chapter Twenty-Three

Miranda hoisted the gun from her lap with shaking hands, leveling it as best she could at the man who'd just tried to kill her—the man who'd made Garrett's life a living hell for the last six years.

"Don't come any closer," she warned, inwardly cursing her unsteady voice. "I'll shoot!"

"You don't have what it takes," Chambers sneered, taking a menacing step forward.

She braced herself against the tree and pushed herself to her feet, all the while the gun remained trained on Chambers' barrel of a chest.

"Give me the gun," he snarled, holding his hand out, taking another step forward.

"I said don't move!"

Covering the distance between them in a few short strides, he reached for her. She slammed herself backward as she tried to elude his grasp, drawn up short by the tree at her back. Then Chambers smiled—the very essence of evil. Miranda's eyes narrowed. She would not cower. She would not show this bastard her fear.

Her hatred, though, that he *could* have.

His expression turned murderous. He charged. She pulled the trigger.

The sound of that single shot seemed to ring through the stillness louder than all the previous shots combined. Her eyes widened in shock when crimson blossomed high on Chambers' shirt near his shoulder. He staggered to a halt, appearing more stunned by the fact she'd actually shot him than by the pain the injury must have caused. His face turned a mottled red, and black rage filled his eyes.

"Bitch!" Chambers roared, lunging at her like a charging bull.

He knocked the gun from her hands with a brutal downward blow of his massive fist to her forearms. Then he backhanded her with another vicious roar. Pain exploded in her cheek. She fell to her hands and knees, her head spinning. Darkness swirled around her, but she fought off the shadows, refusing to faint before this monster. She spit the metallic taste of blood from her mouth. The cut on the inside of her cheek stung.

Defiance forced her back to her feet to face him. She glared at him as she drew the back of her hand slowly over her bloodied mouth. Her cheek throbbed. Even the sight of Draco's gun, now in Chambers' beefy hand, couldn't dim her anger.

All the pain this man had caused...the lives he'd taken and the damage he'd willfully caused Garrett...pushed her over the edge, made her reckless. Her fingers curled; her hands fisted at her sides. She opened her mouth, venomous words pooled on the tip of her tongue. Just as she drew breath to let them fly, the sound of running feet knocked the wind from her sails.

Garrett...

Panic shredded her nerves. Her mind raced. She couldn't let this man hurt Garrett again.

An evil grin stretched his marred features as Chambers shifted the gun, aiming for the darkened yard and the sound of the approaching footsteps. The sight of Garrett dashing into harm's way filled Miranda with a terror that being tied up inside the flaming ranch house hadn't even come close to touching.

With a cry born of rage and fear, Miranda threw herself at Chambers, knocking the arm that held the gun to the side. The gun discharged into the ground, but Chambers snagged a handful of her streaming hair and he jerked, spinning her around, pulling her in front of him, using her body as his shield. Burning pain seared her scalp. She gasped, clawing at his hand.

Unforgiving iron pressed against Miranda's temple, and he gave her hair a ruthless jerk. Tears of pain and rage blurred her vision. She blinked them back and watched Garrett and Draco both skid to a quick stop several yards away. Chests heaving, both of them trained their guns on Chambers. Terror clawed through her. Because of her, Garrett and Draco could both very well die tonight. Cruelly twisting his fist in her hair, Chambers gave a sadistic, satisfied laugh, as if he'd read her thoughts and couldn't be more pleased with the situation.

"That's far enough, McCabe—unless you want her blood on your hands."

Garrett's face was pale beneath the smudges of soot. The barrel of Chambers' gun waved between Garrett and Draco. His hand twisted tighter in her hair, and she winced. He pressed the barrel of the gun harder against her temple, and she squeezed her eyes closed against the pain.

What to do? What to do? She had to think of something. She couldn't let Garrett risk himself for her. She had to figure a way out of this...somehow.

"I can take him," Draco muttered to Garrett, his voice carrying on the breeze to Miranda and her captor.

"No," Garrett hissed. "You might hit her."

"Wise choice, McCabe. Now, put the guns down, boys," Chambers ordered, but Miranda cut in, distracting him before he could see his order through.

"Listen to me," she pleaded. "My family is rich. They'll pay you whatever you want—just please don't hurt Garrett. Let him go, please," she begged.

"I'll go without a fight, just let Garrett go. Please…"

She could see the strained lines her words put on Garrett's face. The telltale muscle leaped along his jaw. He was damned well furious, and some of that fury was now directed at her.

As long as he was alive—and continued to stay that way—she didn't care if he never spoke to her again. He'd be alive. That was all that mattered. She couldn't go on if Garrett died.

There'd be no point.

"You make a good point, my dear," Chambers laughed. "It would be a crime to waste a perfectly good avenue of income. Of course, McCabe doesn't have to be alive for you to still be of use to me."

With that, he turned the gun to Garrett, and time slowed for Miranda. The realization that, rather than risk the possibility of hurting her, Garrett would stand there and let Chambers shoot him, hit her with painful clarity.

"No!" Miranda screamed, twisting against Chambers as the bullet ripped from the gun.

From the corner of her eye, she saw Garrett stagger, heard his pained gasp, and reason fled her. Miranda became a writhing, snarling, she-cat— clawing and pummeling Chambers as she quite literally crawled all over him.

Her fingernails raked across his unmarred cheek leaving deep, blood-welling grooves. She knocked his hat from his head, and her small fist broke his nose. She dug her elbow viciously into the gunshot wound on his shoulder, and kicked him in the groin. There was no reason left inside her, no civility. No sanity.

He'd killed Garrett. Nothing else mattered any more.

Chambers yanked at her hair in a bid to put space between them, cursing and gasping. Tears stung her eyes, but she focused the pain into flailing arms and kicking legs as she slipped, off-balance, to the ground.

Snarling like a rabid dog, Chambers raised the barrel of his gun, aiming it at her chest. There was no mistaking his intention. Miranda sneered at him insolently, welcoming the bullet that would take her from a world without Garrett. She didn't even flinch when the report of rapid gunfire shattered the night. It took her a moment to see the blood as it flowed over Chambers' face and ran down the front of his shirt—a moment more to see the small holes, one in the center of his forehead and the other centered over his black heart. He toppled forward at her feet.

She scrambled back and pushed to her feet, staring down at Chambers' prone body, unable to force herself to turn around and see Garrett—dead. The thought of Garrett's death was more than she could bear. The thought of Garrett dead pushed blackness around the edge of her vision, and she sank to the hard ground, welcoming oblivion.

****

Miranda regained consciousness by slow degrees. Strong arms gently cradled her and a large, calloused hand patted her face, cutting through the fog. She didn't want to surface, didn't want to have to face the darkness that awaited her.

Garrett was gone...

But the voice murmuring against her hair was too insistent.

Sounding too much like...

Miranda forced her eyes open and gazed, wide-eyed, into an emotion-swept sea of stormy-gray. She blinked, stunned.

"You little fool," Garrett hissed, though he continued to stroke her tenderly. "What the devil were you thinking? He could have killed you. You could have..."

Garrett's voice trailed off as he closed his eyes

and bowed his head, touching his forehead to hers. A deep breath shuddered from him. Struggling to sit up, Miranda peered around her. Her gaze flickered over Chambers—a very dead Chambers—and then lit on Draco as he lounged with deceptive negligence against a nearby tree, wearing an impassive expression, watching Garrett hover over her like a mother hen.

A very irate mother hen.

Her gaze flew back to Garrett, and frantic, she searched for a wound, ignoring his angry rebuke. There...a hole surrounded by torn and blood-soaked denim high on his thigh.

"Why couldn't you have just listened for once in your life, woman? Is that too damn much to ask? Why in the hell did you have to be so reckless? You scared ten—*fifteen* years off my life with that little stunt." Garrett continued to rail. "I ought to—"

Struggling out of his grasp, ignoring his threats, Miranda knelt in front of him, peering closely at his leg. Her hands exploring his thigh, temporarily distracted Garrett from his tirade, and his voice choked off on an audible gasp. He was bleeding, so much. She stood and hiked her skirt up, allowing Draco a more than generous glimpse of her legs. She didn't care. Garrett was alive. And he was hurt.

Garrett snarled at Draco, batting at her skirts as he made to rise.

"What the hell are you doing?" Garrett demanded, glaring at Draco's wide grin as he struggled to gain his feet.

"Sit still," she ordered, grasping her petticoat. With a strong tug, she tore off a long length of material, then dropped her skirt back into place. She pushed Garrett back down and set to work binding his injury as tight as she could.

Blasted man. How dare he sit here and berate her? She wasn't the one gushing blood, now was she?

A small sob escaped her as she focused, blurry-eyed, on her task.

****

Garrett glared at the top of her bent head. He'd been about to resume his tirade, when he noticed she seemed to be having trouble knotting the strip of cotton. The tiny sob she tried to hide beneath the guise of a cough brought him up short. He placed his hand over hers. Her hands trembled. Then he felt it—the hot splash of tears on the back of his hand—and his heart jerked, skipping a beat.

Hooking a finger beneath her chin, he tilted Miranda's head up until he could see her face in the golden glow of the fire consuming his home. Tears rolled down her cheeks, one after another, leaving pale trails down soot-stained, blood-smeared cheeks.

His brows drew together, and he stilled.

Tears...

"Miranda," he whispered. In the entire time he'd known her, he'd never—not once—*ever* seen her cry.

Except for the day he'd left her behind.

"Sweetheart, you're crying—"

"I never cry," she huffed, tears rolling unimpeded down her face.

Bemused, beguiled, he wiped a trail of moisture from her cheek with his fingertip, and held his hand up for her inspection, forcing her to face the reality. "You *are* crying!" He shook his head, frowning. "Why are you crying?"

Even to him that sounded like the most idiotic question ever voiced out loud, so he was doubly surprised when she gave one loud, shaking sob and launched herself into his arms, nearly knocking him flat on his back. He strained to hear the words she mumbled against his chest.

"He shot you, Garrett! I thought he'd killed you, you idiot."

Garrett's mouth fell open. For one long moment,

317

he sat motionless, unable to move. Warmth swelled in his chest, swamping his body, setting his nerve endings tingling. He wrapped his arms around her, cradling her to him, even as he continued to sit there, struck speechless.

She'd walked away from a stagecoach robbery, been shot at by a hidden sniper, and stood quiet and stoic beside a dead body in the middle of nowhere—all completely dry-eyed.

But she cried for him.

She'd traveled at grueling paces some men would have been hard-pressed to handle with any kind of aplomb. She'd lost her innocence on the hard ground beside a cold pond and had finally accepted the one thing she'd fought so diligently to avoid...getting married. She hadn't cried once.

Yet she cried for him.

She'd been abducted by a madman, and she'd survived a raging inferno. She'd been shot at, dragged through a hail of gunfire, and been 'just nicked' as she'd so calmly put it. She'd shot a monster and attacked that same monster with her bare hands in defense of *him*. She'd tried to barter her own safety to try to keep Garrett from harm—and she'd done it all without shedding a tear.

But she cried for him.

Garrett's arms tightened around her for a moment, then he pushed her back until he could look into her eyes.

"Don't cry, sweetheart," he murmured, wiping the dampness from her cheeks with both hands. His heart shattered at the sight of her tears. He cupped her cheeks in the palms of his hands. His frantic, determined gaze probed hers. "By the saints, Miranda, I'll do anything—whatever it takes—just don't cry. Please, honey, I love you!"

Miranda hiccupped and smiled at him, so radiant she took his breath away.

"Oh, Garrett!" Miranda sobbed. "I love you, too." Wet, breathless kisses showered his face.

Garrett smiled beneath the assault. "Marry me...please. Be my wife."

"Yes, yes, yes," she exclaimed as she continued to rain kisses on his face with fierce abandon.

Laughing, ignoring Draco's disgusted snort as the bandit stalked away, Garrett captured her head between his hands once more, forcing her to hold still long enough for him to gaze deep into her eyes. "You're sure? Because after this I won't let you take it back. You'll love, honor, and obey and all that? You'll marry me right away, no more fussing about it or trying to get out of it?"

"Yes." She nodded, giving him a watery, joyful smile. But her beautiful eyes twinkled with mischief. "I already love you with all my heart, and I will honor you to the best of my ability, I swear!"

Suspicious, Garrett shot her a mock-stern frown, and narrowed his eyes. "And what about obeying?"

Grinning impishly as she sat on his lap covered in soot and dirt and smears of blood, Miranda cooed, "I wouldn't count on it if I were you."

Chapter Twenty-Four

Draco slipped from the main house at the Bar M and drew a deep breath of cool night air. Miranda stood a few paces away, leaning against the rail, gazing into the dark, starless sky. He knew she was there. He'd deliberately sought her out, waiting to find her alone. It had been a long wait, since they'd made it to the ranch. Garrett barely let her out of his arms, let alone out of his sight.

He stared at her for a few moments and thought of the future he could have had—a future they could have had together. It would have been so easy for him to hate McCabe right now, but Draco knew too well the hell McCabe had lived the last six years.

He also knew that through the last six years, when it would have been so easy for McCabe to let his hatred and his bitterness change him, McCabe had clung to his morals, refusing to bend the law to meet his own ends as so many others did—as Draco himself had done a time or two. McCabe had remained honorable, right up to the last. No, Draco couldn't begrudge him his happiness.

The wind picked up for a moment, stirring the ends of his hair. The cool smell of spring and flowers and fresh starts wafted to him, innocent and unbearably sweet.

Standing out at McCabe's place earlier, surrounded by death and destruction, watching Miranda and McCabe kiss and whisper words of love and devotion, Draco had finally faced what he'd refused to see until just then. McCabe and Miranda belonged together. They fit. They had a wonderful future full of life and love. Perhaps what upset him—more than Miranda choosing McCabe over him—was how downright bleak his own future looked in comparison.

When had his life become such a hollow shell? He'd once had it all, too. That had been so long ago he could hardly remember anymore—at least that's what he told himself so he could sleep at night.

He'd also thought he'd reconciled himself to the life he'd found after his own happily ever after had disappeared. He'd been wrong about that as well.

Miranda had given him a brief glimpse at the possibility of happiness again—a glimpse at something he'd long since given up of ever finding again. He didn't know whether he should thank her for it, or curse her.

Nevertheless, here he was, right back where he started. On to the next job. Preparing to seal himself back inside his cold, ruthless shell—a shell of death and loneliness, justice and revenge. The process was getting harder and harder to do, it seemed. He shrugged and squared his shoulders.

Time to cut ties and move on.

Draco stepped from the shadows and stood beside her, silent as the night around them.

"Someone should sew bells to your coat," she said, glancing over her shoulder at him.

The corner of Draco's mouth hitched up, but he remained silent as he stared into the darkness of the mountains towering in the distance. Miranda turned to face him. She searched his face with wide, wary eyes. He wondered what she saw. Dangerous outlaw or seductive rake. A romantic knight in somewhat tarnished armor, or a ruthless killer when the need arose.

Savior or angel of death...perhaps he was a bit of both.

"Who are you, Draco?" Miranda whispered. Her

voice carried on the breeze.

He stared at her for several long moments. Silent. Contemplative. He'd been trying to figure that answer out for the better part of ten years and not having much luck with it. The stark loneliness of his life stretched out before him, tormenting him. His own personal living hell.

"The less you know, the better," he drawled, trying his best to give her the familiar old, devil-may-care grin.

But his heart wasn't in it, and his eyes must have betrayed him.

She tilted her head and considered him with a shrewd stare. Lord Almighty, he couldn't remember ever suffering the urge to squirm like this before in his life.

"Better for whom?" Miranda pressed at length. "Better for me...or better for you?"

He debated how much to tell her. His instincts told him he could hand over his secrets to her, and he always trusted his instincts. They'd only ever failed him once. Yet he hesitated. The one and only time his instincts had failed him, a woman had been involved then, too.

He was still feeling the burn of that mistake.

Yes, he could trust Miranda. But she was Garrett's woman. He had no claim to her. He gave a slight shake of his head. Was he so lonely then? Where had this yearning come from...this yearning for someone to call his own, someone he could trust with everything?

He could ride into the night and not look back. He'd done it before, time and again, and it had never bothered him. Before. But something made him linger. Maybe it was the promise of trust and friendship he saw in this feisty woman's eyes, maybe it was his newly discovered desire to set down roots again, but he found himself opening up at last—to some extent at least.

He could tell her the basics. Garrett would tell her anyway. The rest—well, that was for another day—and another woman.

"Damian Morgan." Draco let out a pent up breath, speaking the name he hadn't called himself in too many years too count. "My name is Damian Morgan."

The name felt foreign on his tongue, as much as the identity had begun to feel foreign to his soul.

Miranda's eyes widened. He'd been silent for so long she, in all likelihood, thought he wouldn't speak at all. But she remained silent, letting him ramble in his own good time.

He flexed his grip on the railing. "I'm a Pinkerton Agent, Miranda. I've been working undercover on various cases for the better part of ten years."

Miranda let out a tiny gasp and stared in wide-eyed wonder. Who hadn't heard of the Pinkerton's and their daring, heroic exploits? But she must not have considered he could be working on the legal side of the law. Now things must be starting to make more sense. She knew this much...what harm could come of filling in some of the blanks for her?

"I met Garrett just after his brothers died in that bank in Carlisle," he continued. "I and another agent had been working with Nick McCabe and Merle Colby on the Chambers' case. Later on, I passed information to Garrett a time or two and helped him capture two of Chambers' raiders."

"You were there...that day Uncle Milton made Garrett choose...the day Garrett was sworn in as a U.S. Marshal." Surprise and awe glowed in Miranda's eyes. "You testified on his behalf. *You* convinced my uncle to give him a second chance."

Draco knew the hardships Garrett had faced in his years as a marshal. He knew the difficult decisions required of a lawman, knew the many ways a man could be tested. Knew it first-hand. Not many men could live up to the challenge, but Garrett had proven himself. No one else could take credit for that. Therefore, he diverted the conversation.

"I've been tracking the mastermind behind a criminal ring that surfaced a few months back. They've been striking at the rail lines all over this area. I've spent the better part of two years infiltrating the inner workings, but it's a tight-knit organization. I only recently discovered the identity of the man behind the ring," Draco explained.

"Chambers," Miranda murmured.

Draco nodded. He flicked at a splinter of wood on the railing with his fingernail. "Now he's gone, I need to focus on the rest of the ring. The inner workings were far too extensive for it all just to end with Chambers' death. The operation was too elaborate. I believe he had a partner. A silent one. One with a lot of power. A lot of connections."

"So you'll be staying in the area?"

"I'll be around," he hedged. Then he turned his head and pinned her with an unswerving gaze. "You can't tell anyone about me...about who I really am."

There was a warning in his eyes she didn't quite understand as he turned to face her. And that look sent chills through her blood.

"Things aren't as safe around here as they seem," he warned. "You have to be careful. Trust in Garrett to keep you safe, Miranda, and know that if he can't be there to watch over you—you won't be alone."

She smiled despite his dire tone, then she stepped forward and gave him an affectionate, sisterly hug. His arms encircled her and he squeezed, for once his embrace absent of any nefarious intentions.

As she drew back, she captured his hand before

he could turn to leave. His eyes were dark with restless loneliness. Her heart wept for him. "You are a good man, too. Damian Morgan or Draco...I will always consider you a dear friend. You'll always have a place with us." She squeezed his hand. "I hope you find what you're looking for someday."

"Someday..." Draco echoed with a vulnerable smile. Then he drew a deep breath and the mask of seductive outlaw was once again in place. "You know it's not too late yet. We could be long gone before Natalia is done stitchin' up McCabe's leg."

"You are incorrigible!" Miranda shook her head, smiling. Fond warmth filled her.

"Don't you *ever* forget it." Draco offered her a wicked smile before he turned to walk away. After only three steps, however, he abruptly whirled around and closed the distance between them, a devilish twinkle glowing in his eye. Before she could voice protest, he swept her against him and pressed a swift, teasing kiss against her lips. When he released her, he smiled shamelessly, winked, and whispered, "McCabe needs a reminder that if he doesn't treat you right, there's someone who'd be happy to steal you away."

That said, he left her staring after him as he disappeared into the darkness of Matt's stables. A few moments later, a hobbling, growling Garrett joined her on the veranda, and Miranda understood Draco's intentions at last. He'd been deliberately provoking Garrett. Miranda blinked in surprise when Garrett let loose a furious tirade.

"Why can't that bastard keep his damned hands to himself? I'm gonna shoot him the next time he even looks at you wrong! Debt or no debt, I'll tear his lips off that damned arrogant face of his. I'll cut off his—"

Miranda darted close and wrapped her arms around his neck, sealing her lips to his, diverting his focus. Several long, breathless moments later, she drew back and smiled up into smoky-gray, passion-filled eyes.

"But, Garrett," she purred. "You're a much, *much* better kisser than he is."

With a mollified grunt, Garrett pulled her back against him. He fit her snug against his hard body and proceeded to prove her point until she melted in his embrace. When he pulled away, his face was tense, his breathing every bit as ragged as hers. He shifted, leaning on the makeshift crutch propped under his arm, and winced.

"You're hurting," Miranda accused. Taking him by the arm, she lead him slowly back to the door, scolding him with every step. How dare he stand here and kiss her senseless when he was hurt so badly? "You shouldn't be standing on that leg. You should be in bed."

Garrett's lips parted in a seductive smile—a smile that put all Draco's practiced, patently wicked grins to shame—and he drawled, "Will you tuck me in?"

His question, filled with blatant innuendo—his tone husky with desire—drew her up short. She caught the edge of her lower lip between her teeth. Oh, the temptation. He had a way of making her melt with just a look.

No, no, he was hurt. She shouldn't even be considering...

She tamped down on the temptation and glowered at him. "You shouldn't even be walking on that leg, much less—" Heat climbed into her cheeks, and she cleared her throat before plunging on, "You could rip your stitches open if you're not careful."

"Then I guess we better be extra careful, because I don't intend to let you out of bed until you can't even remember what *his* name is," Garrett told her, taking the lead now, tugging an astonished, intrigued Miranda into the house behind him. "In fact," he drawled, aiming a considering stare hot enough to curl her toes over his shoulder at her, "it might be a good idea to stay there an extra day or two—just to be sure."

Epilogue

Humming appreciatively as she admired the view, Miranda set the bucket of cold, well water down on one of the rough-hewn planks propped across a pair of nail kegs. Garrett, stripped to the skin from the waist up, stood a few yards away swinging a hammer. She drew in a long, slow breath at the ripple and play of his powerful muscles. Dark, damp hair curled around his ears and neck. His golden skin glistened in the midday sun. Rivulets of sweat slicked over the ridges and planes of his sculpted body.

A shiver of longing worked its way through her system.

Two full months had passed since the night of the fire. Two months of discovery. Two months of planning. Two months of *living*. She and Garrett were staying with Matt and Natalia at the Bar M, while the charred remains of Garrett's house were cleared away and the framework set.

Uncle Milton's convenient appearance at the Bar M the morning after the fire still made her shake her head. *The sneaky old goat.* He'd tried insisting she return with him to town. Tried, being the operative word. Garrett, of course, made it clear—in no uncertain terms, of course—that she would *not* be leaving his side again.

Ever.

The judge had retaliated by demanding Garrett make her an honest woman. In fact, he'd refused to leave the Bar M until he'd seen to the matter himself...right then and there. She recalled the comment Garrett had made later that same night, and she gave a small shake of her head.

"That uncle of yours had an awfully smug smile all through the ceremony," Garrett had remarked *with calm cynicism.*

She'd thought often of that smug smile herself the last two months.

Insistent yipping snapped her attention back to the present. Glancing down, she spied the small ball of black and white fur wrestling with the folds of her skirts. A fond smile tugged at her lips. Gently shooing the intrepid pup from her hem with the toe of her boot, Miranda jerked the material free of the pup's enthusiastic chewing. Thrilled by the new game of keep-away, the puppy lunged for the material, sinking her sharp little teeth into the fabric once again.

The mixed-breed puppy had been her gift to Garrett. Teasing Garrett about his list of requirements, Miranda had cited the puppy's finer qualities with as close to a straight face as she could manage.

"She's sweet-tempered, loyal, obedient, and guaranteed to never nag or harp." Miranda goaded Garrett with an impish grin.

The frazzled cotton yielded to the pup with a loud rip.

"Lady, stop it," Miranda scolded, pushing the animal away with the toe of her boot again. The dog barked, dodging her boot. Lady had a one-track mind. Heaving a frustrated sigh, Miranda reached for the dog. "Stop it this instant!"

The game of tug turned to a game of catch-me-if-you-can. The pup scampered away but was soon engrossed in sharpening her teeth on the end of a rough plank near the porch steps.

"I see she listens about as well as her mistress," Garrett drawled from behind her.

Miranda almost jumped out of her skin. She'd become so distracted by the antics of the playful pup that she hadn't realized Garrett had joined her. He offered her a smoldering grin as he dipped a dented tin mug into the bucket and took a long drink.

Her greedy gaze slid downward over the glistening, virile length of tawny muscles flexing across his chest and abdomen. She slicked her tongue along her bottom lip and caught the edge of her lip between her teeth. A particularly tempting bead of moisture trickled down the double ridge of muscles on his stomach, headed straight for the buckle of his belt.

Garrett sucked in a sharp breath. All those defined muscles she'd been ogling clenched and rippled, setting off a firestorm of need dancing in the pit of her stomach. He canted his head and seared her with a look of raw hunger, a look so intense her knees went weak.

"Keep eatin' me up with your eyes like that, wife, and this house isn't ever gonna get built." His voice and smoldering stare had a way of melting her from the inside out.

"Why, sir, whatever do you mean?" Miranda purred, feigning innocence as the tip of one finger skated down the middle of his chest, following another rivulet of sweat until it disappeared beneath his waistband. Without warning, Garrett's hands shot around her waist. He yanked her against him, burying his face against the side of her neck with a low, hungry groan.

Hot, moist lips branded their way up the side of her throat, across the ridge of her jaw, and fastened on her mouth with unmistakable purpose. He kissed her until her already weak knees all but knocked together, then released her mouth to trail scorching kisses back down the other side of her throat and over her bodice, loosening buttons as he went. His free hand molded the flesh of her bottom as he pressed her hard against his rigid arousal.

"Garrett," she squeaked, pushing at his shoulders. She couldn't seem to catch quite enough air. Then again, with Garrett's mouth and hands on her like this, she had a difficult time caring about anything as inconsequential as breathing. Still, modesty niggled somewhere in the corners of her conscious. "Antonio and the others will be back anytime now." Her breath caught in the back of her throat as his lips blazed a trail over the now bared valley between her breasts. "Garrett, you have to stop!"

"You've been standing over here all day, tormenting me with those hot, knowing little smiles, and you expect me to stop now that I've got my hands on you?" Garrett growled against the curve of her breast, his voice rough as sandpaper. "Not a chance in hell, sweetheart."

One hand released her bottom to slip inside her loosened bodice and claim her breast. His palm was hot and abrasive with calluses, his fingers long and strong. Oh, but did they feel good. He kneaded and caressed until she closed her eyes and moaned aloud. Her fingers sank into his damp hair and fisted. He suckled the hollow at the base of her throat.

He arched her back over the workbench, his hand slowly, deliberately bunching the material of her skirt.

"You want us to come back later?" Antonio's voice called, humor lacing his tone.

Dragging in a deep, shaky breath, Garrett cursed his luck…and Antonio's rotten timing. Garrett slowly straightened and released his wife, shooting her a burning look that promised he'd be picking back up where he'd left off at the first possible opportunity.

She went up on tiptoe to nuzzle a soft, fleeting

kiss against his lips, tormenting him, and quickly rebuttoned her bodice, concealing all that delectable, creamy flesh from his ravenous gaze. His hands— hell, his entire body—ached for her. Before he could change his mind and tell Antonio and the others to take a hike, Miranda scampered from his embrace with an impish grin. He couldn't wait to get her alone later. He'd take his time peeling those clothes off her and make her pay for all those long, wicked looks she'd been giving him.

Garrett growled frustration low in his throat and reached for a hammer, gripping it in a white-knuckled fist. Damnation, it was hot. Maybe he should toss Miranda on his horse and haul her off to the stream, swollen now from late-season rains. He could think of more pleasurable ways to spend the afternoon than sweating his ass off pounding wood and nails.

He could take the ribbing he was sure to get from Ethan and the others. He stood there for a long moment, wavering in his resolve to get the house finished as soon as possible.

No, no, he had to finish the house. Then he could work on filling it to the rafters with the sound of Miranda's laughter, and the sounds of Miranda's passion.

They could work on filling the house to the rafters with children.

Their children...

Miranda turned to walk away, but then paused, calling over her shoulder, "Oh, and Garrett? I've been thinking about it this last couple of weeks, and now I'm certain. You'd better add on an extra room." She tilted her head and offered him a beaming smile. "Actually, you should probably make that *two* rooms. After all, twins do run in my family."

His brow wrinkled for a split second, then his wide-eyed gaze dropped to where she tenderly cradled her hands over her flat abdomen. Smiling, she spun on her heel and glided away.

Garrett stood rooted to the spot. He gaped at her back, all but gasping for air. Behind him, Antonio and Ethan hooted and guffawed. Matt slapped him on the back so hard he staggered forward two full steps. Her siren's laughter floated back to him on the gentle breeze. And Garrett could do little more than grin like a bewitched fool.

Be damned, if she hadn't gotten the last word...again.

A word about the author...

Always a voracious reader, Brenda Huber closed the cover on a book by one of her favorite authors and said to herself...I can do this!

Brenda writes both historical and paranormal romance. She lives in Iowa with her husband and two children.